Midnight

AT THE

Well of Souls

Jack L. Chalker

A Del Rey Book

BALLANTINE BOOKS • NEW YORK

This book is for Roger Zelazny, Mark Owings, Applesusan, Avedon, and Suzy Tiffany for entirely different reasons.

Contents

vii

Dalgonia

MASS MURDERS ARE USUALLY ALL THE MORE SHOCK-
ing because of the unexpected settings and the past
character of the murderer. The Dalgonian Massacre
is a case in point.

Dalgonia is a barren, rocky planet near a dying sun,
bathed only in a ghostly, reddish light, whose beautiful rays create sinister shadows across the rocky crags.
Little is left of the Dalgonian atmosphere to suggest
that life could ever have happened here; the water is
gone or, like the oxygen, now locked deep in rock. The
feeble sun, unable to give more than the deep reddish
tint to the landscape, is of no help in illuminating the
skyline, which was, despite a bluish haze from the in-
ert elements still present in it, as dark as the shadows.
This was a world of ghosts.

And it was haunted.

Nine figures trooped silently into the ruins of a city
that might easily have been mistaken for the rocky
crags on the nearby hills. Twisted spires and crumbling
castles of greenish-brown stood before them, dwarf-
ing them to insignificance. Their white protective suits
were all that made them conspicuous in this darkly
beautiful world of silence.

The city itself resembled nothing so much as one
that might have been built of iron aeons before and
subjected to extensive rust and salt abrasion in some
dead sea. Like its world, it was silent and dead.

A close look at the figures heading into the city
would reveal that they were all what was known as
"human"—denizens of the youngest part of the spiral
arm of their galaxy. Five were female, four male, the

1

leader a thin, frail man of middle years. Stenciled on his back and faceplate was the name *Skander*.

They stood at the half-crumbled gate to the city as they had so many times before, gazing at the incredible but magnificent ruin.

> *My name is Ozymandias.*
> *Look on my works ye mighty,*
>   *and despair!*
> *Nothing beside remains. . . .*

If those words from a poet out of their near-forgotten past did not actually echo through each of them, the concept and feeling of those lines did. And through each mind, as they had through the minds of thousands of others who had peered and pecked through similar ruins on over two dozen other dead planets, those endless and apparently unanswerable questions kept running.

Who were they who could build with such magnificence?

Why did they die?

"Since this is your first trip as graduate students to a Markovian ruin," Skander's reedy voice said through their radios, startling them out of their awe, "I will give a brief introduction to you. I apologize if I am redundant, but this will be a good refresher nonetheless.

"Jared Markov discovered the first of these ruins centuries ago, on a planet over a hundred light-years distant from this spot. It was our race's first experience with signs of intelligence in this galaxy of ours, and the discovery caused a tremendous amount of excitement. Those ruins were dated at over a quarter of a million standard years old—and they were the youngest discovered to date. It became obvious that, while our race still grubbed on its home world fiddling with the new discovery of fire, someone else—these people—had a vast interstellar empire of still unknown dimensions. All we know is that as we have pressed inward in the galaxy these remains get more and more numerous. And, as yet, we haven't a clue as to who they were."

"Are there no artifacts of any sort?" came a disbelieving female voice.

2

"None, as you should know, Citizen Jainet," came the formal reply in a mildly reproving tone. "That is what is so infuriating about it all. The cities, yes, about which some things can be inferred about their builders, but no furniture, no pictures, nothing of an even remotely utilitarian nature. The rooms, as you will see, are quite barren. Also, no cemeteries; indeed, nothing mechanical at all, either."

"That's because of the computer, isn't it?" came another, deeper female voice, that of the stocky girl from the heavy-gravity world whose family name was Marino.

"Yes," Skander agreed. "But, come, let's move into the city. We can talk as we go."

They started forward, soon coming into a broad boulevard, perhaps fifty meters across. Along each side ran what appeared to be broad walkways, each six to eight meters across, like the moving walkways of spaceports that took you to and from loading gates. But no conveyor belt or such was evident; the walkways were made of the same greenish-brown stone, or metal, or whatever it was that composed the rest of the city.

"The crust of this planet," Skander continued, "is about average—forty to forty-five kilometers thick. Measurements on this and other worlds of the Markovians showed a consistent discontinuity, about one kilometer thick, between the crust and the natural mantlerock beneath. This, we have discovered, was an artificial layer of material that is essentially plastic but seems to have had a sort of life in it—this much, at least, we infer. Consider how much information your own cells contain. You are the products of the best genetic manipulation techniques, perfect physical and mental specimens of the best of your races adapted to your native planets. And yet, for all that, you are far more than the sum of your parts. Your cells, particularly your brain cells, store input at an astonishing and continuing rate. We believe that this computer beneath your feet was composed of infinitely complex artificial brain cells. Imagine that! It runs the entirety of the planet, a kilometer thick—all brain. And all,

3

we believe, attuned to the individual brain waves of the inhabitants of this city!

"Imagine it, if you can. Just wish for something, and there it is. Food, furniture—if they used any—even art, created by the mind of the wisher and made real by the computer. We have, of course, small and primitive versions now—but this is generations, possibly millennia, beyond us. If you could think of it, it would be provided!"

"This Utopian Theory accounts for most of what we see, but not why all this is now ruins," piped in an adolescent male voice, Varnett, the youngest—and probably brightest—but unquestionably the most imaginative of the group.

"Quite true, Citizen Varnett," Skander acknowledged, "and there are three schools of thought on it. One is that the computer broke down, and another is that the computer ran amok—and the people couldn't cope either way. You know the third theory, anyone?"

"Stagnation," Jainet replied. "They died because they had nothing left to live for, strive for, or work for."

"Exactly," Skander replied. "And yet, there are problems with all three suppositions. An interstellar culture of this magnitude would have allowed for breakdowns; they'd have some sort of backup system. As for the amok theory—well, it's fine except that every sign shows that the same thing happened at once, all across their entire empire. One, even several, okay, but not all at the same time. I am not quite willing to accept the last theory, even though it is the one that fits the best. Something nags at me and says that they would have allowed even for that."

"Maybe they programmed their own degeneration," Varnett suggested, "and it went too far."

"Eh?" There was a note of surprise but keen interest in Skander's voice. "Programmed—planned degeneration! It's an interesting theory, Citizen Varnett. Perhaps we'll find out in time."

He motioned and they entered a building with a strange, hexagonal doorway. All the doors were hexagons, it appeared. The interior of the room was very large, but there was no sign as to its purpose or function. It looked like an apartment or a store after the tenants had moved out, taking everything with them.

"The room," Skander pointed out to them, "is hexagonal—as the city is hexagonal, as is almost everything in it if you see it from the correct angle. The number six seems to have been essential to them. Or sacred. It is from this, and from the size and shape of the doorways, windows, and the like—not to mention the width of the walkways—that we have some idea of what the natives must have been like. We hypothesize that they were rather like a top, or turnip shape, with six limbs which may have been tentacles usable for walking or as hands. We suspect that things naturally came in sixes to them—their mathematics, their architecture, maybe they even had six eyes all around. Judging from the doors and allowing for clearance, they were about two meters tall on the average and possibly wider than that at the waist—which is where we believe the six arms, tentacles, or whatever were centered, and that must be why the doorways widen at that point."

They stood there awhile, trying to imagine such creatures living in the rooms, moving up and down the boulevards.

"We'd best be getting back to camp," Skander said at last. "You will have ample time to study here and to poke into every nook and cranny of the place." They would, in fact, be there a year, working under the professor at the University station.

They walked quickly in the lighter gravity and reached the base camp about five kilometers from the city gates in under an hour.

The camp itself looked like some collection of great tents of a strange circus, nine in all, bright white like the pressure suits. Long tubes connecting the tents occasionally flexed as the monitoring computers continually adjusted the temperature and barometric pressure that kept each inflated. On such a dead world little else was needed, and the insides were lined to make punctures almost impossible. If any such did happen, though, only those in the punctured area would be killed; the computer could seal off any portion of the complex.

Skander entered last, climbing into the air lock after

5

making certain that none of his charges or major equipment was left outside. By the time the lock equalized and allowed him into the entry tent, the others were already all or partially out of their pressure suits.

He stopped for a minute, looking at them. Eight representatives from four planets of the Confederation —and, except for the one from the heavy-gravity world, all looked alike.

All were exceptionally trim and muscular; they could be a gymnastic team without any imagination. Although they ranged in age from fourteen to twenty-two, they all looked prepubescent, which, in fact, they were. Their sexual development had been genetically arrested, and would probably continue that way. He looked at the boy, Varnett, and the girl, Jainet—both from the same planet, the name of which eluded him. The oldest and the youngest of the expedition, yet they were exactly the same height and weight, and, with heads shaved, were virtually identical twins. They had been grown in a lab, a Birth Factory, and brought up by the State to think as identically as they looked. He had once asked why they continued to make both male and female models, only half in jest. It was, of course, a redundancy system in case anything happened to the Birth Factories, he had been told.

Humanity was on at least three hundred planets, and of those all but a handful were on the same line as the world that had spawned these two. Absolute equality, he thought sourly. Look alike, behave alike, think alike, all needs provided for, all wants fulfilled in equal measure to all, assigned the work they were raised for and taught that it was the only proper place for them and their duty. He wondered how the technocrats in charge decided who was to be what.

He thought back to the last batch. Three in that number came from a world that had even dispensed with names and personal pronouns.

He wondered idly how different the human race was at this point from the creatures of the city out there.

Even on worlds like his own home world it was like this, really. True, they grew beards and group sex was the norm, something that would have totally shocked these people. His world had been founded by a group

6

of nonconformists fleeing the technocratic communism of the outer spiral. But, in its own way, it was as conformist as Varnett's home, he thought. Drop Varnett into a Caligristian town and he would be made fun of, called names, even, perhaps lynched. He wouldn't have the beard, or the clothes, or the sex to fit into Caligristo's life-style.

You can't be a nonconformist if you don't wear the proper uniform.

He had often wondered if there was something deep in the human psyche that insisted on tribalism. People used to fight wars not so much to protect their own life-style but to impose it on others.

That's why so many worlds were like these people's —there had been wars to spread the faith, convert the downtrodden. Now the Confederacy forbade that —but the existing conformity, world to world, was the status quo it protected. The leaders of each planet sat on a Council, with an enforcement arm capable of destroying any planet that strayed into "unsafe" paths and manned by specially trained barbarian psychopaths. But these weapons of terror could not be used without the actions of a majority of the Council.

It had worked. There were no more wars.

They had conformed the entire mass of humanity.

And so had the Markovians, he thought. Oh, the size and sometimes the color and workmanship of the cities had varied, but only slightly.

What had that youth, Varnett, said? Perhaps they had *deliberately* broken down the system?

Skander's face had a frown as he removed the last of his pressure suit. Ideas like that marked brilliance and creativity—but they were unsafe thoughts for a civilization like the one the boy had come from. It revived those old religious ideas that after perfection came true death.

Where could he have gotten an idea like that? And why had he not been caught and stopped?

Skander looked after their naked young bodies as they filed through the tunnel toward the showers and dorm.

Only barbarians thought that way.

Had the Confederacy guessed what he was up to here? Was Varnett not the innocent student he was supposed to be, but the agent of his nightmares?

Did they suspect?

Suddenly he felt very chilly, although the temperature was constant.

Suppose they *all* were. . . .

Three months passed. Skander looked at the picture on his television screen, an electron micrograph of the cellular tissue brought up a month before by the core drill.

It was the same pattern as the older discoveries—that same fine cellular structure, but infinitely more complex inside than any human or animal cell—and so tremendously alien.

And a six-sided cell, at that. He had often wondered about the why of that—had even *their* cells been hexagonal? Somehow he doubted it, but the way that number kept popping up he wouldn't disbelieve it, either.

He stared and stared at the sample. Finally, he reached over and turned up the magnification to full and put on the special filters he had developed and refined in over nine years on this barren planet.

The screen suddenly came alive. Little sparks darted from one point in the cell to another. There was a minor electrical storm in the cell. He sat, fascinated as always, at the view only he had ever seen.

The cell *was* alive.

But the energy was not electrical—that was why it had never been picked up. He had no idea what it was, but it behaved like standard electrical energy. It just didn't measure or appear as electricity should.

The discovery had been an accident, he reflected, three years before. Some careless student had been playing with the screen to get good-looking effects and had left it that way. He had switched it on the next day without noticing anything unusual, then set up the usual energy-detection program for another dull run-through.

It was only a glimpse, a flicker, but he had seen it —and worked on his own for months more to get a

8

filter system that would show that energy photographically.

He had tested the classical samples from other digs, even had one sent to him by a supply ship. They had all been dead.

But not this one.

Somewhere, forty or so kilometers beneath them, the Markovian brain was still alive.

"What *is* that, Professor?" Skander heard a voice behind him. He quickly flipped the screen off and whirled around in one anxious moment.

It was Varnett, that perennial look of innocence on his permanently childlike face.

"Nothing, nothing," he covered excitedly, the anxiety in his voice betraying the lie. "Just putting on some playful programs to see what the electrical charges in the cell might have looked like."

Varnett seemed skeptical. "Looked pretty real to me," he said stubbornly. "If you've made a major breakthrough you ought to tell us about it. I mean—"

"No, no, it's nothing," Skander protested angrily. Then, regaining his composure, he said, "That will be all, *Citizen* Varnett! Leave me now!"

Varnett shrugged and left.

Skander sat in his chair for several minutes. His hands—in fact, his whole body—began shaking violently, and it was a while before the attack subsided. Slowly, a panicked look on his face, he went over to the microscope and carefully removed the special filter. His hand was still so unsteady he could hardly hold on to it. He slipped the filter into its tiny case with difficulty and placed it in the wide belt for tools and personal items that was the only clothing any of them wore inside.

He went back to his private room in the dorm section and lay down on his bed, staring up at the ceiling for what seemed like hours.

Varnett, he thought. Always Varnett. In the three months since they had first arrived, the boy had been into everything. Many of the others played their off-duty games and engaged in the silliness students do,

9

but not he. Serious, studious to a fault, and always reading the project reports, the old records.

Skander suddenly felt that everything was closing in on him. He was still so far from his goal!

And now Varnett knew. Knew, at least, that the brain was alive. The boy would surely take it the step further—guess that Skander had almost broken the code, was ready, perhaps in another year or so, to send that brain a message, reactivate it.

To become a god.

He would be the one who would save the human race with the very tools that must have destroyed its maker.

Suddenly Skander jumped up and made his way back to the lab. Something nagged at him, some suspicion that things were even more wrong than he knew.

Quietly, he stepped into the lab.

Varnett was sitting at the television console. And, on the screen, the same cell Skander had been examining was depicted *with its energy connectors clearly visible!*

Skander was stunned. Quickly his hands reached for the little pocket in which he kept his filter. Yes, it was still there.

How was this possible?

Varnett was doing computations, checking against a display on a second screen that hooked him to the math sections of the lab computer. Skander stood there totally still and silent. He heard Varnett mumble an assent to himself, as if some problem he had been running through the computer had checked out correct.

Skander stole a glance at his chronometer. Nine hours! It had been nine hours! He had slept through part of his dark thoughts and given the boy the chance to confirm his worst nightmare.

Something suddenly told Varnett he wasn't alone. He sat still for a second, then glanced fearfully around.

"Professor!" he exclaimed. "I'm glad it's you! This is stupendous! Why aren't you telling everyone?"

"How—" Skander stumbled, gesturing at the screen. "How did you get that picture?"

Varnett smiled. "Oh, that's simple. You forgot to

dump the computer memory when you closed up. This is what you were looking at, which the computer held in new storage."

Skander cursed himself for a fool. Of course, everything on every instrument was recorded by the computer as standard procedure. He had been so shook up by Varnett's discovery of his work that he had forgotten to dump the record!

"It's only a preliminary finding," the professor managed at last. "I was waiting until I had something really startling to report."

"But this *is* startling!" the boy exclaimed excitedly. "But you have been too close to the problem and to your own disciplines to crack it. Look, your fields are archaeology and biology, aren't they?"

"They are," Skander acknowledged, wondering where this conversation was leading. "I was an exobiologist for years and became an archaeologist when I started doing all my work on the Markovian brains."

"Yes, yes, but you're still a generalist. My world, as you know, raises specialists in every field from the point at which the brain is formed. You know my field."

"Mathematics," Skander replied. "If I recall, all mathematicians on your world are named Varnett after an ancient mathematical genius."

"Right," the boy replied, still in an excited tone. "As I was developing in the Birth Factory, they imprinted all the world's mathematical knowledge directly. It was there continuously as I grew. By the time my brain was totally developed at age seven, I knew all the mathematics, applied and theoretical, that we know. Everything is ultimately mathematical, and so I see everything in a mathematical way. I was sent here by my world because I had become fascinated by the alien mathematical symmetry in the slides and specimens of the Markovian brain. But all was for nothing, because I had no knowledge of the energy matrix linking the cellular components."

"And now?" Skander prodded, fascinated and excited in spite of himself.

"Why, it's gibberish. It defies all mathematical logic. It says that there are *no* absolutes in mathematics!

11

None! Every time I tried to force the pattern into known mathematical concepts, it kept saying that two plus two equals four isn't a constant but a *relative* proposition!"

Skander realized that the boy was trying to make things baby-simple to him, but he still couldn't grasp what he was saying. "What does all that mean?" he asked in a puzzled and confused tone.

Varnett was becoming carried away with himself. "It means that all matter and energy are in some kind of mathematical proportion. That nothing is actually real, nothing actually anything at all. If you discard the equal sign and substitute 'is proportional to' and, if it is true, you can alter or change *anything*. None of us, this room, this planet, the whole galaxy, the whole universe—none of it is a constant! If you could alter the equation for anything only slightly, change the proportions, anything could be made anything else, anything could be changed to anything else!" He stopped, seeing from the expression on Skander's face that the older man was still lost.

"I'll give a really simple, basic example," Varnett said, calmed considerably from his earlier outburst. "First, realize this if you can: there is a finite amount of energy in the universe, and that is the only constant. The amount is infinite by our standards, but that is true if this is true. Do you follow me?"

Skander nodded. "So you're saying that there is nothing but pure energy?"

"More or less," Varnett agreed. "All matter, and *constrained* energy, like stars, is created out of this energy flux. It is held there in that state—you, me, the room, the planet we're on—by a mathematical balance. Something—some quantity—is placed in proportion to some other quantity, and that forms us. And keeps us stable. If I knew the formula for Elkinos Skander, or Varnett Mathematics Two Sixty-one, I could alter, or even abolish, our existence. Even things like time and distance, the best constants, could be altered or abolished. If I knew your formula I could, given one condition, not only change you into, say, a chair, but alter all events so that you would have always *been* a chair!"

"What's the condition?" Skander asked nervously, hesitantly, afraid of the answer.

"Why, you'd need a device to translate that formula into reality. And a way to have it do what you wished."

"The Markovian brain," Skander whispered.

"Yes. That's what they discovered. But this brain—this device—seems to be for local use only. That is, it would affect this planet, perhaps the solar system in which it lies, but no more. But, somewhere, there must be a master unit—a unit that could affect at least half, perhaps the whole, galaxy. It *must* exist, if all the rest of my hypothesis is correct!"

"Why must it?" Skander asked, a sinking sensation growing in his stomach.

"Because *we* are stable," the boy replied, an awe-struck tone in his voice.

Only the mechanical sounds of the lab intruded for a minute after that, as the implications sank home to both of them.

"And you have the code?" Skander asked at last.

"I think so, although it goes against my whole being that such equations can be correct. And yet—do you know why that energy does not show by conventional means?" Skander slowly shook his head negatively, and the mathematician continued. "It is the primal energy itself. Look, do you have that filter with you?"

Skander nodded numbly and produced the little case. The boy took it eagerly, but instead of placing it in the microscope he went over to the outer wall. Slowly he donned protective coveralls and goggles, used in radiation protection, and told Skander to do likewise. Then he sealed the lab against entry and peeled back the tent lining in the one place where it covered a port—not used here, but these tents were all-purpose and contained many useless features.

The baleful reddish landscape showed before them at midday. Slowly, carefully, the boy held the tiny filter up to one eye and closed the other. He gasped. "I was right!" he exclaimed.

After a painful half-minute that felt like an eternity, he handed the little filter to Skander, who did the same.

13

Through the filter, the entire landscape was bathed in a ferocious electrical storm. Skander couldn't stop looking at it.

"The Markovian brain is all around us," Varnett whispered. "It draws what it needs and expels what it does not. If we could contact it—"

"We'd be like gods," Skander finished.

Skander reluctantly put down the filter and handed it back to Varnett, who resumed his own gazing.

"And what sort of universe would you create, Varnett?" Skander almost whispered, reaching under the protective clothing as he spoke and pulling out a knife. "A mathematically perfect place where everyone was absolutely identical, the *same* equation?"

"Put your weapon away, Skander," Varnett told him, not taking his gaze from the filtered landscape. "You can't do it without me, and if you think about it you'll realize that. In only a few months they'll find our bodies and you here—or dying in the city—and what will that get you?"

The knife hesitated a long moment, then slowly slid back into the belt under the protective garment.

"What the hell are you, Varnett?" asked Skander suspiciously.

"An aberration," the other replied. "We happen, sometimes. Usually they catch us and that's that. But not me, not yet. They will, though, unless I can do something about it."

"What do you mean, an aberration?" Skander asked unsurely.

"I'm human, Skander. A real human. And greedy. I, too, would like to be a god."

It had taken Varnett only seven hours to crack the mathematics, but it would take a lot longer to make the Markovian brain notice them. Their project was so intense that the others began to take notice and inquire, particularly the research assistants. Finally, they decided to take them all in on it—Varnett because he was certain that, once in contact with the Markovian brain, he could adjust the others to his version of events, and Skander because he had no choice. While

14

they worked the lab, the others combed the city and, using small flyers, the other cities and regions of the planet.

"You are to look for some sort of vent, entrance, gate, or at least a temple or similar structure that might mean some kind of direct contact with the Markovian brain," Skander told them.

And time went on, with the others, good Universalists all, looking forward to carrying the news back to the Confederacy that the perfect society was within man's grasp.

Finally, one day, only two months before the next ship was due in, they found it.

Jainet and Dunna, one of the research assistants, noticed through the large filters they had constructed for the search that one tiny area near the north pole of the planet was conspicuous by the absence of the all-pervasive lightning.

Flying over to it they saw below them a deep hexagonal hole of total darkness. They were reluctant to explore further without consultation, and so radioed for the rest to come up.

"I don't see anything," Skander complained, disappointed. "There's no hex hole here."

"But there was!" Jainet protested, and Dunna nodded in agreement. "It was right there, almost directly over the pole. Here! I'll prove it!" She went over and rewound the flyer's nose camera recording disk a little more than halfway. They watched the playback in skeptical silence, as the ground rolled beneath them on the screen. Then, suddenly, there it was.

"See!" Jainet exclaimed. "What did I tell you!"

And it was there, clearly, unquestionably. Varnett looked at the screen, then to the scene below them, then back again. It all checked. There had been a hexagonal hole, almost two kilometers across at its widest point. The landmarks matched—it was at this spot.

But there wasn't a hole there now.

They waited then, almost an entire day. Suddenly the flat plain seemed to vanish and there was the hole again.

They photographed it and ran every analysis test on it they could.

"Let's drop something in," Varnett suggested at last.

They found a spare pressure suit and, hovering directly over the hole, the light on the suit turned on, they dropped it in.

The suit struck the hole. "Struck" is the only word they had for it. The suit hit the top of the hole and seemed to stick there, not dropping at all. Then, after hovering a moment, it seemed to fade before their eyes. Not drop, but fade—for even the films showed that it didn't fall. It simply faded out to nothingness.

A few minutes later the hole itself disappeared.

"Forty-six standard minutes," Varnett said. "Exactly. And I'll bet at the same time gap tomorrow it opens again."

"But where did the suit go? Why didn't it drop?" Jainet asked.

"Remember the power of this thing," Skander told her. "If you were to get to it, you wouldn't descend forty-plus kilometers. You'd simply be transported to the place."

"Exactly," Varnett agreed. "It would simply alter the equation and you would be *there* instead of *here*."

"But where is *there*?" Jainet asked.

"We believe at the control center of the Markovian brain," Skander told her. "There would be one—the same way there are two bridges on a spaceship. The other is for emergencies." Or male and female members on your planet, Skander had almost said.

"We'd best go back and run this all through our own data banks," Varnett suggested. "After all, it's been a long day for us anyway. The hole opens and closes regularly. So we can do the same things tomorrow as we can do today."

They all muttered assent at this proposal, and several suddenly realized how tired they were.

"Someone should stay here," Skander suggested, "if only to time the thing and keep the camera running."

"I'll do it," Varnett volunteered. "I can sleep here on this flyer and you all can go back in the other two. If anything comes up I'll let you know. Then someone can spell me tomorrow."

They all agreed to this, so after a short while everyone but Varnett headed back to base camp.

Almost all went to sleep immediately, only Skander and Dunna taking the extra time to feed their records into the data bank. Then both went off to their own quarters.

Skander sat on the edge of his bunk, too excited to feel tired. Curiously, he felt exhilarated instead, adrenalin pumping through him.

I must take the gamble, he told himself. I must assume that this is indeed the gateway to the brain. In less than fifty days this crew will be replaced, and they'll go home to blab the secret. Then everyone will be in, and the Statists of the Confederacy will gain the power.

Was that what had happened to the Markovians? Had they become so much a communal paradise that they stagnated and died out?

No! he told himself. *Not for them! I shall die, or I shall save mankind.*

He went first to the lab and wiped all information from the data banks. There was nothing left when he finished; then he wrecked the machinery so none could retrieve the faintest clue. Next he went to the master control center. There the atmospheric conditions were set. Slowly, methodically, he turned off all the systems except oxygen. He waited there almost an hour until the gauges read that the atmosphere was now almost entirely oxygen everywhere in the tents.

That done, he made his way carefully to the air lock, anxious not to scrape against anything or to cause any sort of spark. Although nervous at the prospect that one of the sleepers would wake up and make that spark, he took the time to don his pressure suit and then take all the other such suits outside.

Next he took from the emergency kit of one of the flyers a small box and opened it.

Premanufactured items for all occasions. It was a flare gun.

The puncture it would make would be sealed in seconds by the automated equipment, but not before it ignited the oxygen inside.

It was over in one sudden flare, like flash paper.

After, he could see the vacuum-exposed remains of the sleepers whose charred bodies were still in their beds.

Seven down, one to go, he thought without remorse.

He boarded a flyer and headed toward the north pole. He glanced at his chronometer. It took nine hours to fly back, he had been three doing his work, and now there was another nine to return to the pole.

About an hour to spare until that hole opened up again.

Enough time for Varnett.

It seemed like days until he got there, but the chronometer said just a little over nine hours.

As he came over the horizon he searched for Varnett's flyer. It wasn't to be seen.

Suddenly Skander spotted it—down, down on that flat plain at the pole. He braked and hovered over it. Slowly, in the gloom, he made out a tiny white dot near the center of the plain.

Varnett! He was going to be the first in!

Varnett detected movement and looked up at the flyer. Suddenly he started running for his own.

Skander came down on him, skirting the ground so low that he was afraid he would crash himself. Varnett ducked and rolled, but was unhurt.

Skander cursed himself, then decided to set it down. He still had the knife, and that might just be enough. He took the flare pistol which, while it wouldn't necessarily penetrate the suit, might cause a blinding distraction. He was not a large man, but he was a head taller than the boy and the odds were otherwise even in his mind.

Landing near Varnett's flyer, he got out quickly, flare gun in his right hand, knife in his left. Cursing the almost total absence of light and the fact that he had had to take his eyes off Varnett to land, Skander looked cautiously around.

Varnett had vanished.

Before this could sink in, a white figure jumped from atop the other flyer and hit him in the back. He went down, dropping the flare gun.

The two figures, rolling across the rocky landscape, grappled for the knife. Skander was larger, but older

18

and in worse physical condition than Varnett. Finally, with a shove, Skander pushed Varnett away from him and came upon the boy with the knife. Varnett let him get very close; then, as the knife made a quick stab, the boy's arm reached out and caught the older man's wrist. The two struggled and groaned in their suits as Skander tried to press the knife home.

They were in that frozen tableau when, suddenly, the hole opened.

They were both already in it.

Both vanished.

Another Part of the Field

NATHAN BRAZIL STRETCHED BACK IN HIS HUGE, PIL-lowy lounge chair aboard the bridge of the freighter *Stehekin,* nine days out of Paradise with a load of grain bound for drought-stricken Coriolanus and with three passengers. Passengers were common on such runs—there were actually a dozen staterooms aboard —as freighter travel was much cheaper than passenger ships and a lot easier if you wanted to get where you were going in a hurry. There were a thousand freight runs for every passenger run to almost anyplace.

The crew consisted only of Brazil. The ships were now automated, so he was there just in case something went wrong. Food had been prepared for all before takeoff and had been loaded into the automated kitchen. A tiny wardroom was used on those occa-sions when someone wanted to eat outside of his state-room or with the captain.

Actually, the passengers had more contempt for him than he for them. In an age of extreme conform-ity, men like Nathan Brazil were the mavericks, the loners, the ones who didn't fit. Recruited mostly off the barbarian worlds of the frontier, they could take the loneliness of the job, the endless weeks often without human company. Most psychologists called them sociopaths, people alienated from society.

Brazil liked people all right, but not the factory-made ones. He would rather sit here in his domain, the stars showing on the great three-dimensional screens in front of him, and reflect on why society had become alienated from him.

He was a small man, around 170 centimeters tall, slight and thin. His skin was dark-complexioned. Two bright, brown eyes flanked a conspicuous Roman nose which sat atop a mouth very wide, rubbery, and full of teeth. His black hair hung long to his shoulders, but was stringy and looked overgreased and underwashed. He had a thin mustache and thinner full beard that looked as if someone had attempted to grow a full brush and hadn't made it. He was dressed in a loose-fitting but loudly colorful tunic and matching pants, and wore sandals of a sickly green.

The passengers, he knew, were scared stiff of him, and he liked it that way. Unfortunately, they were still almost thirty days out and their boredom and claustrophobia would sooner or later drive them meddling into his lap.

Oh, hell, he thought. Might as well get everybody together. They have huddled back in that small lounge in the stern long enough.

He reached up and flicked a switch.

"The captain," he intoned in a tenor voice that nonetheless had a gravelly undertone to it, making it sound a little harsh and unintentionally sarcastic, "requests the pleasure of your company at dinner today. If you like, you may join me in the wardroom forward in thirty minutes. Don't feel put out if you don't want to come. I won't," he concluded, and switched off the speaker, chuckling softly.

Why do I do that? he asked himself for the hundredth—thousandth?—time. For nine days I chase them around, bully them, and see as little of them as possible. Now, when I start to be sociable, I blow it.

He sighed, then reached over and dialed the meals. Now they would *have* to come up, or starve. He idly scratched himself and wondered whether or not he

20

should take a shower before dinner. No, he decided, I had one only five days ago; I'll just use deodorant.

He picked up the book he had been reading off and on, a blood-and-guts romance on some faraway planet published centuries ago and produced in facsimile for him by a surprised and gratified librarian.

He called librarians his secret agents because he was one of the very few who read books at all. Libraries were usually single institutions on planets and were patronized by only a very few. Nobody wrote books anymore, he thought, not even this garbage. They dredged up whatever information they needed for reference from the computer terminal in every household; even then the vast majority were the vocal types that answered questions. Only the technocrats needed to read.

Only barbarians and wanderers read anymore.

And librarians.

Everybody else could just flip a switch and get a full, three-dimensional, sight-sound-and-smell creation of their own fantasies or those of a crew of dedicated fantasists picked by the government.

Pretty dull shit, he thought. Even the people were bred without imaginations. The imaginative ones were fixed—or gotten rid of. Too dangerous to have a thinker unless he thought the government's way.

Brazil wondered idly whether any of his passengers could read. The Pig probably—his name for Datham Hain, who looked very much like one—but he probably only read up on the stuff he sold or some mundane crap like that. Maybe a manual on how to strangle people twenty ways, he thought. Hain looked as if he'd enjoy that.

The girl with him was harder to figure. Like Hain, she obviously wasn't from the communal factory worlds—she was mature, maybe twenty or so, and, if she didn't look so wasted away, she might be pretty. Not built, or beautiful, but nice. But she had that empty look in her eyes, and was so damned servile to the fat man. Wu Julee, the manifest said her name was. *Julie Wu?* mused a corner of his brain. There it was again! Damn! He tried to grab onto the source of the thought, but it vanished.

21

But she does look Chinese, said that little corner, and then the thought retreated once again.

Chinese. That word meant something once. He knew it did. Where did those terms come from? And why couldn't he remember where they came from? Hell, almost everybody had those characteristics these days, he thought.

Then, suddenly, the thought was out of his mind, as such thoughts always were, and he was back on his main track.

The third one—almost the usual, he reflected, except that he never drew the usual, permanently twelve-year-old automaton on his trips. They were all raised and conditioned to look alike, think alike, and believe that theirs was the best of all possible worlds. No reason to travel. But Vardia Diplo 1261 was the same underneath, anyway: looked twelve, was flat-chested, probably neutered, since there was some pelvic width. She was a courier between her world and the next bunch of robots down the line. Spent all her time doing exercises.

A tiny bell sounded telling him that dinner was served, and he got up and ambled back to the wardroom.

The wardroom—nobody knew why it was called that—merely consisted of a large table that was permanently attached to the floor and a series of chairs that were part of the floor until you pulled up on a little ring, whereupon they arose and became comfortable seats. The place was otherwise a milky white plastic—walls, floor, ceiling, even tabletop. The monotony was broken only by small plaques giving the ship's name, construction data, ownership, and by his and the ship's commissions from the Confederacy as well as by his master's license.

He entered, half expecting no one to be there, and was surprised to see the two women already seated. The fat man was up, intently reading his master's license.

Hain was dressed in a light blue toga that made him look like Nero; Wu Julee was dressed in similar fashion, but it looked better on her. The Comworlder, Vardia, wore a simple, one-piece black robe. He noted idly that Wu Julee seemed to be in a trance, staring straight ahead.

Hain completed reading the wall plaques, then returned to his seat next to Wu Julee, a frown forming on his corpulent face.

"What's so odd about my license?" Brazil asked curiously.

"That form," Hain replied in a silky-smooth, disquieting voice. "It is so old! No such form has been used in my memory."

The captain nodded and smiled, pushing a button under his chair. The food compartments opened up on top and plates of steaming food were revealed in front of each person. A large bottle and four glasses rose from a circular opening in the middle of the table.

"I got it a long time ago," he told them conversationally, as he chose a glass and poured some nonalcoholic wine into it.

"You have been in rejuve then, Captain?" Hain responded politely.

Brazil nodded. "Many times. Freighter captains are known for it."

"But it costs—unless one is influential with the Council," Hain noted.

"True," Brazil acknowledged, talking as he chewed his synthetic meat. "But we're well paid, in port only a few days every few weeks, and most of us just put our salaries into escrow to pay for what we need. Nothing much else to blow it on these days."

"But the date!" Vardia broke in. "It's so very, very old! Citizen Hain said it was three hundred and sixty-two standard years!"

Brazil shrugged. "Not very unusual. Another captain on this same line is over five hundred."

"Yes, that's true," Hain said. "But the license is stamped *Third Renewal—P.C.* How old *are* you, anyway?"

Brazil shrugged again. "I truthfully don't know. As old as the records, anyway. The brain has a finite capacity, so every rejuve erases a little more of the past. I get snatches of things—old memories, old terms—from time to time, but nothing I can hang on to. I

23

could be six hundred—or six thousand, though I doubt it."

"You've never inquired?" Hain asked curiously.

"No," Brazil managed, his mouth full of mush. He swallowed, then took another long drink of wine. "Lousy stuff," he snorted, holding the glass up and looking at it as if it were full of disease cultures. Suddenly he remembered he was in the middle of a conversation.

"Actually," he told them, "I've been curious as to all that, but the records just sort of fade out. I've outlived too many bureaucracies. Well, I've always lived for now and the future, anyway."

Hain had already finished his meal, and patted his ample stomach. "I'm due for my first rejuve in another year or two. I'm almost ninety, and I'm afraid I've abused myself terribly these past few years."

As the small talk continued, Brazil's gaze kept falling to the girl who sat so strangely by Hain. She seemed to be paying not the least attention to the conversation and had hardly touched her food.

"Well," Brazil said, suppressing his curiosity about the strange girl, "*my* career is on that wall and Citizen Vardia's is obvious, but what takes you flitting around the solar systems, Hain?"

"I am—well, a salesman, Captain," the fat man replied. "All of the planets are somewhat unique in the excesses they produce. What is surplus on one is usually needed on another—like the grain you have as cargo on this fine ship. I'm a man who arranges such trades."

Brazil made his move. "What about you, Citizen Wu Julee? Are you his secretary?"

The girl looked suddenly confused. *That's real fear in her eyes,* Brazil noted to himself, surprised. She turned immediately to Hain, a look of pleading in her face.

"My—ah, niece, Captain, is very shy and quiet," Hain said smoothly. "She prefers to remain in the background. You *do* prefer to remain in the background, don't you, my dear?"

She answered in a voice that almost cracked from

disuse, in a thin voice that held no more tonal inflection than Vardia's.

"I do prefer to remain in the background," she said dully, like a machine. A recording machine at that—for there seemed no comprehension in that face.

"Sorry!" Brazil told her apologetically, turning palms up in a gesture of resignation.

Funny, he thought to himself. The one who looks like a robot is conversational and mildly inquisitive; the one who looks like a real girl is a robot. He thought of two girls he had known long ago—he could even remember their names. One was a really sexy knockout—you panted just being in the same room with her. The other was ugly, flat, and extremely mannish in manner, voice, and dress—the sort of nondescript nobody looked at twice. But the sexy one liked other girls best, and the mannish one was heaven in bed.

You can't tell by looks, he reflected sourly.

Vardia broke the silence. She was, after all, bred to the diplomatic service.

"I think it is fascinating you are so old, Captain," she said pleasantly. "Perhaps you are the oldest man alive. My race, of course, has no rejuve—it is not needed."

No, of course not, Brazil thought sadly. They lived their eighty years as juvenile specialist components in the anthill of their society, then calmly showed up at the local Death Factory to be made into fertilizer.

Anthill? he thought curiously. Now what in hell were *ants*?

Aloud, he replied, "Well, old or not I can't say, but it doesn't do anybody much good unless you've got a job like mine. I don't know why I keep on living—just something bred into me, I guess."

Vardia brightened. *That* was something she could understand. "I wonder what sort of world would require such a survival imperative?" she mused, proving to everyone else that she didn't understand at all.

Brazil let it pass.

"A long-dead-and-gone one, I think," he said dryly.

"I think we shall go back to our rooms, Captain," Hain put in, getting up and stretching. "To tell the

25

truth, the only thing more exhausting than doing something is doing nothing at all." Julee rose almost at the same instant as the fat man, and they left together.

Vardia said, "I suppose I shall go back as well, Captain, but I would like the chance to talk to you again and, perhaps, to see the bridge."

"Feel free," he responded warmly. "I eat here every mealtime and company is always welcome. Perhaps tomorrow we'll eat and talk and then I'll show you how the ship runs."

"I shall look forward to it," she replied, and there even seemed a bit of warmth in her flat voice—or, at least, sincerity. He wondered how genuine it was, and how much was the inbred diplomatic traits. It was the sort of comment that was guaranteed to please him. He wondered if he would ever know what went on in those insect minds.

Well, he told himself, in actual fact it didn't make a damned bit of difference—he would show her around the ship and she would seem to enjoy it anyway.

When he was alone in the wardroom, he looked over at the empty dishes. Hain had polished off everything, as expected, and so had Vardia and he— the meals were individually prepared for preference and body build.

Julee's meal was almost untouched. She had merely played with the food.

No wonder she's wasting away, he thought. Physically, anyway. But why mentally? She certainly *wasn't* Hain's niece, no matter what he said, and he doubted if she was an employee, either.

Then, *what?*

He pushed the disposal button and lowered the chairs back to their floor position, then returned to the bridge.

Freighter captains were the law in space, of course. They had to be. As such, ships of all lines had certain safeguards unique to each captain, and some gimmicks common to all but known only to those captains.

Brazil sat back down in his command chair and looked at the projection screen still showing the virtually unchanging starscape. It looked very realistic, and very impressive, but it was a phony—the scene was a computer simulation; the Balla-Drubbik drive which allowed faster-than-light travel was extradimensional in nature. There was simply nothing outside the ship's energy well that would relate to any human terms.

He reached over and typed on the computer keyboard: "I SUSPECT ILLEGAL ACTIVITIES. SHOW CABINS 6 ON LEFT AND 7 ON RIGHT SCREEN." The computer lit a small yellow light to show that the instructions had been received and the proper code for the captain registered; then the simulated starfield was replaced with overhead, side-by-side views of the two cabins.

The fact that cameras were hidden in all cabins and could be monitored by captains was a closely guarded secret, though several people had already had knowledge of the accidentally discovered bugs erased from their minds by the Confederacy. Yet, many a madman and hijacker had been trapped by these methods, and Brazil also knew that the Confederation Port Authority would look at the recordings of what he was seeing live and question him as to motive. This wasn't something done lightly.

Cabin 6—Hain's cabin—was empty, but the missing passenger was in Wu Julee's Cabin 7. A less-experienced, less-jaded man would have been repulsed at the scene.

Hain was standing near the closed and bolted door, stark naked. Wu Julee, a look of terror on her face, was also naked.

Brazil turned up the volume.

"Come on, Julee," Hain commanded, a tone of delightful expectancy in his harsh voice. There was no question as to what he had in mind.

The girl cowed back in horror. "Please! Please, Master!" she pleaded with all the hysterical emotion she had hidden in public.

"When you do it, Julee," Hain said in a hushed but still excited tone. "Only then."

She did what he asked.

Less-experienced and less-jaded men would have been repulsed at the sight, it was true.

Brazil was becoming aroused.

27

After she finished, Wu Julee continued to plead with the fat man to give it to her. Brazil waited expectantly, half-knowing what *it* was already. He just had to see where it was hidden and how it was protected.

Hain promised her he would go get it and then donned the toga once more. He unbolted the door and appeared to look up and down the hallway. Satisfied, he walked out to his own cabin and unlocked the door. The unseen watcher turned his gaze to Cabin 6.

Hain entered and took a small, thin attaché case from beneath the washbasin. It had the high-security locks, Brazil noted—five small squares programmed to receive five of Hain's ten fingerprints in a certain order. Hain's body blocked reading the combination, but it wouldn't have mattered anyway—without Hain's touch the whole inside would dissolve in a quick acid bath.

Hain opened the case to reveal a tray of jewelry and body paint. Normal enough, and the tray seemed deep enough to fill the whole case. No customs problems.

Working a second set of fingerprint-coded combinations through the thin plastic which hid the additional guards, the tray came loose and appeared to be floating on something else. The fat man lifted the tray out.

For the first time Brazil noticed that Hain had on some thin gloves. He hadn't seen them being put on—maybe they were already on during the scene he had just witnessed—but there they were.

The fat man reached in and picked out a tiny object that almost dripped with liquid. The rest of the case bottom, Brazil could see, was filled with the stuff. His suspicions were confirmed.

Datham Hain was a sponge merchant.

The contraband was called sponge because that was what the stuff was—an alien sponge spawned on a distant sea world now interdicted by the Confederacy.

The story came back to Brazil. A nice planet, mostly ocean but dotted with millions of islands connected in a network of shallows. A tropical climate except at the poles. It looked like a paradise, and tests had shown nothing that could hurt the human race. A test colony—two, three hundred people—was landed on the two largest islands for the five-year trial, as per standard procedure. Volunteers, of course, the last remnant of frontiersmen in the human race.

If they survived and prospered, they owned the world—to develop it or do with it what they would. But because man's test instruments could analyze only the known and the theoretical, there was no way to detect a threat so alien it hadn't even been imagined. That was the reason for the trial in the first place.

So those people had settled in and lived and loved and played and built on their islands.

For almost a month.

That was when they started to go mad, the people of that colony. They regressed—slowly, at first, then increasingly faster and faster. They turned into primitive beasts as the thing that had caught them ate away at their brains. They became like wild apes, only without even the most rudimentary reasoning ability. Finally they died, from their inability to cope with even the basics of eating and shelter. Most drowned; some killed one another.

And out of their bodies, eventually, grew the pretty flowers of the island, in new profusion.

Scientists speculated that some sort of elemental organism—based not on carbon or silicon, but on the iron oxides in the rocks of their pretty island—interacted through the air not with them but with the synthetic food rations they brought to help them until they could develop their own native agriculture.

And they had eaten it, and it had eaten them.

But there had been one survivor—one woman who had hidden in the huge beds of alien sponge along a particularly rocky shoreline. Oh, she had died, too—but almost three weeks later than the others. When she no longer returned each evening to sleep in the sponge bed.

The natural secretions of the sponge acted as a retardant—not as an antidote. But as long as a victim had a daily intake of the secretion, the mutant strain seemed inactive. Remove the substance—and the degenerative process began once again. But scientists had taken some samples of the mutant strain and of living sponge with them to study in their labs on far-off worlds. All of it was thought to have been destroyed afterward—but evidently some had not been. Some had been taken by the worst of elements and was developed in their own labs in unknown space.

The perfect commodity.

By secretly introducing the stuff into people's food, you gave them the disease. Then, when the first symptoms came and baffled all around you, the merchant would come. He would ease the pain and cause normality by giving you a little bit of sponge—as Hain was administering a dose to Wu Julee at that very moment.

The Confederacy wouldn't help you. It maintained a sponge colony on that interdicted world for the afflicted, where one could live a normal, if very primitive, existence and soak each night in a sponge bath. If, that is, the victim could be gotten there before the disease became too progressive to bother.

The sponge merchants chose only the most wealthy and powerful—or their children, if their world had families of any sort. There was no charge for the daily sponge supply, oh, no. You just did as they asked when they asked.

There was even the suspicion that so many rulers of the Confederacy were hostage to the stuff now that that was the reason no real search for an antidote or cure had ever been started.

For power was the ultimate aim of the sponge merchants.

Nathan Brazil wondered who Wu Julee was. The daughter of some big-shot ruler or banker or industrialist? Maybe the child of the Confederacy enforcement chief? More likely she was a sample, he thought. No use risking exposure.

She was his absolute slave, no question. The disease had been allowed to incubate in her just short of that critical point when the stuff multiplied exponentially. Human, yes, but probably already with her IQ halved, constantly in mild pain that started to grow as the effects of the sponge antitoxin wore off. An effective demonstration, which would keep the merchant from having to infect some innocent and let things run their full course. That was done, of course, when necessary—but it wasn't good to have a long period of time when it would be obvious to the agents of the Confederacy that a sponge merchant was at large.

He wondered idly why the girl didn't commit suicide. He thought *he* would. A victim is probably too far gone to consider it by the time he realizes it is the only option, he decided.

Brazil looked back up at the screens. Hain had repacked the case and stored it and was preparing to go to sleep. Clever, that case, the captain thought. Sponge is extremely compressible and needs only enough seawater to keep it moist. It even grew in there, he thought. As samples were dispensed, new ones would replace it. That was the reason only the minimum was ever given to a victim—get hold of enough of it, unused, and you could grow your own.

Wu Julee was lying on her own bed, one leg draped down on the side. She was breathing hard but she had a sort of idiot's smile on her face.

Relief for another day, the little sponge cube swallowed, the body breaking down the evidence.

Nathan Brazil's stomach finally turned.

What were you, Wu Julee, before Datham Hain served dinner? he mused. A student or scholar, or a professional, like Vardia? A spoiled brat? A young maiden, perhaps one day expecting to bear children?

Gone now, he thought sadly. The recordings would nail Datham Hain clean—and the syndicate of sponge merchants would let him hang, too. Most he had ever heard of were compulsive suiciders when subjected to any psych probes or the like. They would get nothing from him but his life.

But Wu Julee—without sponge, she needed eighteen days from where they would be at absolute flank speed to make that damned planet colony, and she was already near or at the exponential reproductive stage.

She would arrive a mindless vegetable, unable to

31

do anything not in the autonomic nervous system, having spent most of the voyage as an animal. A day or two after that, it would eat her nervous system away and she would die.

So they wouldn't bother. They'd just send her to the nearest Death Factory to get something useful out of her.

They said Nathan Brazil was a hard man: experienced, efficient, and cold as ice, never a feeling for anything but himself.

But Nathan Brazil cried at tragedy, alone, in the dark, on the bridge of his powerful ship.

Neither Hain nor Wu Julee came to dinner again, although he saw the fat man often and kept up the pretense of innocent friendship. The sponge merchant could actually be quite entertaining, sitting back in the lounge over a couple of warm drinks and telling stories of his youth. He even played a fair game of cards.

Vardia, of course, never joined in the games and stories—they were things beyond her conception. She kept asking *why* they played card games since the only practical purpose of games was to develop a physical or mental skill. The concept of gambling, of playing for money, meant even less to her—her people didn't use the stuff, and only printed it for interplanetary trade. The government provided everyone with everything they needed equally, so why try to get more?

Brazil found her logic, as usual, baffling. All his life he had been compulsively competitive. He was firmly convinced of his uniqueness in the universe and his general superiority to it, although he was occasionally bothered by the universe's lack of appreciation. But she remained inquisitive and continued asking all those questions two cultures could never answer for each other.

"You promised days ago to show me the bridge," she reminded him one day.

"So I did," he acknowledged. "Well, now's as good a time as any. Why don't we go all the way forward?"

They made their way from the aft lounge, along the great catwalk above the cargo.

"I don't mean to pry," he said to her as they walked along, "but, out of curiosity, is your mission of vital importance?"

"You mean war or peace, something like that?" Vardia responded. "No, very few are like that. The truth is, as you may know, I have no knowledge of the messages I carry. They are blocked and only the key from our embassy on Coriolanus can unlock whatever I'm supposed to say. Then the information will be erased, and I will be sent home, with or without a message in return. But, from the tone or facial expressions of those who give me the messages, I can usually tell if it's serious, and this one certainly is not."

"Possibly something to do with the cargo," Brazil speculated as they entered the wardroom and walked through it this time and out onto another, shorter catwalk. The great engines which maintained the real-universe field of force around them throbbed below. "Do you know how bad things are on Coriolanus?"

She shrugged. "Not too bad, I understand. No widespread famine yet. That will happen months from now, when the harvest doesn't come in because the rains didn't come *last* season and the ground is too hard. Then this cargo will be needed. Why do you ask?"

"Oh, just curious, I guess," he responded, an odd and slightly strained tone in his voice.

They entered the bridge.

Vardia was immediately all over it, like an anxious schoolchild. "What's this?" and "How's that work?" and all the other questions poured from her. He answered as best he could.

She marveled over the computer. "I have never seen one that you must write to and read," she told him with the awe reserved for genuine historical antiques. He decided not to respond that people these days were too mechanical for him so he couldn't bear to have a real mechanical person around, but instead he replied, "Well, it's what you get used to. This one's just as modern and efficient as any

33

other; I tried it on and can handle it easier. Although I have little to do, in an emergency I have to make thousands of split-second decisions. It's better to use what you can use instinctively in such a situation."

She accepted his explanation, which was partially the truth, and noticed his small library of paperback books with their lurid covers. He asked her if she knew how to read and she said no, whatever for? Certain professions on her world required the ability to read, of course, but very few—and if that wasn't required, as it certainly wasn't for her job as a reel of blank recording tape, she could see no reason to learn.

He wondered if somewhere they simply had a single Vardia Diplo program, and they read it out, erased the whole thing, then rerecorded it for each trip. Probably, he decided—otherwise, she would have seen bridges before and encountered enough alien culture not to ask those naive questions. Most likely she was just new. It was tough to tell if her kind was fourteen or forty-four.

At any rate, he was glad she couldn't read. He had suffered a very unsettling moment when she had gone over to that computer and he had noticed that he had forgotten to turn off the screen.

The computer had been spewing its usual every-half-hour warning to him.

UNAUTHORIZED COURSE CORRECTION, it said. THIS IS NOT A JUSTIFIED ACTION. COURSE IS BEING PLOTTED AND WILL BE BROADCAST TO CONFEDERACY AS SOON AS DESTINATION IS REACHED.

And she wondered why he didn't have the talking kind of computer.

And so they continued on the new course, all but Brazil and the computer oblivious to their real destination.

A stroke of genius, he congratulated himself after Vardia had left. The courier's answers had eased his conscience on Coriolanus. They would get their grain —just late. In the meantime, Hain would continue to give Wu Julee the sponge, until that day came when they arrived over the sponge world itself. There he would lose two passengers—Wu Julee would have

34

life, and Hain would be introduced to the colony as a pusher.

Brazil didn't think any Admiralty Board in the galaxy would convict him; besides, he already had the largest number of verbal and written reprimands in the service. Vardia, though, would never understand his reasoning.

A loud, hollow-sounding gong brought him out of his satisfied reverie. It reverberated throughout the ship. Brazil jumped up and looked at the computer screen.

DISTRESS SIGNAL FIELD INTERCEPTED, it read. AWAIT INSTRUCTIONS.

Seeing what the message was, he first flipped off the gong then flipped on the intercom. His three passengers were all concerned, naturally.

"Don't be alarmed," he told them. "It's just a distress field. A ship or some small colony is having problems and needs help. I will have to answer the call, so we'll be delayed a bit. Just sit tight and I'll keep you informed."

With that he turned to the computer, giving it the go-ahead to plot the coordinates of the signal. He didn't like the idea at all—the signal had to be coming from a place far off his approved course. That invited premature discovery. Nonetheless, he could never ignore such a signal. Similar ones had saved him too many times, and the odds of anybody else intercepting it were more astronomical than his own odds at happening on it.

The ship's engines moaned, then the throbbing that was a part of his existence subsided to a dull sound as the energy field around the ship merged into normal space.

The two screens suddenly came on with the real, not the fake, galaxy—and a planet. A big one, he noted. Rocky and reddish in the feeble light of a dwarf star.

He asked the computer for coordinates. Its screens were blank for a long time, then it replied, DALGONIA, STAR ARACHNIS, DEAD WORLD, MARKOVIAN ORIGIN, NO OTHER INFORMATION. UNINHABITED, it added needlessly. It was plain that nothing *he* knew could live here.

PLOT DISTRESS COORDINATES AND MAGNIFY WHEN DONE, he ordered, and the computer searched the bleak panorama, quadrant by quadrant. Finally it stopped on one area and put it under intense magnification.

The picture was grainy, snowy as hell, but the scene clearly showed a small camp. Something just didn't look right.

Brazil parked the ship in a synchronous orbit and prepared to go down and see what was wrong. But first, he flipped on the intercom again.

"I'm afraid I'll have to seal you aft," he told his passengers. "I have to check out something down on the planet. If I don't return within eight standard hours, the ship will automatically pull out and take you to Coriolanus at top speed, so you needn't be worried."

"Can I come with you?" Vardia's voice came back at him.

He chuckled. "No, sorry, regulations and all that. You'll be in contact with me through this intercom all the time, so you'll know what's going on."

He suited up, reflecting that he hadn't been in one of the things in years. Then he entered the small bay below the engine well through a hatch from the bridge and entered the little landing craft. Within five minutes, he was away.

The ship's computer took him to the spot by radio link, and he was at the scene in under an hour. He raised the canopy—the little craft had no air or pressurization of its own—and climbed down the side, striking the ground. The lighter gravity made him feel ten feet tall. The ship, of course, was kept at one gee for everybody's convenience.

He needed only a couple of minutes to survey the scene and to report his findings back to the ship's recorders as the passengers anxiously followed his every word. "It's a base camp," he told them, "like the kind used for scientific expeditions. Tent-type units, modular, pretty modern—seem to have exploded somehow. All of them." He knew that was

36

impossible—and he knew they knew—but those were the facts all the same.

He was just wondering aloud as to what could have caused such a thing when he noticed the piled-up pressure suits near what would have been the exit lock. He went over to them and picked one up, curiously.

"The suits are outside the area—empty. As if somebody threw them there. The explosion or whatever couldn't have done it—not without some damage. Wait a minute, let me get over to the area of the dorms."

Vardia listened with growing fascination, and frustration that she could see none of it, nor ask questions.

"*Yuk,*" came Brazil's voice over the intercom. "Pretty messy death. They died when the vacuum hit, if the explosion didn't get them. Hmmm. . . . Seven. I can't figure it out. The place is a mess but the explosion didn't really do more than rip the tents to shreds. But that was enough."

He moved over to another area that caught his eye.

"Funny," he said, "looks like somebody's done a job on the power plant. Well, here's what did it, anyway. Somebody jacked up the oxygen to pure and shut off the rest of the air. Just takes a spark after that. Worries me, though. There are two dozen safeguards against that sort of thing. Somebody had to do it deliberately."

The words sent a chill through all three passengers listening breathlessly to his account. Even Wu Julee seemed caught up in the drama.

"Well, I just counted the beds," Brazil told them, his voice keeping calm but tinged with the concern he felt. "A dorm room for five, another one with three, and a single—probably the project chief's. Bodies in all but the chief's and one of the fivesome. Hmmm. . . . There were seven pressure suits. Should have been nine."

They heard him breathing and moving around, but he was infuriatingly silent for the longest period.

Finally he said, "Two flyers are gone, so the missing ones must be somewhere else on the planet. It's a sure bet that one of them, at least, killed the others."

Again the long silence, punctuated only with breathing sounds. All aboard the freighter were holding their breaths. It took no imagination at all to figure out that one, maybe two, madmen were loose on that planet—and Brazil was alone.

"Now here's the strangest part," the captain reported at last. They strained for every word, cursing him for his maddening conversational tone. "I've gotten to the rescue signal. It's about a kilometer from the camp, on a low ridge. But it isn't turned on."

It was almost two hours more before Nathan Brazil was back aboard the ship. He didn't get out of his suit, although he left the helmet on his chair while he checked the computer. It assured him once again that it was indeed receiving a distress signal from the beacon below.

Only Brazil knew that it wasn't.

It just wasn't possible.

He unlocked the aft compartment and made his way back to the passengers, all of whom were seated in the lounge.

"So what do you make of it, Captain?" Hain asked seriously.

"Well," replied the other hesitantly, "I'm about to start believing in ghosts. *That signal isn't on.* To make sure, I disabled it completely before coming back. But it's still coming in loud and strong up here."

"There must be another signal," Vardia suggested logically.

"No, there isn't. Not only is one the standard issue —and everything else there is standard issue—but a computer that can plot a course in deep space through the underdimensions and get you to a particular port on a particular planet in the middle of nowhere doesn't screw up in plotting the coordinates of a distress signal."

"Let's proceed on what we *do* know, then," Hain suggested. "We know that there *is* a signal—no, no, let me finish!" he protested as Brazil was about to cut in. "As I said, there *is* a signal. It was set or sent by someone who, presumably, is one or both of the people who survived the—ah, disaster. Someone—or something—wants us to come down, wanted us to find the wrecked station, wants *something*."

"A malevolent alien civilization, Hain?" Brazil retorted skeptically. "Come on. We've got—what?—a thousand, give or take, solar systems explored to date, with more every year. We've found remains of the Markovians—one of their cities is near the camp, probably what the group was investigating—and lots and lots of animal and plant life. But no living, present-day alien civilizations."

"But we've done only a trifle!" Hain protested. "There are a billion billion stars around. You know the odds."

"But not here, inside our perimeter," the captain pointed out.

"But, he *is* right, you know," Vardia interjected. "Perhaps someone—or something—discovered *us*."

"No," Brazil told them, "it's not that. There is some simple explanation. What happened down there was cold-blooded human murder by one of the team. For what madness, I can't guess. They can't get off the planet with what they've got. If they don't starve to death first, their pickup ship will get them."

"You mean you aren't going to try to find them?" Vardia asked. "But you must! Otherwise some other ship might answer them and the killers might be able to overpower them before they are forewarned!"

"Oh, the odds against anyone else hearing that signal are astronomical," Brazil replied patiently.

"I assure you," Hain said flatly, "that the last thing I wish to do is stalk a murderer on an unknown world. Nevertheless, Citizen Vardia is correct. If we found them, someone else might."

Brazil's eyebrows shot up in surprise. "Can *you* handle a pistol?" he asked the fat man. "Can you?" he asked Vardia.

"I can," Hain replied evenly, "and have."

"That is left to the military caste," Vardia replied, "but I am an expert with the sword, and I have a ceremonial one with me. It will puncture a pressure suit."

Brazil almost laughed. "A sword? You?"

She ran to her room and came back with a gleaming, handsome blade that glittered as if it were made of the finest silver. "It builds quick reflexes and good muscles," she explained. "Also, for some reason the sword is traditional in our service."

Brazil's face grew serious again. "And what about Wu Julee?" he asked, not of her but of Hain.

"She goes where I go," Hain replied cautiously. "And she will, in a pinch, help protect us with her life."

I'll bet, Brazil thought sourly. You, anyway.

There was never any problem of pressure suits; they expanded or contracted to fit almost any known human wearer, although Hain's did give him a little problem. Each of them had worn one before, at least in the practice drill before the ship left port. They were extremely light, and, once the helmet had been set into place and the seal activated, a person hardly knew he had it on. Air was recirculated and refined through two small, light filters on the side of the helmet. The supply would last for almost a day. In an emergency situation, the lifeboat could recharge the air supply for fifteen people for a month, so there was plenty of air to spare.

Brazil led them first to the distress beacon, if only to prove to himself that he was correct. They examined it carefully, and agreed that there was no way it could be sending.

But the little lifeboat monitor connection to the mother ship still said it was.

So they climbed back in and sped northward, the mystery so pressing on them that they barely noted the Markovian ruins near the camp and along the route. The ship's computer had located the two missing shuttlecraft on a plain near the north pole, and that seemed the next likely place to investigate. If anyone was left alive, he would be there.

"Why do you think they are up there?" Vardia asked Brazil.

"My theory is that the murderer couldn't trap one of them in the base camp and that that one took a shuttle and flew off. There must have been a chase, and that plain is where they met up," the captain replied. "We'll know in a little while, because we're almost there."

Being in a lifeboat with a major spatial propulsion unit, Brazil was able to make the long trip by going back up into orbit and braking back down again. Thus, the nine-hour journey was reduced to just a little over ninety minutes. He braked to the slowest speed he could maintain as they cleared a last mountain range and came upon a broad, flat plain.

"There they are!" Vardia almost shouted, and they all looked ahead at the two craft, small silver disks in the twilight, shown prominently at the edge of a slight discoloration in the plain.

Brazil circled around the spot several times.

"I can see no one," Hain reported. "Not a sign of life, not a pressure suit, nothing. They may still be in the craft," he suggested.

"Okay," Brazil replied, "I'll set down a few hundred meters from them. Hain, you stay back just outside this boat and cover me. The other two of you stay inside. If anything happens to us, the mother ship will reclaim the boat."

There was a soft bump, and they were down on the surface of Dalgonia. Brazil reached into the broad, black belt he wore on the outside of his pressure suit and removed one of two pistols and handed it to Hain.

The pistols didn't look like much, but they could fire short pulses of energy at rates from one per second to five hundred per second, the latter not doing much for aim but able to spread things enough to knock off a small regiment. There was a *stun* setting that would paralyze a man for a half hour or more, but both men placed their weapons on *full*.

There were seven ugly bodies far to the south.

Brazil eased out of the hatch in the eerie silence of a near vacuum, and, keeping the two shuttlecraft always in view, moved to cover behind the lifeboat. That was a relatively safe haven. Since the boat had

41

been built to take a tremendous amount of stress and even friction, it would be impervious to any weapons likely to be in the hands of their quarry.

Hain emerged shortly after, having more trouble climbing down with his bulk despite the weak gravity. He chose a position just forward of the nose where he was mostly sheltered but could still use the edge of the boat to steady his pistol.

Brazil, satisfied, moved cautiously forward.

He reached the nearest craft in less than two minutes. "No sign of life yet," he told them. "I'm going to climb up on top and have a look inside." He mounted the rail-type ladder along the side of the shuttle and walked over to the entry hatch.

"Still nothing," Brazil reported. "I'm going in."

It took only another three minutes to get inside and find nobody home. He then repeated the sequence with the second craft and found it empty too, although this one showed signs that somebody had spent many hours there.

"Come on up, anybody," he called. "There's no one here, or for many kilometers around. See what you make of it."

Hain told Wu Julee to join him. Vardia climbed out last, and they all went over to the captain, who was standing near the second shuttle and looking anxiously at the ground. Brazil noted with some amusement that Vardia clutched her nice, pretty sword.

"Look at the ground here," he said, pointing to the tracks of a person in a pressure suit coming up to a point at which the dust around was greatly disturbed for a large area.

"What do you make of it, Captain?" Hain asked.

"Well, it looks as if my theory's right, anyway. See—the first one was here, then saw the second one land, and he hid out on the back of the shuttle. When the pursuer—the guy who landed second I assume was the murderer—found nobody home, he walked around to here"—Brazil gestured at the mottled dust thrown about—"and was jumped by the first person from on top. They fought here, then one took off across the plain, the other in pursuit. See how we get only the toe tracks coming out of the fight scene?"

Vardia was already following the tracks out onto the plain. Suddenly she stopped short and stared, incredulous, at the ground. "Captain! Everyone! Come here!" she called urgently. They rushed up to her. She was pointing at the ground immediately ahead of her.

The fine dust was thinner here, and the rock changed color from a dull orange to more of a gray, but at first they didn't see what she meant. Brazil went over and stooped down. Then it sank in on him.

At the place where one man had stepped, just where the two strains of rock met, there was half a footprint. Not the running type—it was angled, so that a little less than half of a grown man's footprint, pressure suit pattern and all, was visible in the orange. Where it met the gray, there was unbroken dust.

"How is it possible, Captain?" Vardia asked, awed for the first time in her life—and not a little scared.

"There *must* be an explanation. It's a freakish thing—but I'd believe almost anything after all we've seen. I'm sure we'll find their prints continue farther on. Let's see."

They all walked onto the gray area for some distance. Vardia suddenly looked back to make certain that *they* were making footprints, and was relieved to see that they were. Suddenly she stopped short.

"Captain!" she exclaimed, that toneless voice suddenly tinged with panic and fear. The rest caught it, stopped, and turned. Vardia was pointing back at the ships from which they had come.

There were no shuttlecraft. There was no lifeboat. Only a bleak, unbroken orange plain stretching off to the mountains in the distance.

"Now what the hell?" Brazil managed, looking all around him to see if they had somehow turned around. They hadn't. He looked up to see if he could spot anything leaving, but there was nothing but the cold stars as darkness overtook them.

"What happened?" Hain asked plaintively. "Did our murderer—"

"No, that's not it," Brazil cut in quickly, a cold chill

43

suddenly going through him. "No one person—not even two—could have managed all three craft, and nobody but me could have lifted that lifeboat for another two hours."

There was a sudden vibration, like a small earthquake, that knocked them all off their feet.

Brazil broke his fall and held on in a crouch on his hands and knees. He looked up suddenly.

The whole area seemed bathed in eerie flashes of blue-white lightning, thousands of them!

"Damn me for an asshead!" Brazil swore. "We've been had!"

"But by whom?" Vardia called out.

Wu Julee screamed.

Then there was nothing but darkness and that weird, blue lightning, now laced, it appeared, with golden sparks. They all felt the sensation of falling and turning and twisting in the air, as if they were dropping down some bottomless pit. There was no up, no down, nothing but that dizzy sensation.

And Wu Julee kept screaming.

Suddenly they were lying on a flat, glassy-smooth black surface. Lights were on around them, and there seemed to be a structure—as if they were in some building, like a great warehouse.

Things didn't stop spinning around for a while. They were dizzy, and sick. All but Brazil threw up into their helmets, which neatly and efficiently cleared the mess away. A professional spaceman, Brazil was the first to recover his equilibrium. Then he steadied himself, half sitting up on the black, glassy floor.

It was a room, he saw—no, a great chamber, with six sides. The glassy area was also a hexagon, and around it stretched a railing and what appeared to be a walkway. A single great light, also six-sided, was suspended above them in the curved ceiling. The place was huge, Brazil saw, easily large enough to house a small freighter.

The others were there. Vardia, he saw, was already sitting up, but Wu Julee, it appeared, had passed out. Hain just lay on the floor, breathing hard. Brazil struggled to his feet and made his way unsteadily to Wu

Julee. He checked and saw that she was in fact still breathing but unconscious.

"Everybody all right?" he called. Vardia nodded and tried to rise. He helped her to her feet, and she managed. Hain groaned, but tried, and was game about it. He finally managed it.

"Just about one gee," Brazil noted. "That's interesting."

"Now what?" asked Datham Hain.

"Looks like some breaks in that railing—the closest one is over there to your right. We might as well make for it." Taking their silence for assent, he picked up Wu Julee's limp body and they started off. She weighed hardly anything, he noted, and he wasn't a particularly strong man.

He looked down at her, sorrow in his eyes. *What will happen to you now, Wu Julee? But I tried! God! I tried!*

Her eyes opened, and she looked up into his through the tinted helmet faceplates. Perhaps it was the gentle way he carried her, perhaps it was his expression, perhaps it was just the fact that she saw him and not Hain, but she smiled.

She got much heavier about halfway there, he noted, as his body was drained of the adrenalin that had pumped into him during the—fall? Finally he was straining at the weight, although she weighed no more than half what she should. He finally admitted defeat and had to put her down. She didn't protest, but as they continued to walk she clung tightly to his arm.

No matter what, Hain no longer owned her.

Steps of what looked like polished stone led up to the break in the rail—six of them, they noted. Finally they were all up on some kind of platform from which a conveyor belt stretched out. But it was not moving in either direction.

They all looked to the captain for guidance. For the first time in his life, Nathan Brazil felt the full weight of responsibility. He had gotten them into this—never mind that they had talked him into it, it was his responsibility—and he didn't have the slightest idea what to do next.

45

"Well," he began, "if we stay here we starve to death, or run out of air—or both. We may do so anyway, but we at least ought to see what we're into. There has to be a doorway out of this place."

"Probably six of them," Hain said caustically.

Brazil stepped out onto one of the conveyors, and it suddenly started moving. The movement was so unexpected that he found himself carried along farther and farther away from the rest before anyone could say anything.

"Better get on," he called back, "or you'll lose me! I don't know how to stop this thing!"

He was receding farther and farther, when Wu Julee stepped on. The other two immediately did likewise.

The speed wasn't great, but it was faster than a man could walk briskly. A larger, broader platform loomed ahead before Brazil could see it. So he slid off onto it, stumbled, fell down, and rolled halfway across.

"Watch out! Platform coming up!" he warned. The others saw the platform and him in time to step off, although each one nearly lost his balance in the attempt.

"Apparently you're supposed to be walking on the belt," Vardia said. "That way you just walk onto the platform. See? There are actually several belts just before the platform, each one going at a slightly slower speed."

The belt suddenly stopped.

"No doorway here," Hain noted. "Shall we press on?"

"I suppose so—*whoops!*" Brazil exclaimed as he was about to step out. The other belt had started in the reverse direction!

"Looks like somebody's coming to meet us," Brazil said jokingly, a tone that didn't match his inner feelings at all. Even so, he pulled and checked his pistol, noting that Hain was doing the same. Vardia, he saw, still held onto that sword.

They could see a giant figure coming toward them, and all stepped back to the rear edge of the platform.

As the figure came closer, they could see that it was like nothing in the known universe.

Start with a chocolate brown human torso, incredibly broad, and ribbed so that the chest muscles seemed to form squarish plates. A head, oval-shaped, equally brown and hairless except for a huge white walrus mustache under a broad, flat nose. Six arms—in threes, spaced in rows down the torso—extremely muscular but attached, except for the shoulder pair, on ball-type sockets like the claws of a crab. Below, the torso melded into an enormous brown-and-yellow-striped series of scales leading to a huge, serpentine lower half, coiled, but obviously five or more meters in length when outstretched.

As the creature approached the platform, it eyed them with large, human-looking orbs punctuated with jet-black pupils. As it reached the edge of the platform, the lower left arm slapped the rail. The belt stopped just short of the platform. Then, for what seemed like forever, they just stared at each other—these four humans in ghostly white pressure suits and this creature of some incredibly alien spawning.

The alien finally pointed to them, then with its top pair of arms made a motion to remove their helmets. When it saw they made no move, it pointed again to them, then did what appeared to be a deep-breathing exercise.

"I think it's trying to tell us we can breathe in here," Brazil said cautiously.

"Sure, *he* thinks so, but what does he breathe?" Hain pointed out.

"No choice," Brazil replied. "We're almost out of air anyway. May as well chance it."

"I do," came the unexpected voice of Wu Julee, and, with that, she unfastened her helmet—not without some trouble, for her coordination was shot. Finally the helmet fell to her feet, and she breathed in.

And continued breathing.

"Good enough for me," said Vardia, and she and Brazil did the same. For a short time Hain continued to resist. Then, finally assured that everyone was still breathing, he removed his as well.

47

The air seemed a bit humid and perhaps a little rich in oxygen—they experienced a slight light-headedness that soon passed—but otherwise fine.

"Now what?" Hain asked.

"Damned if I know," Brazil replied honestly. "How do you say hello to a giant walrus-snake?"

"Well I'll be goddamned!" exclaimed the walrussnake in perfect Confederation plain talk, "if it ain't Nathan Brazil!"

Zone
(Enter Ghosts)

NONE OF THE GROUP COULD HAVE BEEN MORE stunned than Nathan Brazil.

"Somehow I knew you'd wind up here," the creature continued. "Sooner or later just about every old-timer does."

"You know me?" Brazil asked incredulously.

The creature laughed. "Sure I do—and you know me, too, unless you've had one too many rejuves. I know, had the same problem myself when I dropped through the Well. Let's just say that people really change around here, and let it go at that. If you'll follow me, I'll make you more comfortable and give you some orientation." With that the creature uncoiled backward, then recoiled at a length about two meters back on the belt. "Step aboard," it invited.

They looked at Brazil. "I don't think we have much choice," he told them. Then, noticing Hain's pistol still drawn and pointed, he said to the fat man: "Put that popgun away until we find out the lay of the land. No use in getting popped yourself."

They stepped onto the belt, which started not when they boarded but only after the rail was given another slap by their alien host. For the first time they could hear noise—giant blowers, it sounded like, echoing throughout the great hall. The belt itself gave off its own steady electric hum.

"Do you—eat what we eat?" Hain called out to the creature.

The alien chuckled. "No, not anymore, but, don't worry, no cannibals around, either. At least, not Type Forty-ones like you. But I think we can round up some food—some *real* food, maybe the first in everybody's except Nate's whole life."

They rode around three belts until they came to a platform much larger than the others. Here the walls curved and twisted away from the Well. Brazil could see why the configuration hadn't been visible from afar.

Then they followed the snakeman—no mean trick, they found, with its enormous serpentine body—down a long corridor. They saw other corridors branching off, but they traveled over a thousand meters before they took one.

It led into a very large room set up something like a reception area. Comfortable, human-style chairs with plush cushions abounded, and a plastic wall covering was decorated with flowers. Here, such amenities seemed as incongruous as the alien would seem to their worlds. The creature had a sort of desk, semicircular in shape and seemingly form-fitted for him to coil comfortably behind. It held only a very ordinary-looking pen, a small pad of paper, and a seal—hexagonal of course—seemingly solid gold cast in clear plastic. The seal featured a snake coiled around a great cross, and it had a superscription around the edges in a script unfamiliar to any of them.

The snakeman lifted up a small part of his desk top to reveal an instrument panel underneath of unfamiliar design and purpose. A large red button was most prominent, and he pushed it.

"Had to reset the Well," he explained. "Otherwise we could get some nonoxygen breathers in and they'd be hung up in storage until somebody remembered to press the button. Let me also punch in a food order for you—you always were a steak-and-baked-potato man, Nate. So that's what it'll be." He punched some

49

buttons in sequence on the console, then closed it. "Ten or fifteen minutes and the food will be here—and it'll be cooked right, too. Medium, wasn't it, Nate?"

"You seem to know me better than I do," Brazil replied. "It's been so long since I had a steak—maybe almost a century. I'd just about forgotten what one was. Where did you know me, anyway?"

A broad yet wistful smile crept across the creature's face. "Can you remember an old bum named Serge Ortega, Nate? Long ago?"

Brazil thought, then suddenly it came to him. "Yeah, sure, I remember him—but that was maybe a hundred years ago or so. A free-lancer—polite name for a pirate," he explained to the others. "A real rascal. Anything for a buck, was wanted almost everywhere—but a hell of a character. But you can't be him—he was a little guy, from Hispaniola, before they went Com and changed the place to Peace and Freedom."

"I'm sorry to hear that," the creature responded sadly. "That means my people are dead. Who was the mold? Brassario?"

"Brassario," Brazil confirmed. "But all this explains nothing!"

"Oh, but it does," the snakeman replied. "Because I *am* Serge Ortega, Nate. This world changed me into what you see."

"I don't see what's wrong with factory worlds," Vardia interjected. They ignored her.

Brazil looked hard at the creature. The voice, the eyes—they *were* dimly familiar, somehow. It *did* remind him of Ortega, sort of. The same crazy glint to the eyes, the same quick, sharp way of talking, the underlying attitude of amused arrogance that had gotten Ortega into more bar fights than any other man alive.

But it had been so long ago.

"Look here!" Hain put in. "Enough of old home week, Ortega or not Ortega. Sir, or whatever, I should very much like to know where we are, and why we are here, and when we shall be able to return to our own ship."

Ortega gave that evil smile. "Well, as to where you are—you're on the Well World. There's no other name

50

for it, since that's exactly what it is. As to where it is —well, damned if I know. Nobody here has ever been able to leave it. I only know that the night sky is like nothing you ever saw before. I spaced almost two hundred years, and none of the extremely prominent features look familiar. At the very least we're on the other side of the galaxy, or maybe even in another galaxy. As to why you're here, well, you somehow bumbled into a Markovian Gate like me and maybe thousands of others did. And here you are, stuck just like the rest of us. You're here for good, mister. Better get used to it."

"See here!" Hain huffed. "I have power, influence—"

"Means nothing here," Ortega responded coldly.

"My mission!" Vardia protested. "I must perform my duties!"

"No duties, nothin' anymore but you and here," the snakeman said. "Understand this: you are on a world built by the Markovians—yes, I said *built*. The whole thing: lock, stock, and core. As far as we know, the whole damned thing is a Markovian brain in perfect working order, and preprogrammed."

"I figured we were inside Dalgonia," Brazil said. "It felt as if we fell down into something."

"No," replied Ortega, "that was no fall. The Markovians really had godlike powers. Matter transmission was a simple thing for them. Don't ask me how it works, but it does, because we got a local version here. I wouldn't understand it if somebody *did* explain it, anyway."

"But such a thing is impossible!" Hain objected. "It is against the laws of physics!"

Ortega's six limbs shrugged. "Who knows? At one time flying was impossible. Then it was impossible to leave a planet, then impossible to leave a solar system, then impossible for anything to go faster than light. The only thing that makes something impossible is ignorance. Here on the Well World the impossible's a fact of life."

At that moment the food arrived, brought in on a small cart that was obviously some sort of robot. It went up to each in turn, and offered a tray of hot food,

51

which, when removed, revealed an identical tray beneath. Brazil removed the cover and just stared for a minute. Finally, he said, in a tone of absolute awe and reverence: "A *real* steak!" He hesitated a moment and looked over at Ortega. "It *is* real, isn't it?"

"Oh, yes," the snakeman assured him. "It's real enough. The potato and beans, too. Oh, not *quite* a cow, not *quite* a potato, and so forth, but so close you'll never be able to tell the difference. Go ahead, try it!"

Hain was already greedily tearing into his, while Vardia looked at the food, bewildered.

"What's the trouble?" Brazil managed between swallows. "Problems?"

"It's quite safe to eat," Ortega assured her. "There are no microorganisms that will give you any real problems here—not until you go out, anyway. The stuff's biologically compatible."

"No, no—it's—" she stammered. "Well, I have never seen food like it before. How do you . . .?"

"Just watch me and follow my example," Brazil laughingly replied. "See? You cut it with a knife and fork like this, then—"

They dug into the meal, Vardia getting the hang of it, although she protested several times that she thought the food tasted terrible. But they were all too hungry to protest.

Ortega's eyes fell on Wu Julee, who just sat there staring at the food, not eating at all. "The girl—she is ill?" he asked them.

Brazil suddenly stopped eating and looked at Hain, who had already finished and was just letting out an extremely noisy belch. The captain's face had a grave expression on it, and the fine food suddenly felt like lead in his stomach.

"She's a spongie," Brazil said softly. Hain's eyebrows rose, but he said nothing.

Ortega's face, too, turned serious. "How far gone?" he asked.

"Fairly bad, I'd say," Brazil replied. "Deep mental maybe five years old, voluntary action basically emotive only." Suddenly he whirled in his chair and faced Hain, cold fury in his eyes. *"How about it, Hain?"* he snarled. *"Would you agree?"*

Hain's piggish face remained impassive, his tone of voice seemed almost one of relief. "So you found out. I *thought* perhaps I was overdoing the routine at that dinner."

"If we hadn't been trapped on Dalgonia, I'd have had you *and* her down on Arkadrian before you realized what was what," Brazil told him.

Hain's face showed both shock and surprise. Brazil's remarks had gotten to him. Then, suddenly, a thought occurred to him and the old, smug self-confidence returned.

"It would seem, then, that I have fallen not into a terrible situation, but into a most fortunate one by this—er, circumstance," he said calmly. "A pity for the lady, though," he added in mock sympathy.

"Why you son of a bitch!" Brazil snarled and leaped at the fat man's throat, spilling food everywhere. The big man was a head taller and twice the weight of the attacker, but Brazil's quickness and the sheer hatred in his soul flowed into his arms and hands as they tightened around the other's neck.

Hain thrashed and tried to push the smaller attacker away, but all he managed was to cause both of them to roll onto the floor, the small man still squeezing. Hain's mouth was open, face red, as he gasped for breath. The expression on Brazil's face was almost demonic; nothing would keep him from his goal.

Vardia watched openmouthed, understanding the situation only in the vaguest way and finding Brazil's actions, both recounted and current, incomprehensible. In her private universe, there were no people, only cells composing a whole body. A diseased cell was simply eliminated. So there was no place in her mind for one who caused such a disease.

Wu Julee watched the two grapple impassively, her meal still on her lap.

Suddenly Ortega bounded over his desk and grabbed Brazil with massive arms. The giant creature moved almost too fast for the eye to follow; Vardia was stunned at the speed and surety with which the creature acted.

Brazil fought to get free of the grip, and Ortega's

middle arm suddenly came from nowhere and punched the small man hard in the jaw. He went slack, still held aloft in the creature's strong grip.

Freed of his attacker, Hain gasped and choked for air, finally rolling flat on his back and lying there, his huge stomach rising and falling. He felt his neck, where the imprint of Brazil's murderous hands could still be seen.

Ortega began examining the unconscious man. Satisfied that no bones were broken, nor permanent damage done, he grunted and put the man down on the floor. Brazil collapsed in a heap, and the snakeman turned his attention to Hain.

"I thank you, sir," Hain gasped, his hand going involuntarily to his throat. "You have surely saved my life."

"I didn't want to do it, nor would I have done so in normal times," Ortega snapped back acidly. "And if Nate ever catches up to you on the outside, I won't be there to save you—and, if I am, I'll cheerfully join him in tearing you limb from limb. *But I will not allow such a thing here!*" He turned his attention back to Brazil, who was just coming around.

Hain seemed taken aback by the creature's comments, then saw that his pulse pistol had fallen when they had tumbled and now was a foot or so from him on the floor. Slowly, his hand crept toward it.

"No!" Wu Julee suddenly screamed, but Hain already had the weapon, and was pointing it at both the snakeman and Brazil, who was sitting up, shaking his head and rubbing his jaw. Ortega's back was to Hain, but Brazil suddenly looked up and spotted the gun. Ortega saw him stare and turned to face the fat man.

"Now both of you behave and I won't do anything rash," Hain told them in that same cool, confident tone he always used. "But I am leaving this charming place right now."

"How?" asked Serge Ortega.

The question seemed to bother Hain, who was used to simple answers to simple questions. "The—the way we came in," he said at last.

"The doorway leads to a corridor. The corridor leads to the Well in one direction—and that is strictly one way," Ortega told him. "In the other direction are more rooms like this—seven hundred and eighty of them, in a honeycombed labyrinth. Beyond them are housing and recreation facilities for the types of creatures that use those offices—seven hundred and eighty different types of creatures, Hain. Some of them don't breathe what you do. Some of them won't like you a bit and may just kill you."

"There is a way out," Hain snarled, but there was desperation in his voice. "There *must* be. I'll find it."

"And then what?" Ortega asked calmly. "You're out in a world that is moderately large. The surface area is best expressed as five point one times ten to the eighth power kilometers *squared*. And you don't even know what the planet looks like, the languages, *anything*. You're a smart man, Hain. *What are the odds?*"

Hain seemed confused, hesitant. Suddenly he looked at the pistol in his hand and brightened. *"This* gives me the odds," he said firmly.

"Never play the odds until you know the rules of the game," Ortega warned softly, and advanced slowly toward him.

"I'll shoot!" Hain threatened, his voice an octave higher than usual.

"Go ahead," Ortega invited, his great serpentine body sliding slowly toward the panicked man.

"All right, dammit!" Hain cried, and pulled the trigger.

Nothing happened.

Hain pulled the trigger again and again. It clicked, making contact with the solenoid firing pin, but did nothing else.

Ortega suddenly moved with that blinding speed, and the gun seemed to vanish from the fat man's hand.

"No weapon works in this room," Ortega said crisply. Hain sat, a stupefied expression on his face, mouth half open. Possibly for the first time in his life that arrogant self-confidence was gone out of him.

"You all right, Nate?" Ortega shot to the small man, who still sat half-rising, holding his sore jaw.

"Yeah, you son of a bitch," Brazil replied mushily, shaking his head to clear it. "Man! You sure as hell pack a wallop!"

Ortega chuckled. "I was the only man smaller than you once in a bar on Siprianos. I was full of booze and dope, and ready to take on the house, all of whom would have cheerfully slit my throat for the floor show. I just started to pick a fight with the bouncer when you grabbed me and knocked me cold. Took me ten weeks before I realized that you'd saved my neck."

Brazil's jaw dropped in wonder, and the pain hit him as he did so and he groaned. Still, he managed: "You *are* Serge Ortega!" in a tone of bewildered acceptance. "I had totally forgotten that. . . ."

Ortega smiled. "I said I was, Nate."

"But, oh, man, how you've changed," Brazil noted, amazed.

"I told you this world changes people, Nate," Ortega replied. "It'll change you, too. All of you."

"You wouldn't have stopped me from finishing the pig in the old days, Serge."

"I guess I wouldn't have," Ortega chuckled. "And I really wouldn't have now—except that this is Zone. And, if you'll sit over there, across the room from Hain," he said, pointing to a backless couch, and, turning to Hain, continued, "and if *you* will stop all your little, petty games and promise to sit quietly, I'll explain just what the situation is here—the rules and lack of them, and a few other things about your future."

Hain mumbled something unintelligible and went back over to his seat. Brazil, still nursing his sore jaw, silently got up and moved over to the couch. He sank down in the cushions, his head against the back wall, and groaned.

"Still dizzy," he complained. "And I'm getting a hell of a headache."

Ortega smiled and moved back behind his desk.

"You've had worse and you know it," the snake-man reminded the captain. "But, first things first. Want some more food? You spoiled yours."

"You know damned well I won't eat for days," Brazil groaned. "Damn! Why didn't you let me get him?"

"Two reasons, really. First, this is—well, a diplomatic legation, you might say. A murder by one Entry of another would be impossible to explain to my government no matter what. But, more than that, she's not lost, Nate, and that makes your motive even flimsier."

Brazil forgot his aches and pains. "What did you say?"

"I said she's not lost, Nate, and that's right. Just as this detour deprived Hain of justice, it also saved her. Arkadrian was no solution, really. Obviously you felt she was worth saving when you decided to detour —but, just here, she's little more than a vegetable. Obviously Hain was decreasing the dosage as she became more and more accustomed to the pain. He was letting her rot out—but slowly enough to make the trip without problems. May I ask why, Hain?"

"She was from one of the Comworlds. Lived in the usual beehive and helped work on a big People's Farm. I mean the dirt jobs—shoveling shit and the like, as well as painting the buildings, mending fences, and suchlike. IQ genetically manipulated to be low—she's a basic worker, a manual laborer, basically mentally retarded and capable of carrying out simple commands—one at a time—but not of much in the way of original thought and action. She wasn't even good at that work, and they used her as a Party whore. Failed at that, too."

"That is a slander of the Com people!" Vardia protested vehemently. "Each citizen is here to do a particular task that needs doing, and is created for that task. Without people such as she as well as ones like me the whole society would fall apart."

"Would you change jobs with her?" Brazil asked sarcastically.

"Oh, of course not," Vardia responded, oblivious to the tone. "I'm glad I'm not anything but what I am. I would be happy at nothing else. Even so, such citizens are essential to the social fabric."

"And you say my people have gone that route," Ortega said sadly, almost to himself. "But—I would think the really basic menial stuff would be automated. A lot of it was in my time."

"Oh, no," Vardia protested. "Man's future is with the soil and with nature. Automation produces social decay and only that necessary to the maintenance of equality can be permitted."

"I see," Ortega responded dryly. He was silent for a while, then he turned back to Hain. "But how did you wind up with the girl? And why hook her on sponge?"

"Occasionally we need a—a sample, as it were. An example, really. We almost always use such people—Comworld folk who will not be missed, who are never much more than vegetables anyway. We control most of them, of course. But it's rather tough to get the stuff into their food, or even to get an audience with members of a Presidium, but, once you've done it, you control the entire world—a world of people programmed to be happy at whatever they're doing and conditioned from birth to blind obedience to the Party. Control the queen and you control all the bees in the hive. I had an audience with a Presidium Member on Coriolanus—took three years of hard work to wangle it, I'll assure you. There are hundreds of ways to infect someone once you're face-to-face. By that point, poor Wu Julee would have been in the animalistic state from progressively smaller doses. She would be the threat to show the distinguished Member what my—er, client, would become if not treated."

"Such a thing would not work on *my* world," Vardia stated proudly. "A Presidium Member so infected would simply have you, her, and the Member all at a Death Factory."

Hain laughed. "You people never cease to amaze me," he chuckled. "You *really* think your Presidium members are like you? They're descendants of the early Party that spread out in past, mostly lost, history. They proclaimed equality and said they dreamed of a future Utopia when there would be no government, nothing. What they really wouldn't even admit to themselves was that they loved power—*they* never worked in the fields, *they* never worked at all, except giving orders and trying out plans and novel experiences. And they loved it! And their children's children's children still love it. A planetload of happy, contented, docile slaves that will do anything commanded of them. And when that pain starts, less than an hour after infection, they will do anything to keep alive. *Anything.*"

"Still mighty risky for you, isn't it?" Ortega pointed out. "What if you're knocked off by an egomaniac despite all?"

Hain shrugged. "There are risks in anything. We lose most of our people as they work themselves up. But all of us are misfits, losers, or people who started at the bottom of society on the worst of worlds. We weren't born to power—we work for it, take risks for it, earn it. And—the survivors get the spoils."

Ortega nodded grimly. "How many—easy, Nate, or I'll clout you again!—how many worlds do you control now?"

Hain shrugged again. "Who knows? I'm not on the Council. Over ten percent—thirty, thirty-five, maybe —and growing. And two new colonies are made for every one we win, so it's an ever-expanding empire. It'll be that someday—an empire." His eyes took on a faraway look, a maniacal glow. "A great empire. Perhaps, eventually, the entire galaxy."

"Ruled by scum," Brazil said sourly.

"By the strongest!" Hain responded. "The cleverest, the survivors! The people who deserve it!"

"I hesitate to let such evil into *this* world," Ortega said, "but we have had as bad and worse here. This world will test you fully, Hain. I think it will ultimately kill you, but that is up to you. Here is where you start. But there's no sponge here, or other addictives. Even if there were, you'd have fifteen hundred and sixty different species to try it on, and some of them are so alien you won't even understand *what* they are, why they do what they do, or whether they do anything. Some will be almost like those back home. But this place is a madhouse, Hain. It's a world created by madness, I think, and it will kill you. We'll see."

They were silent for a while, Ortega's speech having as unsettling an effect on Brazil and Vardia as on Hain. Suddenly, Brazil broke the silence.

"You said she wasn't lost, Serge. Why not?"

"It has to do with this world and what it does to people," the snakeman replied. "I will brief you later.

59

But—not only do you change here, but you also get back what you've lost. You'll return to perfect health, Nate, even get back that memory of yours. You'll even remember things you don't want to remember. And, you'll be prepared—programmed if you like—for whatever and wherever you are. Not in the Comworld sense—what *you* need. This gives you a new start, Nate—but there's no rejuve here. This is a one-shot deal, people—a fresh start.

"But you will die here, sooner or later, the span depending on what you are."

They slept on cots provided by Ortega. All were dead tired, and Brazil was also still smarting from the knockout punch given him by the great creature that seemed to be the reincarnation of his past friend. Hain slept separately from the rest, under lock and key, in an office the location of which was not told to the fiery little captain.

Ortega woke them all up the next morning. They assumed it was morning, although they hadn't actually been outside and, in fact, had no idea what the outside looked like on this strange yet somehow familiar world. An old-style breakfast of what appeared to be normal hen's eggs, scrambled, sausage, toast, and coffee awaited them, served by the same little cart that had brought the previous night's supper. Brazil noted that the mess from flying food had been carefully cleaned away.

Vardia, of course, had trouble with the breakfast.

Wu Julee seemed no worse than the night before, and in no more pain, if, indeed, she was in pain at all. With a lot of coaxing from Brazil she managed to eat some of the breakfast.

After they had finished and had returned the trays to the little cart, which hummed away on small tires with no apparent guidance, Serge Ortega pressed another button on his little hidden console, causing a screen to drop down at his right.

"Time, unfortunately, is limited here—both for you and, because I have a great many other duties, for me as well. When I got dropped into Zone long ago, I had only a brief orientation before I was thrown out on my ass. I wanted to give you a little bit more, to make it a little easier on you than it was for me."

"Just how long ago *did* you drop here, Citizen Ortega?" Vardia asked.

"Well, hard to say. Well over seventy standard years—they still use the same years, don't they, Nate?" Brazil nodded affirmatively, and Ortega continued.

"It was during a low-colonist period, and I was gunrunning to a placer strike on some asteroids out beyond Sirius. I dumped them fine, avoided all the cops, but ran into some damned conduit out in the middle of deep space, before I could go FTL or anything. I'm told that most—maybe a majority—of the gates are on planets, and maybe this was one, too, at one time. Maybe all those asteroids were once a Markovian planet that broke up for some reason."

"How long has this place—this planet—been here, Serge?" Brazil asked.

"Nobody knows. Longer than people were people, Nate. A coupl'a million years, it appears. Since the oldest folk in the planet's oldest race are only four hundred—and they're at death's door—the ancient history of the place is as shrouded in mystery and mythology as our own. You see, all this involves the Markovians—any of you know about them?"

"Nobody knows much," Brazil replied. "Some sort of super race that ran its planets from brains beneath the surface and died out suddenly."

"That's about it," Ortega acknowledged. "They flourished, scientists here think, between two and five million years ago. And they were galaxy-wide, Nate! Maybe even more. Hard to say, but we have a lot of folk dropping through whose knowledge of the universe doesn't match anything we humans know. And that's the weirdest thing—a hell of a lot of them are close to human."

"In what way do you mean that, Serge?" Brazil asked. "Us-human or you-human?"

Ortega laughed. "Both. Humanoid would perhaps be a better term. Well, first let me show you what you're in for, and I'll add the rest as I go along."

The snakeman dimmed the lights, and a map showing two hemispheres flicked on the screen. It looked like a standard planetary map, but the two circles were filled with hexagons from pole to pole.

"The Markovians," Ortega began, "who were nutty over the number six, built this world. We don't know why or how, but we do know *what*. Each of their worlds had at least one gate of the kind that transported you here. You are now at the South Polar Zone, which doesn't show accurately here for obvious reasons. All carbon-based life comes here, and all of the hexes north of us to that thick equatorial line are carbon-based or could live in a carbon-based environment. The Mechs of Hex Three Sixty-seven, for example, aren't carbon-based, but you could live in their hex."

"So the North Polar Zone takes care of the biologically exotic, then?" Hain asked.

Ortega nodded. "Yes, there are the true aliens, beings with which we have literally nothing in common. Their hexes run down to the equator on the north hemisphere."

"Is that black band at the equator just a map dividing line or is it something else?" Vardia asked curiously.

"No, that's not just on the map," Ortega told her, "and you were sharp to notice it. It is—well, the best I can describe it is that it's a sheer wall, opaque and several kilometers high. You can't really see it until you're at it, outside the border of the last hex by a hair. You can't get past it, and you can't fly over it or anything. It's just, well, *there*. We have some theories about it, of course, the best one being that it's the exposed part of the Markovian brain that is, it seems, of the entire core of this planet. The old name for it seems to be the Well of Souls—so it probably is just that. There's an old adage around here: 'Until midnight at the Well of Souls,' which you'll probably hear. It's just an old ritual saying now, although it may have had some real meaning in the distant past of prehistory. Hell, if that's the Well of Souls, then it's *always* midnight somewhere!"

"What do the hexagons represent?" Hain asked.

"Well, there are fifteen hundred and sixty of them

on the planet," Ortega replied. "Nobody knows the reason for that, either, but at least the figure only has one six in it. Each hex is identical in size—each one of the six sides is just a shade under three hundred fifty-five kilometers, and they're a shade under six hundred fifteen kilometers across. Needless to say they didn't use our form of measurements when they built the place, and we don't know what system they had, but that'll give you an idea in our terms."

"But what's *in* the hexes?" Brazil prodded.

"Well, you *could* call them nations with borders," Ortega replied, "but that would be understating things. Each is a self-contained biosphere for a particular life form—and for associated lower life forms. They are all maintained by the Markovian brain, and each is also maintained at a given technological level. The social level is left to whatever the inhabitants can develop or want to have, so you have everything from monarchies to dictatorships to anarchies out there."

"What do you mean technological level?" Brazil asked him. "Do you mean that there are places where there are machines and places where there are not?"

"Well, yes, that, of course," Ortega affirmed. "But, well, you can only get to the level of technology your resources allow within the hex. Anything beyond it just won't work, like Hain's pistol yesterday."

"It seems to me that you would have been populated to death here," Brazil commented. "After all, I assume all creatures reproduce here—and then the Markovian brains keep shuttling people here as well."

"That just doesn't happen," Ortega replied. "For one thing, as I said, people can die here—and do. Some hexes have very cheap life, some species live a comparatively short time. Reproductive rates are in accordance with this death rate. If populations seem to be rising too high, and natural factors—like catastrophes, which *can* happen here, or wars, which also can happen, although they are not terribly common and usually localized—don't reduce the numbers, well, most of the next batch is simply born sexually normal in every way yet sterile, with just a very small number able to keep the breed going. When attrition takes its toll, the species goes back to being born fertile.

Actually the population's pretty stable in each hex—from a low of about twenty thousand to a high of over a million.

"As for Entries like you—well, the Markovians were extensive, as I said, but many of their old brains are dead and some of the gateways are closed forever for one reason or another. Others are so well disguised that a one-in-a-trillion blunder like mine is needed to find the entrance. We get no more than a hundred or so newcomers a year, all told. We have a trip alarm when the Well is activated and some of us take turns on a daily basis answering the alarms. Sheer luck I ran into you, but I take a lot of turns. Some of the folks here don't really like newcomers and don't treat them right, so I take their duty and they owe me."

"There are representatives of all the Southern Hemisphere races here, then?" Vardia asked.

The snakeman nodded. "Most of them. Zone's really a sort of embassy station. Distances are huge, travel is long here, and so here at Zone representatives of all of us can meet and talk over mutual problems. The Gate—which we'll get to presently—will zip me back home in an instant, although, curse it, it won't zip anybody back and forth except from here to his own hex. Oh, yes, there's a special chamber for Northerners here and one for us up at the North Zone just in case we have to talk—which is seldom. They occasionally have something we are short of, or our scientists and theirs want to compare notes, or somesuch. But they are *so* different from us that that's rare."

Brazil wore a strangely fixed expression as he said, "Serge, you've spelled out the world as much as you can, but you've omitted one fact I think I can guess —how did a little Latin shrimp like you become a six-armed walrus-snake."

Ortega's expression was one of resignation. "I thought it would be obvious. When you go out the Gate the first time, the brain will decide which hex could stand a person or four and that's what you will become. You will, of course, also wind up in the proper hex."

64

"And then what?" Hain asked nervously.

"Well, there's a period of adjustment, of course. I went through the Gate the way Nate remembers me, and came out in the land of the Uliks looking like this. It took me a little while to get used to things, and longer for everything to sort itself out in my head, but, well, the change also produces an *adjustment*. I found I knew the language, at least all the analogues to my old one, and began to feel more and more comfortable in my new physical role. I *became* a Ulik, Nate, while still being me. Now I can hardly remember what it was like to be anything else, really. Oh, academically, sure —my mind was never clearer. But *you* are the aliens now."

There was a long silence as they digested the information. Finally, Brazil broke it and asked, "But, Serge, if there are seven hundred and eighty life forms with compatible biospheres, why hasn't there been a cosmopolitanism here in the South? I mean, why is everybody stuck in his own little area?"

"Oh, there is some mingling," Ortega replied. "Some hexes have been combined, some not. Mostly, though, people stick to their own areas because each one is different. Besides, people have never liked other people who were different. Humanity—ours and everybody else's, apparently—has always found even slight pretexts to hate other groups. Color, language, funny-shaped noses, religion, or anything else. Many wars were fought here at various times, and wholesale slaughter took place. Such things are rare now—everybody loses. So, mostly, everybody sticks to his own hex and minds his own business. Besides, there's the factor of commonality, too. Could you *really* be good buddies with a three-meter-tall hairy spider that ate live flesh, even if it also played chess and loved orchestral music? And—could a society based on high technology succeed in capturing and subjugating a hex where none of its technology worked? A balance is kind of maintained that way—technological hexes trade for needed things like food with nontechnological farm hexes where society is anarchistic and only swords will work."

Vardia looked up, eyes bright, at the mention of swords. She still had hers.

"And, of course, in some hexes there are some pretty good sorcerers—and their spells work!" Ortega warned.

"Oh, come on," Hain said disgustedly. "I am willing to believe in a lot—but magic? Nonsense!"

"All magic means is a line between knowledge and ignorance," Ortega responded. "A magician is someone who can do something you don't know how to do. All technology, for example, is magic to a primitive. Just remember, this is an old world, and its people are different from anything in your experience. If you make the mistake—any of you!—of applying your own standards, your own rules, your own prejudices to any of it, it will get you."

"Can you brief me on the general political situation, Serge?" Brazil requested. "I'd like to know a lot more before going out there."

"Nate, I couldn't do it in a million years. Like any planet with a huge number of countries and social systems, everything's in a constant state of flux. Conditions change, and so do rulers. You'll have to learn things as you go along. I can only caution that there is a lot of petty warfare and a lot of big stuff that would break out if one side could figure out a way to do it. One general a thousand years or so ago took over sixty hexes. But he was undone in the end by the necessity for long supply lines and by his inability to conquer several incompatible hexes in his backfield that eventually were able to slice him up. The lesson's been well learned. Things are done more by crook than hook here now."

Hain's eyes brightened. "My game!" he whispered.

"And now," Ortega concluded, "you must go. I cannot keep you here more than a day and justify the delay to my government. You cannot put off leaving indefinitely in any case."

"But there are many more questions that must be answered!" Vardia protested. "Climate, seasons, thousands of needed details!"

"As for the climate, it varies from hex to hex but has no relationship to geographical position," Ortega told her. "The climate is maintained in each case by the brain. Daylight is exactly fifty percent of each full day anywhere on the globe. Days are within a few

66

hours of standard, so that's fourteen and an eighth standard hours of day and the same of night. The axis is straight up—no tilt at all. But it will vary artificially. But—see! I could go on forever and you'd never know enough. It is time!"

"And suppose I refuse?" Vardia challenged, raising her sword.

With that same lightning-quick movement that had marked the previous day's fight, Ortega's snake body uncoiled like a tightly wound spring, snatched the sword, and was back behind the desk in less than half a second. He looked at her sadly. "You have no choice at all," he said quietly. "Will you all now come with me?"

They followed the Ulik ambassador reluctantly but resigned. He led them again down that great, winding corridor through which they had entered the day before, and it seemed to them all that their walk would never end.

Finally, after what was about half an hour, they found that the corridor opened into a large room. Three sides were bare, plastic-like walls similar to those in Ortega's office but without any pattern. The fourth looked like a wall of absolute black.

"That's the Gate," Ortega told them, gesturing to the black wall. "We use it to go back and forth between our own hexes and Zone, and you will use it to be assigned. Please don't be afraid. The Gate will not alter your personality; and, after the adjustment period, you will find that you are even better, mentally, than you were. For the little girl, here, passage through will mean the restoration of normality, cure of the addiction, and a correction of whatever imbalances they used to limit her IQ and abilities. Of course, she may still be a rather dull farm worker, but in no event will she be worse off than she was before she was addicted."

None of them rushed into the Gate.

Finally, Ortega prodded them. "The doorway behind you is closed. No one, not even I, may reenter Zone until he first goes to a hex. That's the way the system works."

"I'll go first," Brazil said suddenly, and he took a

step toward the Gate. He felt a great hand on his shoulder that stopped him.

"No, Nate, not now," Ortega almost whispered to him. "Last." Brazil was puzzled, but realized the intent. The ambassador had something else to say to him without the others hearing. Brazil nodded and turned to Hain.

"How about you, Hain? Or should I go at you again? We're not in the embassy now."

"You caught me by surprise that time, Captain," Hain replied with the old sneer. "But if you stop and think, you'll know I could break you in pieces. Ambassador Ortega saved *your* life back there, not mine. Yet, I will go. My future is out there." And, with that, Hain strode confidently to the blackness and, without hesitation, stepped into it.

The darkness seemed to swallow him up the moment he entered. There was no other visible effect.

Vardia and Wu Julee each stood solidly, not moving from their places near the entrance.

Ortega turned and took Wu Julee's left arm with one of his, urging her on across the room to the dark wall. She didn't seem to protest until she was very near the darkness. Then, suddenly, she stopped and screamed, "No! No!" Her face turned and looked pleadingly at Brazil.

"Go ahead," he urged her gently, but she broke free of Ortega's gentle grip and ran to the captain.

Brazil looked into her eyes with a gentle pity that was almost tearing him apart inside.

"You must go," he told her. "You must go. I will find you."

Still she didn't budge, but tightened her grip on him. Suddenly she was yanked from him with such force and speed that the movement knocked Brazil to the ground. Ortega pulled her away and tossed her into the blackness in one quick motion.

She screamed, but the scream stopped as the blackness absorbed her, so abrupt that it was like a recording suddenly stopped in midsound.

"This business is a bitch sometimes," Ortega remarked glumly. He turned and looked at Brazil, who was picking himself up off the floor. "You all right?"

"Yeah," Brazil replied, then looked into the creature's sad eyes. "I understand, Serge," he said softly. Then, as if to break the mood, his tone took on that of mock anger: "But if you're going to keep beating the hell out of me I'm leaving here no matter what!"

His tone almost broke through the snakeman's melancholy, and Ortega managed a chuckle. He put his right upper arm out and clasped Brazil to him, and there were tears in his eyes. *"God!"* the snakeman exclaimed. "How can the greatness in people be so unloved?"

Suddenly he relaxed and turned his gaze to Vardia, who had remained motionless throughout the whole episode.

Brazil guessed what must be going through her mind now. Raised by an all-embracing state, trained and bred to a particular function, she was simply not programmed for such a disruption of her orderly, planned life. Every day for her had always been a certainty, and she was secure in the knowledge of that sameness and content with the belief that she was performing a useful task.

Now she was, for the first time, on her own.

Brazil thought for a moment, then hit upon what he hoped was a solution.

"Vardia," he said in his best command voice, "we set out to do a job when we landed on Dalgonia. That trail has led us here to this spot. Now it leads through there. There are seven bodies back on Dalgonia, Vardia. Seven, including at least one of your own people. There is still a duty for you to perform."

She was breathing hard, the only sign of inner mental torment. Finally, she turned and faced the other two, then ran at the blackness of the Gate.

And was gone.

Brazil and Ortega were alone in the room.

"What was that about seven bodies, Nate?" the snakeman asked.

Brazil recounted the story of the mysterious distress signal, the mass murder on Dalgonia, and the signs of the two who had vanished as they had.

Ortega's expression was extremely grave. "I wish I had known of this ten weeks ago when those two came through here. It would have changed things a great deal in Council."

Brazil's eyebrows rose. "You know them, then?"

Ortega nodded. "Yes, I know them. I didn't do the processing, but I watched the recordings of their arrival over and over. There was a great deal of debate about them before they went through the Gate."

"Who were they? What was their story?"

"Well, they came through together, and one of them was still trying to kill the other on the Well itself when Gre'aton—he's a Type Six Twenty-two, looks kind of like a giant locust—put a stop to it. A few of the more human-looking boys took over, splitting them up so they didn't see each other again.

"Each of them told a fantastic story, about how he and he alone had discovered some sort of mathematical relationship used by the Markovian brains. Each claimed that everything in the universe was a series of preset mathematical relationships determined by a master Markovian brain. When they were given the standard briefing, both became terribly excited, each convinced that the Well World was the master brain and that they could somehow communicate with it, maybe even run it. Each claimed the other had stolen his discovery, tried to kill the other, and was here to establish himself as god. Of course, each claimed that he was trying to stop the other from doing so."

"Did you believe them?"

"They were mighty convincing. We used some of the standard lie-detection stuff and tried some telepathy using one of the North boys, and the results were always the same."

"And?" Brazil prompted.

"As far as we were able to determine—and we don't have the methods for a really scientific study— *they were both telling the truth.*"

"*Whew.* You mean they're psychos through and through?"

Ortega was solemn. "No, each truly believes he discovered what the code was, and each truly believes the other stole it, and each truly believes that he'd be good for godhead and the other would be horrible."

"Do you really believe that godhead stuff?" Brazil asked.

Ortega turned all six arms into a giant shrug. "Who knows? A number of folk here have similar ideas, but no one's ever been able to do anything about them. We called a Council—a *full* Council, with over twelve hundred ambassadors participating. All were given the facts. Everything was debated.

"The idea explains a lot, of course. All magic, for example. But it is so esoteric. And, as it was pointed out by some of our mathematically minded folk, even if true it probably didn't mean anything, since no one could change the brain anyway. In the end, even though a large number of members voted to kill them, the majority voted to let them through."

"How did *you* vote, Serge?" Brazil asked.

"I voted to kill them, Nate. They are both maniacs, and both are possessed of genius. Each believed he could do what he set out to do, and both seemed to believe that it was destiny that, so soon after the discovery, they were brought here."

"More to the point, do *you* believe it, Serge?"

"I do," the giant replied gravely. "Right now I think those two are the most dangerous beings in the entire universe. And—more to the point—I think that one of them, I can't tell which, has a chance of succeeding."

"What are their names, Serge, and their backgrounds?"

Ortega's eyes brightened. "So God in His infinite wisdom allows mercy after all! You *do* want to get them, and God has sent you to us for that purpose!"

Brazil thought for a moment. "Serge, ever hear of a Markovian brain actually, literally, trapping people by sending out false signals or the like?"

Ortega thought for a moment. "No," he replied, "as far as I know it's always accident or blunder. That's why so few come. Now do you see what I mean about God sending you to me?"

"Somebody sure did, anyway," Brazil acknowledged dryly. "I wish I could see those films and learn a lot

71

about them before I tried to find two invisible needles in a planet-sized haystack."

"You can," Ortega assured him. "I have all the material back in my office."

Brazil's mouth was agape. "But you told us there was no way back!"

Ortega shrugged monstrously again. "I lied," he said.

Several hours later Brazil learned as much as he was going to from the recordings, testimony, and arguments of the Council committees.

"So can you give me any leads on this Skander and Varnett? Where are they now? And what?"

"Newcomers are pretty conspicuous around here, since there are so few of them and they are so obvious," Ortega replied. "And, yet, I can give you nothing on either. The planet seems to have swallowed them up."

"Isn't that unusual?" Brazil asked. "Or, worse, suspicious?"

"I see what you mean. The whole planet saw what you saw and heard what you heard. They could have some natural allies."

"Yeah, that's what I'm most concerned about," Brazil said bluntly. "The odds are that there's a monstrous race going on here, and that this place is the soul of reason compared to what everything we know would become if the wrong side was to win."

"They could both be dead," Ortega suggested hopefully.

Brazil shook his head in a violent negative. "Uh-uh. Not these boys. They're clever and they're nasty. Skander's almost the archetypal mad scientist, and Varnett's even worse—a *renegade*, high-class Com. At least one of them will make it, and he'll have some way to dump his allies afterward."

"You'll have the help of all the hexes who voted to kill them," Ortega pointed out.

"Sure, Serge, and I'll use that when I have to. But this is really a lone-wolf operation and you know it. That Council was politically very slick. They could count. Even a hex voting to kill them knew they wouldn't be killed—so what was the use of their vote?

Getting there might take help—but once there, every friend I have on this world will seek godhead, and never mind that I don't know how to talk to the brain. No, Serge, I have to kill *both* of them, absolutely, irrevocably, and as quickly as possible."

"Getting *where* might take help?" Ortega asked, puzzled.

"To the Well of Souls, of course," Brazil replied evenly. "And before midnight."

Now it was Ortega's turn to look stunned. "But that's just an old saying, like I said before—"

"It's the answer, Serge," Brazil asserted strongly. "It's just that nobody has been able to decipher the code and make use of it."

"There is no answer to that. It makes no real sense!"

"Sure it does!" Brazil told him. "It's the answer to a monstrous question, and the key to the most monstrous of threats. I saw Skander's and Varnett's eyes light up when they first heard the phrase, Serge. They seized on it!"

"But what's the question?" Ortega asked bewilderedly.

"That's what I don't know yet," Brazil replied, pointing his finger at the Ulik animatedly. "But *they* thought it was the answer, and *they* both think *they* can figure it out. If they can, I can.

"Look, Serge, *why* was this world built? No, not the brain; we'll accept that as bringing some sort of stability to the universe. In fact, if they're right, we're all just figments of some dead Markovian's imagination. No, *why all this?* The Well, the hexes, the civilizations? If I can answer *that*, I can answer the bigger question! And I'll find out!" Brazil exclaimed excitedly, half-rising from his chair.

"How can you be so sure?" Ortega responded dubiously.

"Because someone—or something—wants me to!" Brazil continued in the same excited tone. "That's why I was lured here! That's why I'm here at all, Serge! That's what makes even the timing! Even now they've got a ten-week start! You, yourself, said as much back at the Gate!"

73

Ortega shook his head glumly. "That was just my old Latin soul coming forth, Nate. I've been consorting with Jesuits again—yes, we have several here, from the old missionary days, came in a single ship and are out trying to convert the heathen. But, be reasonable, man! You never would have found Dalgonia were it not for the detour. You wouldn't have detoured except for Wu Julee's presence on your ship, and that could hardly have been planned, let alone your act of mercy."

"I think it *was* planned, Serge," Brazil said evenly. "I think I've been conned all along. I don't know how, or by whom, or for what purpose, but *I've been had!*"

"I don't see how," Ortega responded, "but, even if so, how will you ever know?"

"I'll know," Brazil said in a tone that was both firm and somewhat frightening. "I'll know at midnight at the Well of Souls."

They stood once again at the Gate, this time for the last time.

"It's agreed, then," Ortega said to him. "As soon as you pass through and get oriented, you announce yourself to the local ruler. All of them will have been notified of your coming through, with instructions to render any assistance. But at least one of them is sure to be in league with your enemies, Nate! Are you sure? What if you are swallowed up?"

"I won't be, Serge," Brazil replied calmly. "Chessplayers don't sacrifice their queens early in the game."

Ortega gave one last massive shrug. "Believe what you wish—but, be careful, my old friend. If they get you, I shall avenge your death."

Brazil smiled, then looked at the Gate. "Is it best to run at it, walk into it, or what?" he asked.

"Doesn't matter," Ortega told him. "You'll wake up as if coming out of a long sleep, anyway. May you wake up a Ulik!"

Brazil smiled, but kept his thoughts on being a seven-meter, six-armed walrus-snake to himself. He walked over to the gate, then turned for one last look at his transformed old friend.

"I hope I wake up at all, Serge," he said quietly.

"Go with God, you ancient heathen," Ortega said.

"I'll be damned," Brazil muttered, half to himself. "After all these years I might wake up a Gentile." And, with that, he stepped through the Gate.

And in the darkness he dreamed.

He was on a giant chessboard, that stretched off in all directions. Seven pawns were down on his side —the white side. They looked like scorched and frozen bodies, lying on blackened cots.

Through the mostly faceless field of black pieces, he could see Skander and Varnett, queen and king.

Skander was a queen in royal robes, with a scepter in hand. The queen looked around, but could not spot the king. There was Wu Julee, a pawn, out front, and Vardia, a knight with bright sword flashing.

Ortega, a bishop, glided by quickly, and was struck by a black rook with the face of Datham Hain.

The queen glided quickly, trying not to trip over her long skirts, toward Hain, the scepter ready to strike that ugly, pig face, when suddenly Ortega reappeared and pushed him away.

"The black royal family has escaped, Your Highness!" Ortega's voice shouted. "They are heading for the Well of Souls!"

The queen looked around, but there was no trace of the enemy's major pieces. Anywhere.

"But where is the Well of Souls?" screamed the queen. "I cannot get to the king without knowing!"

A sudden burst of overwhelming, cosmic laughter came from beyond the board. It was giant, hollow, and all embracing. A giant hand gripped the queen and moved it far away to the other side of the board. "Here they are!" the great voice said mockingly.

The queen looked around and screamed in terror. The king with Skander's face was but one square right, and the queen with Varnett's face was one square up.

"Our move!" they both said, and laughed maniacally.

Brazil awoke.

He got quickly to his feet. *Odd,* he thought curiously. *I'm more wide awake, feeling better, head clearer than I can ever remember.*

Quickly he examined his body to see what he was. With a shock he looked up around him, to the shores of a nearby lake. There were animals there, and others of his kind.

"Well I'll be damned!" he said aloud. "Of course! That had to be the answer to the first question! I should have figured it out in Serge's office!"

Sometimes the obvious needed to be belabored.

Considering how primitive the place was, Brazil worriedly set out to see if he could find the Zone Gate.

Czill—Spring
(Enter Vardia Diplo 1261, Asleep)

SHE WAS NEVER CERTAIN WHY SHE HAD FINALLY stepped through the Gate. Perhaps doing so was an acceptance of inevitability, perhaps an obedience to authority that was a part of her conditioning.

There were patterns of color, running in and out, pulsating in a rhythmic, cosmic heartbeat: yellows, greens, reds, blues—all forming kaleidoscopic patterns, a mechanical ringing sound accompanying the pulses in an odd symphonic monotone.

Then, quite suddenly, she awoke.

She was on a lush savanna, tall grasses of green and gold stretching out to low foothills in the distance. Some trees, reminiscent of gum trees, dotted the plain, with odd growths that looked like barren stubs of what once had been taller trees showing in some numbers in the distance.

With a start, she realized that the stubby trees were moving. They moved in a syncopated rhythm that was most strange. The trunks were actually legs, she realized, and it seemed as if they were all moving in great strides, yet were somehow arrested. It was like watching a track meet in slow motion. That was deceptive, though; the slower motion was apparently only an illusion, and as she watched, some of them covered pretty good distances in no time.

They all seem to have something to do or someplace to go, she thought to herself. Purpose means some sort of civilization, and I need to find out where I am and what place this is before I can get my own purpose clear.

She started toward the distant forms.

And suddenly stopped as she caught a glimpse of her own body.

She looked down at herself in wonder.

She was a sort of light green, her skin a smooth, vinelike texture. Her legs were thick and yet long and rubbery, without an apparent joint. The trunk of her body showed no signs of breasts or of a vaginal cavity; and though her feet were flat bases, her arms seemed to be of the same nature as her legs, only thinner, ending as tentacles rather than as hands. Another, shorter tentacle grew out of the main arm about ten centimeters from its tip. A thumb, perhaps?

She found that the rubbery arms worked well either way, being pliant and without apparent joint or bone, and she felt her smooth backside. No rectum, either, she found.

She ran her arm over her face. A wide slit was no doubt the mouth, yet it opened only a tiny fraction. The nose appeared to be a single, fixed, hard hole above the mouth. Growing out of the top of her head was something thin, tough, and about the size of a mortarboard, although of irregular shape.

What have I become? she asked herself, feeling fear bordering on panic.

Slowly she tried to regain control of herself. Taking deep breaths had always helped, but she found she couldn't even do that. She was breathing, all right, she could sense that—but that nostril took in only a very tiny part of the air.

She realized it was primarily a sensitive olfactory organ; she was breathing by involuntary muscle actions through the pores in her smooth, green skin.

After a while her panic seemed to subside, and she

77

considered what to do. The distant shapes were still going about their business, she saw. She seemed to be on a road of some sort.

No matter what, she had to contact those creatures and find out just what was happening. She again started for the figures and found, with some surprise, that she covered the distance—almost a kilometer through the tall grass—in a much shorter time than she would have expected.

It *was* a road, she saw—a dirt track, really, but wide and made up of reddish-brown soil.

The creatures using it paid her no attention whatsoever, but she studied them intently. They were like herself, she knew. Those things she couldn't discover from self-examination were now apparent: two large, round, yellow eyes with black pupils, apparently lidless. She suddenly realized that she hadn't been blinking her own eyes, and could not.

The thing growing out of her head proved to be a single large leaf of irregular shape—no two were alike. The stalk was thick and very short. Its color was a much deeper green than the body and it had an almost waxy texture.

Not knowing how to talk to them, and almost afraid to try, she decided to follow the road. It *must* go someplace, she told herself. It really didn't matter which direction—one was as good as the other.

She walked onto the road and set off toward the low hills to her left. The road really wasn't as crowded as she had thought, but at least a dozen—people?—were on the road ahead of her. She gained on a pair, and as she did she became aware that they were talking. The sounds were musical, yet she discovered that she could almost make out what was being said. As she closed to within three or four meters of the pair, she slowed, aware now that she *could* understand the strange, whispering singsong.

" . . . got into the Bla'ahaliagan spirit-strata stuff, and can't even be talked to these days. If the Blessed Elder doesn't get off that crap pretty soon I'm going to transfer over to cataloging."

"Hmmmm. . . . Dull stuff but I can see your point," the other sympathized. "Crindel got stuck under

78

Elder Mudiul on some esoteric primitive game an Entry dropped on us about three hundred years ago. Seems it has almost infinite patterns after the first few moves, and there was this project to teach it to a computer. Couldn't be done. Weird stuff. Almost went off to the Meditations and rotted, Crindel did."

"How'd the Worthy get out of it?" the first one asked.

"Mudiul got a virus and it got the Elder quarantined for nine years," chortled the other. "By the time the Worthy got out the Board had closed down the project and redistributed the staff. The Old One's got off on whether rocks have souls, and that ought to keep the Worthy out of harm's way until rot wipes the Worthy."

They went on like that for some time, and the conversation did little to clear up anything in Vardia's mind. About the only useful fact that came out of the discussion was the obvious limits of third-person-singular pronouns in the language.

She noticed that both wore gold chains around their necks as their only adornment of any kind, but, trying not to be conspicuous, she couldn't see what was fastened to them.

They had been walking for some time now, and several other things came into her mind. First, the locals seemed to live in communities. She passed groups of them here and there, their numbers ranging from three or four to several dozen. Yet there were no signs of buildings. The groupings seemed to be like camp circles, but without the fire. Occasionally she could glimpse mysterious artifacts here and there in the midst of the groups, but nothing large enough to stand out. Some groups seemed to be singing, some dancing, some both, while others were engaged in animated conversations so complex and esoteric that they melded into a tuneful chatter like a blending of insects.

Also, she was aware very suddenly, she felt neither tired nor hungry. That was a good thing, she reflected, since she had no idea what these people ate.

She continued to think in her own, old language,

but had no trouble understanding others with their singsong chirping so alien to her.

The two she had been following took a side path down toward a large grouping that was gathered in a particularly attractive spot. It was a pastoral setting of multicolored flowers and bushes alongside a fast-flowing stream.

She stopped at the junction of the main road and the access trail to the lake, partially blocking the side trail. Someone came up behind her and brushed past her, making her conscious of her blocking.

"I'm sorry," she said automatically and stepped to one side.

"That's all right," the other replied and continued on.

It was almost a full minute before she realized that she had spoken and been understood!

She hurried after the being who had spoken, now far ahead.

"Wait! Please!" she called after the creature. "I need your help!"

The other stopped and turned, a puzzled expression on it.

"What seems to be the trouble?" the creature asked as she came up to him.

"I—I am lost and confused," she blurted out to the other. "I have just—just become one of you, and I don't know where I am or what I'm supposed to do."

Realization hit the other. "A new Entry! Well, well! We haven't had an Entry in Czill in my lifetime! Well, of course you're confused. Come! You shall sleep with us tonight and you will tell us of your origin and we'll tell you of Czill," it said eagerly, like a child with a new toy. "Come!"

She followed the creature down to the grove. It moved very quickly, and eagerly gathered its companions as fast as possible, excitedly telling them that they had an Entry in Riverbend, as the camp was apparently called.

Vardia took all the attention nervously, still bashful and unsure of herself.

They gathered around asking questions by the hundreds, all at once, each one canceling out the others

80

in the general din. Finally, one with a particularly strong voice appealed for quiet over the noise, and after some work, got it.

"Take it easy!" it shouted, making calming gestures. "Can't you see the poor one's scared to death? Wouldn't you be if, say, you went to sleep this night and woke up a Pia?" Satisfied, it turned to Vardia and said gently, "How long have you been in Czill?"

"I—I have just arrived," she told them. "You are the first persons I've talked to. I wasn't even—well, I wasn't sure *how*."

"Well, you've fallen into the worst pack of jabbering conversationalists," the one with the loud voice said, amusement in its tone. "I am Brouder, and I will not try to introduce everyone else here. We'll likely draw a bigger and bigger crowd as word of you gets around."

It was interesting, she thought, that such weird whistlings and clickings should be instantly translated in her mind to their Confederacy equivalents. The creature's name was *not* Brouder, of course—it was a short whistle, five clicks, a long whistle, and a descending series of clicks. Yet that was what the name said in her mind, and it seemed to work in reverse as well.

"I am Vardia Diplo Twelve Sixty-one," she told them, "from Nueva Albion."

"A Comworlder!" someone's voice exclaimed. "No wonder it wound up here!"

"Pay the critics no mind, Vardia," Brouder told her. "They're just showing off their education." That last was said with a great deal of mysterious sarcasm.

"What did you do before you came here?" someone asked.

"My job?" Vardia responded. "Why, I was a diplomatic courier between Nueva Albion and Coriolanus."

"See?" Brouder snorted. "An educated one!"

"I'll still bet the Apprentice can't read!" called out that one in the back.

"Forget the comments," Brouder urged her with a wave of its tentacle. "We're really a friendly group.

81

I was—is something the matter?" it asked suddenly.

"Feeling dizzy," she replied, the ground and crowd suddenly reeling a bit. She reached out to steady herself on Brouder. "Funny," she muttered. "So sudden."

"It comes on like that," Brouder replied. "I should have thought of it. Come on, I'll help you down to the stream."

It took her down to the rushing water, which had a strangely soothing effect on her. It walked her into the water.

"Just stand here a few minutes," the Czillian told her. "Come back up when you feel better."

Automatically, she found, something like tendrils were coming out of small cavities in her feet and were digging into the shallow riverbed. She drank in the cool water through them, and the dizziness and faintness seemed to evaporate.

She looked at the riverbank and saw that they were all watching her, a line of fifteen or twenty light-green, sexless creatures with staring eyes and floppy leaves on their heads. Feeling suddenly excellent once more, she retracted her tendrils and walked stiffly back to the bank.

"Feel all right now?" Brouder asked. "It was stupid of us—you naturally wouldn't have had much water in you. You're the first Entry in some time, and the first one ever for us. Please, if you feel in the least bit strange or ill, let us know. We take so much for granted."

The concern in its voice was genuine, she knew, and she took comfort from it. *All* of them had looked concerned when she had been out in the river.

She really felt she was among friends now.

"Will you answer some of my questions, then?" she asked them.

"Go ahead," Brouder told her.

"Well—these will sound stupid to you all, of course, but this whole business is entirely new to me," she began. "First off, what am I? That is, what are we?"

"I'm Gringer," another approached. "Perhaps I can answer that one. You are a Czillian. The land is called

Czill, and while that explains nothing, it at least gives you a label."

"What does the name mean?" she asked.

Gringer gave the Czillian equivalent of a shrug. "Nothing, really. Most names don't mean anything these days. They probably all did once, but nobody knows anymore.

"Anyway, we are unusual in these parts because we are plants rather than animals of some sort. There are other sentient plant-beings on the Well World, eleven in the South here and nine in the North, although I'm not sure those are really plants as we understand them. We're a distinct minority here, anyway. But there are great advantages to being in the vegetable kingdom."

"Like what?" she asked, fascinated in spite of herself.

"Well, we are not dependent on any sort of food. Our bodies make it by converting light from the sun, as most plants do. Just get a few hours of real or artificial sun a day and you will never starve. You do need some minerals from the soil, but these are common to much of the Well World, so there are few places you can't get along. Water is your only need, and you need it only once every few days. Your body will tell you when—as it did just now. If you get into a regular routine of drinking, you will never feel dizzy or faint nor will you risk your health from its lack. There is also no sex here, none of those primal drives that get the animals in such a neurotic jumble."

"Such things have been minimized on my home planet," she responded. "It would appear from what you say that I will not find this place that far from my own social concepts. But, if you have no sexes, do you reproduce by some artificial means?"

The crowd chuckled at this.

"No," Gringer responded, "all races on the Well World are self-contained biological units that could survive, given certain ecological conditions, without any aids. We reproduce slowly, for we are among the oldest-lived folk on the planet. When something happens to require additional population, then we plant ourselves for an extended period and produce

83

another of ourselves by fission. This is far more practical than the other way, for everything that we are is duplicated, cell for cell, so that the new growth is an exact copy that contains even the same memories and personalities. Thus, even though you will wear out in a few centuries, you will also live forever—for the growths are so identical that not even we are certain which one is which."

Vardia looked around, studying the crowd. "Are there any such twins here?" she asked.

"No," Gringer replied. "We tend to split up, stay far apart, until the years make us into different folk by the variety of experiences. We live in small camps, like this one, drawn from different occupations and interests, so that the camps provide a wide range of folk and keep things from getting too dull."

"What do you do for work?" Vardia asked. "I mean, most—ah, animal civilizations are devoted to food production, building and maintaining shelters, educating the young, and manufacturing. You don't seem to need any of those things."

"This is true," Brouder acknowledged. "Freed from the animal demands of food, clothing, shelter, and sex, we are able to turn ourselves to those pursuits to which other races must, because of the primacy of those needs, devote only a small part of their endeavors."

Vardia was more puzzled than ever. "What sort of activities do you mean?" she asked.

"We think," Brouder replied.

"What Brouder means," Gringer cut in, seeing her uncomprehending look, "is that we are researchers into almost every area. You may think of us as a giant university. We collect knowledge, sort it, play with problems both practical and theoretical, and add to the greater body of knowledge. Had you followed the main road in the other direction, you would have come upon the Center, which is where those of us who need lab facilities and technical tools work and where people following similar lines meet to discuss their findings and their problems."

Vardia's mind tried to grasp it, and could not. "Why?" she asked.

Brouder and Gringer both showed expressions of surprise. "Why what?" Gringer asked.

"Why do you do such work? To what goal?"

This disturbed them, and there were animated conversations through the gathered crowd. Vardia was equally disturbed by the reaction to her question, which she had considered very straightforward. She thought perhaps she had been misunderstood.

"I mean," she said, "to what end is all of this research? You do not seem to use it yourself, so who is it for?"

Gringer seemed about to have a fit of some kind. "But the quest for knowledge is the only thing that separates sentient beings from the most common grasses or lowest animals!" the Czillian said a bit shrilly.

Brouder's tone was almost patronizing, as if addressing a small child. "Look," the researcher said to her, "what do *you* think is the end result for civilization? What is the goal of your people?"

"Why, to exist in happiness and harmony with all others for all times," she replied as if reciting a liturgy —which is what it was, taught from the day she was produced at the Birth Factory.

Gringer's long tentacles showed agitation. Its right one reached down and pulled up a single blade of the yellowish grass that grew for kilometers in all directions. It pushed the long stalk in front of her, waving it like a pointer. "This blade of grass is happy," Gringer stated flatly. "It gets what it needs to survive. It doesn't think or need to think. It remains happy even though I've pulled it up and it will die. It doesn't know that, and won't even know it when it's dead. Its relatives out there on the plains are the same. They fit your definition of the ultimate goal of civilized society. It knows nothing, and in perfect ignorance is its total perfection and its harmony with its surroundings. Shall we, then, create a way to turn all sentient beings into blades of field grass? Shall we, then, have achieved the ultimate in evolution?"

Vardia's mind spun. This sort of logic and these kinds of questions were outside her experience and her orderly, programmed universe. She had no answers for these—heresies, were they? Cornered, but as yet unwilling to give up the true faith, she regressed.

"I want to go back to my own world," she wailed plaintively.

Brouder's expression was sad, and pity swept the crowd, pity not only at her philosophical dilemma but also for her people, the billions blindly devoted to such a hollow goal. Its rubbery tentacle wrapped itself around hers, and pulled her back into the reddish-brown, upturned soil of the camp.

"Any other questions or problems can wait," it said gently. "You will have time to learn and to fit here. It is getting dark now, and you need rest."

The shadows were getting long, and the distant sun had become an orange ball on the horizon. For the first time since waking up, she *did* feel tired, and a slight chill went through her.

"Except under the artificial light of the Center we are inactive in darkness," Brouder explained. "Although we could go indefinitely there, we need the rooting to remain healthy and active. We gain minerals and strength from it, and it is also necessary for mental health."

"How do I—ah, root?" she asked.

"Just pick a spot not too near anyone else, and wait for darkness. You will see," Brouder told her. The Czillian pointed out a good spot, then moved about five long paces from her.

Vardia just stood there for a while, looking at the small community in the gloomy dusk. She discovered that, although her eyes remained open, she was having trouble seeing. Everything looked very dark, as if she were peering through a piece of film that was badly underexposed. Then she felt the myriads of tiny tendrils in her feet creep out in response to some automatic signal and extend deep into the loose soil. The chill and tiredness seemed to lift, and she felt a warmth rising within her. Every cell of her new body seemed to tingle, and she was consumed in an orgasmic feeling of extreme pleasure that canceled out thought.

All over the hex of Czill, all who were not working

in the Center were similarly rooting. To an alien observer, the land would be punctuated with over a million tall, thick vines as motionless as the trees.

And yet the landscape was not motionless. Millions of nocturnal insects set up a chorus, and several small mammals scurried around looking for food and, in the process, moving, aerating, and fertilizing the soil. They provided the carbon-dioxide-from-oxygen conversion needed for atmospheric balance in this hex. The teeming legions of life coexisted with the daylight Czillians in perfect balance. They existed under the thousands of stars in the night sky the sleeping plant-people could not see.

Because her eyes were lidless she saw the awakening even as she underwent it. It was strange to come out of that infinitely pleasurable sleep and see the morning simply fade in. Several of the others were in her field of vision, and she saw that the sleeping position was very stiff. Tentacles ran down and almost blended with the trunk, the legs almost forming a solid front.

She noted absently that picking one's spot for the night was more important than had been first indicated. The unrooting was apparently triggered by the sun's rays falling on the single leaf atop the head, so the more objects scattered about blocked the sun's first rays, the slower one was to be freed. She felt her own tendrils retract and suddenly she could move freely, as if a paralysis had worn off.

Brouder came up to her. "Well? Do you feel better?" it asked cheerfully.

"Yes, much," she replied, and meant it. She *did* feel better, her fears and insecurities fading into a tiny corner of her mind. For the first time she noticed that Brouder wore a neck chain similar to the ones on the two she had followed. Now she looked at the tiny object suspended from it.

It was a digital watch.

Brouder looked at it and nodded. "We're early," it said, then looked somewhat sheepish. "I always say that, even though we always wake up at the same time."

87

"Then why wear a watch?" she asked. "It *is* a watch, isn't it?"

"Oh, yes," the Czillian affirmed. "I need it to tell me the time and day so I can make my meetings at the Center. It's been hectic lately, and I am always afraid that I'm going to get trapped and not be able to come home nights."

"What are you working on?" she asked.

"A very strange project, even for this place," came the reply. "We are attempting to solve a probably unsolvable riddle that is endemic to this world—a great deal of the Center is devoted to it right now. And the worst part is that most of us feel it is unsolvable."

"Then why bother with it?" she asked.

The Czillian looked at her, a grave expression coloring its body movements.

"Because, while we are the best equipped to work on the problem, others are also at work on it. If there is any chance it *is* solvable, the ultimate knowledge will be ours. In others' hands, that knowledge might threaten the very survival of us all."

Here was something Vardia could understand, and she pressed her new friend for more information. But the Czillian dismissed further inquiry for the time being. She had the strong impression that the work was of too high a grade for her to be trusted, even though she was now one of them.

"I am going to the Center now," Brouder told her. "You should come with me. Not only will that give you a chance to see a little of our country—it's your country now, you know—but only at the Center can you be tested and assigned."

She agreed readily and they started off, back down the road she had followed the day before. As they walked, Brouder pointed out the land and vegetation and sketched out the country for her. "Czill is six hundred fourteen point eight-six kilometers across, as is every other hex on the Well World except the equatorial hexes."

She marveled at the knowledge that the measurement it used bore no relationship to the metrics of her own world, yet was translated to the decimal points instantly inside her head.

"We have, of course, six neighbors, two of which are ocean species. Our seven great rivers are fed by hundreds of streams like the one at our camp. The rivers in turn empty into a great ocean—one of three in the South—covering almost thirty hexes. This one of ours is the Overdark Ocean. One of the sea folk is a marine mammal, half-humanoid and half-fish. They are air-breathers, but live most of their lives underwater. They are the Umiau, and you might run into a few at the Center. We are always cooperating on a number of projects, particularly oceanographic studies, since we can't visit their world except in pressure suits. The other ocean species is a nasty group called the Pia—evil characters with great brains and humanoid eyes. But they have ten tentacles with slimy, adhesive suckers and a gaping mouth with about twenty rows of teeth. You can't really talk to them, although they are quite intelligent. They tend to eat anybody not of their race."

Vardia shuddered, imagining such horrors. "Then why don't they eat the Umiau?" she asked.

Brouder chuckled. "They would if they could, but, as with all hexes near antagonistic species on the Well World, natural limitations are designed into the system. The Umiau's land is near the mouth of three rivers and the low salt content isn't to a Pia's liking. Also, the Umiau do have certain natural defenses and can swim faster and quicker. They're in some kind of uneasy truce now, anyway, since the Umiau, although they aren't fanatical about it, can and will eat Pia, too."

They remained silent for a while, until they came to a major fork in the road.

"We go to the left," Brouder said. "Don't ever go down that right fork—it leads to the camps of the diseased and isolated."

"What sort of diseases?" she asked uneasily.

"About the same number as anywhere else," Brouder replied. "But every time we discover an immunizing agent, something new mutates in the viruses. I wouldn't worry about it, however. The average Czillian life span is over two hundred and fifty years, and if nothing serious happens to change that, you'll twin several times anyway. The population's a stable million and a half—crowded, but not so much that we cannot have empty spaces and camp room. Our births and deaths are almost exactly even —the planet's master brain sees to that. Besides, since we don't really age in the sense most other things do, and since we can regenerate most of our parts that go bad or get injured, there's naturally a constant death factor to keep the population in bounds. The master brain only interferes in critical situations."

"Regenerate?" Vardia asked, surprised. "Do you mean that if I lose an arm or leg it will grow back?"

"Just so," Brouder affirmed. "Your entire pattern is held within every cell of your body. Since respiration is direct, through the pores, as long as your brain's intact, you'll come back. It's painful—and we don't experience much pain—but possible."

"So the only area I have to protect is my head," she remarked.

Brouder laughed a high, shrill laugh. "No, not your head, certainly not! Either foot," it said, pointing to her strange feet that looked like inverted bowls with spongy lids for soles.

"Do you mean I'm walking on my brains?" she gasped incredulously.

"Just so, just so," affirmed Brouder. "Each controls half of your body, but each has the total content of the body's input, including thought and memory. If we were to chop you off at the bottom of the stalk, your two feet would dig into the ground and each would sprout a new you. Your head contains sensory input neural circuits only—in fact, it's mostly hollow. Chop it off and you'd just go to sleep and dig in until you grew a new one."

Vardia marveled at this news as much as she had at Ortega back at Zone. But this isn't some alien creature I just met, she told herself. It is *me* it is talking about.

"There's the Center," Brouder said as they came over a rise.

It was a great building that seemed to spread out for kilometers across the horizon. There was a great bubble in the center that reflected light like a mirror, then several arms—six of them, she noted with dry amusement—made of what appeared to be transparent glass—spread out symmetrically. She saw skyscrapers of the same transparent material, a few twenty or more stories, rising around the bubble and opposite the tips of the arms.

"It's incredible!" she managed.

"More than you know," Brouder replied with a touch of pride. "There our best minds work out problems and store the knowledge we obtain. The silvery rails that thread through the walls and ceilings are artificial solar light sufficient to keep us awake and fed through the night, and if you look to the horizon you'll see the River Averil coming in. The Center's built over it, giving us a constant water source. With light and water provided—and some vitamin baths—you can work around the clock for seven to ten days. But sooner or later it catches up with you and the longer you stay awake the longer you will have to plant in the end."

Something made her think of Nathan Brazil and that book he had been reading, the one with the lurid cover.

"You have a library here?" she asked.

"The best," the other boasted. "It has everything we've ever been able to collect, both from our studies on this planet and from Entries like yourself who provide history, sociology, and even technical information."

"Any stories?" she asked.

"Oh, yes," came the reply. "And legends, tales, whatever. The Umiau are particularly fertile in that department. The river's how they get up to the Center."

"What keeps the Pia away, then?" she asked apprehensively.

"They can't take fresh water, and they'd have to breathe it, remember? The Umiau are mammals so they don't care what sort of water they're in."

Brouder went on to explain the social structure of

the Center. It was headed by a small group of specialists called Elders, not because they were old but because they were the best in their fields. Below them were their assistants, the Scholars, who did the research and basic project work. Brouder was a Scholar, as was Gringer. Under them were the Apprentices who learned their fields and waited for their chance to prove themselves and advance. The bottom level was the Keepers—the cleaners, gardeners, and technicians who maintained everything so that everyone could get on with his work. The Keepers chose their own lives and professions and many were retired upper-level folk who had decided they had gone as far as they could, or who had reached dead ends. But some just liked to do what they did.

Brouder took her inside and introduced her to a Scholar whose name was Mudriel. Basically, the Scholar was an industrial psychologist, and over the next several days—weeks, in fact—Vardia was kept busy with interviews, tests, and other experiments to see her total profile. In addition, they began to teach her to read the Czillian language. Mudriel, in particular, was pleased with the speed and ease with which she was mastering it.

Every evening they sent her out to a special camp near the Psych Department but out of the shade of the building. The nights saw a strange forest grow up on all sides of the Center as thousands of workers of all ranks came out and rooted. Some stayed rooted for days, even several days, sleeping off long, around-the-clock stints at work.

Vardia seemed to be Mudriel's only customer, and she remarked on it.

"You are the first Entry to be a Czillian in our lifetimes," Mudriel explained. "Normally, I study various departments and workers to see if they are ruining their health or efficiency, or are misplaced. It happens all the time. Sometimes, whenever possible, we bring Entries from other hexes here for debriefing. When that is not possible, I go to them. I am one of perhaps a thousand, no more, who has been in the Northern Hemisphere."

"What's it like?" she asked. "I understand it's different."

"That's the word for it," Mudriel agreed, and gave a brief shudder. "But we have some just as bad on our side, in one way or another. Ever think of interviewing a Pia in its own domain when it's trying to be helpful and eat you at the same time? I have."

"And yet you've survived," she said in admiration.

Mudriel made a negative gesture. "Not always. I've been down to my feet once, practically wrecked for weeks three or four times, and killed twice."

"Killed!" Vardia exclaimed. "But—"

Mudriel shrugged. "I've twinned four times naturally," it replied matter-of-factly, "and once when I was left with only my brains. There are still four of me. We stay in the same job and take turns on the travel to even out the risk."

Vardia shook her head in wonder, a gesture more human than Czillian.

While most twins were turned to other fields by the Psych Department, ones with critical jobs or super-specialized knowledge and skills often worked together side by side. Vardia met several people at the Center several times to mutual confusion.

One day Mudriel called her into its office, where it was thumbing through an enormously thick file.

"It's time to assign you and go on to other things," the psychologist told her. "You've been here long enough for us to know you better than we know almost any other Czillian. I must say, you've been a wonderful subject, but a puzzling one."

"In what way?" Vardia asked. As time went by she had become more and more accustomed to her new form and surroundings, and less and less had felt the social alienation of that first night.

"You have normalized," Mudriel pointed out. "By this time you are feeling as if you were born one of us, and your past life and that which went with it is a purely intellectual memory experience."

"That's true," Vardia acknowledged. "It almost seems as if all my past happened to someone else, that I just watched it unfold."

"That's true of all Entries," replied Mudriel. "Part

93

of the change process, when the biological changes adjust and remake the psyche. Much of our personality and behavior is based on such biological things. In the animals, its glands, enzymes, and the like, but with us its various different secretions. Hormonal imbalances in your former race cause differences; by artificially injecting certain substances into a male of your species who was sexually developed, he could be given female characteristics, and vice versa. Now, time has rebalanced your mind with your new body, and it is for the best."

"What puzzles you about me, then?" Vardia prodded.

"Your lack of skills," replied the psychologist. *"Everybody* does something. But you were apparently raised to be highly intelligent yet totally ignorant. You could carry messages and conversations with ease, yet do nothing else. Your ignorance of much of your own sector amazes us.

"You were, in effect, a human recording machine. Did you, for example, realize that in the eighty-three days you've been with us you've had a longer existence than ever in your short life?"

"I—I don't know what you mean," Vardia stammered.

Mudriel's expression and tone were of mixed pity and disgust. "They bred you with an extremely high intelligence, but while you grew up, they administered extremely deep programming to make certain you never used it. Over all this was lightly placed the persona known as Vardia Diplo Twelve Sixty-one, a number whose implications are distasteful to me. This made you curious, inquisitive, but only on the surface. You could never act on any information gained, nor did you have any desire to. The persona was mainly to help others feel comfortable. When you reached your destination, an embassy employee would put you under hypnosis, read off the message —and, in the process, wipe your memory. Then the same persona would be reimposed with a reply message, if any. Had you reached Coriolanus, this would have been the case. You now have vivid memories of

94

your Captain Brazil and the other passengers, and of Dalgonia. All of these would have been gone. Any whom you knew who had previously encountered you would be strangers to you. They would just assume, as you would, that it was another Vardia Diplo they knew. Think back—what do you remember of your life before boarding Brazil's ship?"

Vardia thought back with the clarity and detachment she now possessed. She remembered saying good-bye to the Political Office staff, walking out, riding to the spaceport, boarding the shuttle.

Nothing before.

"I never realized—" she began, but Mudriel cut her off.

"I know," the psychologist said. "Part of the deep program. It would never even occur to you. And you didn't even know the message you carried, the one that they would go to these lengths to keep private. By programmed exercises you kept yourself in perfect physical condition, and if challenged or cornered you would fight suicidally to free yourself. If trapped, you would have triggered a series of impulses that would have brought about your suicide." Mudriel saw the mixed apprehension and disbelief in Vardia's eyes.

"Don't worry," the psychologist assured her. "We have removed the deep programming. You will remain you. Would you like to hear the message you carried?"

Vardia nodded dully, her mind in a fog.

The psychologist took out a tiny translucent cube and popped it into a well in a small recorder on a table nearby.

Vardia suddenly heard her voice—her old voice, incredibly, although she no longer possessed the vocal chords to speak that way, saying in a tinny way: "The Commisariat introduces you to Datham Hain, who, with a companion, came on the same ship as the courier. Citizen Hain is on a mission of vital importance to the Commisariat and requires dinner appointments with several Members of the Presidium of Coriolanus, as many as can be accommodated.

You are to follow whatever might be his instructions to the letter, without question or hesitation. Keep the courier until at least one such meeting has been arranged, then reprogram it to report on that meeting, said reprogramming to be in Hain's presence and with his approval. All glory to the People's Revolution, all glory to its prophets."

The psychologist studied Vardia closely as the recording closed. The ex-courier was obviously stunned and shaken, but that shock treatment had to be administered. All over the Entry's body, the Czillian read the mental struggle that had to be taking place within.

It was a terrible thing to destroy someone's complacent world-picture.

Finally, the psychologist asked gently, "Would you like to go root and meditate? Take as long as you want."

Vardia shook her head negatively. "No," she said at last, in a half-whisper, "no, I'm all right."

"I know," the psychologist soothed. "It is a terrible thing to find the lie in life. That is one reason we are dedicated here to the uncovering of truth. There are societies and people just as bad on this world, maybe even worse. Hain himself is here somewhere, and probably has already fallen in with a bad bunch. Such societies are the enemies of all civilization, and it is with them that we war. Will you join us in the fight?"

Vardia stood silent a few moments more. Then, suddenly, something seemed to snap within her, and with a fierceness and intensity that surprised even her she said, "Yes!"

The psychologist gave the Czillian equivalent of a smile and turned back to the file it had before it.

Picking up a stamp, it brought it down on an empty block on the front of the file. In Czillian it read: *Ready for Assignment.*

The last processing was over, and Vardia Diplo 1261 was extinguished.

Vardia the Czillian left the office.

The Akkafian Empire
(Enter Datham Hain, Asleep)

DATHAM HAIN HAD ENTERED THE GATE WITH A FALSE sense of bravado, but he was scared to death. He had nightmares of awful proportions, bringing forth every fear in his long life. These surfaced as the Markovian brain picked, analyzed, and classified each subject according to some long-lost, preset reasoning.

He awoke suddenly, with a start, and looked around. It was the strangest look in his experience.

He realized immediately that he was now color-blind, although instead of merely the blacks, whites, and shades of gray, there was a mild sepia-tone effect that made certain things look fuzzy and others stand out. His depth perception was remarkable, he realized. At a glance he could tell exactly how far everything in view was from everything else, and his vision seemed to be enlarged to a 180-degree field. That was amazing, as amazing as the view itself.

He seemed to be on a ledge overlooking an incredible landscape far below. The land was bleak and sandy, broken only by hundreds of cones that looked almost like perfectly formed volcanoes. He strained to get a better look, and found, suddenly, the scene magnifying itself, each time by a factor of two. As it did, a hardly noticed hairline-split midway in his vision also magnified, so that it became a huge bar separating the scene into right and left views. It was as if he were peering through two windows while standing in front of the post that separated them.

There were things down there, and they were moving. Hain stared in fascination at them, a corner of his mind wondering why he was fascinated instead of horrified or repelled. They were great insects, ranging in

97

size from one to almost four meters long, the median height being almost a meter. They had two large, apparently multifaceted eyes fixed, like a fly's, forward in the head. Below the eyes were huge mandibles flanking a mouth resembling a parrot's beak. With surprise he saw one creature stop while a long, snaky black tongue emerged to clean the face.

The body was oblong and seemed to have hair on it—the resolution of Hain's vision was so fine that he could almost count the hairs. And yet—yes, flush against the body in the hair were wings, several pairs of them. The rear of the body exposed a barren, bony tip that undoubtedly was a stinger.

Hain tried to imagine the fate of anyone stung with something that size.

The head seemed to be on a hinge or circular joint, as some of the creatures moved it slightly in one or another direction.

For the first time he saw the feelers, giant things that seemed to have a life of their own, moving every way but forward—including straight up. They ended in hair-covered nodules.

The eight legs were thick and were also covered with hair, longer and down-angled. They were multijointed, and he saw a pair of the creatures using their forward legs like hands to move a rock away from a pathway it was blocking. He could see that the tips were not hair but spikelike and were covered with a secretion that looked sticky.

The insects moved with amazing speed sometimes, and, every once in a while, one would take to the air briefly. Apparently they couldn't fly very far with all that weight, but could manage a short hop when they felt like it. As Hain watched, he saw that some of them were operating machines! One looked like a snowplow, and it was clearing dust and debris from the roadways as it was pushed forward; others seemed to have no obvious purpose.

With the realization that these were not animals but one form of sentient life on the Well World, something else hit, as well. He tried to turn his head to see himself, but could not. He opened his strangely rigid mouth and stuck out his tongue. It was more than three meters long, as controllable as an arm, and covered with an incredibly sticky substance.

I'm one of them, he told himself, more in wonder than in fear.

He raised his head up and brought his two forward legs into view. He had been right, he saw. Three joints, all bendable in any direction. The tips *were* spikes, like hard rubber, and he experimented by reaching out and picking up a small rock. As his legs touched the rock, a sticky secretion gave him a grip. When he let go, the secetion turned to a solid film and fell away like used skin.

He noticed immediately that, when the dropped rock hit, he did not hear it. Rather, he *felt* it, as a sharp, single pulsation. The antennae, he told himself. They sense air movement, but not as sound.

Suddenly he was aware that he was getting thousands of tiny pulses through them, and, incredibly, he almost sensed the source and distance of each.

This has possibilities, thought Datham Hain.

Using his tongue he surveyed his own body, being careful not to come near the stinger at the rear which he now realized he could feel when he wanted to. No use in possibly poisoning myself this early in the game, he thought cautiously.

He was about three meters long and almost a meter high, he discovered. About medium-sized for those creatures down there.

He flexed his wings—six pairs, he found—long but looking extremely thin and frail to support his weight. He decided he wouldn't try them out until he knew more about his anatomy. Even birds have to be taught to fly, he thought, and sentient creatures probably had less instinct—if any at all—than the lower species.

Now how do I get down off this ledge? he wondered. Finally, he decided to experiment, moving his body close to the edge. As his front legs touched the side they secreted that substance and stuck, he saw with satisfaction.

Emboldened, he pushed off and started walking down the side.

Doing so was incredibly easy, he found, confidence growing with each step. He realized he could probably walk on a ceiling, if the sticky stuff would support his weight. The main problem would be getting used to the fact that there was so much of him in back of his head. The legs worked in perfect coordination, as if he had been born with them; but the body was hard and rigid, and took some practice to maneuver without spilling end over end.

It took several minutes to descend the low cliff, although he realized that, with practice, he could probably come back and do it in seconds. Once down, he faced a problem that his reason wouldn't solve for him. He wanted to get introduced quickly, to get settled in here, and to check out the sociopolitical system, the geography, and the like. Also, he was feeling hungry, and he hadn't the slightest idea what these creatures ate.

But how did they communicate? Not only language, but even the *means* weren't all that apparent.

Well, that Ortega had said that the brain would provide for such things, he told himself; but he was exceedingly nervous as he approached one of the creatures coming down the road.

The other saw him and stopped.

"What are you doing just standing there, Markling?" the newcomer challenged sternly. "Don't you have any work to do?"

Hain was stunned. The language was a series of incredibly rapid pulsations transmitted in some way from the creature's antennae to his own, yet he had understood everything! All but the last word, anyway. He decided to try to talk back.

"Please. I am newly born to this world, and I need help and guidance," he began, then felt his own antennae quiver incredibly quickly as he talked. It worked!

"What the hell?" responded the gruff stranger, although not really in those terms. Hain's brain automatically seemed to translate into familiar symbols. "You sick or something?"

"No, no," Hain protested. "I have just come from Zone, where I have just awakened as one of you."

The other thought about that for a minute. "I'll be

100

damned! An Entry! Haven't had one in over ten years!"
Suddenly the old skepticism returned. "You're not just
saying that to shirk, are you?"

"I assure you that I am what I say, and that up until
a very short time ago I was of a totally different race
and form."

"You adjust pretty well," the other noted. "Most of
'em have the creeping fits for days. Well, I'll take you
over to the nearest government house and it'll be their
problem. I have work to do. Follow me." With that, it
started on down the road, and Hain followed.

His guide was almost a third larger than he was,
Hain saw. Most of the creatures he passed seemed to
be about the same size or smaller than he. A few big
ones were around, and they seemed to be the bosses.

They walked past several of the huge cones, then up
the side of one that looked no different from the rest
and into the hole on top. Hain noted that the opening
was so even because it was rimmed with metal, like
an open hatch. He almost lost his nerve on entering.
The aboveground part of the cone, about ten meters
worth, was hollow to the outside structure. They were
not only walking down, but at an angle.

When they passed ground level, they walked onto
a floor which was also some kind of metal. Tunnels
lined with tile, with neon or some similar lighting
stretching down in long tubes, led away like spokes
on a wheel. They were wide enough to hold two of
the creatures abreast, and they passed several as his
guide led him down a near one.

Doorless openings into large chambers filled with
all sorts of strange stuff, often with dozens of the creatures working, were passed before they reached one
with a hexagon in lights over the doorway. Inside the
hex was a wide gray ring, then a smaller black one,
then a white dot. It reminded Hain with some amusement of the view of his guide's posterior, with its
menacing stinger.

Several small and medium-sized creatures were
working, apparently at some sort of paperwork, Hain
noted with curiosity. Huge printing machines, like
typewriters, were all over, with television screens dis-
playing what the creatures, using their forward legs,

were typing on a strange keyboard. The keyboard was a series of apparently identical cubes, forty or fifty of them, which lit momentarily as they were touched. A crazy dot pattern emerged on the screens in no apparent logical order or pattern. When the screen was filled, a hind leg would kick a large stud and the screen would go blank—and they would be back to typing again.

So I can't read the language, Hain noted to himself. Well, can't have everything.

The guide waited patiently until somebody noticed him and looked up from its keyboard.

"Yes?" asked the worker and the communicated tone was one of irritated nastiness.

"Found this Markling on the road, claims to be an Entry," said the big guide in that same annoyed tone he had used with Hain.

There was that word again. What in seven hells was a Markling, anyway?

"Just a moment," the clerk or whatever it was said, "I'll see if His Highness will see you."

The office worker went into a side door and stayed several minutes. Hain's hunger was increasing, and so was his apprehension. A hereditary empire, he thought. Well, it could be worse.

Finally the clerk reappeared. "His Highness will see the Entry," she said—for some reason Hain automatically thought of his guide as masculine and the receptionist and most of the other workers as feminine. The guide moved forward.

"Just the Entry," said the clerk sharply. "You will return to your duties."

"As you say," the other replied, and turned and left.

Hain gathered up his courage and entered the doorway.

Inside was the biggest creature he had ever seen. But there was something else unusual about him.

The hairs on his body were white.

Hain suddenly realized just how hereditary this monarchy was.

There were some boxes and bags around of more or less conventional design, and one of those typewriters with a much larger screen. Nothing else. The

102

big one reared back on the last four of his eight legs. Hain was impressed and cowed; he hadn't seen anyone else doing that.

"What's your name, Entry?" the big white one demanded imperiously. The tone, Hain realized by now, was conveyed by the intensity of the signal.

"Datham Hain, Your Highness," he replied in the most respectful way he could.

The official ran his tongue over his beak in thought. Finally, he went over to the typewriter and started punching up something—something short, Hain saw, because the screen was still almost empty when the large creature punched the send bar or whatever it was. A moment's wait. Then the screen started to fill with those funny dots.

The official read the message carefully, studying it for several minutes. Finally it turned back to him as he stood there impatiently, needing almost four meters to negotiate the move.

"Ordinarily, Hain, we'd just train and condition you to a position and you'd fit in or die." Hain's heart—if he still had one—sank. "But," the royal official continued, "in this case we have special use for you. Too bad you turned up a Markling, but that's to be expected. You'll be quartered near here—I'll have one of my assistants show you where. There's a commissary three doors down. Most of you Entries come through starving, so go in there and eat your fill. Don't worry about what it is—we can eat just about anything. Wait in your quarters until I get instructions from Imperial Headquarters."

Hain still stood there, digesting all this. Finally, he said, "Your Highness, might I be permitted one question?"

"Yes, yes," the other said impatiently. "What is it?"

"What's a Markling?"

"Hain," replied the official patiently, "life is hard and cheap in the Akkafian Empire. Infant mortality is extremely high, not only from normal factors imposed by nature but for other reasons you'll find out sooner or later for yourself. As a result, to ensure racial continuation, about fifty females are born for every male.

103

"A Markling is a female Akkafian, Hain. You've had a sex change."

Datham Hain was led by one of the office staff to the commissary, which proved to be a large room filled with strange animals, plants, and worms, some still alive. Feeding as an Akkafian was not pleasant, at least to Hain's unnormalized psyche, but it was necessary. The creatures frankly didn't taste all that bad—in fact, they didn't taste very much at all, but they filled the void in what seemed to be multiple stomachs. If he didn't think about what he was eating, the changeling discovered, it went down all right.

That tongue, like a sticky whip, was infinitely controllable. Live prey were simply picked up, thrown to the rear sting area to be paralyzed, then held and fed by the mandibles a little at a time through the beak.

Discovering that he was now a she wasn't much of a shock to Hain; the odds were that sexuality was so different among these people that it probably didn't make much difference anyway. What *was* disquieting was that the males seemed to be in firm charge. The Nirlings, as the males were called, were larger and controlled the government and supervisory positions and the technology that kept them in power. The females, mostly neutered, did the work, apparently compulsively. Hain had seen no evidence of force or coercion; the workers carried out their tasks dedicatedly, unquestioningly, and uncomplainingly. Hain understood the system to a degree. It was not unlike that of the Comworlds, where people were bred to work.

The only trouble, he—no, she—thought, is that I am on the low end of the scale. To be an alien creature, to be totally different—these things she could accept. To be female she could accept. To be a slave to such a system was intolerable.

After feeding they took her to a rest area. This race worked at whatever it did around the clock, and individuals were spelled by others so they would get rest at scheduled intervals.

The staging area rose for several storeys—a large,

underground wall of cubicles each of which was just large enough to hold a single creature. About half were filled as they entered, and Hain was assigned a number and told to go into it and wait for instructions.

Hain climbed up the side easily and entered the assigned cubicle. It was warm, and extremely humid, which felt oddly more comfortable than the drier air of the offices. There was a carpet of some sort of animal hair, and a small control panel with two buttons, one of which was depressed. Curious, she pressed the other one. She had apparently found a radio which was broadcasting a series of sound patterns whose pulses were oddly pleasing and calming. A wave of relief swept over her insect body and she found herself drifting off into a dreamless sleep.

The office clerk noted with some satisfaction that Hain was asleep, then went over to the superintendent's control console at the base of the rest area. The superintendent was emptying the catch trays of waste and other products, and she showed surprise when she recognized a clerk of the baron's household.

"By order of His Highness," the clerk commanded, "the Markling in One Ninety-eight is to be kept asleep until called for. Make certain the pacifier remains on at shift change."

The superintendent acknowledged the order and went into her office. A panel of plastic buttons laid out and numbered corresponding to the cubicles was before her, with many of the buttons lit, including Hain's. The superintendent held down number 198 with one foreleg while punching a small red control off to one side with the other.

Hain was locked into blissful sleep until the button was depressed again.

The clerk expressed satisfaction, and returned to the baron's office to report. The great white Nirling nodded approval and dismissed her back to her desk.

After a while, he went over to his communications console and punched the number for the Imperial Palace. He didn't like to call the palace, since the king and the ambitious nobles surrounding him were unstable and untrustworthy. Barons were low on the pecking order, but they had a much longer survival rate because they *were* away from the palace. Make your quota and the living was pretty good.

Communication was by audio only, so things had to be spelled out. Although the Akkafians had no ears, they "heard" in much the same way as creatures who did. Sound, after all, is a disruption of the surrounding atmospheric pressure by varying that pressure. Although he had never heard a sound as such, the baron's hearing was better than most creatures on the Well World.

After a long period, somebody at the palace woke up and answered. The Imperial Household was getting sloppy and degenerate, the baron reflected. Perhaps one day soon it would be time for a baronial revolt.

Of course, the titles and such were not the same as human equivalents, but if Hain could have overheard the conversation, it would have been translated much like this:

"This is Baron Kluxm of Subhex Nineteen. I have an emergency topic for immediate transmittal to His Majesty's Privy Council."

"The Privy Council is not assembled," came a bored reply. "Can't this wait, Baron?"

Kluxm cursed silently at the insolence and stupidity of even the household help. The operator was probably one of the king's Marklings.

"I said *emergency,* operator!" he emphasized, trying to keep his temper from showing. "I take full responsibility."

The operator seemed unsure of herself, and finally decided in good bureaucratic fashion to pass the buck.

"I will transfer you to General Ytil of the Imperial Staff," she said. "He will decide."

Before Kluxm could even reply he heard the relay switch, and a new, male voice answered. "Ytil," it said curtly.

The baron had even less use for imperial military men; they generally went to war with other hexes when shortages developed every few years, and invariably lost them. However, he decided that Ytil would do for the same purpose as the operator had;

after he explained the situation, it was somebody else's problem.

"I had an Entry today, one of the ones we'd been told to watch for."

"An Entry!" Ytil's voice was suddenly very excited. The waves were so bad that the general's voice started to give Kluxm a headache. "Which one?"

"The one called Datham Hain. As a common Markling breeder," he added.

Ytil's voice still quivered with excitement, although the last plainly disappointed him. "A Markling breeder! Pity! But to think we got one! Hmmmm. Actually, this might work out to our advantage. I've got to go over my files and recordings of Hain at Zone, but, if I remember, he's the greedy and ambitious type."

"Yes, that's what my file said," Kluxm acknowledged. "But she was abnormally respectful and quiet while here. Seems to have adjusted to our form extremely well."

"Yes, yes, that's to be expected," Ytil replied. "After all, no use antagonizing everyone. Hain's smart enough to see the social structure and her limits in it right off. Where is she now?"

"In a rest area near my office," Kluxm replied. "She's on lull music and has a full stomach, so she's out for two or three days until hunger sets in again."

"Excellent, excellent," approved Ytil. "I'll call the Privy Council together and we'll send someone for her when we're ready. You are to be commended, Baron! A fine job!"

Sure, Kluxm thought glumly to himself. For which you'll take all the credit.

But credit was not what was on Ytil's mind as the general scurried down the palace corridor after terminating the conversation. He stopped in a security room and picked up a tiny, black, jewel-like object on a large chain. Carefully he placed it over his right antenna and then went down to the lowest level of the palace.

The guards weren't very curious about him; it was

107

normal to have high-ranking military and diplomatic people using the Zone Gate.

The Akkafian general walked quickly into the darkness at the end of the basement corridor.

And emerged in Zone.

Zone—the Akkafian Embassy

THE MARKLING RECEPTIONIST LOOKED STARTLED AS General Ytil emerged through the Zone Gate.

Each hex had a gate somewhere, which would transport anyone to Zone instantaneously, and from Zone to his home hex. There were 780 such gates to the offices of each of the Southern Hemisphere races, as well as the one master Gate for Classification through which all entries passed and the huge input-only Gate in the center. It made things very easy for interspecies contact.

General Ytil dismissed the startled exclamation and apologies of the receptionist and made his way immediately to the Imperial Ambassador's office.

The Baron Azkfru had barely been tipped off by the clerk when the general rushed in the door. The ambassador could see the obvious excitement and agitation in Ytil's every movement.

"My Lord Baron!" the general exclaimed. "It has happened! We have one of the new Entries as it was foretold!"

"Calm down, Ytil," Azkfru growled. "You're losing your medals for dignity and self-control. Now, tell me rationally what this is about."

"The one called Hain," Ytil responded, still excited. "It turned up earlier today over in Kluxm's barony as a Markling breeder."

"Hmmmm . . ." Azkfru mused. "Too bad she's a

breeder, but it can't be helped. Where is this Entry now?"

"In lull sleep, safe for two or three more days," the general told him. "Kluxm thinks I've notified the Imperial Household and the Privy Council. He's expecting someone to pick her up."

"Very good," Azkfru replied approvingly. "It looks like things are breaking our way. I never put much stock in fortune-tellers and such crap, but if this has happened then Providence has placed a great opportunity in our hands. Who else knows of this besides Kluxm and yourself?"

"Why, no one, Highness," Ytil replied. "I have been most careful."

Baron Azkfru's mind moved quickly, sorting out the facts and deciding on a course of action with a speed that had guaranteed his rise to the top.

"All right, return to your post for now, and nothing of this to anyone! I'll make all the necessary arrangements."

"You're making the deal with the Northerners?" Ytil asked.

Azkfru gave the Akkafian equivalent of a sigh. "Ytil, how many times do you need to be reminded that *I* am the baron? You *take* orders, and leave the questions and answers to your betters."

"But I only—" Ytil began plaintively, but Azkfru cut him off.

"Go, now," the ambassador said impatiently, and Ytil turned to leave.

Azkfru reached into a drawer and pulled out a pulse rifle. *This* one worked in Zone, at least in his offices.

"Ytil!" he called after the other, who was halfway out the door.

Ytil stopped but couldn't turn. "My Lord?" he called back curiously.

"Good-bye, fool," Azkfru replied, and shot the general repeatedly until the white-haired body was a charred ruin.

Azkfru buzzed for his guard, and thought, *Too bad*

I couldn't trust the idiot, but his incompetence would give the show away.

The guard appeared, and looked down at the general's remains nervously but without curiosity.

"The general tried to kill me," he explained without any effort to be convincing. "I had to defend myself. It appears that he and the Baron Kluxm are at the heart of a baronial revolt. After you dispose of this carrion, go to Kluxm's, and eliminate his whole staff and, of course, the baron. Then go to the rest area and bring a Markling named Hain to my estate. Do it quietly. I'll report the revolt."

They nodded, and it took them only a few minutes to eat the body.

After they had left, he buzzed for a clerk.

"You will go to the Classification Gate and enter. It will take you to the North Zone. When you get there don't leave the Gate room, but simply tell the first inquirer that you want to talk to Ambassador Thirteen Forty, and wait for that person. When it comes, tell it who you are, who sent you, and that we are ready to agree. Got that?"

The clerk waved her antennae affirmatively and repeated the message.

Dismissing her, he attended to the last detail. He flipped the intercom to the receptionist's desk.

"The General Ytil wasn't here," he told her. "Understand? You never even heard of him."

The clerk understood all too well, and rubbed out Ytil's appearance in her logbook.

It was a big gamble he was taking, he knew, and it would probably cost him his life. But the stakes! The stakes were too great to ignore!

The Barony of Azkfru, Akkafian Empire

DATHAM HAIN'S MASSIVE BODY, NOW IN A DRUGGED sleep, rested in the center of the lowest floor of the Baron Azkfru's nest. The room was filled with computer banks flashing light-signals and making clicking and whirring sounds. Four large cables were attached to Hain's head at key points, and two smaller ones were fixed to the base of her two antennae. Two neutered Markling technicians with the symbol of the baron painted between their two huge eyes checked readings on various dials and gauges, and checked and rechecked all the connections.

Baron Azkfru's antennae showed complete satisfaction. He had often wondered what the Imperial Household would say if they knew he had one of these devices.

There would be civil war at the very least, he thought.

The conditioner had been developed by a particularly brilliant Akkafian scientist in the imperial household almost eighty years before, when the ambassador himself was just a youngling. It ended the periodic baronial revolts, and assured the stability of the new —now old—order by making revolution next to impossible. Oh, you couldn't condition everyone with certainty, so it was done subtly. Probably every baron dreamed of overthrowing the empire—it let the pressure and frustration out.

But none of them could do it. Because, although they could dream about it, they couldn't disobey a direct imperial command.

But Azkfru could.

His father had duplicated the device here in the earliest days of its development. Here, slowly, methodically, key ones were deconditioned and reconditioned. Even so, he reflected, you couldn't change the basic personality of the conditioned. That was why Ytil had to go—too dumb to keep quiet. As for Kluxm—well, it was known for some particularly strong-willed Nirlings to break free, although never with any prayer of support from the rest of the conditioned leadership.

"We are ready when you are, Highness," called one of the Markling technicians. Azkfru signaled satisfaction and went down to the floor.

Quickly and efficiently two additional cables similar to the ones on Hain were placed on his own antennae. When he now said something, it would be placed in the machine, amplified, processed, and fed directly into the brain of Datham Hain in such a way that it would be taken as acceptable input and engraved in the other's mind.

The baron signaled a go-ahead, and the technicians touched the last controls.

"Datham Hain!" the ambassador's brain called out.

Hain, although unconscious, answered, "Yes?"

"Your past to this point you retain, but it is an academic past, there to call upon if needed but irrelevant to your present and future," the baron told her. "What is important to you, what is the *only* thing of importance to you, is that you are a breeder Markling of the Barony of Azkfru. Your destiny is whatever the Baron of Azkfru wishes, and that is acceptable and normal to you. My will is your will, your *only* will. You exist to serve me alone. You would never betray me, nor allow harm to come to me. You are my own, my property, and that is all that is good and happy in your mind or life. When you serve me you are happy, and when you do not you are unhappy. That is the measure of your joy in life. I am your leader, your lord, and your only god. Your worship is normal. Do you understand this?"

"I understand, my lord," replied Hain mechanically.

The baron signaled to the technicians to break contact, which they quickly did, then unfastened the two cables from his antennae.

"How did it take?" Azkfru asked one of the technicians.

"The subject is receptive," replied one of the technicians, part of whose *own* conditioning was never to consider the idea that she might have been conditioned. "However, her psychological profile is one of extreme selfishness. That might eventually cancel the conditioning, producing mental breakdown."

"What do you advise, then?"

"Go along with the idea," the technician suggested. "Go back into her mind and tell her that her only avenue to wealth and power is through you and no one else. That's something her mind can completely accept, and it will be acted upon in concert with the standard conditioning you've already administered. Then, after she's awake and you are interviewing her, hold out the highest possible position a breeder Markling could attain."

"I *see*," the baron replied, and he did see. That made everything perfect. "Let us complete the conditioning," he commanded.

Datham Hain awoke with a very strange set of feelings and yet not aware that over ten days had passed since she was first introduced to the land of the Akkafian.

A Markling with the insignia of the Baron Azkfru entered and saw that she was awake. "You must be starved," the newcomer said pleasantly. "Follow me and we will take care of that."

Starvation was close to what Datham Hain actually felt at that point, and she needed no further urging to follow the servant. The feeding room was filled with pens of large, white-ribbed worms that were indigenous to the soil of the land. Hain had no qualms this time about eating such prey, and found them most satisfying.

"The baron raises his own *fikhfs*," the guide explained as she gorged herself. "Only the best for this household, till midnight at the Well of Souls."

Hain suddenly stopped eating.

"What was that you just said?" she asked.

"Oh, it's just a saying," the other replied.

Hain forgot it for the moment and continued eating. When it was clear that her hunger had been satisfied, the guide said, "Now, follow me into reception, and you'll meet the baron."

Hain obediently followed down several long and particularly plush corridors to a wide anteroom covered in that downy fur with a low-volume "music" background, pleasant but not lulling as the other had been.

"Just relax for now," the baron's servant told her. "His Highness will call you in when he is ready."

Relaxing was just the thing Hain felt least like doing; extremely awake and alert, she wished idly for something active to do, something to look at. A rack in one corner held a series of scrolls in that funny writing, but it was just random dots.

Not even any pictures, she thought glumly.

She paced nervously, awaiting the baron's pleasure.

The baron was already entertaining a guest—or guests, he wasn't sure which. Although he had communicated with a representative of whatever government this creature or creatures had, he had never met any of them and knew nothing about them. He still didn't, he realized sourly, and he didn't like the situation, either. The Northern Hemisphere was a place so alien to him that he felt more kinship with the most different of the Southern races compared to the closest of the North.

The object of his speculation and apprehension was floating about three meters in front of him. Yes, floating, he decided—no visible means of support or locomotion. It looked like a slightly upcurved strip of crystal from which a set of dozens of small crystal chimes hung down, the whole thing about a meter long and ending just short of the floor. On top of the crystal strip floated a creature that seemed to consist of hundreds of rapidly flashing lights. Their pattern and their regularity suggested that they existed in a transparent ball fitting in the crystal holder—but, try as he would, he couldn't make out the ball he somehow felt was there.

114

The Diviner and The Rel might be looking at him in an equally odd and uneasy way, he realized, but he would never know. He would not like to be, would not ever be, in its world. But it was in his, and that gave him a small measure of comfort.

"Will this Hain stay loyal to you?" The Rel asked, apparently using its chimes to form the words, which gave it a total lack of tone or coloration.

"My technicians assure me so," replied Azkfru confidently. "Although I fail to see why she is necessary to us in any event. I feel uneasy trusting everything to someone so new and unknown."

"Nevertheless," replied The Rel, "it is necessary. Remember that The Diviner predicted that you would receive one of the outworlders, and that the solution to our problems was not possible without an outworlder present."

"I know, I know," Azkfru acknowledged, "and I am grateful that it was me who was contacted by your people. We have as much stake in this as you, you know." He fidgeted nervously. "But why are you sure that this one is the outworlder needed?"

"We're not," The Rel admitted. "The Diviner only knows that one of the four who came in that party is needed to open the Well. One was destined for Czill, one for Adrigal, one for Dillia, and one for here. Of the four, yours was known to be psychologically the most receptive to our offer."

"I see," Azkfru said, uncertainty mixed with resignation in his tone. "So twenty-five percent was better than zero percent. Well, why not just grab the others so we're sure?"

"You know the answer to that one," The Rel responded patiently. "If we missed just one of these Entries, it would hide and we couldn't monitor it. This way, we will know where they are and what they are doing."

"Um, yes, and there's the second prediction, too."

"Quite so," The Rel affirmed. "When the Well is opened all shall pass through. Thus, if we keep one of them with us, we will stand the best chance of going through with them."

"I still wish I were going with you," the baron said. "I feel uneasy that the only representative of my people will be a conditioned alien of known untrustworthiness."

"One of you is going to be conspicuous enough," The Rel pointed out. "Two of you is an advertisement for hundreds of other uneasy governments. Right now, neither of us knows if our agreement is duplicated by others with any or all of the other three."

That idea made Azkfru more uncomfortable than ever.

"Well, damn it, you—or half of you, or whatever —is The Diviner. Don't you *know?*"

"Of course not," replied The Rel. "The present is as closed to The Diviner as it is to you. Only random snatches of information are received, and that in rather uncontrolled fashion. Getting this much is more than we usually get on anything. Hopefully more pieces will fit together as we progress."

Rather than disturbing him further, this news reassured him instead. So the damn thing wasn't omnipotent, anyway. Still, he wished he knew more about the creature that stood before him. What *were* its powers? What tricks did it have up its sleeve?

The fear that most consumed him was of a double cross.

The Diviner—or The Rel—seemed to sense this, and it said, "Our hexes are as alien as can be. We have no commonality of interest or activity. You are an incomprehensible people to us, and your actions are equally so. Never would we be here, in peril of our sanity, were it not for the urgent single commonality our races share: survival. We are satiated in the summing process, and active in the coefficient of structure. Our sole object is to keep everything just the way it is."

The baron didn't understand any of it, but he *did* understand that mutual survival was a common bond, and the assurance that they wanted to preserve the status quo. The trouble was, he could say exactly the same thing and not mean a word of it.

And now all of his future rested on Datham Hain.

116

The baron gave the Akkafian equivalent of a sigh of resignation. He had no choice in the matter. That conditioning *must* hold!

"How soon do you wish to begin?" he asked the Northerner.

"A lot depends on your end," The Rel pointed out. "Without Skander the whole scheme falls apart, the sum clouds and changes to an infinite number."

"And you can point him out, only you," the baron replied. "I'm ready when you are."

"No more than a week, then," The Rel urged. "We have reason to suspect that Skander will move out of reach shortly after that."

"Very well," the baron sighed, "I'll condition two of my best Markling warriors. You don't need Hain for this part, do you?"

"No," responded The Rel. "That will do nicely. We'll have to work at night and hide out during the day, so it will take a good day to set us up once there. Another two days to get there, inconspicuously, if possible. Can you be ready within a day period from this moment?"

"I think so," the baron replied confidently. "Anything else?"

"Yes. While you prepare the two assistants I should like to talk to one who understands structures and electrical systems. Is that possible?"

"Well, yes," the baron affirmed with some surprise. "But why?"

"It will be necessary to perform some minor sabotage to ease our task," The Rel explained enigmatically. "Although we have studied it, we want to confirm our necessary actions to be doubly certain, hopefully with one who comprehends such things."

"Done," Azkfru told the creatures. "Now I must attend to other matters. Go out the side there and an assistant will take you to a room that will be private. I will send the technicians to you."

"We go to prepare," intoned The Rel, and floated out the designated exit.

Azkfru waited several minutes until he was certain the Northerner was well away, then went over to the

117

doorway to his main waiting room and pressed the opening stud with his right foreleg.

"Enter, Mar Datham," he said imperiously, and quickly got back to the dais that served as his work area. He struck his most awesome pose.

Datham Hain entered on the words, a shiver going through her at their majesty. Almost hypnotically, she entered the office.

She stopped as she saw him, and bent down automatically in a gesture of extreme subservience. Orgiastic spasms shook her, and she cowed in awe and fear.

He is God, she thought with absolute conviction. He is the epitome of greatness.

"My Lord and Master, I am your slave, Datham Hain. Command me!" she intoned and meant every word of it.

The sincerity carried over to Azkfru, who received it with satisfaction. The conditioning had stuck.

"Do you give yourself to me, Mar Datham, body and soul, to do with as I would, forever?" he intoned.

"I do, Master, my Lord God, I do! Command me to die and I shall do so gladly."

Great now. Forever, if she was around all the time. But she would have only a few interviews until he had to trust her with all he had. Well, here goes the kicker, Azkfru thought.

"You are the lowest of the low, Mar Datham, lower than the *fikhfs* that breed to be eaten, lower than the defecations of the least of those *fikhfs*," he intoned.

And it was so, she realized. She felt as low and as small as she could ever get. She felt so tiny and unimportant that she found it hard to think at all. Her mind was a complete blank, yet basking on pure emotion in the presence of Him who was All Glory.

"You will remain lowly scum," the Master pronounced, "until I have other use for you. But as you are the lowest of the low, so can you be raised to the heights by my command." Now came the clincher. "A great task will be placed in your hands, and your

118

love and devotion to me above all else will determine all that is in your future, whether it be the mindless cleaners of the defecation pits or," he paused for added emphasis, "perhaps even the chief concubine of a king."

Hain groveled all the more at this thought suddenly placed in her witless head.

"And your name shall now be *Kokur,* nor will you answer to any other but it, and so you will stay and so you will be until you have successfully carried out my tasks. Then only will you be restored to a name, and then that name will be great. Go, now. My servant shall show you your duties until I shall call you for the task."

She turned and left the office quickly, on quivering legs.

When the door closed behind her, the baron relaxed.

Well, he thought, it is done. For the next few days, if The Diviner and The Rel were successful, Datham Hain would truly be as low as one could get. Although consciously obedient and happy, that nasty subconscious would be helplessly humiliated by the job and the status, and that was perfect. After a few days, Hain would be willing to do anything to get out of there, and she would be offered a permanent return to that miserable state as opposed to elevation as high as she could possibly reach.

Hain would serve him, he felt confidently.

Kokur wasn't a name, it was a job description.

Until The Diviner and The Rel returned, Datham Hain would work in the defecation pits, piling up the huge amounts of crap his barony produced—including her own—and then treating it with a series of chemicals and agents that would change its composition into a horrible but physically harmless mess. Hain would not only work there, she would sleep in it, walk in it, and, as her sole diet, eat it. And the only name she could respond to or think of herself as was *Kokur,* which meant dung-eater.

When off with The Diviner and The Rel, it would be a constant and humiliating reminder of her lowly status and her lifelong fate for failure, a reminder that would even reach others through the translating devices used around the Well World.

Datham Hain would be a most obedient slave.

Actually kind of attractive, he thought. Too bad she's a breeder.

Dillia—Morning
(Enter Wu Julee, Asleep)

WU JULEE AWOKE FROM A DREAMLESS SLEEP AND looked around. She felt strange and slightly dizzy.

The overriding fact that hit her was that the pain was gone.

She closed her eyes and shook her head briskly. The dizziness worsened for a moment, then things seemed to steady.

She looked around.

She was in a beautiful forest, the likes of which she had never seen before. Trees grew straight as poles fifty or more meters in the air, almost disappearing into a slight morning mist. The undergrowth was equally lush and a vivid green. Beautiful flowers grew wildly all around her. There was a trail nearby, a nicely maintained one made of deep sawdust lined with small, irregular stones. There was a slight but steady roaring sound in the distance, but it didn't seem threatening, only curious.

The path seemed to lead toward the roar in one direction, and she decided to follow it. Walking felt strange to her, but she thought little of it. She felt strange all over. She walked slowly down the trail about a kilometer, and it led her to the source of the increasing roar.

She came upon a waterfall, dropping majestically in three stages down the side of a mountain whose gray rocks were well worn by uncounted years of erosion. The falls fed a stream, or river, which flowed swiftly but rather shallowly over a rocky bottom seen clearly through the greenish tinge to the water's surface. Here and there, she saw logs and remnants of logs that had fallen due to weathering or age. Many were covered with mossy yellow-green growths and several were nurse trees, their dead and decaying limbs providing a haven from which newer trees of a different type were growing. Small insects hummed and buzzed all around, and she watched them curiously.

A sudden crackle of underbrush made her turn with a start. She saw a small, brown-furred mammal with a rodent's face and a broad flat tail jump into the stream carrying a twig in its mouth. Her eyes followed it until it made the opposite shore and ran into the underbrush formed by swampy weeds and long grains of grassy plants diagonally opposite her.

Still acting without conscious thought, like a newborn child seeing the world for the first time, she went up to the stream just far enough down that she wasn't caught in the spray from the great falls.

She looked down at her reflection. She saw the face of a young woman barely in her teens, a face that looked back at her. Not beautiful, but pleasant, with long brown hair falling down over small but well-formed breasts.

She reached up with one hand and brushed back the hair on one side. Her skin was a light brown, her palms a slightly lighter color but seemingly made of a tougher skin. I've got pointy ears, she thought, seeing them revealed by the brushed-back hair. And they *were* pointed, the insides a soft pink. Although not really large, she realized that they would probably protrude slightly if she stood perfectly erect. On some sort of impulse, she tried to wiggle her ears—and they moved noticeably!

Then she looked down at her body. At the waist the very light down that began just below her breast thickened into hair of the same color as her skin. Her eyes moved down to two stocky legs that ended in large, flat hooves.

That's strange, she thought. Hooves and pointed ears that wiggle.

For no reason in particular she turned her body at the waist almost halfway around, and looked in back of her. A long, sturdy-looking equine body supported by two hind legs was clearly visible—and a tail! A big, brushy tail she found she could wiggle.

What am I? she thought in sudden fear. Where is this?

She tried to remember, but could not.

It's as if I was just born, she thought. I can't remember anything. Not my name, not anything.

The reflection and the body looked totally strange to her.

I remember the words, she thought. I know that this is a stream and that is a waterfall and that that person in the water is a reflection of me, and I'm a young girl.

She hadn't even realized she was a girl until then.

There was a term for this, she thought, and she tried to remember it. Amnesia, that was it. People who couldn't remember their past. Somehow she felt that she had never been to this place before, and that something was different about her, but she couldn't think of what. She just stood there by the edge of the stream for several minutes in stunned silence, not knowing what else to do. Several insects buzzed around her rear, and with an automatic motion she brushed them away with her tail.

Suddenly her ears picked up the sound of laughing —a girl and a boy, she thought. They were coming down the trail! Quickly, almost in panic, she looked around for a place to hide, but found none before the pair came trotting down the path. They look like the top half of people stuck onto the bodies of working ponies, her mind thought. Her face turned quizzically at the thought. What were people anyway, if not these? And what were ponies?

The two beings were not really large, but the boy was almost a head taller and proportionately larger than the girl. The male was a golden color, with silver-white hair down to his shoulders and a full beard, neatly trimmed, of the same color. The girl, curiously, was a mottled gray mixed with large black spots, and this coloration extended to her upper torso. Her hair was a mixed gray and black, her gray breasts much fuller than the amnesiac onlooker's.

No navels, she thought inanely. We don't have navels.

The pair saw her and stopped almost in midlaugh. They surveyed her curiously, but without any trace of hostility or alarm. "Hello!" called the boy—he looked no more than fourteen or fifteen, the girl about the same. The voice was a pleasant tenor, with a slight, indefinable accent. "I don't think we've seen you here before."

She hesitated a moment, then replied hesitantly, "I—I don't think I've ever been here before. I—I just don't know." Tears welled in her eyes.

The two centaurs saw that she was in some distress and rushed up to her.

"What's the matter?" the girl asked in a high-pitched adolescent voice.

She started to cry. "I don't know, I can't remember anything," she sobbed.

"There, there," the boy crooned, and began to stroke her back. "Get it all out, then tell us what's going on."

The stroking had a calming effect, and she straightened up and wiped her eyes with her hand.

"I don't know," she managed, coughing a little. "I—I just woke up down the trail and I can't remember anything—who I am, where I am, even what I am."

The boy, who was even larger in comparison to her than he was to his companion, examined her face and head, and felt the skull.

"Does it hurt anywhere when I do this?" he asked.

"No," she told him. "Tickles a little all over, that's all."

He lifted up her face and stared hard into her eyes.

"No glaze," he commented, mostly to himself. "No sign of injury. Fascinating."

"Aw, come on, Jol, what'd you expect to find?" his companion asked.

"Some sign of injury or shock," he responded, almost in a clinical tone. "Here, girl, stick out your tongue. No, I mean it. Stick it out."

She did, feeling somewhat foolish, and he examined it. It was a big tongue, flat and broad, and a gray-pink in color.

"All right, you can stick it back in now," he told her. "No coating, either. If you'd have had some kind of shock or disease, it'd show."

"Maybe she's been witched, Jol," the spotted gray centaur suggested, and drew back a little.

"Maybe," he conceded, "but, if so, it's nothin' to concern us."

"What d'you think we oughta do?" his girlfriend asked.

Jol turned and for the first time Julee saw he had some kind of saddlebag strapped around his waist.

"First we take our shower," he answered, removing an irregular bar of what must have been soap, some cloths, and towels from the bag, then unstrapping it and letting it fall to the ground. "Then we'll take our mystery girl here to the village and let somebody smarter than we are take over."

And they proceeded to do just that. After some more hesitation, she joined them, following their actions and sharing a towel.

"You don't have to get too dry," the girl, whose name was Dal, told her. "You'll air-dry pretty good."

Together the three of them set off back down the trail.

As they left the forest the village and lands beyond came into view.

It was a beautiful land, she thought. The stream flowed out of majestic, snow-capped mountains which spread out on both sides to reveal a rich valley and gently rolling hills.

The village—a collection of rough but sturdy log buildings by the side of a blue-green lake—bustled with activity. The fields were properly plowed and planted, and she saw a few centaurs checking and tending between stalks of unknown grain.

The whole place didn't seem as if it could support,

124

or had, more than a few hundred people, she thought and commented on that to her companions.

Jol laughed. "That proves you must be from down-lake," he said. "Some pretty big communities down there. Actually, there's close to a thousand in the valley, here, but we're spread out all over the land-scape. Only fifty or sixty live in town all the time."

The main street was broad and maintained much like the trails, of which she had seen quite a few, a thick covering of sawdust making the paving.

Most of the buildings had an open side facing the street. The largest building was the first one they reached. It contained a huge forge on which several male and female centaurs worked hot metal. She saw with curiosity one woman lift a hind leg while a brawny male, wearing a protective bib, hammered something on her foot, apparently painlessly.

Other buildings proved to be stores selling farm implements, seed, and the like. There was even a barbershop and a bar, closed at the moment but unmistakable in its huge kegs and large steins.

"Is it always this warm and humid here?" she asked Jol.

He chuckled again in that friendly way he had about him. "No, this is a four-season hex," he explained enigmatically. "Then we all get out our *gammot* fur coats and hats and gloves and romp in the cold snow."

A *gammot,* she discovered, was one of the large rodents she had spied down by the stream.

"It must be a huge coat," she remarked, and Dal and Jol both laughed.

"You *really* do have amnesia!" Dal responded. "The hair on our bodies and a nice, thick layer of fat put on in summer and fall are pretty good insulators. Only our hairless parts need protection."

"You can see the fireplaces and chimneys," Jol pointed out. "In the fall the fronts are put back on and they become warm as today inside."

Julee started to ask what happened when it rained, but she saw that the roofs and ledges were angled and the buildings so placed that it would take a really terrible storm to get much rain inside.

"It looks as if anyone dishonest could steal anything he wanted here," Julee commented.

They both stopped and looked at her strangely. "That just isn't done here—not by any Dillian," he huffed.

His reaction startled her, and she apologized. "I— I'm sorry. I don't know why I think like that."

"We do get some alien traders from other hexes in once in a while and they've tried taking stuff," Dal put in to defuse the issue. "Won't do 'em no good here, though. Only way in is by the lake—forty kilometers, almost as deep as it is long. Nobody can beat us in the woods, and anybody who wants to climb six kilometers of mountain at steep grade and below zero temperatures would lose more than he could take."

They reached a small building about two-thirds of the way down the thirty or so buildings of the town's lone street. A wooden sign hung on a post, a hexagonal symbol of two small trees flanking a huge one, burned in with some sort of tool. Inside stood an elderly centaur with long, white hair and unkempt beard reaching down below his nipples. He had once been coal black, she realized, but now the body hair was flecked with silvery white.

He would look very officious standing there at his cluttered desk, she thought, amused, if he wasn't sound asleep and snoring loudly.

"That's Yomax," Jol told her. "The closest thing we've got to a government in the village. He's sort of the mayor, postmaster, chief forester, and game warden here. He always opens up at seven o'clock like the duty book says, but since the boat doesn't get in until eleven-thirty, he usually goes back to sleep until just before then." He yelled, "Hey! Yomax! Wake up! Official business!"

The old man stirred, then wiped his eyes and stretched, not only his arms but also his entire long body.

"Hmph! Whazzit?" he snorted. "Some damned brat's always foolin' with me," he muttered, then turned to see who stood there.

His eyes fixed on Wu Julee, and he suddenly came fully awake.

"Well! Hello!" he greeted in a friendly but puzzled tone. "I don't remember seein' you around before."

"She's lost her memory, Yomax," Jol explained. "We found her down by Three Falls."

"She don't know nothin' about nothin'," Dal put in. "Didn't even know 'bout winter and coats and all."

The old man frowned, and came up to her. Ignoring Jol's protests that he had done it already, Yomax proceeded to go through the same examination Julee had had earlier—with similar negative results.

Yomax scratched his beard and thought. "And you don't remember *nothin'?*" he asked for the fifth or sixth time, and for at least that many times she answered, "No."

"Mighty strange," he said. Then, suddenly, he brightened. "Lift your right foreleg," he instructed. She did, and he grasped the hoof firmly and turned it up.

"I think she's been witched," Dal maintained.

"Com'mere and lookit this," Yomax said softly. The other two crowded in to see.

"She ain't got no shoes!" Dal exclaimed.

"Not only that," the old one pointed out, "there's no sign that she ever had any."

"Don't prove nothin'," Dal persisted. "I know lots'a folks what don't wear shoes, particularly up-valley."

"That's true," admitted Yomax, dropping the leg and straightening up, for which Julee was thankful. She felt circulation start to return. "But," the old centaur continued, "that's a virgin hoof. No deep stains, no imbedded stones, nothing. Hers are like a newborn's."

"Aw, that ain't possible," Jol said scornfully.

"I told ya she was witched," Dal insisted.

"You two get along and do your chores or whatever," Yomax told them, waving them away with his hands. "I think I know at least part of what this is about."

They left reluctantly and then started to return. Yomax had to bellow at them several times.

"Now, then, young lady," he began, satisfied of some privacy at last, "let me throw some names at you. Let's see if any of 'em strike a bell."

"Go ahead," she urged him, intrigued.

"Nathun Brazzle," he began, trying to make do with the strange names on a paper he had fished from a crowded drawer in his desk. "Vardya Dipla Twelve Sixty-one. Dayton Hain. Wo Jolie. Anythin'?"

She shook her head slowly from side to side. "I've never heard any of those names before," she told him. "At least—I don't think so."

"Hmmm . . ." the old man mused. "I'm sure I'm right. Only possible explanation. Well, tell you what. Got one test when the boat comes in. Old Entry from the same neck of the woods as these folks—ten, fifteen years ago. He pilots the ferry now, since old Gletin refused to see how old he was and went overboard in a storm 'couple years back," Yomax told her. "He'll still remember the old language. I'll git him to spout some of that alien gibberish at ya, and we'll see if ya understand it."

They passed the time talking until the ferry arrived, the old man telling about his land and people with pride and affection. During the course of his rambling but entertaining memoir/travelogue, which she was sure was almost half-true, a great many facts emerged. She learned about the Well World, and what the hexes were. She learned about Zone and gates, and the strange creatures that wandered around. She found that, although the Dillians lived to be well over a hundred Well World years on the average, the population was relatively small. Females went into heat only every other year, then only for a short period, and invariably bore but a single young—which had about an even chance of surviving its first year.

If you made it through puberty, about a twenty percent chance, then you would live a long life—because you would already be immune to most of what would kill you.

The various colors—Yomax said there were hundreds of combinations—of the people didn't seem

128

to meld with interbreeding, she was told, since all color genes were recessives.

"Rank comes with age," Yomax told her. "When you get too old to plow, or build, or chop and haul wood, they put you in charge of things. Since nobody likes to admit they're old when the job's so little—you saw how much respect I got from the young ones—I wound up bein' about everything the village needs."

The mother was the ultimate authority in child-rearing, he explained, but the family group shared moral responsibility. Since customs like marriage and inheritances were unknown—everything was simplistically communal—people formed family groups with other people they liked, without much regard to sex. The groups were mostly traditional now, but occasionally new ones of three to six would be formed by the young after puberty.

The entire hex was a collection of small towns and villages, she learned, because of the low birthrate and also because of innate limits on technology here. Anything more ambitious than the most basic steam engine just wouldn't work in Dillia.

That kept things extremely simple and pastoral, but also stable, peaceful, and uncluttered.

"In some hexes you can't even tell what sort of place it once was," Yomax told her. "All them machines and smelly stuff, everybody livin' in air-conditioned bubbles. Then they want to come *here* to get back to nature! They do some tourist business in other parts of the country, but this place is so isolated nobody's discovered it yet. And, when they do, they'll find us damned hostile, I can tell you!"

With that impassioned statement, there came the long, deep sound of a steam whistle, its call echoing across the mountains.

Yomax grabbed a simple cloth sack tied with twine and invited her down to the lakefront about 150 meters from town. She saw a simple wooden wharf with several huge posts, nothing more. A few townspeople waited just off the dock, apparently having business downlake or awaiting passengers.

Coming up on the wharf was the strangest craft she

129

had ever seen. A giant oval raft, it looked like, with another raft built on top of it and supported by solid log cross-bracing. In the middle was a single, huge, black boiler, with a stack going up through the second tier and several meters beyond, belching white smoke.

A single centaur, black and white striped all over, a crazy-looking broad-brimmed hat on his head, stood at a large wheel, which was flanked by two levers. The levers went down through to the boiler level and seemed to do nothing but signal a brown centaur-engineer to turn some control or other on the boiler. The boiler was attached by what looked more like thick rope than chain to a small, wooden paddle wheel in the back.

About twenty varicolored Dillians stood on the first deck, some between oaken trunks full of unguessable cargo. Under the cross-bracing there seemed to be a counter and some kegs and steins. A large bale of grain flanked it.

Wu Julee could guess that this was the snack bar. She had already had a brunch with Yomax and discovered that the centaurs were herbivores who occasionally cooked various dishes but mostly ate raw grains and grasses grown in their fields. Tasted good, too, she had found.

Ropes from wooden posts on the side of the primitive steamer were tossed to a couple of villagers on the dock who tied the boat off. Satisfied, the captain went to the back and came down an almost disguised grooved ramp to the first deck.

Yomax tossed the mail to a crewman who idly threw it toward the center of the boat. The captain picked up a similar sack and jumped off to the dock, clasping hands with Yomax and then handing the old official the sack.

Yomax introduced the steamer captain to Wu Julee.

"This here's Klamath," the old man told her. "Not a proper name for a good Dillian, but he was born with it."

"Please to meet you, Lady um . . .?" The captain's expression prompted a lead.

"She don't know her name, Klammy," Yomax explained. "Just kinda showed up all blanked out early this mornin'. I think she's an Entry, and thought maybe you could help." Quickly he explained his language idea to the captain.

"Harder than you think," the captain replied thoughtfully. "It's true that I think in the old tongue, but everything's instantly and automatically translated in and out. It'd be easier if I could write something for her."

Julee shook her head sadly. "I am certain that I never learned to read. I just know it."

"Hmmm. . . . Well, Yomax, you're the control," Klamath said. "It's going to take a lot of concentration to get out some old word stuff through the translation process, and I'm not really going to know if I'm successful or not. It all sounds the same to me. If she understands it and you don't, then we'll have it made."

Klamath took chin in hand in a thoughtful pose, trying to think of something he could do to break through the barrier. Suddenly he brightened. "Worth a try," he said at last, "but even if she doesn't understand it, it won't prove much. Well, here goes.

"Using the Three KY spectroanalysis program, stellar motion can be computed by phase-shifting observations using the infraspectrometer circuits in the navigational matrix for visual course plots," Klamath intoned. Suddenly he stopped and turned to Yomax. "How was that?" he asked.

"I got maybe one word in four," the old man replied. "How about the lady here?"

Julee shook her head in bewilderment. "A lot of big words but I didn't understand what they meant."

"Can you remember a big word?" Klamath prompted.

She thought for a minute. "Ma—matrix, I think," she said hesitantly, and, she looked totally perplexed, "phase shifting?"

Klamath smiled. "Good old basic navigation manual!" he exclaimed. "You're from my part of the universe, all right. There's just no equivalent for that stuff in this language."

Yomax nodded, an expression of satisfaction on his face. "So she's one of the last four."

"Almost certainly," Klamath nodded. "I've been keeping track of them since I know one, at least slightly. He's almost a living legend among spacers, and we know where he is and where the one called Vardia is. You must be that girl that was sick; that would explain the memory problems."

"Who am I, then?" she asked excitedly. "I want to know."

"Probably a girl named Wu Julee," Klamath told her.

"Wu Julee," she repeated. The name sounded strange and totally unfamiliar to her. She wasn't sure she liked it.

"I'll be heading back downlake in an hour or so, and when I get to Donmin I'll see the local councilman and pass the word along," Klamath said. "In the meantime, you might as well stay here. It's about the best place to relax and enjoy things, and that might be just what you need."

Their course of action agreed to, they all went to the local bar. She felt somewhat left out of the conversation after that, and the thick, dark ale made her slightly giddy. She excused herself and wandered out onto the main street.

Jol and Dal were there, and, seeing her, rushed up for the news.

"They say I'm an Entry," she told them. "Someone named Wu Julee. They said I was sick."

"Well, you're healthy now," Jol replied. "And whatever you had got cured on the way in. Maybe your memory will come back, too, after a while." He stopped and fidgeted nervously for a time, glancing once in a while to Dal. Finally the spotted female threw up her hands.

"All right, all right. May as well," she said enigmatically.

"Sure it's all right with you?" Jol responded.

"Why not?" his girlfriend replied, resigned.

Jol turned back to Wu Julee. "Look," he said eagerly, "we—Dal and me—we been thinkin' of putting together our own family, particularly with Dal pregnant and all. There's so few folks our age up here, and

132

we aren't gettin' along with our own families too good now. Why don't you come in with us?"

Julee hesitated a moment, then replied, "I'd like that —if it's all right with Yomax."

"Oh, he won't mind," Dal replied. "He's been itchin' to see us take jobs anyhow, and if we form the group we'll have to to get our share of the harvest."

And it *was* that easy.

They picked a spot fairly deep in the woods upvalley and started by building a primitive but efficient trail to the site. It required little clearing, but it did wind in and out between the giant trees. Borrowing a large handsaw and with some help from a forester they chopped down two trees near a tiny creek and burned out the stumps. Villagers helped them clear the area and cut up the trees into useful sizes, as well as providing smaller, more useful logs and hauling reddish clay used for insulation.

Wu Julee—the others nicknamed her Wuju, which she liked better—threw herself into the work, putting any thoughts of Klamath and governmental problems out of her mind. She hadn't seen the captain after the first day, since the boat came only once a day and stayed barely over an hour. Weeks passed.

They put in the sawdust floor, and built a stone cairn to use as a stove and winter heater, fueled with wood left over from the project. The cabin had a large central area with crude tables and a work area, and five stalls—bedrooms, really, with leaning supports, since the Dillians slept standing up. The extra stalls were for Dal's increasingly obvious new arrival and a spare in case someone else would join them. Jol and Dal took her trapping in the woods, and showed her how to skin and weave the animal furs and the skin from various plants into clothing. Once settled in, she and Jol were assigned to survey and check some back-country trails, particularly noting log bridges that might not stand the weight of winter snows. It was easy and pleasant work, and she enjoyed the peace and natural wonder of the mountains. When winter came they would help dig out snowed-in cabins and ensure safe paths around the small lakeside community.

In late summer Dal dropped her foal, large and fully

formed but barely covered in a soft, neutral, downy fur, with reddish, wrinkly skin that made the boy-child look like a wizened old man.

Although born looking physically eight or nine in size and proportion—and able to stand, walk, even run within a few hours of birth—the child would be toothless for over a year and could only feed by nursing. It needed almost constant supervision, even though hair developed in the first few weeks affording a measure of protection. Born only with the instincts of a wild animal, the boy would have to learn how to reason, to speak, to act responsibly. It was difficult for Julee to get used to at first, since after the first month the child looked like a boy of about ten.

But he would look that way for years, they told her, perhaps eight or ten, until puberty. Until then they would be his world; after that, he would have to pull his own load.

But this peaceful, almost idyllic existence was interrupted by the start of her nightmares. They often involved racing pain, torture, and an evil, leering monstrous face that demanded horrible things of her. Many nights she woke up screaming, and it took hours to calm her down.

She began seeing the town Healer—the Dillian wasn't a doctor, because they had never been able to talk one into moving up into the isolated wilderness, but she could treat minor injuries and illnesses and set broken bones and the like. Anything really serious required using the old treadmill-powered raft to get the patient downlake. That was not really as difficult as it sounded because there was a fairly strong current that led to the falls at the downlake town.

Talking to the Healer helped, but the sleeping powders didn't. As fall started turning the leaves a riot of colors, and the snow began to creep down from the mountaintops, with occasional cold winds breaking through the still comfortable warm air, she was drawn and looked not at all well. Drinking the warm, potent ale seemed to help for a while, but she was more and more in a state of intoxication which made her less useful and harder to live with.

134

The villagers and her two companions were concerned but felt helpless as she seemed to deteriorate daily. The nightmares became worse and more frequent, the drinking increasing to compensate. She had been there almost twelve weeks, and she was miserable.

One particularly chilly day she came from the little bar in a high state of inebriation that even the cold wouldn't moderate, wandering down to the dock as the steamboat came in. She stared at a figure dressed in rugged furs sitting on the top deck, outside the little pilothouse that had been erected when the season changed.

It was alien. It looked human, but had only two legs and no hindquarters. Its features were hidden under a big fur hat, but it seemed to be smoking a pipe—a habit only a few of the oldest around did because of the difficulty of getting the weeds to stuff into it. She wasn't sure if this was a creature of her drunk or of her nightmares, and she just stared at it.

The boat tied up and the creature, or vision, joined the captain in walking down to the first level and onto the dock. Klamath spotted her, and pointed. The funny two-legged creature, so small next to the Dillians, nodded and walked over to her.

She drew back apprehensively, stifling a sudden and overwhelming urge to run.

The creature approached her cautiously and called out, in Dillian, "Wu Julee? Is that you, Wu Julee?" The voice seemed familiar, somehow. He stopped about two meters from her, took the huge, curved pipe from his mouth, and pulled off the furry headpiece.

Wu Julee screamed and screamed, then suddenly seemed to collapse, hitting the ground hard in a dead faint.

Klamath and many of the villagers rushed up to her in concern.

"Damn!" said the creature. "Why do I always have that effect on women?"

For the shock of seeing his face had brought it all back to her suddenly and in full force. The only change the Well World had made in Nathan Brazil was his clothes.

The Barony of Azkfru,
Akkafian Empire

THE BARON AZKFRU WAS FURIOUS.

"What do you mean he wasn't there?" he stormed.

The Diviner and The Rel remained impassive and apparently unperturbed as usual.

"We had no problems concealing ourselves through the first day," The Rel reported, "and acted about an hour after nightfall. When we approached the structure where Skander almost had to be, The Diviner sensed a change in the balancing equation. A new factor had been introduced. Skander had been there, but had left."

"What do you mean a new factor?" snarled the Baron.

"In the most basic terms," The Rel explained patiently, "someone knew we were coming and what we were after. So either by direct warning or the indirect action of others, Skander was not there when we were. It was much too dangerous to remain there any length of time awaiting a possible return, so we broke off and returned here."

Azkfru was stunned. "A leak? Here? But, that's impossible! It couldn't have been any of my people—they're too thoroughly under my control. And, if anyone from the Imperial Palace had a reconditioned plant here, I wouldn't still be alive now. If there's a leak, it must be on your side."

"It is possible our intentions were divined in the same way we divine the actions of others," The Rel admitted, "but it is impossible for any in my own leadership to have betrayed us, and you, yourself, saw to the security when we came cross Zone. A release of information on your side remains the most likely explanation."

136

"Well, we'll dismiss the blame for now," Azkfru said more calmly, "and proceed from here. What do we do now?"

"Skander is still the only link we have to concrete knowledge of the puzzle," The Rel pointed out. "And, its location is known, if presently unattainable. The Diviner states that Skander's research was incomplete, and it must return to the learning place sooner or later. We are now attuned to that, and will know when. It is suggested that we bide our time until this Skander is again within our grasp. We did not compromise the plan, we just about proved it. It is still workable."

"Very well," growled Azkfru. "Will you stay here?"

"We miss our homeland and constructive endeavor," The Rel replied, "but the mission is too vital. We will remain. Our needs are few, our requirements simple. A dark, bare cell will be sufficient, and an avenue to the surface every once in a while to stand beneath the stars. Nothing more. In the meantime, I would check your own security. It will profit us little if such a thing happens again!"

Soon after The Diviner and The Rel were seen to, the baron flew to the Imperial Palace and, securing a Zone pass, returned to his office in Zone. He was confident that he wouldn't be alive if it were any of his own people, so that left alien intervention—which meant Zone.

The offices, even the walls, were practically torn apart. It took almost two days and the destruction of more than half the embassy to find it. A tiny little transmitter inserted in his communications unit in his own office! His technicians examined it, but could be of little help.

"The range is such that it would carry to over four hundred other embassies," one explained to him. "Of the four hundred, almost three hundred are functional and used, and, of those, more than half are technologically capable of creating such a device, while the rest could probably purchase it untraceably, and almost all could place the device during a slow period when you were away."

He had most of his office staff ritually executed anyway, not that it made him feel any better—just less foolish.

Someone had heard him kill General Ytil.

Someone had spied when The Diviner and The Rel had come through, and listened to their initial conversations in his office.

No more, he knew. But that was bad enough.

Someone else now knew at least *what* Skander was.

He had no choice, though, he realized. He had to wait.

Almost fifteen weeks.

The Center in Czill

VARDIA WAS ASSIGNED A BASIC APPRENTICE'S JOB, DOing computer research. She learned fast—almost anything they taught her—even though she couldn't make a great deal of sense out of her part of the project she was on. It was like seeing only one random page from a huge book. In itself, nothing made any sense. Only when put together with thousands of other pages did a picture finally emerge, and even then the top researchers had the unenviable job of fitting all the pages together in the proper order.

She enjoyed the life immensely. Even though she didn't understand her work, it was a constructive function with purpose, serving the social need. It was a comfortable niche. Here, indeed, is social perfection, she thought. Cooperation without conflict, with no basic needs beyond sleep and water, doing things that meant something.

After a couple of weeks on the job she began feeling somewhat dizzy at times. The spells would come on her, apparently without cause, and would disappear just as mysteriously. After a few such episodes she went to the central clinic. The doctors made a few very routine tests, then explained the problem to her.

"You're twinning," the physician said. "Nothing to be concerned about. In fact, it's wonderful—the only surprise is that it has happened so fast after joining us."

Vardia was stunned. She had met some twins off and on at the Center, but the idea that it would happen to her just never occurred to her.

"What will this do to my work?" she asked apprehensively.

"Nothing, really," the doctor told her. "You'll simply grow as each cell begins its duplication process. A new you will take shape growing out from your back. This process will make you a bit dizzy and weak, and, near its completion, will cause some severe disorientation."

"How long does the process take?" she asked.

"Four weeks if you continue a normal schedule," was the reply. "If you're willing to plant day and night, about ten days."

She decided to get it over with if she could. Although everyone else seemed excited for her, she, herself, was scared and upset. Her supervisor was only too glad to give her time off, as she had not worked on the project long enough to be irreplaceable. So she picked a quiet spot away from the Center and near the river and planted.

There was no problem during the nights, of course, but during the day, when she had to root by exercising the rooting tendrils voluntarily, she quickly became bored. Except for early morning and just before dusk, she was alone in the camp or else surrounded by unconscious Czillians sleeping off long round-the-clock work periods.

On the third day, she knew she had to have water and uprooted to go down to the stream. Doing so was more difficult than she would have thought possible. She felt as if she weighed a ton, and balance was a real problem. She could reach back and feel the growth out of her back, but it didn't make much sense.

At the river's edge she saw a Umiau.

She had seen them at the Center, of course, but only going from one place to another. This was the first one she had seen close up, and it just seemed to be lying there, stretched out on the sand, asleep.

The Umiau had the lower body of a fish, silvery-blue scales going down to a flat, divided tail fin. Above the waist it remained the light blue color, but the shiny scales were gone, leaving a smooth but deceptively tough skin. Just below the transition line was a very large vaginal cavity.

The Umiau had two large and very firm breasts, and the face of a woman who, were she in Brazil's world, would have been considered beautiful despite hair that seemed to flow like silvery tinsel and bright blue lips. The ears, normally covered by the hair, were shaped like tiny shells and set almost flush against the sides of the head, and, Vardia saw, the nose had some sort of skin flaps that moved in and out as the creature breathed, probably to keep water out when swimming, she guessed. The long, muscular arms ended in hands with long, thin fingers and a thumb, all connected by a webbing.

Vardia stepped in to drink, and, as she did so, she saw other Umiau on and off along the banks, some swimming gracefully and effortlessly on or just beneath the surface. The river was shallow here, near the banks, but almost two meters deep in the center. On land they were awkward, crawling along on their hands or, at the Center, using electric wheelchairs.

But, as she saw from the swimmers in the river's clear water, in their own element they were beautiful.

Most, like the sleeper nearby, wore bracelets of some colorful coral, necklaces, tiny shell earrings, or other adornments. She had never understood jewelry as a human, and she didn't understand it now.

They all looked alike to her except for size. She wondered idly if they were all women.

Finishing her drink, she made her way, slowly, to the shore. She made large splashes and was terrified she would fall.

The noise awakened the sleeper.

"Well, hello!" she said in a pleasant, musical voice. The Umiau could make the sounds of the Czillian language, and most of them at the Center knew it.

Czillians could not mock any other, so all conversations were in the Czillian tongue.

"I—I'm sorry if I awakened you," Vardia apologized.

"That's all right," the Uniau replied, and yawned. "I shouldn't be wasting my time sleeping, anyway. The sun dries me out and I have a fever for hours after." She noticed Vardia's problem. "Twinning, huh?"

"Y-yes," Vardia replied, a little embarrassed. "My first time. It's awful."

"I sympathize," the mermaid said. "I passed the egg this cycle, but I'll receive it next."

Vardia decided to root near the stream for a while, and did. "I don't understand you," she told the creature hesitantly. "Are you, then, a female?"

The Umiau laughed. "As much as you," she replied. "We're hermaphrodites. One year we make an egg, then pass it to another who didn't, where it's shot with sperm and develops. The next year, you get the egg passed to you. The third year you're a neuter; then the cycle starts all over again."

"You cannot abstain, then?" Vardia asked innocently.

The Umiau laughed again. "Sure, but few do, unless they get themselves sterilized. When the urge hits, honey, you do it!"

"It is pleasant, then?" Vardia persisted innocently.

"Unbelievably," the Umiau replied knowingly.

"I wish this was," Vardia pouted. "It is making me miserable."

"I wouldn't worry about it," the Umiau told her. "You only do it two or three times in your very long lives." The mermaid suddenly glanced at the sun. "Well, it's getting late. It's been pleasant talking with you, but I have to go. Don't worry—you'll make out. The twin's coming along fine."

And, without another word, it crawled into the water more rapidly than Vardia would have suspected possible and swam away.

The next few days were mostly boring repetitions of the earlier ones, although she did occasionally talk to other Umiau for brief periods.

On the ninth day when she needed water again, she discovered she had little control over herself. Every forward movement seemed to be countered by the twin now almost fully developed on her back. Even her thoughts ran confused, every thought seeming to double, echoing in her mind. It took immense concentration to get to the water, and, in getting out, she fell.

She lay there for some time, feeling embarrassed and helpless, when she suddenly realized a curious fact, a thought that echoed through her mind.

I'm I'm seeing seeing in in both both directions directions, her mind thought.

Getting up was beyond her, she knew, and she waited most of the afternoon for help. The confusing double sight didn't help her, since both scenes seemed to be double exposures.

She tried to move her head, but found she couldn't without burying it in the sandy bank. Finally, an hour or two before sunset, others came for rooting and pulled her out and helped her back to a rooting spot.

The tenth day was the worst. She couldn't think straight at all, couldn't move at all, couldn't judge scenes, distances, or anything. Even sounds were duplicated.

The sensation was miserable and it seemed to go on forever.

On the eleventh day nothing was possible, and she was in a delirium. About midday, though, there was a sudden release, and she felt as if half of her had suddenly, ghostlike, walked out of her. Everything returned to normal very suddenly, but she felt so terribly weak that she passed out in broad daylight.

The twelfth day dawned normally, and she felt much better, almost, she thought, euphoric. She uprooted and took a hesitant step forward. "This is more like it!" she said aloud, feeling light and in total control again.

And, at exactly the same moment, another voice said exactly the same thing! They both turned around with the same motion.

Two identical Vardia's stood looking, amazed, at each other.

"So you're the twin," they both said simultaneously.

"I'm not, you are!" they both insisted.

Or am I? each thought. Would the twin know?

Everything was duplicated. Everything. Even the memories and personality. That's why they kept saying and doing the same things, they both realized. Will we ever know which is which? they both thought. Or did it matter? They both came out of the same body.

Together they set out for the Center.

They walked wordlessly, in perfect unison, even the random gestures absolutely duplicated. Communication was unnecessary, since each knew exactly what the other was thinking and thought the same thing. The procedure was well established. Once at the reception desk, they were taken to different rooms where doctors checked them. Pronounced fit and healthy to go back to work, each was assigned to a part of the project different from that she had previously been working on, although with similar duties.

"Will I ever see my twin again?" asked the Vardia who was in Wing 4.

"Probably," the supervisor replied. "But we're going to get you into divergent fields and activities as quickly as possible so each of you can develop a separate path. Once you've had a variety of experiences to make you sufficiently different, there's no reason not to see each other if you like."

In the meantime the other Vardia, having asked the question sooner and having received the same answer, was settling in to a very different sort of position, even though the basic computer problem was the same.

She began working with a Umiau, for all the world identical to the one she had talked with along the riverbank. Her name—Vardia's mind insisted on the feminine for them even though they were neither—and both—was Endil Cannot.

After a few days of feeling each other out, they started talking as they worked. Cannot, she thought, reminded her of some of the instructors at the Center.

Every question seemed to get a lecture.

One day she asked Cannot just what they were looking for. The work so far consisted of feeding legends and old wives' tales from many races into the computer to find common factors in them.

"You have seen the single common factor already,

143

have you not?" Cannot replied tutorially. "What, then, is it?"

"The phrase—I keep hearing it off and on around here, too."

"Exactly!" the mermaid exclaimed. "Until midnight at the Well of Souls. A more poetic way of saying forever, perhaps, or expressing an indefinite, like: We'll keep at this project until midnight at the Well of Souls—which seems likely at this rate."

"But why is it important?" she quizzed. "I mean, it's just a saying, isn't it?"

"No!" the Umiau replied strongly. "If it were a saying of one race, perhaps even of bordering races, that would be understandable. But it's used even by *Northern* races! A few of the really primitive hexes seem to use it as a religious chant! Why? And so the saying goes back as far as antiquity itself. Written records go back almost ten thousand years here, oral tradition many times that. That phrase occurs over and over again! Why? What is it trying to tell us? That is what I must know! It might provide us with the key to this crazy planet, with its fifteen hundred and sixty races and differing biomes."

"Maybe it's literal," Vardia suggested. "Maybe people sometime in the past gathered at midnight at some place they called the Well of Souls."

The mermaid's expression would have led anyone more knowledgeable in all-too-human emotions to the conclusion that the dumb student had finally grasped the obvious.

"We've been proceeding along that tack here," Cannot told her. "This is, after all, called the Well World, but the only wells we know of are the input wells at each pole. That's the problem, you know. They are *both* input, not opposites."

"Must there be an output?" Vardia asked. "I mean, can't this be a one-way street?"

Cannot shook her statuesque head from side to side. "No, it would make no sense at all, and would invalidate the only good theory I have so far as to why this world was built and why it was built the way it was."

"What's the theory?"

Cannot's eyes became glazed, but Vardia could not tell if it was an expression or just the effect the Umiau had when closing the inner transparent lid while keeping the outer skin lid open.

"You're a bright person, Vardia," the mermaid said. "Perhaps, someday, I'll tell you."

And that was all there was to that.

A day or two later Vardia wandered into Cannot's office and saw her sitting there viewing slides of a great desert, painted in reds, yellows, and oranges under a cloudless blue sky. In the background things got hazy and indistinct. It looked, Vardia thought, something like a semitransparent wall. She said as much aloud.

"It is, Vardia," Cannot replied. "It is indeed. It's the Equatorial Barrier—a place I am going to have to visit somehow, although none of the hexes around it are very plentiful on water, and the trip will be hard. Here, look at this," she urged, backing the slides up several paces. She saw a view taken through the wall with the best filters available. Objects were still indistinct, but she could see just enough to identify one thing clearly.

"There's a walkway in there!" she exclaimed. "Like the one around the Zone Well!"

"Exactly!" the mermaid confirmed. "And that's what I want to know more about. Do you feel up to working through the night tonight?"

"Why, yes, I guess so," she replied. "I've never done it before but I feel fine."

"Good! Good!" Cannot approved, rubbing her hands together. "Maybe I can solve this mystery tonight!"

Stars swirled in tremendous profusion across the night sky, great, brilliantly colored clouds of nebulae spreading out in odd shapes while the starfield itself seemed to consist of a great mass of millions of stars in swirls the way a galaxy looked under high magnification. It was a magnificent sight, but one not appreciated by Vardia, who could not see it with her coneless eyes as she worked in the bright, artificial

145

day of the lab, or by unseen onlookers out in the fields to the south.

At first they looked like particularly thick grains of the wild grasses in the area. Then, slowly, two large shapes rose up underneath the stalks, shapes with huge insect bodies and great eyes.

And—something else.

It sparkled like a hundred trapped fireflies, and seemed to rest atop a shadowy form.

"The Diviner says that the equation has changed unnaturally," said The Rel.

"Then we don't go in tonight?" one of the Akkafian warriors asked.

"We must," replied The Rel. "We feel that only tonight will everything be this auspicious. We have the opportunity of an extra prize that increases the odds."

"Then the balance—this new factor—is in our favor?" asked the Markling, relieved.

"It is," The Rel replied. "There will be two to carry back, not one. Can you manage it."

"Of course, if the newcomer isn't any larger than the other," the Markling told The Rel.

"Good. They should be together, so take them both. And—remember! Though the Czillians will all sleep as soon as the power-plant detonator is triggered, the Umiau will not. They'll be shocked, and won't see too well or get around too much, but there may be trouble. Don't get so wrapped up in any struggle that you sting either of our quarry to death. I want only paralysis sufficient to get us back to the halfway island."

"Don't worry," the warriors assured almost in unison. "We would not fail the baron like that."

"All right, then," The Rel said in a voice so soft it was almost lost in the gentle night breeze. "You have the detonator. When we rush at the point I have shown you, I shall give a signal. *Then* and only then are you to blow it. Not sooner, not later. Otherwise the emergency generators will be on before we are away."

146

"It is understood," the Markling assured the Northerner.

"The Diviner indicates that they are both there and otherwise alone in their working place," The Rel said. "In a way, I am suspicious. This is too good fortune, and I do not believe in luck. Nonetheless, we do what we must.

"All right—*now!*"

Dillia—Uplake

WU JULEE GROANED AND OPENED HER EYES. HER head was splitting and the room was spinning around.

"She's comin' around!" someone's voice called out, and she was suddenly conscious of a number of people clustering around her.

She tried to focus, but everything was blurry for a few moments. Finally, vision cleared enough for her to see who each was, particularly the one non-Dillian in the crowd.

"Brazil!" she managed, then choked. Someone forced a little water down her throat. It tasted sour. She coughed.

"She knows you!" Yomax yelled, excited. "She remembers things agin!"

She shut her eyes tightly. She *did* remember— everything. A spasm shook her, and she vomited the water.

"Yomax! Jol!" she heard the Healer's voice call. "You louts take her behind! Captain Brazil, you pull; I'll push! Let's try and get her on her feet as soon as possible!"

They fell to their tasks and managed to pull it off with several tries. No thanks to me, Brazil thought. Man! These people have muscles!

She was up, but unsteady. They put side panels

padded with cloth under her arms and braced them so she could support herself. The room was still spinning, but it seemed to be slowing down. She still felt sick, and started trembling. Someone—probably Jol —started stroking her back and that seemed to calm her a little.

"Oh, my God!" she groaned.

"It's all right, Wu Julee," Brazil said softly. "The nightmares are past, now. They can't hurt you anymore."

"But how—" she started, then threw up again and kept gagging.

"All right, all of you outside now!" the Healer demanded. "Yes, you, too, Yomax! I'll call you when I'm ready."

They stepped out into the chill wind. Yomax shrugged, a helpless look on his face.

"Do you drink ale, stranger?" the aged centaur asked Brazil.

"I've been known to," Brazil replied. "What do you make it out of?"

"Grains, water, and yeast!" said Yomax, surprised at the question. "What else *would* you make ale out of?"

"I dunno," Brazil admitted, "but I'm awfully glad you don't either. Where to?"

The three of them went down the main street, Brazil feeling like a pygmy among giants, and up to the bar, front on now.

The place was full of customers—about a dozen— and they had trouble squeezing in. Brazil suddenly became afraid that he would be crushed to death between equine rumps.

The conversation stopped when he entered, and everyone looked at him suspiciously.

"I just love being made to feel welcome," Brazil said sarcastically. Then, to the other two, "Isn't there a more, ah, private place to talk?"

Yomax nodded. "Gimme three, Zoder!" he called, and the bartender poured three enormous steins of ale and put them on the bar. He handed one to Jol and the other to Brazil, who almost dropped it when he found out how heavy the filled stein really was.

148

Using two hands, he held on and followed Yomax down the street a few doors to the oldster's office.

After Jol stoked the fire and threw some more wood in, the place seemed to warm and brighten spiritually as well as literally. Brazil let out a long sigh and sank to the floor, resting the stein on the floor beside him. As the place warmed up, he took off his fur cap and coat. Underneath he didn't seem to be wearing anything.

The two centaurs also took off their coats, and both of them stared at him.

Brazil stared back. "Now, don't you go starting that, or I'll go back to the bar!" he warned. The Dillians laughed, and everybody relaxed. Brazil sipped the brew, and found it not bad at all, although close to two liters was a bit much at one time for him.

"Now, what's all this about, mister?" Jol asked suspiciously.

"Suppose we swap information," he offered, taking out his pipe and lighting it.

Yomax licked his lips. "Is that—is that *tobacco?*" he asked hesitatingly.

"It is," Brazil replied. "Not very good, but good enough. Want some?"

Yomax's expression, Brazil thought, was as eager and unbelieving as mine was when I saw that steak at Serge's.

Was that only a few months ago? he asked himself. *Or was it a lifetime?*

resembled a giant corncob and proceeded to fill it.

Yomax dragged out an old and battered pipe that Lighting it with a common safety match, he puffed away ecstatically.

"We don't get much tobacco hereabouts," the old man explained.

"I never would have guessed," Brazil responded dryly. "I picked it up a fair distance from here, really —I've traveled nine hexes getting here, not counting a side trip to Zone from my home hex."

"Them rodent fellas are the only ones in five thousand kilometers with tobacco these days," Yomax said ruefully. "That where?"

Brazil nodded. "Next door to my home hex."

"Don't think I remember it," the old official prodded curiously. "Except that you look like us, sort of, from the waist up, I don't think I ever seen your like before."

"Not surprising," Brazil replied sadly. "My people came to a no-good end, I'm afraid."

"Hey! Yomax!" Jol yelled suddenly. "Lookit his mouth! It don't go with his talkin'!"

"He's using a translator, idiot!" snapped Yomax.

"Right," the small man confirmed. "I got it from the Ambreza—those 'rodent fellas' you mentioned. Nice people, once I could convince them that I was intelligent."

"If you and they was neighbors, why was *that* a problem?" Jol asked.

The sadness crept back. "Well—a very long time ago, there was a war. My people were from a high-tech hex, and they built an extremely comfortable civilization, judging from the artifacts I saw. But the lifestyle was extremely wasteful—it required enormous natural resources to sustain—and they were running out, while the by-products curtailed good soil to the point where they were importing eight percent of their food. Unwilling to compromise their life-style, they looked to their neighbors to sustain their culture. Two hexes were ocean, one's temperature was so cold it would kill us, two more weren't worth taking for what they had or could be turned into. Only the Ambreza Hex was compatible, even though it was totally nontechnological. No steam engines, no machines of any kind not powered by muscle. The Ambreza were quiet, primitive farmers and fishermen, and they looked like easy prey."

"Attacked 'em, eh?" Yomax put in.

"Well, they were about to," Brazil replied. "They geared up with swords and spears, bows and catapults—whatever would work in Ambreza Hex—with computers from home telling them the best effective use. But my people made one mistake, so very old in the history of many races, and they paid the price for it."

"What mistake was that?" asked Jol, fascinated.

"They confused ignorance with stupidity," the man

explained. "The Ambreza were what they appeared to be, but they were not dumb. They saw what was coming and saw they had to lose. Their diplomats tried to negotiate a settlement, but at the same time they scoured other hexes for effective countermeasures—and they found one!"

"Yes? Yes? And that was . . .?" Yomax prompted.

"A gas," Brazil said softly. "A Northern Hemisphere hex used it for refrigeration, but on my people it had a far different effect. They kidnapped a few people, and the gas worked on them just as the Northerners said it would. Meanwhile the only effect on the Ambreza was to make them itch and sneeze for a while."

"It killed all your people?" asked Yomax, appalled.

"Not killed, no—not exactly," the small man replied. "It made, well chemical changes in the brain. You see, just about every race is loosely based on, or related to, some animal past or present."

"Yup," Yomax agreed. "I once tried to talk to a horse in Hex Eighty-three."

"Exactly!" Brazil exclaimed. "Well, we came from —were a refinement of, really—the great apes. You know about them?"

"Saw a few pictures once in a magazine," Jol said. "Two or three hexes got kinds of 'em."

"That's right. Even the Ambreza are related to several animals in other hexes—including this one, if I recall," Brazil continued. "Well, the gas simply mentally reverted everyone back to his ancestral animalism. They all lost their power to reason and became great apes."

"Wow!" Jol exclaimed. "Didn't they all die?"

"No," Brazil replied. "The climate's moderate, and while many of them—probably most of them—did perish, a few seemed to adapt. The Ambreza moved in and cleared out the area afterward. They let them run free in small packs. They even keep a few as pets."

"I ain't much on science," the old man put in, "but I *do* remember that stuff like chemical changes can't

151

be passed on. Surely their children didn't breed true as animals."

"The Ambreza say that there has been slow improvement," answered the small man. "But while the gas has to be extremely potent to affect anybody else, it appears that the stuff got absorbed by just about everything—rocks, dirt, and everything that grows in it or lived in it. For my people, the big dose caused initial reversion, but about one part per *trillion* keeps it alive. The effect is slowly wearing out. The Ambreza figure that they'll be up to the level of basic primitive people in another six or seven generations, maybe even start a language within five hundred years. Their—the Ambreza's, that is—master plan is to move the packs over into their old land when they start to improve. That way they'll develop in a non-technological hex and will probably remain rather primitive."

"I'm not sure I like that gas," Yomax commented. "What worked on them might work on us." He shivered.

"I don't think so," Brazil replied. "After the attack, the Well refused to transport the stuff anymore. I think our planetary brain's had enough of such things."

"I still don't like the idea," Yomax maintained. "If not that, then somethin' else could get us."

"Life's a risk anyway, without worrying about everything that *might* happen," Brazil pointed out. "After all, you could slip on the dock and fall in the lake and freeze to death before you got to shore. A tree could fall over on you. Lightning could strike. But if you let such things dominate your life, you'll be as good as dead anyway. That's what's wrong with Wu Julee."

"What do you mean?" Jol asked sharply.

"She's had a horrible life," Nathan Brazil replied evenly. "Born on a Comworld, bred to do farm labor, looking and thinking just like everybody else, no sex, no fun, no nothing. Then, suddenly, she was plucked up by the hierarchy, given shots to develop sexually, and used as a prostitute for minor visitors, one of whom was a foreign pig named Datham Hain."

152

He was interrupted at this point and had to try to explain what a prostitute was to two members of a culture that didn't have marriage, paternity suits, or money. It took some doing.

"Anyway," he continued, "this Hain was a representative of a group of nasties who get important people on various worlds hooked on a particularly nasty kind of drug, the better to rule them. To demonstrate what it did if you didn't get the treatment, he infected Wu Julee first and then let the stuff start to destroy her. There's no cure, and on most worlds they just put such people to death. Most of those infected, finding their blood samples matching Wu Julee's blood, played Hain's game, taking orders from him and his masters.

"The stuff kind of does to you, but very painfully, what that gas did to my Hex Forty-one, only it also depresses the appetite to nonexistence. You eventually mindlessly starve to death."

"And poor Wuju was already pretty far gone," Jol interpolated. "In pain, practically an animal, with all that behind her. No wonder she blotted all memories out! And no wonder she had nightmares!"

"*Life's* been a nightmare to her," Brazil said quietly. "Her physical nightmare is over, but until she faces that fact, it still lives in her mind."

They just stood there for several minutes, there seeming to be nothing left to say. Finally, Yomax said, "Captain, one thing bothers me about your gas story."

"Fire away," the man invited, sipping more of the ale.

"If that gas stuff was still active, why didn't it affect you, at least slightly?"

"I honestly don't know," Brazil responded. "Everything says I should have been reduced to the level of the hex, including Ambreza chemistry. But I wasn't. I wasn't even physically changed to conform to the larger, darker version of humanity there. I couldn't explain that—and neither can the Ambreza."

The Healer stuck her head in the door, and they turned expectantly.

"She's sleeping now," she reported. *"Really* sleeping, for the first time in more than a month. I'll stay with her and see her through."

They nodded and settled back for a long wait.

Wu Julee slept for almost two days.

Brazil used the time to tour the village and look at some of the trails. He liked these people, he decided, and he liked this isolated place, cut off from everything civilized except for the one daily boat run. Standing on a ledge partway up a well-maintained cross-country trail, he was oblivious to the cold and the wind as he looked out at the mass of snow-covered mountains. He realized suddenly that almost the whole mountain range was in the next hex, and he speculated idly on what sort of denizens lived in that kind of terrain.

After spending most of a day out there, he made his way back to the village to check on Wu Julee's progress.

"She came around," the Healer informed him. "I got her to eat a little something and it stayed down. You can see her, if you want."

Brazil *did* want, and went in.

She looked a little weak but managed a smile when she saw him.

She hasn't really changed radically, he thought, at least not from the waist up. He would have known her anywhere—despite the different coloration and the lower body, the pointy ears, and all. She actually looked healthier than she had under the influence of that vicious drug, the product of eating better and of exercising.

"How are you feeling?" he asked, idly wondering why that stupid question was always the first asked of obviously sick people.

"Weak," she replied, "but I'll manage." She let out a small giggle. "The last time we saw each other I had to look up to you."

Brazil took on a pained expression. "It never fails!" he wailed. "Everybody always picks on a little man!"

She laughed and so did he. "It's good to see you laugh," he said.

"There's never been much to laugh about, before," she replied.

"I told you I'd find you."

"I remember—that was the worst part of the sponge. You *know*, you are aware of all that's happening to you."

He nodded gravely. "Throughout the history of man there's always been some kind of drug, and people stuck on it. The people who push the stuff are on a different kind of drug, one so powerful that they are not aware of its own, ravaging, animalistic effect on them."

"What's that?"

"Power and greed," he told her. "The ugliest—no, the second ugliest ravager of people ever known."

"What's the ugliest, then?" she asked him.

"Fear," he replied seriously. "It destroys, rots, and touches everyone around."

She was silent for a moment. "I've been afraid most of my life," she said so softly he almost couldn't make out the words.

"I know," he replied gently. "But there's nothing to fear now, you know. These are good people here, and this is a spot I could cheerfully spend the rest of my life in."

She looked straight at him, and her youthful looks were betrayed by the eyes of someone incredibly old.

"They *are* wonderful," she admitted, "but it's *their* paradise. They were born here, and they know nothing of the horrors around them. It must be wonderful to be that way, but I'm not one of them. My scars seem huge and painful just because of their goodness and simplicity. Can you understand that?"

He nodded slowly. "I have scars, too, you know. And some of them are more than I can take at times. My memory's coming back—slowly, but in extreme detail. And, like Serge said, they're mostly things I don't want to remember. Some good times, some wonderful things, certainly—but some horrors and a lot of pain, too. Like you, I blotted them out, more successfully it seems, but they're coming back now—more and more each day."

155

"Those rejuve treatments must have done a lot to your memory," she suggested.

"No, nothing," he said slowly. "I've never had a rejuve treatment, Wu Julee. Never. I knew that when I blamed them for such things."

"Never—but that's impossible! I remember Hain reading your license. It said you were over five hundred years old!"

"I am," he replied slowly. "And a lot more. I've had a hundred names, a thousand lives, all the same. I've been around since Old Earth, and before."

"But that was bombed out centuries ago! Why, that was back almost before history!"

His tone was casual, but there was no doubting his sincerity. "It's been dropping like a series of veils, little by little. Just today, up in the mountains, I suddenly remembered a funny, little, Old Earth dictator who liked me because I wasn't any taller than he was. "Napoleon Bonaparte was his name. . . ."

He slept on furs in Yomax's office for several days, seeing Wu Julee gain some strength and confidence with every visit.

But those eyes—the scars in her eyes were still there.

One day the steamboat came in, and Klamath almost fell in the lake rushing out to meet him.

"Nate! Nate!" the ferry captain called. "Incredible news!" From his expression it was nothing good.

"Calm down, Klammy, and tell me about it." He spied a block-printed newspaper in the waterman's hand, but couldn't read a word of the language.

"Somebody just busted into that university in Czill and kidnapped a couple of people!"

Brazil frowned, a funny feeling in his stomach. That was where Vardia was, where he was going next.

"Who'd they snatch?" he asked.

"One of yours, Vardia or something like that. And a Umiau—they're sorta mermaids, Nate—named Cannot."

The little man shifted uneasily, chewing on his lower lip.

"Anybody know who?"

"Got a good idea, though they deny it. Bunch o' giant cockroaches with some unpronounceable name. Some of the Umiau spotted them in the dark when they shorted out the power at the Center."

Slowly the story came out. Two large creatures resembling giant flying bugs blew the main power plant, causing the artificial sunlight to fail in one wing of the Center. Then they crashed through the windows of the lab, grabbed Vardia and Cannot, and took them away. The leaders of the culprit's race were confronted at Zone, but pointed out that there were almost a hundred insectival races on the planet and denied they were the ones. Their tight monarchy, resembling a Comworld with fancy titles, was leakproof —so nobody was sure.

"But that's not the most sensational part!" Klamath continued, his voice rising again. "These Umiau got superupset at all this, and one of them let slip the truth about Cannot.

"Seems they and the top dogs of the Center had a real secret to keep. Cannot was Elkinos Skander, Nate!"

Brazil just stood there, digesting the information. It made sense, of course. Skander would use the great computers of the Center to answer his big questions, getting everything he needed so that, when he was ready, he could mount an expedition under his direction to the interior of the Well World. Power and greed, Brazil thought sourly. Corrupting two of the more peaceful and productive races on the planet.

Well, they wanted it all, and now all they've got left is their fear, he reflected.

"I'll have to go to Czill now," he told the ferry captain. "It looks as if my job is starting."

Klamath didn't understand, but agreed to hold the boat until Nathan could say good-bye to Wu Julee.

She was standing unsupported and looking through a book of landscape paintings by local artists when he entered. His expression telegraphed his disquiet.

"What's the matter?" she asked.

"They've broken into a place a couple of hexes

157

over and kidnapped Vardia and Skander, the man who might be the killer of those seven people back on Dalgonia," he told her gravely. "I have to go, I'm afraid."

"Take me with you," she said evenly.

The thought had never occurred to him. "But you're still weak!" he protested. "And here is where you belong. These are your people, now. Out there is nothing but worse and worse. It's no place for you!"

She walked over to him and looked down with those old, old eyes.

"I have to," she told him. "I have to heal the scars."

"But there're only more scars out there," he countered. "There's fear out there, Wu Julee."

"No, Nathan," she replied sternly, using his first name for the first time. She tapped her forehead. "The fear is in here. Until I face it, I'll die by inches here."

He was silent for a while, and she thought he still wouldn't take her.

"I'm easier to care for than you are," she pointed out. "I'm tougher of skin, more tolerant of weather, and I need only some kind of grass and water."

"All right," he said slowly. "Come if you must. You can get back to Dillia through a gate from anywhere, anyway."

"That's what I've got to know, Nathan," she explained. "I'm cured of sponge, but I'm still hooked on that ugliest drug, fear."

"You sure you're well enough?"

"I'm sure," she replied firmly. "This will give me what I need."

She put on a coat and they went outside. When they told Yomax and the others that she was going along, the same round of protests started all over again, but her mind was made up.

"I'll tell Dal and Jol," Yomax said, tears welling in his eyes. "But they won't understand, neither."

"I'll be back, old man," she replied, her voice breaking. She kissed him lightly on the cheek.

Klamath sounded the steam whistle.

They stepped on the board first floor of the steamship and entered the partially closed cargo door that enclosed the lower deck from the colder weather.

158

Five hours later they landed in the much larger village of Donmin downlake. Compared to the uplake community, it was a bustling metropolis of fifteen or twenty thousand, stretching out across broad, cleared plains. The streets were lit with oil lamps, although Brazil had no idea what sort of unrefined, natural oil they used. It smelled like fish, anyway.

He reclaimed a well-made but crude backpack from the shipping office and said good-bye to Klamath, who wished them luck.

The packs, Wu Julee found, were largely filled with tobacco, a good trade commodity. One pouch had some clothing and toiletries.

Using the tobacco, Brazil managed to trade for some small items he thought they would need, then got a room for them at a waterfront inn, where they spent the night.

The next day they set out early across the trails of Dillia toward the northeast. She had trouble staying back with him, having to walk in almost uncomfortable slow motion. After several kilometers of particularly slow going, she suggested, "Why don't you ride me?"

"But you're already carrying the pack," he protested.

"I'm stronger than you think," she retorted. "I've hauled logs heavier than you and the pack put together. Come on, climb on and see if you can keep from falling off."

"I haven't been on a horse since I went to the first Wilson inauguration," he muttered incomprehensibly. "Well, I'll try."

It took him three tries, even with her help, to mount her broad, stocky body that reminded him so much of a Shetland pony. And he fell off twice, to her derisive laughter, when she started to trot. She finally had to put her arms behind her to give him something to hold on to. When her circulation started going, he had to hold on to the much-less-reassuring pack. His own circulation was in no great shape. His legs discovered a hundred new muscles he had never known before, and the agony almost obliterated the soreness of his rump from bouncing.

But they made good time, the kilometers flying by. Near dusk they reached the Dillian border, through the last village and seeing here and there only an isolated farmhouse. It started to snow, but it was only a flurry at first and didn't really bother either of them.

"We're going to have to quit soon," he called to her.

"Why?" she mocked. "Scared of the dark?"

"My body just won't take much more of this," he groaned. "And we'll pass into the Slongorn Hex in a little while. I don't know enough about it to want to chance it in the dark."

She slowed, then stopped, and he got off. Pain shot through him but it was the aching sort, not the driving sharpness of riding. She was amused at his discomfort.

"So who couldn't make the trip because they were too weak?" she teased. "Look at the brave superman now! And we've already stopped five times!"

"Yeah," he grunted, stretching and finding that that only made it hurt in different places. "But that was only so you could eat. Lord! Do you people stuff yourselves!"

And they did, he thought, consume an enormous quantity to support their large bodies.

"Will we have to camp here?" she asked, looking at the darkening woods with no sign of lights nearby. "If we do, we'd better get some good shelter. It looks like the snow may pick up."

"If that road we passed about a kil and a half ago was the turnoff to Sidecrater Village, there should be a roadhouse not too much farther on." He checked a frayed and faded map he had in the pack.

"Why not go back to the village?" she suggested.

"Almost eight kils down a dead end?" he replied skeptically. "No, we'll go on and hope the roadhouse is still in business. But I'll walk for a while, no matter what!"

As darkness fell the snow did pick up, and started to stick. The wind whistled through the trees, keeping time with the subtle, quiet sound of the snow hitting against trees, bushes, and them.

Visibility dropped to almost zero.

"Are we still on the road?" she yelled to him.

"I don't know," he admitted. "We should have come to that roadhouse by now. But we don't have any choice. We'd never build a fire in this stuff now. Keep going!"

"I'm getting real cold, Nathan!" she complained. "Remember, more than half of me is exposed!"

He stopped, and brushed the snow off her backside. Insulating layer of fat or not, he realized she couldn't continue too much longer.

"I'm going to climb on!" he yelled above the wind. "Then go on as fast as you can! We've *got* to come to something sooner or later!"

They pushed forward, he clinging to her back, but it was slow going against the wind. They continued on for what seemed like hours in the blowing cold and darkness.

"I don't know how much longer I can go on!" she called to him at last. "My ass is frozen solid now."

"Come on, girl!" he shouted. "Here's that adventure you wanted! Don't give up now!"

That spurred her on, but it seemed hopeless as the snow continued to pile up.

"I think I see something ahead!" she shouted. "I can't be sure—I think my eyes are covered with icicles!"

"Maybe it's the roadhouse!" he shouted. "Head for it!"

She pushed on.

Suddenly, as if they passed through an invisible curtain, the snow was gone—and so was the cold. She stopped suddenly.

He got off and brushed the snow from him. After a few moments to catch his breath, he walked back several steps.

And back into the blowing snow and cold.

He went back to her.

"What is it, Nathan?" she asked. "What happened?"

"We must have missed the roadhouse," he told her. "We've crossed the border into Slongorn!"

Her body began to thaw rapidly, and painfully. Her eyes misted, then started to clear.

161

Looking back, she could see nothing but billowing, snowy fog.

In any other direction, the spectacular night sky of the Well World shone cloudlessly around them.

"We might as well camp right here," he suggested. "Not only am I too tired to go any farther, but there's no use chancing unfamiliar territory. Anything that might cause us problems is unlikely to be this close to the border, and we always have a convenient if chilly exit if we find any real problems."

"It's hard to believe," she said as he unstrapped the pack and removed a couple of towels, wiping his face and hair, then starting to give her the much more difficult rubdown. "I mean—coming out of that awful storm and into this—winter to summer, just like that."

"That's the way it can be," he replied. "Sometimes there's no clear dividing line, sometimes it's dramatic. But, remember, despite the fact that things interlock on this world—tides, rivers, oceans, and the like—each hex is a self-contained biological community."

"All of a sudden I'm starting to sweat," she noted. "I think I'll take these heavy fur clothes off."

"I'm ahead of you," he responded, drying her rear and tail. She twisted around and saw that he had removed almost all of his clothing. He looks even punier naked, she thought. You can just about see every rib on his body, even through that carpet of black chesthair.

He finished and came around to her front. Together they stood and looked at the landscape eerily illuminated in the bright starlight.

"Mountains, trees, maybe a small lake over there," he pointed out. "Looks like a few lights off in the distance."

"I don't think we're on the road," she commented. They seemed to be on a field of short grasses. She reached down almost automatically and picked a clump.

"I'm not sure you ought to eat that right now," he warned. "We don't know all the ground rules here."

She sniffed the grass suspiciously. Although Dillians were moderately nearsighted, their senses of smell

162

and hearing were acute. "Smells like plain old grass," she said. "Kind of short, though. See? It's been cut!"

He looked at the stuff and saw that she was right. "Well, this is logically either a high-technology hex or a nontechnological one, judging from the pattern I've seen," he noted. "From the looks of things, it's high."

"The grass has been cut in the last day or two," she observed. "You can still smell it."

He sniffed, but didn't notice much, and shrugged. He never had much of a smeller despite the Roman nose, he thought.

"I'm going to chance it," she decided at last. "It's here, and I need it, and we have two or three days before we'll get through here." She took about three steps, then stopped.

"Nathan?"

"Yes?"

"What kind of people live here? I mean, what—"

"I know what you mean. I couldn't get a really good description out of anyone. It's not the most traveled route, mostly a through route. The best I could get was that they were two-legged vegetarians."

"That's good enough for me," she replied, and started picking clumps of grass and chewing them.

"Don't get too far away!" he called. "It's too damned hot to build a fire, and I don't want to attract the wrong people. We might be—probably are—trespassing."

Satisfied as long as he could still see her, he stretched out the furs to dry and stripped completely. After discovering that some of the grass was stiff and sharp, he spread the three wet towels out to form a mat, then got out a couple of large bricks of cooked confection he had bought back in Donmin. He sat on the towels and ate about half of one bar, which was hard and crunchy but filling, and then came down with a terrible candy-thirst.

He reached for the flagon containing water, but decided to leave its half-empty contents if he could. No telling what the water was like here.

He got up and went over to the border, only a few meters away. He could hear the howling winds and see the blowing snow. Some of the cold radiated out a

163

few centimeters from the border. He got down on his knees, reached into the cold, and came up with a handful of snow.

That did the job.

He went back and stretched out on the towels. He still ached from the day's ride, but not nearly as bad. He knew the pain would come back when he mounted the next day, though. Maybe in three or four days he would get used to riding. By his own estimates, they were still almost nine hundred kilometers from the Center.

She came back after a while and surveyed him lying there on the towels.

"I thought you'd be asleep," she said.

"Too tired to sleep," he responded lazily. "I'll get off in a little while. Why don't you get some? You're doing all the work, and there's a lot yet to do. In the next few days we'll sure find out if they have pneumonia on this world."

She laughed and the laugh developed into a major yawn.

"You're right," she admitted. "I'll probably fall over in the night, though. Nothing to lean on here."

"Ummm-humm," he half-moaned. "Can you sleep lying down?"

"I have, once or twice, mostly on the end of drunks," she replied. "It's not normal, but if I don't crush my arm, I can. Once we go to sleep we're just about unconscious and unmoving for the night."

She came up close to him and knelt down, then slowly rolled over on one side, very close to him and facing him.

"Ahhh . . ." she sighed. "I think this is going to work, tonight, at least."

He looked at her, still half-awake, and thought, Isn't it funny how human she looks like that? Some of her hair had fallen over in front of her face, and, on impulse, he reached over and put it in back of her gently. She smiled and opened her eyes.

"I'm sorry, I didn't mean to wake you," he whispered.

"That's all right," she replied softly. "I wasn't really asleep. Still ache?"

"A little," he admitted.

"Lie with your back to me," she told him. "I'll rub it out."

He did as instructed and she twisted a little to free her left arm then started a massage that felt so good it hurt.

After a few minutes he asked her if there was something he could do in return, and she had him stroking and rubbing the humanoid part of her back and shoulders. Doing so was awkward, but she seemed satisfied. Finally, he finished and resumed his position on the towels.

"We really ought to get some sleep," he said quietly. Then, almost as an afterthought, he leaned over and kissed her.

She reached out and pulled him to her, prolonging the embrace. He felt terribly uncomfortable, and, when she finally let him go, he rolled back onto the towels.

"Why did you *really* come with me?" he asked her seriously.

"What I said," she replied in a half-whisper. "But, also, I told you I remember. I remember *all* of it. How you gambled to save my life. How you held me up in the Well. And—how you came out of your way to find me. I saw the map."

"Oh, *hell*," he said disgustedly. "This will never work. We're two different kinds of creature, alien to each other."

"You've been wanting me, though. I could feel it."

"And you know damned well our bodies don't match. Anything like sex just won't work for us now. So get those ideas out of your head! If that's why you're here, you should go back in the morning!"

"You were the only clean thing I ever ran into in that dirty old world of ours," she said seriously. "You're the first person I ever met who *cared*, even though you didn't know me."

"But it's like a fish falling in love with a cow," he retorted in a strained, higher-than-normal tone. "The spirits are there but they happen to come from two different worlds."

"Love isn't sex," she replied quietly. "I, of all people, know that better than anyone. Sex is just a physical act. Loving is caring as much or more about someone else than you do about yourself. Deep down inside you have the kind of feeling for others that I've never really seen before. I think some of it rubbed off. Maybe, through you, I'll face down that fear inside of me and be able to give myself."

"Oh, *hell!*" Brazil said sourly, turning his back to her.

In the quiet that followed, they both went to sleep.

The centaur was huge, like a statue of the god Zeus come to life, and it mated with the finest stallion. He came out of his cave at the sound of footsteps, then saw who it was and relaxed.

"You're getting careless, Agorix," the man said to him.

"Just tired," the centaur replied. "Tired of running, tired of jumping at every little noise. I think soon I will go into the hills and end it. I'm the last, you know."

The man nodded gravely. "I have destroyed the two stuffed ones in Sparta by setting the temple on fire."

The centaur smiled approvingly. "When I go, there will be naught but legends to say that we were here. That is for the best." Suddenly tears flowed from his great, wise eyes. "We tried to teach them so much! We had so much to offer!" he moaned.

"You were too good for this dirty little world," the man replied with gentleness and sympathy.

"We came of our own choice," the centaur replied. "We failed, but we tried. But it must be even harder on you!"

"I have to stay," the man said evenly. "You know that."

"Don't pity me, then," the centaur responded sharply. "Let me, instead, mourn for you."

Nathan Brazil awoke.

The hot sun was beating down on him, and had he not already been tanned from earlier travels, he would have had a terrible sunburn.

What a crazy dream, he thought. Was it touched off

by last night's conversation? Or was it, like so much lately, a true memory? The latter scared him a little, not because the dream was obscure, but because it would explain a lot—and in a most unpleasant direction.

He put it out of his mind, or tried to.

Suddenly he realized that Wu Julee was gone.

He sat up with a start and looked around. There was a large indentation in the grass where she had been, and some divots kicked up where she had gotten up, but no sign of her.

He looked around, noting several things about the landscape.

For one thing, they had been fairly lucky. Although the area around *was* a grassy hill, it sloped down into dank, swampy wetlands not far away. There were odd buildings, like mushrooms, scattered about near the swamp and through it, but no sign of any real activity. He looked back at the border. It was a snowy forest scene that greeted him, but the storm had passed and the sky was quickly becoming as blue there as it was overhead. He walked over to the border, got some snow, and rubbed his face with the cold stuff.

Blinking the sleep from his eyes, he turned back to look for Wu Julee. He spotted her at last, coming back toward him at full gallop.

He turned and packed the towels away in the pack, removing from the clothing pouch a bundle of black cloth. He unfolded it and looked at it. He had had it made in another hex, awfully nonhuman, but it had seemed right when he had tried it on.

The pants fitted, and his feet slipped into shoe-shaped bottoms with fairly tough, leathery soles on the outside. The material was of the stretchy type, and it seemed to adhere to him like a second skin, as did the pullover shirt. He had two of the latter, and chose the one with no sleeves over the other, which had form-fitting gloves.

It works, he thought to himself, and fairly comfortable, too. But it's so form-fitting and so thin I still feel naked. Oh, well, at least it'll keep the sun out.

He wished for sunglasses, not for the first time. But

167

the first group he had hit who made them were the Dillians, and the smallest was a bit too large for him.

Wu Julee came up to him at that point, looking excited.

"Nathan!" she called, "I've been out exploring and you'll never guess what's over the next hill!"

"The Emerald City," he retorted, even though he knew that expression would draw a blank look. In fact, it went right past her.

"No! It's a road! A *paved* road! And it has cars on it!"

He looked puzzled. "Cars? This close to the border? What kind of cars?"

"Electric ones, I think," she replied. "They don't go all that fast, and there aren't many of them, but there they are. There's a little parking lot up by the border. The Dillian roadhouse is a hundred meters or so farther on!"

"So we did miss it in the storm and got off the track!" he said. "They must supply the roadhouse with various things, and use the roadhouse as a business base. Funny you never heard of them."

"I've been uplake all my time here," she reminded him. "The only others I ever heard about were the mountain people, and I never saw any of them."

"Well, what do these people look like?" he asked curiously. "We'll have to travel through most of their hex."

"They're the strangest—well, you'll have to see. Let's get going!"

He strapped the pack on her and climbed aboard. She seemed particularly happy and eager and, well, *alive* this morning, he thought.

They moved along at a fast clip, and the old pains came back almost immediately, although he was getting to the point where he was going up when she was and down when she did. It helped a little, but not much.

They cleared the top of the hill in about five minutes, and he saw immediately what she meant. A half-dozen vehicles were parked in a little paved area near the border. They were mostly open, except for one with

168

a roof of canvas or something like it. None of them had seats, and, from the looks of the one with the top, their drivers were very tall and drove by a two-lever combination. The road was wide enough for one car to pass another, and it had a white line painted down the center of the black surface.

She stopped near the lot. "Look!" she said. "Now you'll see what I mean by weird people!"

And she was most definitely right, Brazil decided. The last time he had seen anything remotely resembling it was on a long-ago, month-long bender.

Imagine an elephant's head, floppy ears and all, but no tusks, with not one but *two* trunks growing from its face, each about a meter long and ending in four stubby, jointless fingers grouped around the nostril opening. Mount the head on a body that looked too thin to support such a head, armless and terminating in two short, squat, legs and flat feet that made the walker look as if he were slightly turning from side to side as he walked. Now paint the whole creature a fiery red, and imagine it wearing green canvas dungarees.

Nathan Brazil and Wu Julee didn't have to imagine it. That was exactly what was walking at a slow pace toward them.

"Oh, wow!" was all he could manage. "I see just what you mean."

The creature spotted them and raised its trunks, which seemed to grow out of the same point between and just below the eyes, in a greeting. "Well, hello!" it boomed in Dillian in a voice that sounded like an injured foghorn. "Better weather on this side of the line, hey?"

"You can say that again," Brazil responded. "We almost got caught in the storm and missed the roadhouse. Spent the night over in the field, there."

"Heading out, then?" the Slongornian asked pleasantly. "Going to tour our lovely country? Good time of year for it. Always summer here."

"Just passing through," replied Brazil casually. "We're on our way to Czill."

The friendly creature frowned, which gave it an even

169

more comical aspect that was hard to ignore. "Bad business, that. Read about it last night."

"I know," Nathan replied seriously. "One of the victims—the Czillian—was a friend of mine. Ours," he quickly corrected, and Wu Julee smiled.

"Why don't you go into the roadhouse, have breakfast, and try to bum a ride through?" the creature suggested helpfully. "All of these trucks'll be going back empty, and you can probably hitchhike most of the way. Save time and sore feet."

"Thanks, we'll try it," Brazil called after the Slongornian as that worthy climbed into the covered truck and started backing it out, controlling the steering with a trunk on each lever. The truck made a whirring noise but little else, and sped off down the road at a pretty good clip.

"You know, I bet he's doing fifty flat out," he said to Wu Julee as the truck disappeared from view. "Maybe we can move faster and easier than we figured."

They walked over the border to the incongruously snow-clad roadhouse. The cold hit them at once, Wu Julee being unclad except for the pack, and his clothing not much more than protection from the sun. They ran to the roadhouse, and she was inside almost a minute ahead of him.

Five Slongornians stood at a counter shoving what appeared to be hay down their throats with their trunks. One drained a mug of warm liquid somewhat like tea and then squirted it into its mouth. The innkeeper was a middle-aged female Dillian who looked older than her years. Two young male centaurs were sorting boxes in the back, apparently arranging the deliveries the Slongornians had made.

And there was one other.

It's a giant, man-sized bat! Brazil thought, and that is what it did look like. It was taller than he was by a little bit, and had a ratty head and body with blood-red eyes; its sharp teeth were chewing on a huge loaf of sweetbread. Its arms were slightly outstretched and they melded into the leathery wings, the bones extended to form the structural support for the wings. It had long, humanoid legs, though, with a standard knee covered in wiry black hair like gorillas' legs, and ending in two feet that looked more like large human hands, the backs covered with fur. The thing was obviously double- or triple-jointed in the legs, since it was balanced on one with no apparent effort while holding the loaf in the other, the leg brought up level with the mouth.

The creature seemed to ignore them, and no one else in the place seemed to pay any attention. They turned and ordered breakfast, a thick porridge in a huge bowl served steaming hot with wooden spoons stuck in the stuff. Wu Julee just ordered water with it, while Nathan tried the pitch-black tea. It tasted incredibly strong and bitter, and had an odd aftertaste, but he had found from the days he had spent in Dillia that the tea woke him up and got his motor started.

It didn't take long for one of the Slongornian truck drivers to strike up a conversation. They seemed to be an extraordinarily friendly and outgoing people, and when curious about this strange-looking one in their midst felt no hesitancy in starting things off. Between comments about the weather, the porridge, and the hard and thankless life of truck drivers, Brazil managed to explain where he was going and as much of his reason as he had told the one in the parking lot.

They sympathized and one offered to take them the nineteen kilometers to his base in the nearest Slongornian city, assuring them that they could probably hitch rides from terminal to terminal across the country.

"Well, Wu Julee, no exercise and no aches today," Nathan beamed.

"That's nice," she approved. "But, Nathan—don't call me by that name anymore. It's somebody else's name—somebody I'd rather not remember. Just call me Wuju. That's Jol's nickname, and it's more my own."

"All right," he laughed. "Wuju it is."

"I like the way you say it," she said softly. He reflected to himself that he didn't feel comfortable with the way *she* had said *that*.

"Excuse me," said a sharp, nasal, but crystal-clear voice behind them, "but I couldn't help overhearing you on your travel plans, and I wondered if I could tag along? I'm going in the same direction for a while."

171

They both turned, and, as Brazil expected, it was the bat.

"Well, I don't know . . ." he replied, glancing at the willing truck driver who cocked his head in an unmistakable why-the-hell-not attitude.

"Looks like it's all right with the driver, so it's all right with us, ah—what's your name? You've already heard ours."

The bat laughed. "My name is impossible. The translator won't handle it, since it's not only a sound only we can make but entirely in the frequencies beyond most hearing." The creature wiggled his enormous bat ears. "My hearing has to be acute, since, though I have incredible night vision, I'm almost blind in any strong light. I depend on my hearing to get around in the day. As for a name, why not call me Cousin Bat? Everyone else does."

Brazil smiled. "Well, Cousin Bat, it looks as if you're along for the ride. But why not just fly it? Injured?"

"No," Cousin Bat replied, "but this cold's done me no good, and I've traveled quite a distance. Frankly, I'm extremely tired and sore and would just as soon let machines do the work instead of muscle."

The bat went over to settle his bill, paying in some kind of currency that Brazil guessed was valid in Slongorn, which would be used to pay for the supplies.

He felt a sudden, hard pressure on his arm, and turned. It was Wu Julee—Wuju, he corrected himself.

"I don't like that character at all," she whispered in his ear. "I don't think he can be trusted."

"Don't be prejudiced," he chided her. "Maybe he feels uncomfortable around horses and elephants. Did you have bats on your home world?"

"Yes," she admitted. "They were brought in years ago to help control some native bugs. They did, but they were worse than the bugs."

Brazil shook his head knowingly. "I thought so. Well, we'll meet some even more unpleasant characters along the way, and he seems straight enough. We'll find out. If he's honest, he'll be a great night guard and navigator."

She resigned herself, and the matter was settled for the moment.

Actually, Brazil had an ulterior motive. With Cousin Bat around, there was less likelihood of the emotions of the night before getting aired or strengthened, he thought.

The ride was uneventful. Cousin Bat took the floor next to the Slongornian driver and promptly went to sleep, while Wuju and Brazil sat in the rear bed, the only place she could fit.

The Slongornian city was modern enough to have traffic jams as well as signals and police. Had it not been for the mushroom-shaped buildings and the total incongruity of the inhabitants, it would have been very comfortable. They waited there for two hours before another truck going in their direction was sufficiently empty to fit Wuju in the back, and even then she was uncomfortably cramped. Still, it was faster than her own speed.

Shortly after nightfall, they were more than halfway across the hex. Cousin Bat was wide awake by this time. Since there were no inns that could accommodate someone of Wuju's size and build, they made camp in the field of a friendly farmer.

The bat had looked like a cartoon version of a villain by day, but in the dark he took on a threatening aspect, his red eyes glowing menacingly, reflecting any light.

"You going to fly on now, Cousin Bat?" Brazil asked after they were settled.

"I will fly for a while," the creature replied, "partly for the exercise, and partly because there are some small rodents and insects roaming about here. I am sick and tired of wheat cakes and the like. My constitution is not constructed for such fare. However, Murithel, which is the next hex, is a bit nasty I'm told. I'll stick with you to Czill, if you'll have me."

Brazil assured him he would, and the bat leaped up into the evening sky with a flurry of leathery wings and vanished.

"I still don't like him," Wuju insisted. "He gives me the creeps."

173

"You'll have to get used to him," he told her. "At least, until I find out what his game is."

"What?" she yelped.

"Oh, he's a phony, all right," Brazil said. "Remember, in the old life I was nothing much but a truck driver like these folks here. I was even delivering grain. Truck drivers see a little of everybody and everything, know isolated facts about all sorts of things from the people they run into. They knew where our flying companion's home hex was. It's nine hexes north-northwest of here—almost exactly the opposite direction to the way we're going, at least the wrong point on a V."

"Now who's getting nervous?" she retorted. "He could be going someplace on business. He certainly hasn't told us much about what he does."

"I know what he does," Brazil replied evenly. "One of the other drivers saw him flying south, toward Dillia, two days ago."

"So?"

"He was coming to meet us, Wuju. He stayed at that roadhouse knowing we'd have to come that way to get to Czill. He almost missed us in the storm, but we managed to blunder into him anyway."

"Then let's get away, Nathan. Now. He might—kill us, or kidnap us, or something."

"No," he said thoughtfully. "Nobody goes that far out of his way to kill somebody. You just hire it done and that's that. If it's kidnap, it's the same gang that got Vardia and Skander, and if we joined it would solve one of my problems. But I smell something different here—I don't think he's one of their side, whoever they are."

"Then he's on our side?" she asked, trusting his judgment.

Nathan Brazil turned over on his towels and yawned. "Baby, you better remember now that the only side anybody's ever on is his own."

He slept far better than she that night.

Cousin Bat, looking tired, woke them up in the morning, but it was hours before they got a ride, and they made poor time. Brazil was plainly worried.

"I'd hoped to get to the border before nightfall," he

174

told them, "so we could see what was what tomorrow. Now, we won't get there until midday, and not really in until nightfall."

"That suits me," the bat replied. "And both of you can make do in the dark. I suggest we make the border, look over the terrain, but not enter until darkness falls. Better to keep to the dark for movements."

Brazil nodded approval. "Yeah. At least that'll put the Murnies on the same footing, and with your eyes we ought to be able to even out the odds."

Wuju looked alarmed. "What are the Murnies?" she asked.

"I see we've got the same information," Cousin Bat said. "The Murnies are the folk of Murithel, of which we have over three hundred kilometers to traverse. They are a nasty bunch of carnivorous savages that seem to be half-plant and half-animal. They'll try to eat anything that doesn't eat them."

"Can't we go around them, then?" she asked, appalled at the idea of crossing such a land.

"No," Cousin Bat replied. "Not from here. An arm of the ocean comes in to the east, and from what I've heard of the Pia we'll take the Murnies on dry land. To go up the other way we'd go through Dunh'gran, a land of nicely civilized flightless birds, but then we'd have to cut through Tsfrin, where the giant, crablike inhabitants are quite antisocial—not to mention armor-plated—and down in through Alisst, about which I know nothing. Not to mention about fourteen hundred kilometers."

"He's right, Wuju," Brazil said. "We'll have to try to sneak through the Murnies."

"Any weapons?" Cousin Bat asked.

"I've got a light-pistol," Brazil told him. "In the pack, there."

"No good," the bat replied. "Nontechnological hex. Those great weapons are never any use where you need them."

Brazil rooted around in the pack and pulled out a gleaming short sword. Looking at Wu Julee, he asked, "Remember this?"

"It's that Com girl's!" she exclaimed. "So that's

what that damned thing was that kept hitting me on the side! How in the world did you wind up with it?"

"It was left in Serge's office at Zone," he reminded her. "I went back there a few days after arriving in my home hex. I found the Zone Gate, dodged Ambreza guards, and jumped in, managing to get word to Ortega before those giant beavers made me into a domesticated pet. Old Serge gave it to me. Said it might come in handy. Ever used one?"

She looked at it strangely. "I—I don't think I've ever even killed a bug. I don't know if I could."

"Well, you'll have to find out now," he told her. "Your arm muscles and speed make it a better weapon for you than for me."

"What will you use, then?" she asked.

"Five thousand safety matches and a can of flammable grease," he replied cryptically. "You'll see. What about you, Cousin Bat?"

"Carrying a weapon would keep me off-balance, but I can always pick and drop rocks," the creature replied. "Besides, my teeth and my airborne punch are extremely effective."

"Okay, then," Brazil nodded, reasonably satisfied. "We're as good as we're gonna get. Remember, our *best* hope is no fight at all—to sneak through and that's that."

Wuju took the sword and tried a few awkward thrusts. She didn't look sure or confident. "What—what do I aim at if I have to use it?" she asked uncertainly.

"The head's always the best," Cousin Bat told her. "Even if it isn't the brain, at least it's the eyes, nose —things that matter. A second choice is the genitals, if any."

No roads led to the Murithel border, and they had to walk the last several kilometers in the dark.

"We'll stay on this side through tomorrow," Brazil said tensely. "Then, near sundown, we'll go."

They spent the night talking, except for an hour or so when Cousin Bat left for his nightly feeding. Brazil tried to keep Wuju awake most of the night, so they would sleep the following day, but well before the night was half over she had succumbed.

He decided to let her sleep, and spent the earlier hours talking to the bat. The creature was easy to talk to, but gave little useful information and rather glib lies.

Brazil resisted the temptation several times to come right out and ask Cousin Bat who he really was and what he wanted, but never quite got to the point of doing so.

Both finally were asleep by morning.

Wuju was up first, of course, but she didn't stray far from them. Brazil slept until almost midday, and Bat finally had to be awakened later on when he showed every sign of sleeping until dark.

Murithel was clearly visible from their camp. It didn't look very menacing; in fact, it looked beautiful.

Brazil had one of those uneasy memories again. He remembered a place long vanished and forgotten. He'd been standing on a barren hill overlooking some rough but scenic landscape. A couple of thousand meters from that hill ran a line of trees lending color to the landscape. What he could see of Murithel reminded him of that long ago day, and gave him the same feelings, for the river that had fed those trees was something called the Little Bighorn, and a few years before he had seen it, others had as well. He bet that that landscape had looked as quiet and peaceful as this one did to that general who came into primitive territory.

How many Indians are behind those rocks and trees? he asked himself.

The landscape was formed of low, rocky mountains and rolling hills, some made up of bright orange rock eroded into strange and eerie patterns. Others were more a dull pink, with clumps of trees here and there and grass on the tougher portions. A line of trees betrayed a small river or stream off to their left. The sky was cloudy and the sun reflected strange shadows off the landscape.

177

"I think it's beautiful," Wuju said. "But it looks so *strange*. Even the sky seems to be a lighter blue, with yellows and greens in it. But it's so rough and rugged—how will we know that we're going the right way?"

"No problem on a clear night," Brazil replied. "Just head toward the big, bluish-orange nebula. Looks as if it's clouding up in there, though."

"I agree," the bat put in, concern in his voice. "We might have some rain. Bad for navigation, bad for flying if need be. It'll slow us down."

"But it'll also keep the Murnies down," Brazil pointed out. "If we get rain, we keep going as long as it's possible. The Slongornians say that that low pinkish range of hills with the little bit of green goes pretty much northeast for almost half the distance. I'd say we get to it and follow it. Looks as if there may be caves and shelters there, too."

The bat nodded approval. "I agree. If I were to live in such a place, I'd make my camps and villages along river and stream courses, on the flats but in defensible positions. If we stay away from such places unless absolutely necessary, we might just make it."

"As close to sunset as possible, I want you to reconnoiter the area from the air," Brazil told Cousin Bat. "I want to know as much about what's in there, reasonable paths and the like, before we go." He went over and pulled the sword out of the pack, and changed his shirt to the long-sleeved one with gloves. With Bat's help, they tore the shirt he had been wearing, twisted and tied it to make a makeshift scabbard fixed around Wuju's neck and draped to one side so all but the hilt was in the shirt.

"That ought to hold," he said with satisfaction, "if the sword doesn't tear through the material and if you remember to hold the cloth when taking out the sword." Next he removed a small, battered tin and took out something that looked like oily grease.

"What's that?" she asked, curious.

"Slongornian cooking fat," he replied, applying the stuff to his face and neck. "Something in it is like a dye. Bat's black and you're brown, but my light skin will be a giveaway in close quarters. I want to be able to blend in."

Satisfied, they settled back to wait for sundown.

The Barony of Azkfru, Akkafian Empire

VARDIA REGAINED CONSCIOUSNESS SLOWLY. EVEN WITH the aid of what looked like a sunlamp, it was almost half an hour before she could make any movement at all.

The Umiau she knew as Cannot groaned softly. With great effort she turned her head a little and saw that the mermaid was having a similar struggle to regain muscle movement.

"Son of a bitch!" the Umiau swore in Confederacy plain talk.

She would have gasped had she the physical equipment for it. She recognized the dialect at once, though she hadn't heard it since she was in Ortega's office in Zone.

"You—are—from—the—Confederacy," she managed, the voice sounding strangely distant and fuzzy.

"Of course," the mermaid growled. "That's what all this is about. I am Elkinos Skander."

Vardia stretched and flexed, feeling far surer of herself with every passing moment.

The Umiau stared at her for a moment, a puzzled frown on her face. "You mean you really haven't any idea about what's going on?"

Vardia shook her head. "No, nothing."

Skander was thunderstruck. It simply hadn't occurred to her that anyone hadn't known at least part of the story. "Look," she began, "you're Vardia, right? You came in with that party from Dalgonia?" She nodded, and the mermaid continued. "Well, I came in a few weeks ahead of you."

Now it was Vardia's turn to be astonished. "Then you—it was *your* tracks we followed!"

"Indeed they were!" Skander replied and proceeded to tell her the entire story—the discovery, the opening of the gate, even the murders. Only the point of view had changed on the latter.

"I returned to the camp instead of staying on station," Skander lied. "By the time I arrived, this rascal Varnett had already killed them. There was no way out, no chance of holding him off, so I made for the Gate. I hadn't any real idea where it would take me, or if it would kill me; but I was being chased by a madman. I had no choice. When I arrived, the Gate had not yet opened, and Varnett caught me. We struggled—he was much younger, but I was in far better condition—and the Gate opened beneath us."

He went on and told how they were separated, interrogated for several days, and finally allowed to pass through the same Gate she had gone into. "I don't know what happened to Varnett," Skander finished. "I woke up a Umiau and damned near drowned those first few hours. The Umiau spotted me and I was taken immediately to government Center by two police. They kept me locked up until I normalized, and while there I was apprised of the unique situation here and of my own new situation. When I heard about the Center and the contacts with your people, we decided to strike a bargain—me with my new people, and my people with yours—to solve the problem of this planet once and for all and," the mermaid concluded, with a strangely fiery look in her eyes like those of a religious fanatic, "whoever does solve it will control this world at the very least, and perhaps all of them."

"But none of our people has ever sought power," she objected.

"*All* people seek power," Skander replied firmly. "Few, however, are ever given the opportunity to grab it."

"I still can't see my people wanting to rule the world or whatever," she said stubbornly. "Perhaps yours, but not mine."

Skander shrugged. "Your people are a mystery to me, just as mine would be to yours. Maybe they only wanted to add the ultimate knowledge. Maybe they still wouldn't have done it, but for one factor."

"Which is?" she asked, still unwilling to accept what she was hearing.

"Varnett, of course. He's out there; he has the same formulae I do for contacting the brain, and he's at least as smart, perhaps smarter than myself. We couldn't take the chance. If anyone was to break the final puzzle and control the brain of this world, it would better be the Umiau—and the Czillians, of course," the scientist added hastily.

"So how did we come to this?" Vardia asked, waving her tentacles around at the barren dirt chamber with its incongruous electrical outlet.

"Because I was stupid," Skander replied harshly. "Someone found out who I was—how I don't know. But our ambassador at Zone got a warning that someone was out to kidnap me, and so I cleared out and lay low for several weeks. I relied on the fact that most species can't tell individuals of another species apart. I came back, eventually, using a colleague's name and office, and tried to complete the last few days' work. That's why we were pushing it around the clock. I'd already solved half the puzzle and hoped I could crack the rest. I even had you transferred up —not for what you *were* doing, but because I could talk conversationally to you about the Dalgonian Gate and your own experiences."

Now she was really puzzled. "Why would my experiences be any different than yours?"

"Because the Gate should have closed behind us!" Skander exclaimed excitedly. "We—Varnett and I— opened it when we cracked the code. Our minds opened it. But there's no reason why the thing remained active—if it has. The resupply ship should have been in shortly after you and gone through the same motions—then most of them should have arrived here."

Vardia thought back, and told about the strange emergency signal.

"Another funny thing. I hadn't really thought about it, but—"

"Go on!" Skander prompted. "What was it?"

"I—I'd swear that your two ships *vanished*—just weren't there—before the Gate opened."

The Umiau was suddenly very excited. "Vanished! Yes, that would explain it! But, tell me, who else was in your party? I glanced at the information but didn't pay much attention at the time."

"There was a big, ugly fat man, I don't remember his name," she recalled, straining. It all seemed so long ago. "He turned out to be a sponge merchant— and he had this girl, Wu something, who was all fouled up on the stuff."

"No one else? Wasn't there a pilot?"

"Oh, yes, Nathan Brazil. A funny little man no bigger than I was. But old—his pilot's license was pre-Confederacy!"

Suddenly Skander laughed and rocked back against the wall on her long fish's tail, clapping her hands once in amusement.

Vardia didn't understand at all and said so.

"They've kidnapped the wrong person!" the Umiau replied, still chuckling.

"That's very interesting, Dr. Skander, but where does that leave us?" came a weird, unearthly yet quiet voice that seemed to be made up of pulses and chimes, although both kidnap victims understood every word. They both turned, as The Diviner and The Rel glided out of a nook hidden in shadows.

"What the hell are you?" Skander said, more in wonder than in fear.

"We are, I'm afraid, behind your rough treatment and discomfort," The Rel replied.

"You're not from around Czill," Vardia observed almost accusingly. "Nothing like you is related to the kind of life we have here."

"We are from the Northern Hemisphere," The Rel explained. "However, we were obliged, upon learning of Dr. Skander's mission through means not worth explaining to you, to forge an alliance. You are in the Akkafian Empire, on the other side of the ocean from Czill."

"Those big bugs," Vardia put in. "The ones that came through the glass—they're not . . ."

"They are," The Rel replied. "I fail to see why that should disturb you. So far we haven't found much difference in any of you Southern races."

"No difference!" Vardia exclaimed, upset by the comment. "Why, just look at the two of us! And—how can you compare us to those bugs?"

"Form doesn't matter," observed The Rel. "Only content. I find most of your actions and reactions incomprehensible, but consistent. As for those bugs, we'll have one with us for quite some time, I fear. I have arranged it so that we draw only the weakest link in this society, but it takes no deduction to assume that the creature will be incredibly brave and loyal in our defense until that final moment when we are at the controls of the planetary brain. Then, of course, it will kill us all."

Skander opened her mouth but said nothing. The score was perfectly clear, except The Diviner and The Rel's role and side.

"That's all very well," Vardia said at last, "but won't these people think of that?"

"Oh, they will perform what is known as the double cross," The Rel replied casually in that same, even tone. "But The Diviner's talents are real. We will make it—all but one of us. We shall do this."

"Which one?" Skander asked quietly.

"I have no idea, and neither does The Diviner," replied The Rel. "Perhaps it's one of you, or the Akkafian. Perhaps it is we, for no Diviner can foretell its own demise."

They digested that awhile. Finally, Skander broke the new silence.

"You say you're not like us. But here you are, kidnapping me, trying for the same goal as all the other races would if they had the chance. Power is still the name of the game."

"You misunderstand us," The Rel said. "We have

183

power. We have powers we choose not to reveal at this time. We have no wish to interfere in your petty goals, wars, sex, politics, or anything else. Our goal is simply to make certain that no one ever gets into that control center again."

"Well, so you say," Skander replied skeptically. "But the fact remains that, for now, you're our only hope of getting out of here and getting away from the bugs."

"Remember that!" The Rel said. "I am your only protection. And—oh, yes, for some additional measure of protection, I would suggest that Czillian Vardia change its name for the entire expedition, and that you both remember to use that different name. I will make certain that our companion does not know your identity, either."

"But why?" Vardia asked, particularly puzzled now. "Who is this companion."

"A greatly changed and mentally preconditioned Datham Hain, the fat man of your party," The Rel told her. "It would be better if it did not know that one of our party knows everything about its past activities. Although a conditioned slave, deep down Hain is still Hain. I suggest you remember what it did to others before, what kind of person it is."

"Oh," was all she could manage. She thought for a moment. "Then I'll call myself Chon, which is a common name in Czill, and easy to remember and respond to."

"Very good," The Rel replied. "Remember it. We will leave as soon as possible. In the meantime, may I remind you of several facts. First, let me point out, Dr. Skander, that there is little water in this land. These people can move on the ground at close to ten kilometers per hour, up to twice that in the air; and they have nasty stingers. As for you, Czillian, move out of the sunlight and you'll root. You know that. That lamp is all that keeps you awake. The light here is not intense enough on its own to keep you awake." And with that it glided out the door.

184

Skander beat her fist on the hard ground, and Vardia stayed still, but the message had been received and understood.

There was no escape.

Murithel—One Hour from Dawn

WUJU HAD SOME TROUBLE WITH THE UNEVEN, ROCKY ground, but they had managed to advance more than forty kilometers into the hex without meeting any of its dominant life form.

There was a flutter of wings and Cousin Bat landed just ahead of them. "There's a fairly good cave with rock cover a little farther up," the dark one whispered. "It's a good place to make camp. There's a small tribe of Murnies over on the other side of those trees, there, but they look like a hunting party, likely to stay on the plains and river basin."

Brazil and Wuju looked where the bat pointed, but could see nothing but pitch darkness.

Cousin Bat led the way up to the cave. It was already getting light when they approached it, and they lost no time at all in getting in. It was a good location, high up on the cliff atop some ancient rock slide. They could see for kilometers but, thanks to the shape of the rocks and boulders around the cave, could not be seen from the plain below. It was damp and had a small family of tiny, toadlike reptiles living there, but these were quickly chased. It wasn't all that deep a cave, but it would hide the three of them.

"I'll take the first watch," Brazil said. "Wuju's dead tired now, and you, Bat, have been flying around half the night. All I've been doing is riding."

They agreed, and he assured them he would call Wuju when he was too tired to carry on.

Brazil took a comfortable perch near the cave mouth and watched the sun rise.

Still light-headed over this air, he thought. It was obviously quite different in composition from what he was used to, although he had been through worse getting to Dillia from his own ill-fated Hex 41. Much richer in oxygen, lower in nitrogen, he decided. Well, the other two had gotten used to it and he would, too, in time.

The air was cool and crisp but not uncomfortable. Probably eighteen degrees Celsius, he thought, with high humidity. The threatened rainstorm still looked threatening, but hadn't materialized yet.

The sun was well over the distant mountains when he saw his first Murnies. There they were—a small bunch, less than a dozen, running with spears after a deerlike creature. They were over two meters high, he guessed, although it was hard to figure at a distance. They were almost rectangular, a uniform light green in color, very thin—incredibly so, for he almost lost ones that turned sideways. They were kind of lumpy, looking at the distance something like light-green painted bushes. Two arms, two legs—but they melted into a solid when one stood straight and still.

He was amazed that he could see some features from this far away. Their big yellow eyes must be larger than dinner plates, he thought, and those mouths —huge, they seemed to go completely across the body, exposing a reddish color when they were opened wide. And they had teeth—even from here he could see they were pointed daggers of white of a size to fit those mouths.

They were sloppy hunters, but eventually they cornered the brownish deer-thing, surrounded it, and speared it to death.

Don't they ever throw the spears? he wondered. Maybe those thin, wide arms couldn't get enough strength or balance.

As soon as the creature fell, they pounced upon it, ripping pieces of it and shoving it into their mouths, fighting each other to get extra bites. Those hands must have pretty good claws to tear like that, he thought.

In just a few minutes, they had finished off the entire deer-thing, which must have weighed at least 150 kilos, he guessed. They even ate the bones. When they finally picked up their spears and went off down the plains, there was no sign of the prey they had eaten except a torn-up patch of dirt and grass.

Seven days, he thought. At the rate we're going, seven days in *their* country. And that's if everything goes *right*. And there's bound to be lots more of them, a lot thicker group.

No problem alone, of course. Even easier with Cousin Bat, whoever he worked for.

Why the hell did I allow her to come along?

Why had he?

That act of courage in taking off her pressure helmet in Zone? Was that what he liked in her, deep down?

Pity, maybe. Certainly that had motivated him at the start.

Thinking back, he kept remembering how she had clung to him in Zone, looked to him for support, defying Hain even that close to the end.

What was love, anyway? he mused. She said it was *caring,* caring more about someone else than about yourself.

He leaned forward and thought a minute. Did he *really,* deep down, care if the Murnies got the bat? He realized he wouldn't shed a tear for the creature. Just one more in a long list of dead associations. Was he going to Czill because Vardia was kidnapped? No, he decided, luck of the draw, really. He was going to Czill because it was the only lead he had to Skander, and that project was—well, wasn't that caring?

What's it to me if Skander takes over and remolds the universe in his own crazy image? He had met a lot of nice people, happy people, old friends and new acquaintances, in his long life and here on the Well World. He cared about them, somehow, even though he knew deep down that, in a pinch, they probably wouldn't do the same for him. Maybe it's for that unknown one who would, he thought. Nathan Brazil, ever the optimist.

Had anybody ever cared?

He thought back, idly watching a much larger group of Murnies chasing a fair-sized herd of the deer-things. How many times had he been married, legally or socially? Twenty times? Thirty? Fifty? More?

More, he thought wonderingly. About every century. Some had been nice lookers, some real dogs. Two of them had even been men. Had any of them really *cared* about him?

Not one, he thought bitterly. Not one, deep down in their selfish little hearts. Lovers, hell. The only friends who hadn't betrayed him in some manner or the other were those who hadn't had the chance.

Would he really care if the Murnies ate *him?*

Just tired, the centaur had said. *Tired of running, tired of jumping at every little noise.*

I'm tired, too, he thought. Tired of running nowhere, tired of that tiny belief, often foresworn, that somewhere, somewhere, was someone who would *care.*

If all that were true, why *did* he care about the Murnies? Why did he feel fear?

The wild ports, the happy drugs, the whores and dives, the endless hours alone on the bridge.

Why have I lived so long? he asked himself. Not aging wasn't enough. Most people didn't die of old age, anyway. Something else got them first.

Not him.

He had always survived. Banged up, bleeding, nearly dead thousands of times, and yet something in him would not let him die.

He remembered the Flying Dutchman suddenly, sailing the world's oceans with a ghost crew, alone but for one short leave every fifty years, doomed until a beautiful woman would love him so much that she would give up her life for him.

Who commands the Dutchman? he asked the winds. *Who curses him to his fate?*

It's psychology, he thought. The Dutchman, Diogenes—I'm all these people. It's why I'm different.

All those millions over the centuries who killed themselves when nobody cared. Not me, I'm cursed. I can't accept the universality of shallow self-interest.

188

That fellow from—what was the name of that country? England. Yes, England. Orwell. Wrote a book that said that a totalitarian society sustains itself by the basic selfishness of everybody. When the chips were down, his hero and heroine betrayed each other.

Everybody thought he was talking of the fears of a future totalitarian state, Brazil thought bitterly. He wasn't. He was talking about the people around him, in his own enlightened society.

You were too good for this dirty little world, he had said, but he had stayed. Why? In failure?

Whose failure? he wondered, suddenly puzzled. He almost had the answer, but it slipped away.

There was movement in back of him and he jumped and jerked around.

Wuju came up to him slowly. He looked at her curiously, as if he had never seen her before. A chocolate brown girl with pointy ears welded to the working half of a brown Shetland pony. And yet it worked, he thought. Centaurs always looked somehow noble and beautiful.

"You should have called one of us," she said softly. "The sun's almost straight up. I thought you were asleep."

"No," he replied lazily. "Just thinking." He turned back to gaze over the valley, now seemingly swarming with Murnies and deer-things.

"About what?" she asked casually, starting to massage his neck and shoulders.

"Things I don't like to think about," he replied cryptically. "Things I hid away in little corners of my mind so they wouldn't bother me, although, like all ghosts, they haunt me even when I don't know it."

She leaned over and kissed him on the cheek. "I do love you, Nathan," she whispered.

He got up and walked toward the back of the cave, patting her gently on her equine rump as he did so. There was a puzzled half-smile on his face, and he said, as he stretched out near Cousin Bat, in a voice so low it was really to himself, "Do you, Wuju? Do you, really?"

The Barony of Azkfru, Akkafian Empire

THE BARON WAS, IF ANYTHING, MORE MAJESTIC THAN before, and Datham Hain was at her lowest ebb, at the brink of suicide from weeks now in the dung pits.

"You have your name back, now, Mar Hain," the baron pronounced in that godlike tone he had.

That was a small gesture, yet to Hain it was as momentous as being crowned supreme ruler of the galaxy, for it restored a measure of her self-respect. It also bound the Entry all the more to the baron, from whom all blessings flowed.

"I have now a task for you, of the utmost difficulty," the baron told her. "It will require loyalty and devotion, as well as all of your intelligence and cunning. If you fail me, you are lost forever; if you succeed, you shall sit beside me in an honored place as chief concubine of, not your baron, but at the very least the emperor, perhaps not only of this empire."

"You have but to instruct this humble slave and I will obey though there be no reward and the cost be my life," Hain groveled.

I'll bet, the baron thought sarcastically. Once more he regretted having to trust such a one as this on so important a mission. Blast that Northerner! Yet, The Diviner had so far been a hundred percent correct on everything, and he dared not go against the creature, at least not until the final moments.

"Listen well, Mar Hain," the baron said carefully. "Soon you will meet three aliens. You will have a translation device implanted so that you can follow all conversations. Also, two of them are Entries, and may be able to communicate in the nontranslatable tongue of your old life—so it is better if you feign both ignorance and stupidity whenever possible.

"You will be going on a great journey together. Now, here is what you are to do. . . ."

"Those filthy bugs!" Vardia, now calling herself Chon, exclaimed as they set her down on a road with the others and flew off, making irritating buzzing noises as they did so.

"Let's have no racial slurs," Hain said sternly. "They think even less of you, and they are my people."

"Come on, you two, cut it out!" Skander snapped. Unable to walk, they had built a saddle which left the mermaid perched only mildly comfortable atop Hain's back. "We have a long and probably difficult journey ahead of us. Our lives may depend on each other, and I don't want all this carping!"

"Quite so," The Rel agreed. "Please remember, you two, that although you were kidnapped, we all have a common goal. Save all disputes for the time we reach our goal, not during the journey."

They were at the imperial border, manned by bored sentries. The change in the landscape was tremendous. The arid, hilly, pinkish-gray land of the Akkafians ended abruptly as if there were some physical barrier, perfectly straight, stretching from horizon to horizon.

"All of you put on your respirators," The Rel instructed, needing none for itself. They still didn't know if it breathed. Hain's was bulky, the great insect looking as if she were wearing some sort of giant, distorted earmuffs behind her eyes. Vardia's hung on a strap around her neck and was attached to her lower legs by two cables ending in needles which were inserted in her skin. Skander's was a simple mask over mouth and nose, with tubes leading to a tank also on Hain's back. Vardia's alone contained not an oxygen mixture but pure carbon dioxide. There was a mechanism by which the waste contents in her canister could be exchanged with those of Skander and Hain.

The hex they faced was bleak enough; the sky showed not the various shades of blue common to much of the world, but an almost irritatingly bright yellow.

"Sound will travel, but slowly and with great distortion," The Rel told them. "The atmosphere has enough trace elements to allow us to get by with such simple devices, but that is mostly due to seepage—the other hexes surrounding it naturally leak a little. We will be able to refresh our tanks from supplies along the way, but under no circumstances remove your masks! There are elements all about which will not harm your exteriors but will, nonetheless, cause physical problems or even death if taken in great quantities in the lungs for any period of time."

Vardia looked out over as much of the landscape as the glare permitted her to see. A very jagged, burnt-orange landscape, filled with canyons and strange, eroded arches and pillars. What erodes them? she wondered idly. And what sort of creatures could live in such a hostile place? Carbon-based life? All the South was supposed to be, yet there could be nothing carbon-based about anything able to stand such a place.

"Hain," The Rel instructed, "remember to keep your beak tightly shut at all times. You don't want to swallow the stuff. And, Skander, keep that blanket tightly on your lower parts and you'll get and retain enough moisture to keep you from drying up. The respirator's been designed that way. All set? Then, any last-second questions?"

"Yes, I have a couple," Vardia said nervously. "What sort of creatures will we meet, and how will we possibly cross this place and survive?"

"The creatures are basically autonomatons, thinking machines," The Rel replied. "This is a high-technological hex; more so, in fact, than the one we've been in. The only reason they coexist is that the Akkafians couldn't exist here for very long, nor is there anything of use to them in The Nation, while the people of this hex would break down in an atmosphere more conducive to your form of life. Come! We've wasted enough time! You'll see how we survive as we go along."

With that The Diviner and The Rel floated quickly across the border. Vardia, a helpless feeling inside her, followed; and Hain and Skander brought up the rear.

Skander and Vardia both had the same impression: as if they were suddenly in an environment of kerosene. The odor permeated their bodies and penetrated their breathing. The atmosphere also felt heavy, almost liquid; and, while invisible, it rippled against their bodies like a liquid, even though it was plainly a gas. Moreover, it burned slightly, like a strong alcohol. It took them awhile to get used to it.

The Rel paced them at close to Vardia's maximum stride; Hain followed at the same pace, between eight and ten kilometers per hour. In less than an hour they came upon a paved road, although the paving stone looked like a single long ribbon of smoothly polished jade. And, as with most roads and trails in the various hexes, this one contained traffic.

The first thought they all had was that no two denizens of The Nation were alike. There were tall ones, thick ones, thin ones, short ones, even long ones. They moved on wheels, treads, two, four, six, and eight legs, and they had every imaginable type of appendage and some not very imaginable as to purpose. Although all obviously machines of dull-silver metal, all looked as if they had been fashioned in a single stroke. No bolts, joints, or any other such were visible; they bent and flexed the metal like skin, and in any way they wanted.

Vardia understood and marveled at this.

Each one was made for a single purpose, to fulfill a single need of the society. It was built to order to do a job, and this it did where and when needed. It was, she thought, the most practical of all the societies she had seen, the perfection of social order and utilitarianism—a blend of the best of the Comworlds' concepts with the lack of physical dependencies of the Czillians.

She only wished she understood what the people of The Nation were doing.

There were structures, certainly, more and more of them as they went on. Some were recognizable as buildings, although as varied and oddly shaped as the inhabitants of this strange land. Other structures seemed to be skeletal, or spires, twisted shapes of metal, and even apparently girders of some sort arranged in certain deliberate but baffling ways. Functionally built workmen rushed to and fro. Some were building, of course, but many seemed to be digging holes and filling them up again, while others carried piles of sand from one point and dumped them to form new piles of sand elsewhere. None of it made sense.

They continued to follow The Diviner and The Rel. They went on through this landscape for hours without stopping and without any of the creatures taking the slightest notice of them. More than once, in fact, both Hain and Vardia had had to move out of the way quickly to avoid being run over by some creature or by the creature's load.

They came upon a building that seemed to be made of the same stuff as the creatures themselves, but was shaped something like a large barn. The Diviner and The Rel surprised them by turning in at the building's walkway. It waited until they were all at the rather large sliding doorway, then glided up to a very large button, then back, up again, and back again.

"Do you wish me to push it?" Vardia asked. The response sounded like garbled nonsense to her own ears. The Rel jumped up and down, and The Diviner's lights blinked more agitatedly, and so Vardia pushed the button. The door slid aside with entirely the wrong sounds, and the strange creature that led them glided inside. They followed and found themselves in a very large but barren chamber. Suddenly the door slid shut behind them, and they were in total darkness, illuminated only by the oddly nonilluminating blinks of The Diviner.

They had gotten so used to the strange sensations produced by the atmosphere of the place that the gradual absence of them was almost as harsh as their original exposure to them.

There were whirring, clicking, and whooshing noises all around them, going on for what seemed to be several minutes. Then, finally, an inner door slid open to reveal another large barren chamber, this one lit by some kind of indirect lamps in the ceiling. They went in.

"You may remove your breathing apparatuses now," The Rel told them clearly. "Skander, will you pull Mar Hain's up and off? Thank you. Now, Hain, can you gently—gently—remove the two tubes from Citizen Chon's legs? Yes, that's right."

They all breathed in fresh air. It was stuffy, weak, and slightly uncomfortable to Vardia; to the others, it was exhilarating.

"You'll be all right in a little while, Citizen Chon," The Rel assured her. "The atmosphere is mostly pure oxygen, with just a trace of carbon dioxide. This will be added, both from our companions and artificially, in a little while."

There was another hissing sound, and one of the metallic creatures came out of a side door that had been almost invisible in the back wall. It was humanoid, about the same height as Vardia's 150 centimeters, and was featureless except for a triangular screen on the head.

"I trust all is satisfactory?" it said, in a voice pleasantly and unexpectedly filled with human tonality. It sounded, in fact, like an eager, middle-aged hotel clerk, far more human than The Rel's monotone.

"The green one, there, the Czillian, is a plant, not an animal," The Rel told the creature. "It requires carbon dioxide of at least point five percent. Will you raise the level? It is in much discomfort."

"Oh, I am so very, very sorry," the robot replied so sincerely that they almost believed it. "The matter is being adjusted."

Just like that Vardia *could* sense a difference, growing with every minute. She found it much easier to breathe, and the feeling that she was going to black out evaporated. Obviously these things were all linked together. The Czillian marveled at their efficiency, quietly envying their unity.

"What environments do you require?" the creature asked.

"Types Twelve, Thirty-one, One Twenty-six, and Thirteen Forty," The Rel told it. "Adjoining, with private intercom, please."

"It is being prepared," the robot assured them, and bowed slightly.

"What sort of a place *is* this?" Skander asked sharply.

The robot reared back, and Vardia swore that its featureless face had a shocked expression to match the tone of the reply.

"Why, this is a *first*-class transient hotel, of course. What else?"

One at a time they were taken to their rooms by small wheeled robots with place for luggage and the like. They put all their gear in storage, except for the air tanks, which were ordered cleaned and refilled, with particular attention to Vardia's getting the right gas.

Strong hands lifted Skander gently out of the saddle and onto the back of one of the carts. The scientist found herself traveling at high speed down a lighted tunnel, and deposited next to a room with no apparent exterior markings. It opened automatically, and the cart glided inside and stopped.

Skander was amazed. It was a swimming pool, with a dry slope going gently down into blue water which became deeper and deeper as it went toward the back of the room—the pool was perhaps fifteen meters long by about ten wide. In the water, clearly visible, were several small fish of the kind the Umiau liked the most, and clumps of the blue-green seaweed that was the other staple of their diet.

Skander rolled off and happily plunged into the water. It was only about four meters deep at its deepest point, but it felt wonderful.

The little cart left, the door closing behind it. It returned for Hain, who was too large for it. Another cart appeared in seconds, and the two, working in concert, took Hain down the same tunnel to the next door, which was furnished in the *zagrt* fur of the best nobles and was stocked with a nice supply of the juicy white worms.

Next, Vardia was taken to a room that had a rich black soil and good artificial sunlight. The room even had a chain dangling from its center, labeled, in

196

Czillian, *Pull for darkness. All guests awakened in eight hours after darkness pulled or twelve hours after occupancy.* There was a small pool of clear water in the corner, and even a small desk with paper and pen.

She guessed from her own surroundings what the others' must be like, and only wished she could see The Diviner and The Rel's room. That would almost certainly tell more about the mysterious creatures than anything seen so far.

There was a mild crackling sound in their rooms, and then The Rel's odd, toneless voice came to the other three.

"Please enjoy this night at the baron's expense," it said. "Tomorrow I shall arrange transportation for us which will take us to the border. We shall not have such pleasant and easy accommodations after this, so enjoy it. After tomorrow, things get tough."

Vardia took a long drink and then sank her roots into the rich soil that felt incredible, indescribable. With a feeling of total well-being, she turned off the lights.

Skander was the last to sleep, since the Umiau had been cooped up in the saddle harness and was enjoying the freedom of the waters. At last she, too, crawled up the bank and pressed the light switch on the wall.

Each of them slept soundly (except possibly for The Diviner and The Rel, who didn't seem to need it—the others weren't sure), and all were awakened not only by the automatic turning on of the lights but by the voice of The Rel.

The creature conveyed emotion for the first time, not by tone but by the sharp, fast, excited way it spoke. "Something is terribly wrong!" it told them. "We are being detained for some technicality! We cannot leave today!"

"Do you mean," Skander's voice came to all of them in a tone of almost total disbelief, "that we're under arrest?"

"It would seem so," replied The Rel. "I cannot understand it."

Murithel—Somewhere in the Interior

"WE'RE IN SOME KIND OF TROUBLE," NATHAN BRAZIL said half under his breath.

For three days now they had moved along the rocky mountain ledges, mostly under cover of darkness guided by Cousin Bat's exceptional night vision and inbred sonar. They had passed hundreds, perhaps thousands of the bloodthirsty Murnies, often coming close to their villages in the dark, quietly working around their dulled campfires.

They had been exceptionally lucky, and they knew it. But now they had run out of mountains.

The mountains—hills, really—ended abruptly in a jagged cliff, stretching off at an angle away from the direction they had to go. Ahead, toward the east, flat, unbroken prairie spread out to the horizon.

The land was still dry this time of year, yet yellow grasses topped with pinkish blossoms carpeted the prairie. Also covering the plains were herds of thousands, perhaps tens of thousands, of the antelope that were the Murnies' staple diet.

Murnie camps also dotted the plains, in small groups of three or four skin tents, never more than seven groups in a bunch, arranged in a circle.

Even as Brazil looked at the scene, appreciating their position, something, some wrongness ahead of him, nagged at his mind.

"How the hell are we ever going to get through them?" Wuju asked nervously. "We can't fight them all, even in the dark."

"Well, let's camp here for the day," Cousin Bat suggested, "and tonight I'll take a trip across and see how far we really have to go to reach cover. Maybe you'll think of something by the time I get back."

They agreed it was the only thing they could do, so they carved out a niche in the rocky ledge and tried to sleep, first Brazil on guard, then Bat, and finally Wuju. The sequence was almost a routine by now.

Nathan Brazil was dreaming more of his strange dreams when he felt hands gently shaking him. "Nathan!" Wuju whispered urgently. "Wake up! It's almost dark!"

He got up and tried to shake the sleep from his eyes. He was dizzy and upset from the small amount of food he had allowed himself from the dwindling supply in the packs. The deprivations were taking their toll on him. Wuju had it almost as bad, since there was precious little grass on the trail for one of her bulk. Yet she had never complained.

They all smelled like concentrated sweat and feces, and Brazil wondered idly if Murnies had good smellers. With no baths for three days and only leaves for toilet paper, he was certain that, in reverse circumstances, he could smell his party five kilometers upwind.

Cousin Bat was already waiting for the sun to sink completely behind them. Brazil went up to him quietly.

"You ready, Bat?" he asked the night creature.

"Not bad," came the reply. "The wind's wrong. If that plain's too broad I might have to come down at least once. I don't like that."

Brazil nodded. "Well, I want you to land if possible, or at least skim close enough to get me a handful of those weeds."

"Got something in mind?" the other asked.

"Maybe," he replied. "If we're lucky—and if we don't have to run to the border."

"I'll see what I can do," the bat replied dryly. "We've got to clear this bunch in one sweep, you know. Once committed, we'll have no place to hide."

Brazil looked at the creature strangely. "You know, I can't quite figure you out," he said.

"What's to figure?" Bat replied. "It's my neck, too, you know."

"Why not just fly over and away? You might not make it all the way in a stretch, but you could pick your own places. Why stick with us?"

The bat gave that ratty smile, exposing those triple rows of sharply pointed little teeth.

"To tell you the truth, I thought about it a number of times, particularly in the last few days. It's extremely tempting—all the more so now—but I can't do it."

"Why not?" pumped Brazil, puzzled.

The bat thought for a minute. "Let's just say that, once before, I was in a position to help some people I knew were in danger. I don't want more people on my conscience."

"We all have our crosses to bear," Brazil said in an understanding tone. "Myself more than most."

"It boils down to more than just conscience, Brazil," responded Cousin Bat earnestly. "I've known some other men. They, like me, wanted power, wealth, fame—all the reasons for striving. They'd lie, cheat, steal, torture, even kill for those. I want these things, too, Brazil, but what more right do I have to them than they? Perhaps, though I don't know for sure, the fact that they would abandon you and I would not makes me superior to them. I'd like to think so."

And with that, as the last rays of the sun disappeared behind the rocks to the west, Cousin Bat took off into the dark.

A few seconds later, Wuju sidled up behind Brazil. "What a strange man," she said wonderingly.

He gave a mirthless chuckle. "Bat, you mean? He let his guard down more there than I'd expected. It's the most personal thing we've gotten in all these days. But, no, strange is not the correct word for him. Unusual, perhaps, even uncommon. If he was telling the complete truth there, he's also a good friend, a particularly nasty enemy—and, quite possibly, one of the most potentially dangerous men I've yet met on this planet."

She didn't understand what he was talking about but didn't pursue it, either. Something much more important was on her mind.

"Nathan," she asked softly, "are we going to die?"

"I hope not," he replied lightly, trying to break the mood. "With luck—"

"The truth, Nathan!" she interrupted. "What are our chances?"

"Not good," he responded truthfully. "But I've been in spots as bad or worse in my long life. I survive, Wuju. I—" His voice broke off abruptly, and he averted his eyes from hers. She understood, and there were small tears in her eyes.

"But the people around you don't," she finished. "That's it, isn't it? That's *your* cross. How many times have you been a lone survivor?"

He looked out into the darkness for a minute. Then, without turning, he said, "I can't count that high, Wuju."

Cousin Bat returned in a little over an hour. Brazil and Wuju were doing something just inside the shelter, and he was curious.

They looked up from their work as he approached, and Brazil asked the simple but all-important question: "Well?"

"Five kilometers, give or take," the bat replied evenly. "Before you get any farther there's a steep drop to a river valley, mud sides with slow, shallow water. It's barely flowing."

Brazil seemed to brighten at the news, particularly of the river's speed and shallowness. "Can we get a straight run, more or less?" he asked.

The bat nodded. "Once we get down, I'll position you and point you in the right direction. I'll stay over you once you get started to keep you on the right track."

"Good! Good!" Brazil enthused. "Now, what about the antelope?"

"Tens of thousands of them," the other replied. "Together in big groups. Nothing too near us, though."

"Excellent! Excellent!" Brazil seemed to get more excited with every word. "And now the clincher—did you get some of that grass?"

Cousin Bat turned and walked back to where he had landed, picking up a clump of straw with one foot. Holding it, he hobbled back to them and dropped the grass at Brazil's feet.

The man picked it up expectantly, feeling it, even biting it. It was somewhat brittle, and gave a slight snap when it was bent too far.

"Just out of curiosity, what are you doing?" the bat asked.

Brazil reached down into a pouch and removed a small handful of the tiny sticks inside.

"Safety matches," he explained. "Haven't you noticed it, or thought about it, you two? Haven't you *seen* out there on the plain?"

They both looked at him with blank expressions. "I haven't seen anything except antelope, Murnies, and grass," said Wuju, trying to think.

"No! No!" Brazil responded, shaking his head animatedly. "Not what you *see!* What you *don't* see! Look out there into the darkness! Tell me what you see."

"Nothing but pitch darkness," Wuju said.

"Nothing but sleeping antelope, Murnies, and grass," Bat said.

"Exactly!" Brazil said excitedly. "But what you *don't* see, anywhere out there, is something we've seen in every Murnie camp we've passed up to this point."

They still didn't see it, and he continued after a pause. "Look, why do the Murnies build campfires? Not to cook their food—they eat it raw, even live. It's because they think this is cold! And to protect themselves from the dog packs at night, of course. It must be very important to them or we wouldn't have seen the campfires so consistently. *But there are no fires out there on the plains!* No dots of light, no sparks of any kind! And the riverbed's wide but slow and shallow is it flowing. You see what it means?"

"I think I do," Wuju replied hesitantly. "It's the dry season. Out there on the grasslands, the danger of a brushfire exceeds their fears of the dogs or their desire for warmth."

"It must be like a tinderbox out there," Brazil pointed out. "If they are afraid of any fire at all, it must be so dry that anything will set it off. If the wind's right, we can make things so hot for them down

202

there that the least thing they'll be concerned about is us."

"Wind's about as right as you can get," the bat said quietly.

"Okay, then," Brazil responded. He removed all his clothes, and jumped, stark naked, up on Wuju's back, his back against hers. He pulled the shirt around his chest just under his armpits. "Take the ends on both sides, Wuju, and tie them tight around you. No! Pull it *tight,* damn it! As tight as you can! Yes, that's better." Next the stretchy pants were pulled around his waist and tied in front of her. It was several minutes before he was satisfied that he was solidly attached to her, riding backward. Tied just in front of him were the packs, the two pouches full of safety matches within easy reach. Then he applied the rest of the Slongornian cooking fat to as much of his exposed parts as he could. It was a sloppy job, but it would do in the dark.

Cousin Bat nodded approvingly. The two men looked at each other wordlessly, and the bat turned and started down the rocky ledge. Wuju followed, Brazil cursing to himself at his inability to see anything ahead of them, thinking he forgot something, and feeling with every step that he was slipping off even though the knots remained secure.

"Stop!" he yelled suddenly, and everyone froze. "Your hair, Wuju! Tie it down. Use the scabbard— you have to hold the sword anyway. I don't want to set it on fire or have it blowing in my face."

She did what he asked silently, draping her hair forward and over her left breast so it wouldn't interfere with the sword in her right hand. Now Brazil was roped in three ways, and he felt as if he were cut in pieces. Which was just the way he wanted it.

They had gone over the plan many times, but he was still nervous. Wuju could sprint at more than thirty-five kilometers per hour, but that was just for short distances. She would have to go all out for over five kilometers, then down into a ditch, and keep running as long as she could.

Cousin Bat took off and circled for what was only a minute but seemed to be an hour. Finally they heard him come up behind them. "Now!" the flying creature ordered. *"Go!"*

Wuju took off across the plains at full speed.

Brazil watched the grasses disappear behind her and held onto the pack for dear life. He was sitting on a bony place and being bounced around for all he was worth. Although it was a clear night and he had excellent night vision, Brazil already could not see the rocky hills they had left.

Come on, Wuju! he thought tensely to himself. *Keep going!*

"Turn slightly right." Bat's voice came from somewhere above, and she did as instructed. "Too much!" She heard the bat's voice, probably just two or three meters above her head: "That's it! Now straight!"

Brazil panicked as he felt the upper bindings loosen, and he grabbed all the harder on the pack sides. And still she roared ahead at top speed! He could hear her take sobbing breaths and feel her horselike half inhale and exhale mightily, but still they went on.

We're going to make it! he thought excitedly. *If I can only hold on to this goddamn pack for a few more minutes, we'll be through them before they realize what happened!*

Suddenly the knots from the top two bands broke, sending the elastic clothing into the night and propelling him forward, headfirst, into the pack.

"Nathan!" he heard her call breathlessly at the break and jerk.

"I'm all right!" he called back. "Keep going!"

Suddenly there were sounds around them, grunts, groans, and yells.

"Nathan!" she screamed. "They're ahead of us!"

"Run right at them at top speed!" he yelled. "Slash with your sword!" He grabbed at the matches, struck several against the hard leather straps. They flared, but immediately went out because of the wind caused by her rapid movement.

Suddenly she was heading into them, and they were roaring and clawing at her. She knocked the first several down and found, to her surprise, that the sword seemed to slice into them like butter. Once, twice more, she slashed at them, and they screamed in deep agony and clutched at wounds.

And then she was through them!

"Any ahead?" Brazil yelled.

"Not yet," came Bat's voice. "Keep going!"

"There's plenty behind us!" Nathan called. "Slow down to a gallop so I can get at least one match lit!"

Wuju slowed and he tried again. They stayed lit in his hands, but went out before they hit the ground.

"Brazil!" Bat's voice called urgently. "A whole bunch of them! Coming up fast to your right!"

Suddenly a group of six or seven came at them out of the grasses. Nathan felt a searing pain in his right leg. One Murnie jumped and hit Wuju's backside, tearing a deep gash in her just in front of the pack. She screamed, stopped, and reared, slashing out at them with her sword.

Brazil hung on somehow, and tore off one of the pouches of matches with strength that surprised him. He struck one and threw it into the pouch. The matches caught with a *whoomph* and he threw the pack out onto the grass.

Nothing for a minute, and she bolted for the Murnies at an apparent opening. They had formed a hunting circle and their spears were ready.

They expected the charge, but their traditional ways didn't allow for their quarry to have a sword, and the formation broke.

Suddenly the whole world caught fire.

The suddenness and volatility was what stunned them all.

My god! Brazil thought suddenly. *It's as if the stuff were made of cellulose!*

He could see Cousin Bat, saw the creature come down on a Murnie and kick with those powerful, handlike feet rolled up as fists. The giant green savage went down and didn't move.

The whole world suddenly became bright. Ahead she saw the stream valley, like a crack in the land.

The Murnies started running and screaming. The

antelope panicked and ran in all directions, trampling many Murnies underfoot to get away.

She jumped into the ravine, and the momentum and steep sides caused her to lose her balance. She went sprawling down the hill. Brazil felt himself suddenly free as he was flung away onto the bank. He was stunned for a minute, then he picked himself up and looked around. There was a glow still from the fire above, but down in the valley there was a still, near-absolute darkness.

Feeling numb and dizzy, he ran down the valley in the direction Cousin Bat had said the river flowed. He looked around for Wuju but couldn't see her anywhere.

"Wuju!" he screamed hoarsely. *"Wuju!"* But his voice was no match for the riot of noise above him, the cries of burning animals and panicked Murnies, many of whom were plunging over the bank into the valley.

He ran down the muddy shore and into the river and followed it. The rocky bottom cut his feet. But he was oblivious to pain, running like a scarecrow, mindlessly, aimlessly down the river.

Soon the glow and the sounds were far behind him, but still he pressed on. Suddenly he tripped and fell facedown in the water. He continued, crawling forward, then somehow picked himself up and started again.

The fetid odor of swamp mud was all around him and all over him, yet he continued. Until, quite abruptly, everything caught up to him and he collapsed, unconscious before he hit the water, stones, and mud.

The Nation—a First-class Hotel

THEY HAD NOT, AS IT HAPPENED, BEEN ARRESTED. They had been quarantined. The way the robot manager explained it, an analysis of the particles found in their waste gases had revealed two of them to have certain microscopic life forms that could cause corrosion problems in The Nation. They were, therefore, being held until their laboratories could check out the organisms, develop some sort of serum, and introduce it to them so they could safely get across the country without causing difficulties.

For Hain this was her first real vacation since entering this crazy world, and she lazed, relaxed, and seemed in no hurry to go on.

The Diviner and The Rel accepted the situation indignantly but with resignation; it kept pretty much to itself.

Since their hosts had evacuated the wing in which the four were staying, they were allowed to visit one another. Vardia was the only mobile person who cared to do so; she started going to Skander's room regularly.

The Umiau welcomed the company, but refused to talk about her theories on the Well World or to discuss the object of their journey for fear that other ears were listening.

"Why do we have to go through with this?" Vardia asked the scholar one day.

The Umiau raised her eyebrows in surprise. "We're still prisoners, you know," she pointed out.

"But we could tell the management," the Czillian suggested. "After all, kidnapping is a crime."

"It is, indeed," the mermaid agreed, "but that is also unheard of cross-hex. The fact is, these people don't *care* if we're prisoners, victims, or monsters. It just isn't their concern. I've tried."

"Then we must escape once we're back on the road," she persisted. "I've already seen a map—it's in a desk in my room. The next hex borders the ocean."

"That won't work," Skander replied firmly. "First of all, we have no idea as to the powers of this Northerner, and I don't want to test them. Secondly, Hain can fly and walk faster than you, and either one of us is just a few good mouthfuls for her. No, put that out of your mind. Besides, we'll not be ill-served in this. In the end, I have the ultimate control over us all, because they can't do a thing without the knowledge I possess. They are taking me where I want to go and could not get myself. No, I think we'll go along with them—until midnight at the Well of Souls," she added with a devious chuckle.

"That's about how long we'll be kept here," Vardia said grumpily.

The Umiau reclined lazily in the shallow end of the pool. "Nothing we can do about this. Meantime, why not tell me something about yourself? You know all about me, really."

"I really don't have much of a history before coming here," she responded modestly. "I was a courier—wiped clean after every mission."

The mermaid clucked sympathetically. "But surely," she urged, "you know about your world—the world of your birth, that is. For instance, were you born or hatched? Were you male or female? What?"

"I was produced by cloning in Birth Factory Twelve on Nueva Albion," she said. "All reproduction is by cloning, using the cellular tissues of the top people in history of each occupational group. Thus, all Diplos on or of Nueva Albion were cloned from the Sainted Vardia, who was the go-between in the revolution several centuries ago. She kept contact between the Liberation Front on Coriolanus and the Holy Revolutionaries in reactionary Nueva Albion. Thus, I carried her genes, her resemblance, and her job. My number, Twelve Sixty-one, said I was the sixty-first Vardia clone from Birth Factory Twelve."

Skander felt a sourness growing in her stomach. So that's what mankind has come to, she thought. Almost two-thirds of mankind reduced to clones, numbers—less human than the mechs of this absurd Nation.

"Then you were a woman," the Umiau said conversationally, not betraying her darker inner thoughts.

"Not really," she replied. "Cloning negates the need for sexes, and sexes represent sexism which promotes inequality. Depending on the clone model, development is chemically and surgically arrested. All glands, hormone production, and the like are removed, changed, or neutralized permanently, in my case on my eleventh birthday. We are also given hysterectomies, and males are castrated, so that it is impossible to tell male or female after the turning age. Every few years we were supposed to get a complete treatment that kept the aging processes arrested and freshened the body, so that one couldn't tell a fifty-year-old from a fifteen-year-old."

Outwardly the Umiau remained impassive, but internally Skander was so depressed that she felt nauseated.

Ye gods! the archaeologist swore to herself. A small, carefully bred cadre of supermen and superwomen ruling a world of eunuch children raised to unquestioning obedience! I was right to have killed them! Monsters like that—in control of the Well! Unthinkable!

They should all be killed, she knew, hatred welling up inside of her. The masters who were the most monstrous of spawn, and the masses of poor impersonal blobs of children—billions of them, probably. Best to put them out of their misery, she thought sadly. They weren't really people anyway.

Suddenly her thoughts turned to Varnett. Same idea, Skander thought. Although the boy hadn't come from a world as far gone as Nueva Albion, it would go that way in time. Names disappear on one world, sex on another, then all get together to form a universe of tiny, mindless, sexless, nameless organic robots, programmed and totally obedient—but so, so happy.

Varnett—brilliant, a truly great mind, yet childish, immature, in thousands of ways as programmed as his cousins whom he despised. What sort of a world, what sort of a universe, would Varnett create?

The Markovians had understood, she reflected. They knew.

I won't betray them! she swore intensely. I won't let anyone wreck the great dream! I will get there first! Then they'll see! I'll destroy them all!

Murithel—Somewhere in the Interior

COUSIN BAT CIRCLED AROUND FEELING HELPLESS. Maybe I can pick him up, he thought, looking at Brazil's battered and bleeding body in the mud. He's not a very big fellow, and I've moved some pretty heavy rocks with these legs.

He was about to give it a try when a group of Murnies came running up the valley. They got to Brazil's unconscious body before Bat could do anything at all, and the night creature thought, It's all over. They'll chomp him into pieces for a late snack now.

But they didn't. Four of the savages stayed with the body, while two others made for the top of the valley and the plains above. Fascinated, Bat stayed with them, balancing on the air currents.

The two returned a few minutes later with a litter made with tough branches for poles and, apparently, woven grass for the stretcher. Carefully they placed Brazil on the litter. One Murnie picked up the front, the other took the rear. They climbed the bank effortlessly, and Bat followed them, still invisible in the dark.

Darkness had returned to the plain as well. Bat was amazed to see hundreds, perhaps thousands, of Murnies beating a large, smoldering area about a thousand meters from the valley where they had plunged. It was a well-coordinated, well-rehearsed fire brigade, with the bulk of the Murnies beating out the last sparks with skin blankets, while an apparently endless chain of the creatures ran a bucket brigade from the creek all the way to the fire scene.

These are savages? Bat asked himself wonderingly. The teamwork and skillful handling of the fire he could not reconcile in his mind with the toothy carnivores who chased live prey with primitive spears and attacked them fiercely with spear and claw.

Brazil's unmoving form was hauled into a small camp away from the fire scene. A particularly huge Murnie, his light green skin laced with dark brown, examined the man and started barking orders. Even though Bat's translator would—should—pick up what the big one was saying, he dared not get close enough to hear.

The big Murnie got a bucket of water and started to wash Brazil's wounds with a gentleness that surprised the bat. Others brought a large hide case and a number of leaves. The big one opened the laces on the case, and from its interior pulled out varicolored jars of what looked like mud and more leaves, some apparently kept soaked in some solution in jars.

Slowly, methodically, the big one administered the muds to Brazil's open wounds, and used the leaves to form a compress for the man's head.

He's a doctor! Cousin Bat realized suddenly. They're treating him!

Bat felt better, almost relaxed enough to leave, but he did not.

Those wounds are tremendous, he noted. The man's lost huge amounts of blood, and probably has multiple breaks, concussion, and shock. Even if the medicine man knew the art of transfusion, there is none to give the blood.

Brazil will be dead within hours, no matter what magic this creature can work, Bat realized sadly. But what can I do? And, if they somehow cure him—what then? Prisoner? Pet? Plaything? Slave?

The Murnie medicine man gestured, and a smaller tribesman came into camp leading a huge stag antelope. It was the largest such animal Bat had ever seen, light brown with a white stripe running from the back of the head to the stubby tail, a large set of eerie-looking antlers atop that head. The stag was docile, too much so to be normal, Bat knew. It was drugged or something. He saw with amazement that the deer-like animal wore a collar of carefully twisted skin, from which a small stone dangled.

Someone owns that animal, Bat reflected. Do these savages of the plain breed their food?

Into camp from different directions came five more Murnies, looking like the witch doctor—really large ones, with that curious brown discoloration, more pronounced on some than others.

Six, thought the bat. Of course it would be six. Primitives went in for mystic numbers, and if any number had power here that one certainly did.

They put the stag so that it faced Brazil, and all six moved close. Three of them placed their right hands on the unflinching stag, and took the right hands of the other three in their left. The other three all placed their left hands on Brazil's body.

Bat stayed aloft as long as he could, but finally decided he had to land. He was just coming out of the fight, and the exhilaration and extra pep that had flowed through him had waned. Reluctantly, he made for the valley and flew along until he found a place with no Murnies in the immediate vicinity. He landed, breathing hard, thinking of what he could do.

In a few minutes he had his wind back, and decided on a plan that the odds said were ridiculous.

He had to try.

No more running, he told himself. If I can do it, I'll do it.

He took off and flew back to the camp, seeing that he was in luck. The stag was staked to a post in the ground, apparently asleep, away from Brazil, who was covered with the mud compounds and leafy stuff, still in the open.

Brazil weighed around fifty kilos, he guessed. The litter? Five more? Ten? I can't do it, he thought suddenly, fear shooting through him. That much weight, for all that distance!

212

Suddenly he thought of the Dillian girl. He had lost track of her while following Brazil, but he couldn't take the time now. Nothing he could do in her case regardless, he knew. But she had run all out, all that distance on the ground, never stopping, cut and speared—way beyond her limits, while hungry and weak.

You've been eating well, Bat told himself sternly. You're as big and strong and healthy as you'll ever be. If she can do it . . .

Without another thought he swooped down to Brazil, and took one side of the litter, folding it over so he held both branches in his feet with Brazil wrapped in the middle. He took a quick glance around. So far so good. Now—could he take off, no ledge, no running start, with this load?

He started beating his great wings furiously, aided by a timely gust of wind that rustled the grass across the plain. He rose, and beat all the more furiously. Too low! he thought nervously. Got to get height!

The furious flapping brought Murnies running from their tents, including the big one.

"No! No! Come back!" the medicine man screamed, but the wind picked up and Bat was on his way, over the stream and down along its course, the unconscious Brazil hanging from the folded litter. Cousin Bat did not believe in gods or prayers, yet he prayed as he struggled to keep up speed, height, and balance. Prayed he would make it to Czill and to modern medicine without killing Brazil, himself, or both.

With shock and dismay the medicine man watched Bat fly into the darkness.

"Ogenon!" he called in a deep, rough voice.

"Yes, Your Holiness?" a smaller, weaker voice replied.

"You saw?"

"The body of the honored warrior has been taken by the one who flies," Ogenon responded in a tone that seemed to wonder why such a stupid question had been asked.

"The flying one is ignorant of us and our ways, or he would not have done this," the medicine man said as much to himself as to his aide. "He flew east, so

213

he's taking the body to Czill. I'll need a strong runner to get to the border. Now, don't look at me like that! I know how foul the air is over there, but this has to be done. The Czillians must realize when they see the warrior's body and hear the winged one's story what has happened, but, if the body survives—not likely—they will not know of the survival of the essence. Go!"

Ogenon found a warrior willing to make the trip in short order, and the medicine man instructed him what to say and to whom, impressing on the runner the need for speed. "Do the message in relays," the old one said. "Just make sure it is continuous and that it is not garbled."

Once the instructions were given and the runner was off into the darkness, the large Murnie turned again to his aide, who was looking extremely bleary-eyed and was yawning repeatedly.

"Get awake, boy!" snapped the elder. "Now, locate the six-limbed creature and tell me where it is."

"That's simple, Your Holiness," Ogenon responded sleepily. "The six-limbed one is under treatment at the Circle of Nine. I saw it being dragged there."

"Good," the old one replied. "Now, you'll have to go to the Base Camp and bring an elder to me, Elder Grondel by name."

"But that's—" Ogenon started to protest, yawning again.

"I know how far it is!" the big one roared. "You can make it there and back before dawn!"

"But suppose the Revered Elder won't come," the aide wailed, trying to get out of the assignment and to get back to sleep.

"He'll come," the medicine man replied confidently. "Just describe to him the three alien creatures we've had here this night, and tell him particularly of the honored warrior and of what has happened. He'll beat you here, I'll wager, even though he's eighty years old! Now, off with you! *Now!*"

Ogenon went, grumbling about how everybody kicked him around and he always had to do everything.

Once out of sight, the elder couldn't hold back his own yawns anymore, yet he didn't return to his tent

214

and mat but sat down in the, for him, very chilly night air.

All he could do now was wait.

Wuju relived the nightmare run for hours, then, suddenly, woke up.

I must still be dreaming, she thought. Everything was fuzzy and she was feeling quite high. She couldn't believe what she saw.

She was in a Murnie camp, in the earliest light of dawn, and there were horribly loud and grotesque snores all around her. Sitting in front of her, arms around its knees, was the biggest Murnie she had ever seen—taller than she, and she stood over two meters. It was also oddly colored, on the whole a deeper brown than she, laced only here and there with spots of the light green that was the usual color of these strange creatures.

From a distance they had looked like walking rectangular bushes. But here, up close, she saw that they had a rough skin that folded and sagged, like partially melted plastic, all over their body. They looked like a large trunk of a body with no head, she thought. The eyes, huge as dinner plates, were located where the breasts should be, and perhaps thirty centimeters below them was that enormous mouth, a huge slit that seemed almost to cleave the trunk in two. There was no sign of hair, genitals, or, for that matter, a nose and ears.

The drug or whatever it was seemed to be wearing off more and more. This isn't a dream! she thought suddenly, as fear ran through her. She tried to move, but found her legs were all roped to stakes deep in the ground, and her hands were tied behind her. She struggled in panic to pull free, and the sound woke up the big brown Murnie. Its huge eyes opened, deep yellow with perfectly round, black irises that reflected the light almost like a cat's.

"Do not struggle," the creature said to her. The words were mushy, as if they were uttered in the midst of a roar, but they were understandable. It was speaking a language it knew but its mouth was not suited to its use.

215

"I said do not struggle!" the Murnie repeated, getting up and stretching in a very human fashion. "You are quite safe. No one will harm you. Can you understand me? Nod if you can."

Wuju nodded fearfully, panic still all over her face.

"All right, now listen well. It is difficult for me to speak this tongue, and I must concentrate carefuly to get the words out. You can understand me, but I cannot understand you, I don't think. Say something."

"What—what is all this?" she almost screamed.

The Murnie scratched his behind with his huge, wide hand. The arms were almost to the ground when drooping by his side. "I thought so. I could not understand a word. You have no translator. You must concentrate hard, like me. Think, then answer. What language am I using?"

She thought for a second, then suddenly realized the truth. "Confederacy!" she exclaimed, amazed. "You are an Entry!"

"All right. I got Confederacy but nothing else. That is because all Entries continue to think in their original tongue. What they say is automatically transformed in the neural passages to the language of the native hex. You can understand me, therefore you can speak it as I do if you think hard, make your mouth form the word you think. Take it slowly, one word at a time. Tell me your name and the name of your companions. Then try a simple phrase, one word at a time."

Wuju concentrated, the fear and panic evaporating. Once this one had been one of her own kind! A potential friend she would need most of all here. As she started to speak she saw what he meant, and adjusted.

"I-ahm-Wuju," she managed, and it almost sounded right. Her mouth and tongue wanted to make a different set of words. "Moy frandiz ahar Nathan Brazil ind Cooseen Baht."

"Nathan Brazil!" the big Murnie exclaimed excitedly, suddenly very wide awake. The rest of what he said was unintelligible.

My god! she thought. Does everybody on this crazy planet know Nathan?

The Murnie suddenly frowned, and scratched the

216

side of his head thoughtfully. "But the other was an old-culture man by description," he mused, suddenly looking at her again with those huge yellow eyes. "You mean he still looked like his old self?" She nodded, and his great mouth opened in surprise. "I wonder why he wasn't changed in the Well?"

"Whahr est Nathan?" she managed.

"Well, that's really the problem," the Murnie answered. "You see, he's sort of in two places at once."

He was a former freighter pilot like Brazil, the native told her, on the line for over two hundred years, facing his fourth rejuve and with all his family and friends dead, his world so changed he couldn't go home. He had decided to commit suicide, to end the loneliness, when he got a funny distress signal in the middle of nowhere. He had veered to investigate, when suddenly his ship had seemed to cease to exist around him, and he had fallen into the Zone Well and wound up a Murnie.

"They are good people," he told her. "Just very different. They can use nothing not found in nature or made by hand. No machines at all. They are bisexual, like us—although an alien couldn't tell who was who. Strong families, communal, with a strong folk art and music—herdsmen who breed the antelope we eat. Very hostile to strangers, though—they would have killed you last night."

"Den woi om I ailoif?" she managed.

"You're alive," he replied, "because you killed about two dozen warriors, directly that is, plus the fire and the like."

She didn't understand, and said so.

"The Murnie nation accepts death naturally," he explained. "We don't fear it, nor dwell on it. We live for each day. It's far more enjoyable that way. What are respected most and valued most are honor and courage. You all displayed that last night! It took raw courage to run the plain, and great honor to keep going until you dropped rather than give in. If you had surrendered, they would still have killed you. But they found both you and Brazil, badly wounded, unconscious in different parts of the stream bed. It would

217

have been cowardly and dishonorable to have killed you. You had gained respect—so they dragged each of you to the camp nearest where you were found, and your injuries were tended to. Our medicine is quite advanced—this is a rough hex."

"Nathan!" she exclaimed. "Ist hay arriot?"

"He was banged up much worse than you," the Murnie replied gravely. "You're going to hurt for a while when the herbal anesthetic wears off, but you have nothing more than four or five deep scratches on your back and a lot of bruises. We have treated them, but they will ache." He paused for a second. "But Brazil, he was much worse. I don't know how he kept going. It's not possible. He should be dead, or, at best, totally paralyzed, yet he walked almost a kilometer down that streambed before collapsing. What an incredible will he must have! The Murnies will sing stories of him and tell of his greatness for centuries! In addition to the hundreds of minor bone breaks, the enormous amount of blood he lost from gaping wounds, and a badly lacerated leg, he had a broken back and neck. He got a kilometer with a broken back and neck!"

She thought of poor Nathan, twisted and bleeding, paralyzed and comatose. The thought made her sick, and it was several minutes and several attempts before she could concentrate on speaking Confederacy again. Tears welled up in her eyes, and she couldn't stop crying for several minutes. The fierce-looking Murnie stood there feeling helpless and sympathetic.

Finally she managed, "Ist—hay ist stull aliff?"

"He is still alive," the Murnie replied gravely. "Sort of."

"Hay ist oncun—uncrunchus?"

"Unconscious, yes," the Murnie replied. "I said, remember, that this was a rough hex that prized honor and courage, and had a lot of knowledge and wisdom within its limits. Because Murithel is totally nontechnological, the inhabitants have turned, aside from herbal compounds and muds, to the powers of the mind. Some of these doctors—and they *are* doctors—have enormous mental powers. I don't understand the

218

powers, and I doubt if they do. These people study and concentrate over half their lives to develop the powers. By the time they're strong enough to be useful, the wise men—Holy Ones we call them—are elderly, sometimes with only a few years to live and to teach the next generation." He paused again, and started pacing nervously, trying to think of how to say it.

"When Brazil was brought in so battered and close to death," he said carefully, "he was already, because of his tremendous courage, the most legendary character ever to be here. The Holy One who examined him did what he could, but saw that death was probable no matter what. He summoned five others—six is a magic number here, for obvious reasons—and they performed a Transference of Honor. It has only been done three or four times since I've been here—it shortens the life spans of the Holy Ones by a year or more. They reserve it for the greatest of honor and courage." He stopped again, his tone changing. "Look, I can see you don't understand. It is difficult to explain such things when I don't understand it, either. Umm. . . . Are you a follower of any religion?"

The idea of religion was extremely funny to her, but she answered gently, "No."

"Few of us are—or were, in my day, and I'm sure it's worse now. But here, against these hills and on these plains, you learn that you are ignorant of almost everything. Call it mechanical, if you will, a part of the Markovian brian's powers, like our own transformations and this world itself, but accept it: that which is us, our memories, our personality, whatever, can be not only transformed but transferred. Now I—stop looking at me like that! I am *not* insane. I've seen it!"

"Arrh sou stelling moi daht Nathan ist naow e Murnie?" she asked, unwilling to believe but unwilling to disbelieve, either. Too much had already happened to her on this crazy world.

"Not a Murnie," he replied evenly. "That would involve superimposing his—well, they call it his 'essence' —on somebody else. No, when someone's so respected that he rates a Transference of Honor, he is transferred to the best thoroughbred breeding stag or doe.

Don't look so shocked—they are of such high quality that they are instantly recognized. No one would eat them, or even bother them.

"If, then, the body can be successfully brought back to health—which is rare or the Holy Ones would never do the Transference in the first place—he is switched back. If not, he is revered, cared for, and has a happy and peaceful life on the plains."

"Nathan est un ahntlupe?" she gasped. It was becoming easier to talk, although her pronunciation was still terrible.

"A beautiful pure stag," the Murnie acknowledged. "I've seen him. He's still drugged. I didn't want him coming out of that state until you and I were both there to explain it to him."

"Ist der—ist der unny chants dot hes boody wall liff?" she asked.

"Will his body live?" the Murnie repeated. "I'm sure I don't know. I honestly doubt it, but I would have said that the Transference of Honor was more likely than going a kilometer with a game leg, a broken back, and busted neck. The outcome will depend on how much damage he receives beyond what's already done."

Then he told her of Cousin Bat's rescue. "He obviously could not consider us civilized or Brazil anything more than the victim of primitive medicine. Would you? So he plucked Brazil's body up and is even now taking it to Czill where they have a modern hospital. If the body survives the trip—and from what was told me I doubt if it survived the night, let alone the trip—the Czillians will know what happened. One of our people is getting the news to them sometime today just in case. They can sustain the body's functions indefinitely if it's still alive, though an empty vessel. Their computers know of the Transference of Honor. If they can heal the body, it can be returned here for retransference, but that is not something to pin your hopes on.

"I said I experienced three Transferences in my eighty years. Of them all, none of the bodies lasted the night."

Nathan Brazil awoke feeling strange. Everything looked strange, too.

He was on the Murnie plain, he could see that—and it was daylight.

So I've survived again, he thought.

Things looked crazy, though, as if they were seen through a fish-eye camera lens—his field of vision was a little larger than he was used to, but it was a round picture vastly distorted. Things around the periphery looked close up; but as the view went toward the center of the field of view, everything seemed to move away as if he were looking down a tunnel. The picture was incredibly clear and detailed, but the distortion as things around the field of view bent toward the fixed center made it difficult to judge distances. And the whole world was brown—an incredible number of shades of brown and white.

Brazil turned his head and looked around. The distortion and color blindness stayed constant.

And he felt funny, crazy, sort of.

He thought back. He remembered the mad dash, the fire, falling off Wuju—then everything was dark.

This is crazy, he thought.

His hearing was incredibly acute. He heard everything crystal-clear, even voices and movements far away. It took him several minutes to sort out the chatter, finally assigning about eighty percent of it to things he could see.

There were Murnies moving around, and they all seemed to be light brown to him, although he remembered them as green. Suddenly he heard footsteps near him, and he turned to see a huge Murnie that was all very deep brown coming toward him.

I must be drugged, he told himself. These are aftereffects of some drug they gave me.

The big Murnie ambled up to him.

I must be standing upright on a rack or something, he thought. I'm as tall as he is, and he's at least two meters, judging by his size, large compared to the run-of-the-Murnie crowd around.

Two grossly distorted Murnie hands took his head, lowered it slightly, so the creature was looking right into Brazil's eyes.

221

The Murnie grunted, and said, in Confederacy, "Ah! Awake, I see! Don't try to move yet—I want to let you down easy before that. No! Don't try to talk! You can't, so don't bother."

The creature walked a few steps in front of him and sat down tiredly on the grass.

"I haven't slept in over a day and a half," the Murnie said with a sigh. "It feels good just to relax." He shifted to a more comfortable position, and considered where to begin.

"Look, Nate," he began, "first things first. You know I'm an Entry, and I've been told I'm not the first one who knew you that you've run into here. It kinda figures. Well, if your mind can go back ninety years, you might remember Shel Yvomda. Do you? If so, shake your head."

Brazil thought. It was an odd name, he should remember it—but there were so many people, so many names. He tried to shrug, found he couldn't, and so moved his head slowly from side to side.

"Oh, well, it doesn't matter. They call me the Elder Grondel now, Elder because I've lived longer than fifty years here and that makes for respect. Grondel is their name—means The Polite Eater, because I continue to be civilized. I'm one of two people in Murithel who can still speak Confederacy. We would have lost it, except we ran into each other and practice for old times' sake. Well, enough of that. I guess I'd better tell you what happened. You aren't gonna like this, Nate."

Brazil was stunned, but he accepted the situation and understood why they had done it and why they had thought it necessary. He even felt a deep affection for Cousin Bat in spite of the fact that he had fouled up the works.

As they sat there, the last of the drug wore off, and he suddenly found himself free to move.

He looked as far down as possible first, and thought, crazily, This is what Wuju must have seen when she first appeared in Dillia. Long, short-furred legs, much more graceful than hers, with dark hooves.

He turned his head and saw his reflection against the tent nearby.

He was a magnificent animal, he thought with no trace of humor. And the antlers! So that's why his head felt so funny!

He tried to move forward, and felt a tug. The Murnie laughed, and unfastened him from the stake.

He walked around on four legs for the first time, slowly, just around in circles.

So this is what it feels like to be changed, he thought. Strange, but not uncomfortable.

"There are some hitches, Nate," Grondel said. "It's not like a transformation. The body you have is that of a great animal, but not a dominant species. You've got no hands, tentacles, or any other thing except your snout to pick things up with, and you've got no voice. These antelope are totally silent, no equipment to make a noise. And your only defenses are your speed —which is considerable, by the way, cruising at fifteen or more kilometers per hour, sprints up to sixty—and a tremendous kick with the rear legs. And the antlers —those are permanent; they don't shed and won't grow unless broken off."

Brazil stopped walking and thought for a while. Arms he could do without if necessary, and the rest— but not being able to talk bothered him.

Suddenly he stopped and stared at himself. All the time he had been thinking, he had been automatically leaning over and munching grass!

He looked back at Grondel, who just was watching him curiously.

"I think I can guess what you just realized," the Murnie said at last. "You just started munching grass without thinking. Right?"

Brazil nodded, feeling stranger than before.

"Remember—you, *all* of that inner self that's you —was transferred, but it was superimposed on the remarkably dull antelope brain and nervous system. Superimposed, Nate—not exchanged. Unless you directly countermand it, the deer's going to continue acting like a deer, in every way. That's automatic, and instinctive. You're not man *into* deer, you're man *plus* deer."

Brazil considered it. There would be some prob-

223

lems, then, particularly since he was a brooder, given to introspection. What did a deer do? Ate, slept, copulated. Hmmm. . . . The last would cause problems.

There were, as Grondel had said, many hitches.

How do I fit inside this head? he wondered. All of my memories—more, perhaps, than any other man. Weren't memories chemical? He could see how the chemical chains could at least be duplicated, the brainwave pattern adjusted—but how did this tiny brain have room for it all?

"Nate!" He heard a call, and looked up. Grondel was running toward him from whatever distance this fish-eye vision couldn't tell him. He would get used to it, he thought.

He had moved. As he brooded, he had wandered out of the camp and over almost to the herd! He turned and ran back to the camp, surprised at the ease and speed with which he ran, but he slowed when he realized that the distorted vision would take some getting used to. He almost ran the Murnie down.

He started to apologize, but nothing came out.

The Murnie sympathized. "I don't know the answer, Nate. But get used to it before doing anything rash. Your body's either dead or it'll be even better the longer you give it in Czill. Hey! Just thought of something. Come over here to this dirt patch!"

He followed the Murnie curiously.

"Look!" Grondel said excitedly, and made a line in the dirt with his foot. "Now you do it!"

Brazil understood. It was slow and didn't look all that good, but after a little practice he managed to trace the letters in the dirt with his hoof.

"WHERE IS WUJU?" he traced.

"She's here, Nate. Want to see her?"

Brazil thought for a second, then wrote, very large, "NO."

The Murnie rubbed out the old letters so it was again a virgin slate. "Why not?" he asked.

"DOES SHE KNOW ABOUT ME?" Brazil wrote.

"Yes. I—I told her last night. Shouldn't I have?"

Brazil was seething; a thousand things raced through his mind, none of them logical.

"DON'T WANT," he had traced when he heard Wuju's voice.

"Nathan?" she called more than asked. "Is that really you in there?"

He looked up and turned. She was standing there, looking awed, shaking her head back and forth in disbelief.

"It's him," Grondel assured her. "See? We've been communicating. He can write here in the dirt."

She looked down at the marks and shook her head sadly. "I—I never learned how to read," she said, ashamedly.

The Murnie grunted. "Too bad," he said. "Would have simplified things." He turned back to Brazil. "Look, Nate, I know you well enough to know that you'll head off for Czill as soon as you're confident of making the trip. I know how you feel, but you *need* her. *We* can't go, wouldn't if we could. And somebody's got to know you're you, to keep you from straying, and to do your talking for you. You need her, Nate."

Brazil looked at them both and thought for a minute, trying to understand his own feelings. Shame? Fear?

No, dependence, he thought.

I've never been dependent on anyone, but now I need somebody. For the first time in my long life, I need somebody.

He was dependent on Wuju, almost as much as she had been dependent on him in the early stages of their relationship.

He tried to think up logical reasons for that not being the case, to rationalize his feelings, but he could not.

He traced in the dirt, "BUT I'M NOW BIGGER THAN YOU ARE."

Grondel laughed and read it to her. She laughed, too.

Then he wrote: "TELL HER ABOUT DEER PART." Grondel understood, and explained how Brazil was really two beings—one man, one animal—and how he had already lapsed into deer while thinking.

She understood. When still, such as during the night,

225

he would have to be staked like a common deer to keep him from wandering away. And he couldn't even drive his own stake!

Dependence. It grated on him as nothing ever had, but it had the feel of inevitability.

He hoped fervently that his body was still alive.

Grondel had finally collapsed in sleep and was snoring loudly in a nearby tent.

Brazil and Wuju were alone for the first time, he suffering the indignity of being staked so he couldn't wander off.

They had worked most of the day on his getting used to the body, adjusting to the vision and color blindness, the supersensitive senses of hearing and smell. The speed in his sprint amazed him and Wuju both. As fast as she had seemed when he was human, she now seemed terribly slow, ponderous, and exhausted while he was still feeling great. He also discovered that his hind-leg kick could shatter a small tree.

A few things were simplified, of course. No packs needed now, he could eat what she ate. No drag on speed—he could run as fast as Cousin Bat could fly, maybe faster for short periods.

If only he could talk! Make some sort of sound!

Wuju looked at him admiringly. "You know, you're really beautiful, Nathan. I hope they have mirrors in Czill." She still talked mildly distorted, but Grondel had been forcing her to use the old language so much during the past day and a half that it was becoming easier, like a second language.

She came and stood beside him, pressing her equine body against his sleek, supermuscled antelope body. She started to rub him, actually pet him gently.

His mind rebelled, though he didn't try to pull away or stop her.

I'm getting excited as hell! he thought, surprised. And, from the feel of it, there was a lot of him to get excited.

His first impulse was to stop her, but instead he moved his head over and started nuzzling her neck

226

with his muzzle. She leaned forward, so his antlers wouldn't get in the way.

Is it the animal, or do I want to do this? a corner of his mind asked, but the thought slipped away as irrelevant, as was the thought that they were still two very, very different species.

He stroked her equine back with the bottom of his snout and got to the bony hind end. She sighed and slipped off the leash that was attached to his hind leg. They continued.

This was a crazy, insane way to have sex, but the deer in him showed him how.

Wuju finally had what she wanted from Nathan Brazil.

Brazil awoke feeling really fine, the best in many long years. He glanced over at Wuju, still asleep, although the sun had been up for an hour.

Isn't it funny, he thought. The transformation, the commitment, the crisis, and the way those people had served me have all come together to do what nothing else had.

He remembered.

He remembered it *all*, all the way back.

He understood, finally, what he had been doing before, what he was doing now, why he survived.

He considered the vessel he wore. Not of his own choosing, of course, but it was serviceable if he could just get a voice.

How great a change to know it all! His mind was absolutely clear, certain, now that everything was laid out before him. He was in total control now, he knew.

Funny, he thought, that this doesn't change anything. Knowledge, memory, wisdom aside, he was the culmination of all of the experiences in his incredibly long life.

Nathan Brazil. He rolled the name around in his mind. He still liked it. Out of the—what?—thousand or more names he had had, it had the most comfortable and enigmatic ring.

He let his mind go out across the land. Yes, definitely some sort of breakdown. Not major, but messy.

Time dulls all mechanisms, and the infinite complexity of the master equation was bound to have flaws. One can represent infinity mathematically but not as something real, something you can see and understand.

And yet, he thought, I'm still Nathan Brazil, still the same person I was, and I'm here in Murithel in the body of a great stag and I've still got to get to the Well before Skander or Varnett or anyone else does.

Czill. If what he had heard was right, they had computers there. A high-technology hex, then. They could give him a voice—and news.

Grondel emerged from a tent and came over to him. He strained at the rope on his left hind leg, and the Murnie understood and freed him. He went immediately to the big patch of bare dirt that was his writing pad. Grondel followed, grumping that he hadn't had anything to eat yet, but Brazil was adamant and anxious.

"What's on your mind, Nate?" he asked.

"HOW FAR HERE TO CZILL CENTER" Brazil traced.

"Already, huh?" Grondel muttered. "Somehow I knew it. Well, about a hundred and fifty kilometers, maybe a little more, to the border, then about the same into the Czillian capital. I'm not sure, because I've never left this hex. We don't get along well with our neighbors, which is fine with us."

"MUST GO," he scratched. "IN CONTROL OF SELF NOW. IMPORTANT."

"Ummm. . . . Thought you weren't going there across Murithel for a vacation. All right, then, if I can't dissuade you. What about the girl?"

"SHE COMES TOO," he scratched. "WILL WORK OUT EASY CODE FOR BASIC STUFF, STOP, GO, EAT, SLEEP, ETC."

And that was the way they worked it out, Brazil thinking of as many basic concepts as he could and using a right leg, left leg, stomping code for them. Twelve concepts were the most he could work on short notice without fear that she would mix them up. He also had to assure them several times that he would not wander away or stray again. She accepted it, but seemed dubious.

They ate their fill of the grasses. Grondel would

ride Wuju with them to the border. Though Nathan was safe as a branded, purebred stag, she was not. A Murnie accompanying them would ease her passage.

They followed the stream, passing first the spot where his body had lain, the mud and bottom still disturbed from the action. They made exceptionally good time, and Brazil enjoyed the experience of being able to move quickly and effortlessly, so powerful that the mud couldn't trap him, nor could the brisk pace tire him. He just wasn't built for riding, though; and Wuju had to carry Grondel, which slowed her more than usual. It didn't matter.

They made the border shortly after dark on the second day. On the morning of the third, after Grondel had refreshed Wuju on the stomp code, they bade him good-bye and crossed into Czill. The air was extremely heavy with an almost oppressive humidity, the kind that wets you with a fine, invisible mist as you move through it. The air was also oppressive with carbon dioxide, which seemed to make up one or more percent of the atmosphere, although oxygen was so far above their previous norms that it made them feel a little light-headed. Were it not for the great humidity, Brazil thought, this would be a hell of a place for fires. As it was, he would be surprised if a match would burn.

They ran into Czillians soon enough, strange-looking creatures that reminded him of smooth-skinned cactuses with two trunks and carved pumpkin heads. Neither he nor Wuju had a translator now, so communication was impossible, but at the first village center they reached, they managed a primitive sort of contact.

The place looked like a great, transparent geodesic dome, and was one of the hundred or more subsidiary research villages outside the Center. The Czillians were surprised to see a Dillian—they knew what Wuju was, but as far as any could remember none of her race had ever reached Czill before. They regarded Brazil as a curiosity, an obvious animal.

About the only thing Wuju could get across to them were their names. She finally gave up in frustration and they continued on the well-maintained road. The

Czillians sent the names and the information of their passage on to the Center, where it was much better understood.

Brazil paid a lot of attention to Wuju, and their lovemaking continued nightly. She was happy now and didn't even wonder how Brazil, who led, was picking the right direction at every junction as if he had been there before. In her mind the only question that mattered was about his human body. She felt a little guilty, but she hoped the body would not be there or would be dead.

She had him now, and she didn't want to lose him.

Late in the morning of the second day, they came to what was obviously the main highway of the hex, and followed it. It was another day and a half before they got to the Center, though, since it was not in the center of the hex as Grondel had thought, but was situated along the ocean coast.

They arrived just as darkness was falling, and Brazil stomped that they would sleep first. No use going in when there was only minimum staff, he thought.

As he made love to her that night, part of her mind was haunted. The rest of him is inside that building, she thought, and it upset her. This might be their last night.

Cousin Bat woke them up in the wee predawn hours.

"Brazil! Wuju! Wake up!" he shouted excitedly, and they both stirred. Wuju saw who it was and greeted him warmly, all her past suspicions forgotten.

Bat turned to Brazil unbelievingly. "Is that *really* you in there, Brazil?"

Brazil nodded his antlered head affirmatively.

"He can't talk, Cousin Bat," Wuju explained. "No vocal cords of any kind. I think that upsets him more than anything else."

The bat grew serious. "I'm sorry," he said softly to Brazil. "I didn't know." He snorted. "Big hero, plucking the injured man from the jaws of certain death. All I did was make a mess of it."

"But you *are* a hero!" Wuju consoled him. "That was an incredibly brave and wonderful thing." Well, there was no avoiding it. The question had to be asked.

"Did he—is his body still alive?" she asked softly.

"Yes, it is, somehow," Bat replied seriously. "But —well, it's a miracle that it's alive at all, and there's no medical reason for it. It's pretty battered and broken, Wuju. These doctors are good here—unbelievable, in fact. But the only thing that body will ever be good for is cloning. If Brazil were returned to it, he'd be a living vegetable."

They both looked at Brazil expectantly, but the stag gave no indication whatsoever of emotion.

Wuju tried to remain normal, but the fact that a great deal of tension had suddenly drained from her was obvious in the lighter, more casual tone she used. "Then he's to stay a deer?"

"Looks that way," Bat responded slowly. "At least they told me that the injuries were already too severe for me to have caused the final damage. They can't understand how he survived the Murnie blows that broke his neck and spinal column in two places. Nobody ever survived damage like that. It's as good as blowing your brains out or getting stabbed through the heart."

They talked on until dawn, when the still landscape suddenly came alive with awakening Czillians. Bat led them into the Center, and took them to the medical wing, on the river side.

The Czillians were fascinated by Brazil and insisted on checking him with electroencephalographs and all sorts of other equipment. He was impatient but submitted to the tests with growing confidence. If they were this far advanced, perhaps they could give him a voice.

They took Nathan down to a lower level after a while and showed him his body. Wuju came along, but one quick glance was all she needed and she rushed from the room.

They had him floating in a tank, attached to hundreds of instruments and life-sustaining devices. The monitors showed autonomic muscle action, but no cranial activity whatsoever. The body itself had been repaired as much as possible, but it looked as if it had

231

been through a meat grinder. Right leg almost torn off, now sewn back securely but lifeless in the extreme. The giant, clawed hand that had ripped the leg had also castrated him.

Brazil had seen enough. He turned and left the room, climbing the stairs back to the clinic carefully. They were not built to take something his size and weight, and the turns were difficult. He didn't fit in the elevators, which were designed for Umiau in wheelchairs.

Having a 250-plus-kilo giant stag walk into your office can be unsettling, but the Czillian doctor tried not to let it faze it. The doctor heard from Bat, who had heard it from Wuju, that Brazil could write. Since soft dirt was one thing that was very plentiful in Czill, it had obtained what appeared to be a large sandbox filled with dry, powdery gray sand from the ocean shore.

"What do you want us to do?" the doctor asked.

"CAN YOU BUILD ME VOICE BOX," Brazil scratched.

The doctor thought a minute. "Perhaps we can, in a way. You might know that the translator devices, which we import, sealed, from another hex far away, work by being implanted and attached to neural passages between the brain and the vocal equipment— whatever it is—of the creature. You had one in your old body. We now have nothing to attach the translator to in your case, and putting anything in there would interfere with eating or breathing. But if we could attach a small plastic diaphragm and match the electrical impulses from your brain to wires leading to it, we might have an external voice box. Not great, of course, but you could be understood—with full translator function. I'll tell the labs. It's a simple operation, and if they can come up with anything, we might be able to do it tomorrow or the next day."

"SOONER THE BETTER," he scratched, and started to leave to find Bat and Wuju.

"Just a minute," the doctor called. "As long as you're here, alone with me, I'd like to take up something you might not know."

Brazil stopped, turned back to it, and waited expectantly.

"Our tests show you to be—physically—about four and a half years old. The records show that the average life span of the Murthiel antelope is between eight and twelve years, so you can expect to age much more rapidly. You have four to eight more years to live, no more. But that is at least that many years longer than you would have lived without the transfer." It stopped, looking for a reaction. The stag cocked his head in a gesture that was unmistakably the equivalent of a shrug. He walked back to the sandbox.

"THANKS ANYWAY," he scratched. "NOT RELEVANT," he added cryptically, and left.

The doctor stared after him, puzzled. It knew that everyone said Brazil might be the oldest person ever to live, and certainly he had shown incredible, superhuman life and stamina. *Maybe he wants to die,* it mused. *Or maybe he doesn't think he can, even now.*

The operation was a simple one, performed with a local anesthetic. The only problem the surgeon had was in isolating the correct neural signals in an animal brain so undesigned for speech of any kind. The computers were fed all the neural information and some samples of him attempting speech. They finally isolated the needed signals in under an hour. The only remaining concern was for the drilling in the antlers, but when they found that the bony growths had no nerves to convey pain, it simplified everything. They used a small Umiau transistor radio—which meant it was rugged and totally waterproof. Connections were made inside the antler base, and the tiny radio, only about sixty square centimeters, was screwed into the antler base. A little cosmetic surgery and plastic made everything but the speaker grille blend into the antler complex.

"Now say something," the surgeon urged. "Do it as if you were going to speak."

"How's this?" he asked. "Can you hear and understand me?"

"Excellent!" the surgeon said enthusiastically, rubbing its tentacles in glee. "A landmark! There's even a suggestion of tone and emphasis!"

Brazil was delighted, even though the voice was

ever so slightly delayed from the thought, something he would have to get used to. His new voice sounded crazy to his ears, and did not have the internal resonance that came with vocal cords.

It would do.

"You'll have a pretty big headache after the anesthetic wears off," the surgeon warned. "Even though there are no pain centers in the antlers, we did have to get into the skull for the little wire contacts."

"That won't bother me," Brazil assured them. "I can will pain away."

He went out and found the bat and Wuju waiting anxiously in the outer office.

"How do you like my new voice?" he asked them.

"Thin, weak, and tinny, very mechanical-sounding," Bat replied.

"It doesn't sound like you at all, Nathan," Wuju said. "It sounds like a tiny pocket radio, one that a computer was using. Even so, there's some of you in it—the way you pause, the way you pronounce things."

"Now I can get to work," Brazil's strange new voice said. "I'll have to talk to the Czillian head of the Skander project, somebody high up in the Umiau, and I'll need an atlas. In the meantime, Wuju, you get yourself a translator. It's really a simple operation for you. I don't want to be caught in the middle of nowhere with you unable to talk to anybody again."

"I'll go with you," said the bat. "I know the place fairly well now. You know, it's weird, that voice. Not just the tiny sound from such a big character. It doesn't seem to come from anywhere in particular. I'll have a time getting used to it."

"The only part that's important is your calling me a big character," Brazil responded dryly. "You don't know what it's like to go through life being smaller than everybody else and suddenly wind up the largest person in a whole country." Brazil felt good; he was in command again.

They walked out, and Wuju was left alone, internally a mass of bewildering emotion. This wasn't turning out the way she had thought at all. He seemed so cold, so distant, so *different*—it wasn't Nathan! Not the voice, she thought. It was something *in* the voice, a manner, a coldness, a crispness that she had never felt before.

"Get a translator" he had told her, then walked out to business without so much as a good-bye and good luck.

"I want to go down to the old body one last time," Brazil said to the bat, and they made their way down the stairs to the basement room.

Bat, too, had noticed a change in his manner, and it disturbed him. He wondered whether the transformation had altered or changed Brazil's mind. Some forms of insanity and personality disorders are organic, he thought. Suppose the deer brain isn't giving the right stuff in the right amounts? Suppose it's only partially him?

They walked into the room where his body was floating, still alive according to all the screens and dials. Brazil stood by the tank, just looking at the body, for quite some time. Bat didn't interrupt, trying to imagine what he would be thinking in the same circumstances.

Finally Brazil said, almost nostalgic in tone, "It was a good vessel. It served me for a long, long time. Well, that's that. A new one's as easy as repair this time. Let it go."

As he uttered the last word, all the meters fell to zero and the screens all showed a cessation of life.

As if on command, the body had died.

Brazil turned and walked out without another word, leaving Bat more confused than ever.

"There's no question that Skander solved the riddle," the Czillian project chief, whose name was Manito, told Brazil and Cousin Bat. "Unfortunately, he kept the really key findings to himself and was very careful to wipe the computer when he was through. The only stuff we have is what was in when he and Vardia were kidnapped."

"What was the major thrust of his research?" Brazil asked.

"He was obsessed with our collection of folklore

and legends. Worked mostly with those, and keying in the common phrase: *Until midnight at the Well of Souls.*"

Brazil nodded. "That's safe enough," he replied. "But you say he dropped that line of inquiry when he returned?"

"Shortly after," the Czillian replied. "He said it was the wrong direction and started researching the Equatorial Barrier."

Brazil sighed. "That's bad. That means he's probably figured the whole thing out."

"You talk as if you know the answer, too," the project chief commented. "I don't see how. I have all the raw data Skander did and I can't make sense of it."

"That's because you have a puzzle with millions of pieces, but no concept of the size and shape of the puzzle even to start putting things together," Brazil told her—he insisted on thinking of all life forms that could do the act of reproducing, growing a new being, as she. "Skander, after all, had the basic equation. There's no way you can get that here."

"I can't understand why you let him use you so," Bat put in. "You—both races—gave him a hundred percent protection, cooperation, and access to all the tools he needed without getting anything in return."

The Czillian shook her head sadly. "We thought we were in control. After all, he was a Umiau. He couldn't exist outside his own ocean because he couldn't travel beyond it. And there was, after all, the other—the one who disappeared. He was a mathematician. Whose data banks was he consulting? Was he brilliant enough not to need them? We couldn't afford *not* to back Skander!"

"Any idea where they are?" Brazil asked.

"Oh, yes, we know where they are—fat lot of good it does us. They are currently being held captive in a nation of robots called, simply enough, The Nation. We received word that they were there, and, since we have a few informational trades with The Nation, we pulled in all our IOU's to hold them there as long as possible."

Brazil was suddenly excited. "Are they still there? Can we get them out?"

"Yes, they're still there," Manito replied, "but not for long. There's been hell to pay from the Akkafians. Their ambassador, a Baron Azkfru, has threatened to bomb as much of The Nation as he can—and he can do a good deal of damage if that's all he's out for. That's the line. They'll be released today."

"Who's in the party?" Bat asked. "If it's weak enough we might be able to do something yet."

"We've thought of that already," the Czillian responded. "Nothing that wouldn't get our person killed along with the rest. Aside from Vardia and Skander, there's an Akkafian—they are huge insects with great speed, the ability to fly, and nasty stingers, and they eat live prey—named Mar Hain, and a weird Northerner we know little about called The Diviner and The Rel. If they're one or two I can't find out."

"Hain!" Brazil exclaimed. "Of course, it would be. That son of a bitch would be in the middle of anything dirty."

"You know this Hain?" Bat asked curiously.

Brazil nodded. "The gang's all here, it looks like." He turned to Manito suddenly. "Did you bring the atlas I asked for?"

"I did," the Czillian replied, and lifted a huge book onto a table. Brazil walked over to it and flipped it open with his nose, then started turning pages with his broad tongue. Finally he found the Southern Hemisphere map and studied it intently. "Damned nuisance," he said. "Antelope don't need very good vision."

"I can help," the Czillian said, and walked toward the stag. "It is in Czillian, anyway, which you can't read."

Brazil shook his head idly from side to side. "It's all right. I see where we are now, and where *they* are. We're about even—two hexes up on this side to the Ghlmon Hex at the northern tip of the ocean. They've gotten two up the eastern side of the same ocean to pretty much the same spot."

"How can you possibly know that?" the Czillian

blurted out, stunned. "Have you been here before? I thought—"

"No," Brazil replied. "Not *here*." He flipped a few more pages, studying a close-up map of a particular hex. Then he flipped again, studied another, then to yet another. All in all, he carefully examined five hexes. Suddenly he looked up at the confused Czillian.

"Can you get me in touch with some Umiau big shot?" he asked. "They owe us something for Skander. They've got Slelcron, which is a nontech hex and so is fine from our point of view, and Ekh'l, which could be anything at all these days. We've got Ivrom, which I don't like at all, but there's no way around it, and Alisstl, which will make Murithel look like a picnic. We can contend with Ivrom, I hope, but if we went through the Umiau hex, on a boat of some kind, we could avoid the nasty one and maybe even gain some time on the others. If they stick near the coast—and I think they will, because those are the best roads by far—we might just beat them there and intercept them here," he pointed with his nose to the map, "at the northern tip of the bay here, in Ghlmon."

"Just out of curiosity," Bat said, "you said that the Umiau were warned the first time about a kidnap try on Skander. Now, you said you heard they were in The Nation. Who told you those things?"

"Why, we don't know!" the Czillian answered. "They came as, well, tips, passed in common printer-machine type in our respective languages, to our ambassadors at Zone."

"Yes," Bat persisted, "but who sent them? Is there a third set of players in the race?"

"I was hoping *you* could tell me that," Brazil said flatly.

Bat's eyes widened. "Me? All right, I admit I knew who you were back in Dillia, and that I joined you on purpose. But I don't represent anyone except myself, and the interests of my people. We got word the same way the Czillians and Umiau did, at Zone. Said where you'd be, approximately when, and that you were going after Skander and Varnett. We couldn't find who sent it, but it was decided that we had a stake in the outcome. I was elected, because I've done more traveling than most of my people. But—me? The third party? No, Brazil, I admit only to not being truthful with you. Surely by now you know that I'm on your side—all the way."

"That's too bad," Brazil replied. "I would very much like to know our mysterious helper, and how he gets his information."

"Well, he seems to be on our side," Bat said optimistically.

"Nobody's on any side but his own," Brazil snapped back. "Not you, not me, not anybody. We're going to have a tough enough time just dealing with the Skander party. I don't want to reach the goal of this chase and have our helpful third party finish off the survivors."

"Then you propose to give chase?" the Czillian asked stupidly.

"Of course! That's what all this is about. One last question—can you tell me the last major problem Skander fed to the computer?"

"Why, yes, I think so," the Czillian replied nervously. She rummaged through some papers, coming up with two. "He asked two, in fact. One was the number of Entries into hexes bordering the Equatorial Zone, both sides."

"And the answer?"

"Why, none on record. Most curious. They're not true hexes anyway, you know. Since the Equatorial Barrier splits them neatly in half, they are two adjoining half-hexes, each side—therefore, twice as wide as a normal hex and half the distance north and south, with flat equatorial borders."

"What was the second question?" Brazil asked impatiently.

"Oh, ah, whether the number six had any special relation to the Equatorial Zone hexes in geography, biology, or the like."

"And the answer?"

"Still in the computer when the unfortunate, ah, incident occurred. We did, of course, get the answer, even though it was on a printout which the kidnappers apparently took with them. The material was still in storage, and so we got another copy."

"What did it say?" Brazil asked in an irritated tone.

"Oh, ah, that six of the double half-hexes, so to speak, were split by a very deep inlet all the way up to the zone barrier, evenly spaced around the planet so that, if you drew a line from zone to zone through each of the inlets, you'd split the planet into absolutely equal sixths."

"Son of a bitch!" Brazil swore. "He's got the whole answer! Nothing will ever surprise me again!"

At that moment another Czillian entered the room and looked at the bat and the stag confusedly. Finally she picked the bat and said, shyly, "Captain Brazil?"

"Not me," Bat replied casually, and pointed a bony wing at the stag. "Him."

She turned and looked at the creature that was so obviously an animal. "I don't believe it!" she said the way everyone did. Finally she decided she might believe it and went over to the great Murithel antelope, and repeated, "Captain Brazil?"

"Yes?" he answered pleasantly, curious in the extreme. *Captain* Brazil?

"Oh," she responded softly, "I—I realize I've changed a great deal, but nothing like *you*. Wow!"

"Well, who are—um, that is, who *were* you?" he asked, intrigued.

"Why, I'm Vardia, Captain," she replied.

"But Vardia was kidnapped by the bugs!" Bat exclaimed.

"I know," she replied. "That's what's really upset me."

A Road in the Nation

"QUARANTINE, HELL!" SKANDER GRUMBLED, STRAPPED in again atop Hain's back, irritated by the yellowish atmosphere and the discomfort of the breathing apparatus. Her voice was so muffled by the mask that none could understand a word.

"Stop grumbling, Skander," The Rel responded. "You waste air and can't be understood by anybody but me anyway. You are quite right, though—we've been stalled."

Vardia, whose head and vocal mechanism were not related in any way to her respiratory system, asked, "Who could be responsible? Who knew we were here, would be staying at that particular hotel? Perhaps our people have tracked you down." There was hope in her voice.

"Don't get yourself that excited, Czillian," The Rel replied. "As you can see, the delaying action slowed us but did not stop or deter us—nor did it liberate you. No, this smells of darker stuff. Of the one who planted the hidden listening device in the baron's office at Zone and prevented our escapade weeks earlier."

This was the first Vardia had heard of that incident, and it made her think back to the many things that had happened to her. That distress signal where one could not have been operating. The vanishing of the two shuttlecraft on Dalgonia, and the disappearance of their lifeboat. The opening of the Well Gate only after they were all securely in it. Captain Brazil's firm belief that he was being suckered by someone.

That strange snakeman, Ortega. Over seven hundred chances, and Brazil is met by the only person at Zone who knew him. Coincidence?

She suddenly felt furious, thinking of all of it in detail. Someone *was* using her—using all of them—moving them like pieces in a game.

What about the hex assignments? Skander to a place where she had all the tools at her disposal, corrupting a peaceful people in the process. She to the hex next door, assigned—actually *assigned!*—to work with Skander and kidnapped with her. By whom? Someone working for that bastard Datham Hain!

And Captain Brazil! She had gotten the word when Brazil had entered Zone, looking exactly the same as he had before. Why didn't the Gate change him? And that pathetic little addict—dumped into a hex almost perfect for getting back to being human without pressures. Brazil had been hung up on her, she recalled. Probably they were together now.

Why? she wondered. Sex? That was something the animals did, she told herself. She had never understood it, or why people liked it; and if her own twinning was any indication, it was a most unpleasant experience. Why was a distinguished, high-ranking person of such a responsible position as Captain Brazil willing to jeopardize his career and his life for the sake of some wasted girl he never knew—didn't know, in fact, even through Zone? Even if he had saved her, she wouldn't have contributed anything. She was practically an animal then. More sense to get her to a Death Factory where her remains would help fertilize a field.

Perhaps this was why the Com philosophy was developing and spreading, she thought. It was rational, planned. Like being a plant, or one of these robots. Even Hain's dirty crew couldn't stop the march of such perfection of order, she felt sure. The sane hexes here proved it.

"We will have better service, and a shorter stay, at other hotels," The Rel informed them, breaking Vardia's reverie. "I think we will be out of this place where we are so unpopular in two days. Slelcron will be no faster but easier. No one communicates with the Slelcron. We will be ignored but unimpeded. As for Ekh'l—well, I have no information there, but I feel confident that, no matter what happens, we will not be beaten."

"You seem pretty sure of yourself," Vardia commented. "More prophecy from The Diviner?"

"Logic," The Rel replied. "We were impeded for someone's purpose. Why? To what end? So they can beat us to the equator? I doubt it. It would be easier to kill us than detain us so. No, they will have to come out to us at the equator. They want to be there when we arrive because they know who and where we are, but not what Dr. Skander knows—how to get to the Well. They want in with us—indeed, they may be allies, since they will assuredly take steps to see that no one else beats us to the goal. And make no mistake about it, there is another expedition. The Diviner has said that we will not enter until all the recent Entries combine. That is fine—as long as we are in charge."

"We will be," Hain suddenly said.

Near the Ivrom Border in the Umiau Nation

THEY PRESENTED A SIGHT UNPRECEDENTED ON THE Well World: a broad raft of logs, pulled along by ten Umiau wearing harnesses. On the raft were a Dillian centaur, a giant stag, a two-meter-tall bat, and a Czillian, plus a well-depleted bale of hay and a box of dirt.

"Why can't the Umiau just take us all the way up?" Vardia asked Brazil.

The stag turned his head. "I still can't get used to the idea that you are in two places at once, so to speak," he said through his radio speaker. The splashing and sound of the wind on the water made it hard to hear his little box if you weren't positioned just right.

"I have a hard time thinking that the little captain I came here with is a huge deer," she replied. "Now answer the question."

"Too dangerous," he told her. "We're going as far up as possible, but you eventually start getting some nasty currents, whirlpools, and other stuff. They don't get along too well with the inhabitants, either. The Umiau would make out, but those nasty fish with the twenty rows of teeth would chew up this raft and us before we could be properly introduced. No, we'll take our chances with a hundred and sixty kilometers of Ivrom."

"What is Ivrom, Nathan?" Wuju asked. She had gotten the translator, and overcome most of her reservations. He treated her gently, and said only the right things, and she had eased up. There was still that something different about him, that indefinable something they all sensed but couldn't put their fingers on.

Wuju had talked it out with Cousin Bat. "How would you feel," Bat had asked her, "if you'd awakened not a Dillian but a regular horse? And looked down at your own dead body? Would you still be the same?"

She had accepted that explanation, but Bat didn't believe it himself. What had changed in Brazil was the added air of total command, of absolute confidence and certainty. And he had as much as admitted he knew the answer to the total puzzle. He could get in to the control center, control the world—or more.

Bat was more encouraged now, really. So much the better. The man with the answers had no hands, couldn't even open a door by himself. Let him get in, Bat thought smugly. Let him show how to work things.

"Nathan!" Wuju said louder. "What is Ivrom? You haven't told us!"

"Because I don't know, love," he replied casually. "Lots of forest, rolling hills, plenty of animals, most familiar. The atlas said there were horses and deer there. It's a nontechnological hex, so it's the sword-and-spear bit again, probably. The intelligent life form is some kind of insect, I think, but nobody's sure. Those active volcanoes to our left—that's Alisstl, and it's a formidable barrier. The people there are thick-skinned reptiles who live in temperatures close to boiling and eat sulfur. Probably nice folks, but nobody drops in."

She looked over at the range of volcanic mountains. Most were spouting steam, and one had a spectacular lava fountain along a side fissure. She shivered, although it wasn't cold.

"This is the way to travel if you can!" Brazil said with enthusiasm, taking a deep breath of the salty air. "Fantastic! I used to sail oceans like this on big ships, back in the days of Old Earth. There was a romance to the sea, and those who sailed it. Not like the one-man space freighters with their computers and phony pictures of winking dots."

"How soon will we land?" Wuju asked him, a bit

ill at the rolling and tossing he liked so much. She was happy to see him obviously enjoying himself, talking like his old self again, but if it was at the cost of this kind of upset stomach, she would take land.

"Well, they've gone exceptionally fast," he replied. "Strong devils, and amazing in their element. I'll have to remember that strength. Wouldn't do to underestimate our Dr. Skander."

"Yes, but *how long?*" she insisted.

"Tomorrow morning," he replied. "Then it'll be no more than a day or so to Ghlmon—we won't have to cross the whole hex of Ivrom, just one facet—and another day to the top of the bay in Ghlmon."

"Do you really think we'll meet them—the others, that is—up there?" Vardia asked. "I'm most anxious to free my other self—my sister—from those creatures."

"We'll meet them," Brazil assured her, "if we beat them—and we certainly should at this rate. I know where they have to go. When they get there, we'll be ready for them."

"Will I be able to scout this Ivrom tonight?" Cousin Bat called out to him. "I'm sick and tired of fish."

"I'm counting on you, Bat," Brazil replied laughing. "Eat up and tell us what's what."

"No more midnight rescues from the jaws of death, though," Bat replied in the same light vein.

"You never know, Bat," Brazil replied more seriously. "Maybe this time I'll rescue *you.*"

The Umiau had been remarkably uninformed about Ivrom, which wasn't as strange on the face of it as it would seem. The Umiau were water creatures, and their need was for technological items they could not manufacture. An alliance with the Czillians was natural; their other neighbors they at least knew from watery experience, even if they didn't get along too well with all of them, and Alisstl was too hot to handle. Ivrom, named from the old maps and not by the inhabitants, was peaceful forests and meadows, no major rivers, although it had hundreds of tiny creeks and streams. It was a nontechnological hex, so it wasn't easy to get to, even harder to move around in, and probably not worth the trouble. Of course, the major problem was that no one who had ever set out for Ivrom—to study, for contact, or to go through it —had ever been seen or heard from again. For that reason the party stopped on a reef, over a submerged shoal in deep water, and anchored for the night even though there would still have been time when they arrived to have made camp on or near the beach.

It did look inviting, too. The air was sweet and fresh, about twenty degrees Celsius, surprisingly comfortable humidity for a shore area because of the inland breeze, a few light, fluffy clouds but nothing that looked threatening, and a deep blue sky.

The shoreline revealed a virgin sandy beach, flat and yellow and stretching down the coast. The breakers and some obvious storms had forced driftwood onto the shore, where it had built up near the beginning of the forest. It was a very dense forest, rather dark from the thickness of the underbrush and giant evergreens, but nothing looked suspicious or sinister. As twilight deepened, they could make out an occasional small deer and a number of other animals much like muskrats, marmots, and other woodland creatures.

It reminded Brazil of a number of really pleasant places on Old Earth before they were paved over. Even the animals and birds, now flocking to roosts in the tall trees, seemed very Earthlike—far more than even the most familiar hexes he had been through.

He wished he could recall more about the place, but he couldn't. Nobody could keep track of everything, he thought, even though the mind behind Ivrom had obviously paid a great deal of attention to a Type 41 habitat.

Insects, his mind kept telling him. But that was the kind of fact that you heard once or twice rather than recalled from personal experience, and it registered but was not something you had paid attention to at the time. Everything has changed so much it probably wouldn't matter anyway, he thought. Evolution and natural processes like erosion and deposition, diastrophism and the other forces operated in accordance with the logic of each hex, so things were constantly changing on the Well World as they were everywhere in the universe.

Darkness totally obscured the shoreline for all but Cousin Bat, who reported that he couldn't see anything they hadn't seen by day.

"Well, maybe something," Bat corrected. "I can't be sure at this distance, though. Looks like tiny, little, blinking lights, on and off, on and off, all over the forest—moving around, too, but slowly."

Lightning bugs, Brazil thought. Was he the only person from their little corner of the galaxy who could remember lightning bugs?

"Well, go on in, then," Brazil told the bat after a while, "but be careful. Looks peaceful, but the place has a really spooky reputation, and except for the fact that my mind keeps insisting that the life form there is insects, I can't think of anything else to tell you. Just watch out for insects, no matter how small or insignificant—they might be somebody we'd rather make friends with."

"All right," Bat responded calmly. "Insects are a normal part of my diet, but I won't touch them if I can help it. Just a quick survey, then I'll be back."

They agreed and Bat took off into the darkness.

When the sun came up the next morning, Cousin Bat still had not returned.

Just over the Nation—Slelcron Border—Morning

THE REL STOPPED JUST AHEAD AS THE AIR SUDDENLY cleared and they walked into bright sunshine.

"You may all remove your breathing apparatuses and discard them," it told them. "The air is now quite safe for all of you."

Skander reached up and took off her mask, but stowed it in the pack case. "I'll keep mine, and I think you others should, too," the Umiau cautioned. "I have no idea what the interior is like, but it's possible we may need the couple hours of air left in these tanks. If the mechanism is self-operating, it may not exist in any atmosphere."

"I am well aware of that, Doctor," The Rel replied. "I, too, can not exist in a vacuum—The Diviner requires argon and neon, and I require xenon and krypton, which, thankfully, have been present in the quantities we need in all of the hexes so far. We had weeks to prepare for this expedition, you know, and I fully expected us ultimately to have to face a vacuum —in which those little respirators will do us no good whatsoever. The packs contain compressed pressure suits designed for each of us."

"Then why didn't we use them in that hellhole we just went through?" Hain grumbled, outraged. "That stuff burned!"

"That was a hex of sharp edges and abrasives where the suits might have suffered premature damage," The Rel replied. "It was a discomfort, no more. I thought it best not to take any risks with pressurized equipment until we have to."

Hain grumbled and cursed, and Skander wasn't much better—she was drying out rapidly and itched terribly. Only Vardia was now perfectly comfortable—the sun was very strong, the sky was blue and cloudless, and she even somehow sensed the richness of the soil.

"What is this place, anyway?" Skander asked. "Any chance of a shady stream where I can wet down?"

"You'll survive," The Rel responded. "We will alleviate your discomfort as soon as we can. Yes, there are almost certainly streams, lakes, and ponds here. When I find one shallow enough and slow enough that it will not be your avenue away from us, you will get your wish."

The place was thinly forested, but had tremendous growth of bushes and vines, and giant flowers—millions of flowers, as far as the eye could see, rising on stalks from one to three meters high, bright orange centers surrounded by eighteen perfectly shaped white petals.

Huge buzzing insects went from flower to flower, but the actions were individualistic, not as they would move in a swarm. Each was about fifty centimeters long, give or take, and very furry; and though their basic color was black, they had stripes of orange and yellow on their hind sections.

"How beautiful," Vardia said.

"Damned noisy, if you ask me," Skander yelled, noting the tremendous hum the insects' wings made as they moved.

"Are the insects the life form?" Hain asked. The Rel had to move back close to the huge beetle to be heard.

"No," the Northerner replied. "As I understand it, it is some sort of symbiosis. The flowers are. Their seeds are buried by the insects, and if all goes well the braincase develops out of the seed. Then it sprouts the stalk and finally forms a flower."

"Then maybe I can eat a few of the buzzing bastards," Hain said eagerly.

"No!" The Rel replied quickly. "Not yet! The flowers drop seeds, so they do not reproduce by pollination. The bees bury the seeds, but little else—yet they are obviously gaining their food from the center of the flowers. See how one lands there, and sticks its proboscis into the orange center? If the flowers feed them, they must do something for the flower."

"They can't uproot," Vardia said sympathetically. "What's the use of having a brain if you can't see, hear, feel, or move? What kind of a dominant species is that?"

The ultimate Comworld, Skander thought sarcastically, but said aloud, "I think that's what the insects do. If you keep watching one long enough, it goes to one other flower, then returns to the original. It might go to dozens of flowers, but it returns between trips to a particular one."

Vardia noticed a slight lump in the grass just ahead of them. Curiously she went over to it and carefully smoothed the dirt away.

"Look!" she called excitedly, and they all came to see. "It's a seed! And see! An egg of some kind attached to the outside! Each insect attaches an egg to each seed before burying it! It's grown attached! See where the seed case is growing over the egg, secreting that film?"

Skander almost fell out of her saddle peering over Hain's hard shell to see, but the glance she got told the story.

"Of course!" the scientist exclaimed. "Amazing!"

"What?" they all asked at once.

"That's how they communicate—how they get around, don't you see? The insect's like a robot with a programmable brain. They grow up together—I'll bet the insect hatches fully formed and instinctively able to fly when the flower opens. Whatever it sees, hears, touches, it communicates to the flower when it returns. I'll bet after a while they can send the creatures with messages, talk to each other. And every time the insect gets to another flower, the old hands give information for it to take back. The creatures live, but they live their lives secondhand, by recording, as it were."

"Sounds logical," The Rel admitted. "Hain, I would suggest you eat anything *but* those flowers and the black, striped insects. You could get huge numbers of them, we all could, but if we upset them we could face a programmed army of millions of the things. I want to be peaceful."

"All right," Hain agreed grumpily. "But if there's nothing else to eat, the hell with them."

At that moment one of the huge insects flew right into their midst and started carefully but quickly reburying the exposed seed and egg. Satisfied, it flew off to a nearby flower and buried its head in the flower's center. They watched it carefully, both for intent and out of curiosity. Finally it seemed satisfied and backed out, flying over to them and hovering menacingly in front of them, darting from one to the other. They stayed still, but Hain's antennae radiated, "If that thing makes one wrong move, I'll eat it regardless."

Finally the creature got to Vardia, flew all around her, then suddenly jumped on her head, and before she could make a move it pushed its sharp, mosquito-like proboscis into the top of her head just under the leafy growth. They were all too stunned to move for several seconds. Suddenly Hain said, "I'll zap it."

"*No!*" Skander shouted violently. "You might leave that thing in her. Wait a minute and let's see what happens."

Vardia had no pain centers but she did have sensitive nerves, and they felt the thing enter and probe until it touched a particular set of nerves, the ones that sent messages to and from her head and brains.

Quite suddenly everything went dark, and a strange voice much like her own thoughts, only stronger, asked, "Who and what are you and what are you doing here?"

She could think of nothing but answering. The alien thought was so powerful it was hypnotizing. It was more demand than question.

"We are just passing through your hex on our way to the equator."

She felt the proboscis withdraw, and the lights came on again. She was in control and saw the thing heading away at high speed.

"Va— Chon," Skander corrected. "What happened?"

"It . . . it spoke to me. It asked who we were, and I said we were just people going through the hex toward the equator. Man! It's strong! I have the strangest feeling that I would have to answer anything it asked —and do whatever it said."

The Rel drifted over and lifted itself up so it could examine her head with whatever it used for sensory equipment. As it drifted just a few centimeters from her up to her head, she felt a strange tingling. Obviously it did not float—something supported it.

The Diviner and The Rel seemed satisfied and floated back down. "No sign of a wound of any kind," the creature said. "Amazing. One of the flowers got curious, and since you were the only member of the vegetable kingdom around, it picked you. Stay still and let it happen again. Assure them we'll do no harm and get through as quickly as possible. Tell them we're following the coast and will take care."

"I don't think I can tell them anything they don't ask," Vardia responded weakly. "Oh, oh, here it comes again!"

The creature did not have to probe the second time;

251

it went straight to the proper nerve endings. "READ-OUT!" came the command, and suddenly she felt herself being drained, as if that which was her very essence was being sucked up into a bottle through a straw. The process took several minutes.

"Look!" Skander cried. "My god! She's rooted! Unmoving in bright daylight! What did that thing do to her?"

The insect moved back into the mass of flowers.

"We can't do anything but wait," The Rel cautioned. "We don't know the rules here. At least those insects seem to be dominant only on the plants. Take it easy and let things run their course."

Hain and The Rel both moved toward her, where she stood rooted and motionless. Hain pressed against her skin, and got no response, nor any from the blank eyes.

"Are we going to have to camp here?" Hain asked at last in a disgusted tone. "Why not just leave her?"

"Patience, Hain," The Rel warned. "We can't afford to proceed until this drama plays itself out, even if it takes hours. We have only a little more than two hundred kilometers in this hex but we want to survive it."

They waited, and it took hours.

Vardia felt suspended in limbo, unable to see, hear, feel, or do anything else. Yet it wasn't like being asleep—she knew that she existed, just not where.

Suddenly she felt that sucking feeling again, and suddenly she was aware of someone else. She couldn't understand how she knew, but something else was there, all right. Suddenly that force of thought she had felt when the insect had first penetrated her head was all around her.

"I MELD WHAT IS YOURS TO ME AND WHAT IS ME TO YOU," the voice that was pure thought said, and it was so.

There was an explosion in her mind, and she clung desperately to control, to her own personality, even as she felt it being eroded away, mixed into a much larger and more powerful, yet alien, set of thoughts, memories, pictures, ideas.

Why do you resist? asked a voice that might have been her own thoughts or someone else's. Submit. This is what you have always wanted. Perfect union in uniformity. Submit.

The logic was unassailable. She submitted.

"It's coming back!" Skander yelled, and the other two followed the path of the insect to Vardia's head and watched it bury its sharp proboscis as before. This time it stayed an abnormally long time—perhaps three or four times longer than it had the last trip. Finally it finished and withdrew, buzzing off back to its home flower. They watched as her body came back to life, the eyes moving, looking about. She uprooted, and moved her tentacles around, shook her legs.

"Chon! Are you all right?" Skander called out, concerned.

"We are fine, Dr. Skander," replied Vardia in a voice that was hers yet strangely different. "We may proceed now, without any problems."

The Diviner's little flashing lights became extremely agitated. The Rel said, "The Diviner says that you are not the one of our party. Who or what are you? The equation has been altered."

"We are Chon. We are everything that ever was Chon. The one you call Chon has been melded. It is no longer one but all. Soon, as even now it happens, all will be Chon and Chon will be all."

"You're that damned flower!" Hain said accusingly. "You swapped minds with the Czillian somehow!"

"No swap, as you call it, was involved," it told them. "And we are not that damned flower as you said, but *all* the flowers. The Recorders transfer and transmit as you surmised, but the process may be and usually is total at first sprout, or how else should we get our information, our intellect? A new bloom is a blank, an empty slate. We merge."

"And you merged with the Czillian?" The Rel said more than asked. "You have all of its memories, plus all that was you?"

"That is correct," the creature affirmed. "And, since we have *all* of the Czillian experience within us, we are aware of your mission, its reason, and goal, and we are now a part of it. You have no choice, nor do we, since we cannot meld with you."

Skander shivered. Well, Vardia got her wish at last, the mermaid thought. And we've got problems.

"Suppose we refuse?" Skander shot at the new creature. "One gulp from Hain here and you're gone."

The creature in Vardia's body stepped boldly in front of Hain and looked at the big insect's huge eyes.

"Do you want to eat me, Hain?" it asked evenly.

Hain started to flick her sticky tongue, but something stopped her. Suddenly she didn't want to eat the Czillian, not at all. She liked the Czillian. It was a good creature, a creature that had the interest of the baron at heart. It was the best friend she had, the most loyal.

"I—I don't understand," Hain said in a perplexed tone. "Why should I want to eat it? It's my friend, my ally. I couldn't hurt it, never, or the pretty flowers and insects, either."

"It's got some kind of mental power!" Skander screamed, and tried to free herself from the saddle in panic. Suddenly Hain spread out, lowering her shell to the ground, legs extended outward.

Skander was free of the harness and looked around for a place to leap. Her darting eyes met the lime disks of the Czillian, and suddenly all panic fled. She couldn't remember why she was afraid in the first place, not of the Czillian, anyway.

The thing came right up to the mermaid, so close they could touch. A Czillian tentacle stroked the Umiau's hair, and the mermaid smiled and relaxed, content.

"I love you," Skander said in a sexy voice. "I'll do anything for you."

"Of course you will," the Slelcronian replied gently. "We'll go to the Well together, won't we, my love? And you'll show me everything?"

The Umiau nodded in ecstasy.

The Slelcronian turned to The Diviner and The Rel, who stood there a few meters away, viewing the scene dispassionately.

"What are you going to do with me?" The Rel asked in the closest it could come to sarcasm. "Look me in the eye?"

For the first time the creature was hesitant, looking

uncertain, puzzled, less confident. It reached out its mind to the Northern creature, and found nothing it could contact, understand, relate to. It was as if the creature was no longer there.

"If we cannot control you, you are at least irrelevant to us," Vardia's voice said evenly. The Diviner and The Rel didn't move.

"I said the equation had changed," The Rel said slowly. "I didn't say which way. The Diviner is always right, it seems. Until this moment I had no idea whatsoever how we were to control Skander once in the Well, or why the addition of the Czillian tipped things more in our favor. It's clear now."

The Rel paused for a moment. "We have been in charge of this project from its inception," The Rel continued. "We have used a judicious set of circumstances and The Diviner's amazing skills to make our own situation. We lead. Now we lead without worry."

"What power do you possess to command us?" scoffed the new Vardia. "We are at this moment summoning the largest of our Recorders to crush you. You are no longer necessary."

"I have no power at all, save speech and movement," The Rel admitted as eight huge insects hummed thunderously into view over the flowery fields. "The Diviner has the power," The Rel added, and as it spoke the flashing lights of The Diviner grew in intensity and frequency. Suddenly visible bolts shot out from the blinking creature and struck the eight Recorders at the speed of light.

The Recorders' outlines flashed an electrical white. There was a tiny roll of thunder as each of the creatures vanished, caused by air rushing in to take the place where it had been. It sounded like eight distant cannon shots.

"Hmmm . . ." The Rel said in its flat tone, "that's a new one. The Diviner is full of surprises. Shall we go? I should not like to spend more than two nights in your charming land."

The Slelcronian mind in Vardia's body was staggered and crushed. Something seemed to deflate inside, and the confident glow in its eyes was replaced by respect mixed with something new to its experience—fear. "We—we didn't know you had such powers," it almost gasped.

"A trifle, really," The Rel replied. "Well? Do you want to join us or not? I hope you will—it's so much simpler than what The Diviner would have to do to get Skander's cooperation, and I'm certain that, in the interest of your people, both of them, you'd rather we made it before anyone else."

The stunned creature turned to Skander and said, shakily, "Get back into your harness. We must go."

"Yes, my darling," Skander replied happily, and did so.

"Your lead, Northerner," the Slelcronian said.

"As always," The Rel replied confidently. "Do you know anything about Ekh'l?"

The Beach at Ivrom—Morning

"LOOKS PEACEFUL ENOUGH," VARDIA COMMENTED AS they unloaded the raft onto the beach. "Very pleasant, really."

"Reminds me of the Dillian valley area, upvalley in particular," Wuju added, as they strapped the bulky saddlebags around her.

"Something in here doesn't like people, though," Brazil reminded them. "This hex has no embassy at Zone, and expeditions into it have always vanished, as Bat did last night. We have only this one facet of the hex to travel, but that's still over one hundred kilometers, so I think we'll stick to the beach as long as possible."

"What about Bat, then?" Wuju asked in a concerned voice. "We can't just abandon him, after all he's done for us."

"I don't like doing so any more than you do, Wuju," Brazil replied seriously, "but this is a big hex.

He can fly at a good speed and over obstacles, and by now he could be just about anywhere. We might as well be looking for a particular blade of grass. As much as I'd like to help him, I just can't take the risk that whatever's here will get one or all of us."

"Well, I don't like it," Wuju said adamantly, but there was no assailing his logic on any grounds except emotion. "We survived the Murnies," she reminded him. "How much worse can it be here?"

"Much," he replied gravely. "I survived Murithel by luck, as did you——and we knew who the enemy was and the problems. This is even more chancy, because we *don't* know what's here. We've *got* to leave Bat to the Fates. It's Bat or all of us." And that settled that.

With Bat gone, Brazil regretted more and more his lack of arms or other appendages that could hold and use things. Although this was a nontechnological hex, several good and somewhat nasty items would be usable, and these were given to Wuju and Vardia. The centaur was given two automatic, gunpowder-powered projectile pistols, worn strapped to gunbelts worn in an X—and carrying extra ammunition clips— across her chest. Vardia had two pistols of a different kind. They squirted gas kept under pressure in attached plastic bottles. When the trigger was pulled hard, a flint would ignite the gas, which could be liberated at a controlled rate. The flamethrower was good for about ten meters, and needn't be very directional to be effective. Wuju, of course, had never fired a pistol and had no luck with the little practice gotten in in the ocean. But these were still effective short-range weapons, psychologically if nothing else, and they made a lot of noise going off.

"We stick to the beach," Brazil reminded them. "If we're lucky, we'll be able to get the whole way without going into the forest."

As satisfied as they could be, they thanked the Umiau who had pulled them this far, and the mermaids left.

Brazil said "Let's go," in a voice more filled with tension than excitement.

The sand and huge quantities of driftwood slowed

their progress, and they found on several occasions that they had to walk into the shallows to get around some points, but the journey went well.

They made good time. By sundown, Brazil estimated that they had traveled more than halfway. Since his vision was extremely poor after nightfall, and Vardia was better off rooting, they stopped for what they all hoped would be their only night in the mysterious hex.

The sandy soil was not particularly good for the Czillian, but she managed to find a hard, steady place near the beginning of the woods and was set for the night. He and Wuju relaxed nearby as the surf crashed on hidden rocks just beyond the shoreline, then gently ran up with a sizzling sound onto the beach.

Something was bothering Wuju and she brought it up. "Nathan," she said, "if this is a nontechnological hex like Murithel, how come your voice works? It's still basically a radio."

The idea had never occurred to Brazil and he thought about it. "I can't say," he replied carefully, "but on all the maps and the like this is nontech, and the general logic of the hex layout dictates the same thing. It can't work, though, unless it's a by-product of the translator. They work everywhere."

"The translator!" she said sharply. "Feels like a lump in the back of my throat. Where do they come from, Nathan?"

"From the North," he told her. "From a totally crystalline hex that grows them as we grow flowers. It's slow work, and they don't let many of them go."

"But how does it work?" she persisted. "It's not a machine."

"No, not a machine in the sense we think of machines," he replied. "I don't think anyone knows how it works. It was, if I remember right, created in the same way as most great inventions—sheer accident. The best guess is that its vibrations cause some kind of link with the Markovian brain of the planet."

She shivered a little, and Brazil rubbed close to

258

her, thinking the dropping temperature was the cause. "Want a coat?" he asked.

She shook her head negatively. "No, I was thinking of the brain. It makes me nervous—all that power, the power to create and maintain all those rules for all those hexes, work the translators, even change people into other things. I don't think I like the idea at all. Think of a race that could build such a thing! It scares me."

Brazil rubbed her humanoid back with his head, slowly. "Don't worry about such things," he said softly. "That race is long gone."

She was not distracted. "I wonder," she said in a distant tone. "What if they *were* still around, still fooling around. That would mean we were all toys, playthings—all of us. With the power and knowledge to create all this, they would be so far above us that we wouldn't even know." She shook him off and turned to face him. "Nathan, what if we were just playthings for them?"

He stared hard into her eyes. "We're not," he responded softly. "The Markovians are gone—long dead and gone. Their ghosts are brains like the one that runs this planet—just gigantic computers, programmed and automatically self-maintained. The rest of their ghosts are the people, Wuju. Haven't you understood that from what you've learned by this trip?"

"I don't understand," she said blankly. "What do you mean the people are the Markovian ghosts?"

" 'Until midnight at the Well of Souls,' " he recited. "It's the one phrase common to all fifteen hundred and sixty hexes. Think of it! Lots of us are related, of course, and many people here are variations of animals in other hexes. I figured out the solution to that part of the puzzle when I came out of the Gate the same as I went in—and found myself in a hex of what we always thought of as 'human.' Next door were one-and-a-half-meter-tall beavers—intelligent, civilized, highly intellectual, but they were basically the same as the little animal beavers of Dillia. Most of the wildlife we've seen in the hexes that come close to the type of worlds our old race could settle are related to the ones we had back there. There's a relationship for all of them.

"These hexes represent home worlds, Wuju," he said seriously. "Here is where the Markovians built the test places. Here is where their technicians set up biospheres to prove the mathematics for the worlds they would create. Here's where our own galaxy, at least, perhaps all of them, was engineered ecologically."

She shivered again. "You mean that all these people were created to see if the systems worked? Like an art class for gods? And if it was good enough, the Markovians created a planet somewhere that would be *all* like this?"

"Partly right," he replied. "But the creatures weren't created out of the energy of the universe like the physical stuff. If so, they'd be the gods you said. But that's not why the world was built. They were a tired race," he continued. "What do you do after you can do it all, know it all, control it all? For a while you delight in being a race of gods—but, eventually, you tire of it. Boredom sets in, and you must be stagnant when you have no place else to go, nothing else to discover, to reach." He paused, as the breaking waves seemed to punctuate his story, then continued in the same dreamy tone.

"So their artisans were assigned to create the hexes of the Well World. The ones that proved out were accepted, and the full home world was then made and properly placed mathematically in the universe. That's the reason for so much overlap—some artisans were more gifted than others, and they stole and modified each other's ideas. When they proved out, the Markovians came to the Well through the gates, not forced but voluntarily, and they passed through the mechanism for assignment. They built up the hexes, struggled, and did what none else could do as Markovians—they died in the struggle."

"Then they settled the home worlds?" she gasped. "They gave up being gods to suffer pain and to struggle and die?"

"No," he replied. "They settled on the Well World. When a project was filled, it was broken down and

260

a new one started. What we have here today is only the youngest worlds, the youngest races, the last. The Markovians all struggled here, and died here. Not only all matter, but time itself, is a mathematical construct they had learned and overcome. After many generations, the hexes became self-sufficient communities if they worked. The Markovians, changed, bore children that bred true. It was these descendants, the Markovian seed, who went to the Well through the local gates to what we now call Zone, that huge Well we entered by. On the sixth day of the sixth month of each six years they went, and the Well took them, in a single sweep like a clock around the Well, one sweep in the middle of the night. It took them, classified them, and transported them to the home world of their races."

"But surely," she objected, "the worlds had their own creatures. There is evolution—"

"They didn't go physically," he told her evenly. "Only their substance, what the Murnies called their 'essence,' went. At the proper time they entered the vessels which had evolved to the point of the Well. That's why the translator calls it the Well of Souls, Wuju."

"Then we are the Markovian children," she breathed. "They were the seeds of our race."

"That's it," he acknowledged. "They did it as a project, an experiment. They did it not to kill their race, but to save it and to save themselves. There's a legend that Old Earth was created in seven days. It's entirely possible—the Markovians controlled time as they controlled all things, and while they had to develop the worlds mathematically, to form them and create them according to natural law, they could do millions of years work rather quickly, to slide in their project people at the exact moment when the dominant life form—or life forms—would logically develop."

"And these people here—are they all Entries and the descendants of Entries?" she asked.

"There weren't supposed to be any," he told her. "Entries, that is. But the Markovians inhabited their own old universe, you know. Their old planets were

261

still around. Some of the brains survived—a good number if we blundered into even one of them in our little bit of space. They were quasi-organic, built to be integral with the planet they served, and they proved almost impossible to turn off. The last Markovian couldn't shut his down and still get through, so they were left open, to be closed when time did to the old worlds what it does to all things left unmaintained."

"Then there are millions of those gates still open," she speculated. "People could fall in all the time."

"No," he replied. "The gates only open when someone wants them to be open. It doesn't have to be a mystical key—although the boy Varnett, back on Dalgonia, caused it to open by locking into his mind the mathematical relationships he observed. It doesn't happen randomly, though. Varnett was the exception. The key *is* mathematical, but anyone near one doesn't have to know the key to operate the Gate."

"What's the key, then?" she asked, puzzled.

"Spacers—thousands of them have been through the Well, not just from our sector but from all over. I've met a number. It's a lonely, antisocial job, Wuju, and because of the Fitzgerald Contraction and rejuve, it is a long one. All those people who came here through gates got signals on the emergency band that lured them to the gates. Whether they admit it or not, they all had one thing in common."

"What was that?" she asked, fascinated.

"They all wanted to or had decided to die," he replied evenly, no trace of emotion in his voice. "Or, they'd rather die than live on. They were looking for fantasy worlds to cure their problems.

"Just like the Markovians."

She was silent for a while. Suddenly she asked, "How do you know all this, Nathan? The people here don't, those children of the Markovians who didn't leave."

"You got that, did you?" he responded admiringly. "Yes, when the last were changed, they sealed the Well. Those who didn't want to go, lost their nerve, or were happy here—they stayed, with only a memory, perhaps even regret once it was done, for they

262

kept the phrase 'until midnight at the Well of Souls' alive as the symbol of forever. How do I know all this? I'm brilliant, that's why. And so is Skander— that's why we're going where we have to go."

She accepted his explanation, not noticing the evasion. "But if everything is sealed, why bother?" she asked. "Skander can't do any harm, can he?"

"Deep beneath our feet is a great machine," he told her seriously. "The Markovian brain is so powerful that it created and maintained the home worlds as it maintains this one; the brain keeps the equations that sustain all unnaturally created matter, that can undo the fabric of time, space, and matter as it created them. Skander wants to change those equations. Not just our lives but our very existence is at stake."

She looked at him for a long time, then turned idly, staring into the forest, lost in her thoughts.

Suddenly she said, "Look, Nathan! The flying lights are out! And I can hear something!"

He turned and looked into the forest. They *were* insects of some kind, he thought, glowing as they flitted through the forest. The light, he saw, was constant—the blinking that had been apparent from shore was an illusion, caused by their passage behind the dense foliage. The darkness was too complete for his deer vision to get any detail, but the floating, gliding lights were clear. There was something very familiar about them, he thought. I've never been here, yet I've seen this before.

"Listen!" Wuju whispered. "Hear it?"

Brazil's fine-trained ears had already picked it up even over the crashing of the waves.

It was music, haunting, strange, even eerie music, music that seemed to penetrate their very bodies.

"It's so strange," Wuju said softly. "So beautiful."

The Faerie! he thought suddenly. Of course there'd be Faerie! He cursed himself for not thinking of it before. This close to the equator there was bound to be magic, he realized. Some of those authoritarian sons of bitches had snuck onto Old Earth and it had been hell getting rid of them. He looked anxiously at Wuju. She had a dreamy look on her face, and her upper torso was swaying in time to the music.

"Wuju!" he said sharply. "Come on! Snap out of it!"

She pushed him away and started forward, toward the woods. He rushed up and tried to block her way, but she wouldn't be deterred. He opened his mouth and tried to grab her arm, but it wouldn't hold.

"Wuju!" he called after her. "Don't go in! Don't desert us!"

Suddenly a dark shape swooped down from the sky at him. He ducked by lowering his forelegs and started running. It swooped again, and he cursed the poor vision that kept him from taking full advantage of his reflexes.

He heard maniacal laughter above him, and the mad thing swooped again, brushing him this time.

They're forcing me into the forest! he realized. Every time he moved in any direction but in the creature's, laughing and gibbering, it would swoop in and block his way.

"Cousin Bat! Don't do it! It's Nathan Brazil!" he called to the dark shape, knowing the effort was futile, that the bat was under a Faerie spell.

Brazil was in the woods now, where Bat couldn't follow by flying. He saw the creature standing there, outlined in the starlight glare on the ocean, looking up and down the beach.

He looked around, and barely made out a large form heading away about eight meters farther in.

It's useless, he realized. The music's got her and Bat's got me.

I've faced them down before, he thought, and won. Maybe again, because they don't know that. No choice here, though. If I don't follow they'll send some other creatures after me.

He could barely see despite the light from the flitting bugs that grew thicker and thicker as he entered the forest, but he smelled Wuju's scent and followed it.

After what must have been twenty minutes, he emerged into a clearing in the woods.

A toadstool ring, he thought grimly.

Under a particularly huge tree was a wide ring composed of huge brown toadstools. The music came from here, made by the thousands of insects that swarmed in the center of the ring. Wuju was in the ring, too, almost covered by the creatures, so thick now that they lit up the place like a lamp. She was dancing and swaying to the eerie music of their wings, as were a number of other creatures, of varying shapes and sizes.

The music grew in intensity and volume as more and more of the creatures of light came to the ring. Sitting in the hollow of the great tree, still and observing, was a glowing insect much, much larger than the others—perhaps close to a meter. It had the oval shape of a beetle, and a light, ribbed underside that was highly flexible. Two long, jointed hind legs were held in front of it in a bent but relaxed position, and two forelegs, longer and with sharp-toothed ridges, that seemed to be leading the insect orchestra, waving in perfect time. It sat like this, underside exposed, leaning against the tree, a face on a telescoping neck down on the chest, watching things. The face was strange, not insect-like at all, nor was the position of the sitter nor the fact that it had only four limbs. It appeared to have a tiny, scruffy moustache, topped by a perfectly round and black nose, and two almost human eyes that reflected the glare of the proceedings with an evil and ancient leer.

There was a sudden darkness above, and Cousin Bat landed in the middle of the circle, bowed to the large onlooker, and joined the dance. The strange eyes of the lead bug darted around the circle, then over to Brazil, whose form was just barely visible still hidden by the forest.

Suddenly the leader's forelegs went into a V shape, and the music stopped, everyone staying perfectly still; even the bugs seemed frozen in midflight.

The lead bug, who Brazil knew was the Swarm Queen, spoke to Cousin Bat, and Brazil found it interesting that the translator carried it as the voice of an incredibly tiny and ancient old woman.

So are the legends of witches born, he thought sardonically.

"You have brought only two! I charged you to bring all three!" the Swarm Queen accused Bat.

Bat bowed, his voice flat and mechanical. "The other is a plant, Highness. It is rooted for the night, asleep beyond any recall except the morning sun."

"That is unacceptable," the Swarm Queen snapped. "We have dealt with this problem before. Wait!" She turned to Brazil, and he felt the piercing eyes fall on him.

"Deer! Come into the circle!" the Swarm Queen ordered, and Brazil felt himself moving slowly, haltingly, toward the circle despite no order on his part. He felt the energy grow to almost overpowering proportions as he crossed the toadstool ring.

"The ring binds you all! Bound be ye till my return, or till morning, till midnight at the Well of Souls," she intoned, then flipped over on her stomach, supported by all four legs. The back had long, integral wings and seemed to glow with the same stuff as her underside, although Brazil knew that was mostly reflection.

"You will show me," she said to the bat, and Bat immediately took off, the Swarm Queen following with a tinkling sound that was like a single note in the eerie Faerie symphony.

Brazil tried to recross the circle of toadstools, found he couldn't. He idly kicked at one, but it proved to be more rock than toadstool, and his hoof met with a clacking sound but nothing else.

He looked at the inhabitants of the circle. All, like Wuju, were frozen, like statues, although he could see that they were breathing. There was a monotonous, yet pleasant, hum from the Faerie, marking place.

Many of the other creatures were vaguely humanoid; all were small, a few monkey-like, but all were distorted, hellish versions of their former selves.

Brazil remembered the encounters on Old Earth. Since the Faerie created their own press to suit themselves, they had a pretty good reputation in folklore and superstition. He had never discovered how they had managed to get in. Oh, some representatives of many other races had—some as volunteers to teach the people, some because their home worlds had closed before they personally had reached maturity and Old Earth had the room and a compatible biosphere.

He wondered idly if those primitive peasants who told such wonderful stories of the Faerie would still like them if they knew that these folk doubled as the basis for witches and many evil spirits. Once created by some Markovian mind, they could not be wiped out; they had to run their course and survive or fail as the rules said.

They had done too well. They worked their magic and dominated their own hex, using the collective mental powers of the swarm directed and guided by the Swarm Queen who was mother to them all, and tried to spread out. They managed to interfere in thirteen other Southern hexes where the mathematics did not forbid their enormous powers, before the Markovians finally moved to limit them to their own hex.

Here they were in their own element, and supreme. How many thousands, maybe hundreds of thousands, of swarms existed in this hex? Brazil wondered. I beat them outside of their own element once, but can I do it here?

About an hour passed, with Brazil, the only moving thing in the ring, getting more and more nervous; yet he held onto a streak of optimism deep inside. If they couldn't succeed with Vardia before daybreak, these nocturnal creatures would go back to their tree burrows, Swarm Queen included. How long to dawn? he wondered.

A sudden thought came to him, and he started carefully to draw a pentagram around the circle. He tried to be casual, so it didn't look as if he were doing much of anything; but his hoof managed to make the mark in the grassy meadow. This was a long shot, he knew, but it might stall the Swarm Queen until morning.

He was about halfway around when brush crackled

267

and he saw Vardia walk onto the knoll and into the circle, the Swarm Queen resting on her sun leaf. There was a shadow above, and Bat landed back in the circle. As soon as Vardia was across the toadstool ring, the Swarm Queen flew back over to her seat under the tree and resumed that casual and unnatural sitting position.

Too late, he thought, and stopped the pentagram. I'll have to accept the spell and break it.

The Swarm Queen looked thoughtful for a few minutes. Then, quickly, she looked at the circle. "Be free within the circle," she said almost casually in that tiny, old-woman's voice.

Bat staggered a few seconds, then caught himself and looked around, surprised. He saw the others and looked amazed.

"Brazil! Vardia! Wuju! How'd you get here?" he asked in a puzzled tone.

Wuju looked around strangely at the assemblage. She saw Brazil and went over to him. "Nathan!" she said fearfully. "What's happening?"

Vardia looked around and barely whispered, "What a strange dream."

Bat whirled, spied the Swarm Queen, and started to walk toward her. He got to the circle, and suddenly couldn't make his feet move. He flapped his wings for a takeoff, but didn't go off the ground.

"What the hell is this?" Bat asked strangely. "Last I remember I was flying near the shoreline when I heard this strange music—and now I wake up here!"

"These creatures seem to—" Wuju began, but the Swarm Queen suddenly snapped, "Stand mute!" and the Dillian's voice died in midsentence.

The Swarm Queen glanced up at the barely visible sky.

"There's a storm coming," she said more to herself than to anyone. "It will not be over until after dawn. Therefore, the simplest thing should be the best." She looked up at the buzzing swarm, then flipped over and walked into the circle. Brazil could feel the power building up. The Swarm Queen flipped again lightly, and sat on the side of a toadstool, inside the ring, forelegs behind her to steady her.

"What shall we do with the interlopers?" she asked the swarm.

"Make them fit," came a collective answer from the swarm.

"Make them fit," the Swarm Queen echoed. "And how can we make them fit when we have so little time?"

"Transform them, transform them," suggested the swarm.

The Swarm Queen's gaze fell on Wuju, who almost withered at the look and clung to Brazil.

"You wish him?" the Swarm Queen asked acidly. "You shall have him!" Her eyes burned like coal, and the humming of the swarm intensified to an almost unbearable intensity.

Where Wuju had been, there was suddenly a doe, slightly smaller and sleeker than Brazil's stag. The doe looked around at the lights, confused, and then leaned down and munched a little grass, oblivious to the proceedings.

The Swarm Queen turned to Vardia. "Plant, you want so much to act the animal, so shall you be!"

The buzzing increased again, and where Vardia had stood was another doe, identical to the one that had been Wuju.

"It's easier to use something local, that you know," the Swarm Queen remarked to no one in particular. "I have to hurry." She turned her gaze on Cousin Bat.

"You like them, be like them!" she ordered, and Bat, too, turned into a doe identical in every way to the other two.

Now she turned to Brazil. "Stags should not think," she said. "It is unnatural. Here is your harem, stag. Dominate them, rule them, but as what you are, not what you pretend to be!"

The swarm increased again, and Brazil's mind went blank, dull, unthinking.

"And finally," pronounced the Swarm Queen, "so that so complex a spell, done so hurriedly, does not break, I bequeath to the four the fear and terror of all but their own kind, and of all things which disturb the beasts. They are free of the circle."

Brazil suddenly bolted into the dark, the other three following quickly behind.

There was the rumble of thunder, the flash of lightning.

"The circle is broken," intoned the Swarm Queen.

"We go to shelter," responded the swarm as it dispersed. The other creatures came alive, some gibbering insanely, others howling, as the lightning and thunder increased.

The Swarm Queen flipped and walked quickly over to her tree and into the base.

"Sloppy job," she muttered to herself. "I hate to rush."

The rain started to fall.

Even though it *was* a sloppy spell, it took Brazil almost a full day and night to break it. The flaw was a simple one: at no time during the encounter had the Swarm Queen heard him talk, and it just hadn't occurred to her that he could. The input-output device on the translator continued to operate, although it did little good for the rest of the night in the storm and throughout the next day, when the nocturnal Faerie were asleep.

When the creatures emerged at nightfall, though, they talked. The conversations were myriad, complex, and involved actions and concepts alien to his experience, but they did form words and sentences which the transceiver mounted in his antlers delivered to his brain. These words, although mostly nonsense, gave a continual input that banged at his mind, stimulated it, gave it something to grab onto. Slowly self-awareness returned, concepts formed, forced their way through the spell's barrier.

That spark inside of him that had always ensured his preservation would not let him lapse or quit. Concepts battered at his brain, forcing word pictures in his mind, building constructs which burst into his consciousness.

It was like a war against an invisible barrier, something inside him attacking, always beating at the blocks that had been placed.

Suddenly, he was through. Memories crowded

back, and with them came reason. He felt exhausted —he was totally worn out from the struggle, yet he knew that precious time had been wasted, and more roadblocks raised.

He looked around in the dark. It was very hard to see anything except the flitting shapes of the Faerie, but he knew that he must be deep inside the hex. He looked around. Asleep nearby were the three transformed members of the expedition, absolutely identical even to scent. The Swarm Queen *had* been in a hurry and had used but a single model.

Realizing there was little that could be done until shortly before dawn, lest he give himself away to some curious Faerie by acting undeer-like, he relaxed and waited for the sky to lighten.

With daylight came safety, and the freedom to move. He spent over an hour trying to make some kind of contact with the three does, but their stares were blank, their actions totally natural. The spell could not be broken from without as far as they were concerned.

For a while he considered abandoning them; they would follow him to the border, of course, but would be unable to cross it. The stakes certainly warranted it; logic dictated it.

But he knew he couldn't do it. Not without a good try.

He started off, wishing he could trace the wild, crazy route they had used to get where they were. He decided that the best thing to do would be to head due east; no matter what, that would bring him to the ocean sooner or later, and from there he could get his bearings.

He moved with the swiftness that only a deer could have in the forest, and the three followed him loyally, almost slavishly. Part of the spell, he guessed. The Swarm Queen had bound Wuju to him, and then duplicated her transformation precisely on the other two, which simplified things a great deal.

He made the ocean before nightfall, but had no way of telling if he were north or south of the Faerie colony he sought. He decided that he had accomplished enough for one day, and that the next day would tell the story.

He awoke later than intended, the sunlight already glaring down on the ocean, causing diamond-like facets to cover the surface.

Which way? he wondered. Am I north or south of our last position?

He finally decided to go north; at worst, this would take him to the Ghlmon border and where he had to go. If he didn't run into the place he was looking for, he would have to abandon them for a while and return later to straighten the matter out. About an hour up the beach he came upon the packs, still sitting in the sand where they had camped the first night. They were wet and sand-blown, but still intact.

As the does romped in the surf or sniffed at the strange-smelling things in the sand, he worked feverishly, cursing his lack of hands. It took ten minutes to open a pack, and several more to work one of the flame guns that Vardia had carried out of the pack. The next task was somehow to pick it up.

He finally managed a grip of sorts with his mouth. It was awkward, and he dropped it many times as he went back into the forest, but each time he patiently turned it just right and handled it again.

It seemed like hours getting the flame pistol through that forest, but at last he came upon the clearing of ominously familiar character: the toadstool ring and the great tree. It was too well etched in his memory to be simply a similar place of some other swarm, and his deer's nose confirmed the proper scents.

Carefully he searched for a large, uneven rock, and with great difficulty rolled it to within a meter of the hollow area that was the Swarm Queen's throne, at the base of the big tree. He managed to prop the flame gun sideways against the rock, so that it was mostly upright and pointed at the hollow.

Satisfied, he went and got sticks from the forest and built a crude pentagram around the pistol and rock. Next he positioned himself so his forelegs were on either side of the pistol, the left one serving as a backstop for the grip area which also contained the gas, the right one just to the right of the trigger.

He nodded to himself in satisfaction, and briefly checked the sun and the location of his three does, all of whom were idly grazing nearby. About two hours to sundown, he thought. Just about right.

He brought his right foreleg to bear on the trigger. The pistol jiggled but remained in the right general direction. There was a hiss of escaping gas, but no flame. He released it, realizing that the flint igniter mechanism would require a hard and quick jerk on the trigger.

He knew that, if he did that, he might lose control of the gun, even have it suddenly jump up and burn him. He sighed and made up his mind. Tensely, he planted his left foreleg against the gun butt and his right just touching the large, unguarded trigger made for Czillian tentacles.

Suddenly, in one sudden motion, he pulled against the trigger hard with his right leg. It jumped a little, but stayed firm.

And remained unignited.

Steeling himself, he tried again. Once more it failed to ignite, because he had flinched and not pushed the trigger straight back. He wondered idly if he could succeed, given his physical limitations. If not, he would just have to abandon his companions.

He tried one more time, using extra force. The pistol ignited, but the thing almost jerked out of his precarious hold. Carefully, without releasing the trigger, he gingerly managed to point the thing back in the general direction of the tree. Just to the left of the tree the area was smoldering, some of it still afire.

Now the jet of flame focused on the tree hollow, and he could see the bark smolder and catch, the fire almost enveloping the tree like something liquid and living. Smoke billowed up, the scent disturbing to his nostrils. Birds screeched, and forest animals ran for cover in panic.

Suddenly he heard what he had been waiting for: a tiny, weak voice coughing.

The Swarm Queen had more than one exit available, and she crawled dizzily out of the top of the tree trunk, near the point where the four main branches went off. She was blind, sick, and groping feebly, starting to make her way up the side of one of the branches.

"Swarm Queen!" he called, not letting up on the flame. "Shall I burn you or will you meet my conditions under pain of reversal?"

"Who are you that dares do this to me?" she managed, coughing and groaning in fear and misery as she maintained her dignity.

"He who was wronged by you, and he who drove your ancestors off distant planets!" he replied boldly, but idly and somewhat fearfully wondering how much more of a charge the pistol had. "Do you yield under pain of reversal?"

The large bug hadn't made it up the branch, almost overcome by the smoke and feeling the flames. Brazil was suddenly afraid she would fall into the fire before she yielded.

"I—I yield!" she called. "Turn off your cursed fire!"

"Say the whole thing!" he demanded.

"I yield under pain of reversal, dammitall!" she screamed nervously.

At that moment the charge ran out of the gun and it sputtered and died. Brazil let go, and looked at it strangely. A few seconds longer, he thought, and I'd have lost.

"Get me down before I burn!" screamed the Swarm Queen, who was still very much in danger. The flames continued to smolder in the tree and around the trunk, although without the added fire they were slowly turning to glowing red against the charred and blackened side.

"Jump straight ahead and fly to the ground," he told her. "You know the distance."

She could have done so before, of course, but the heat and fire always induced panic in these creatures.

She landed shakily and sat, trembling, for several minutes. Finally she regained her composure and peered up at him with those old and evil semihuman eyes, squinting. She was not totally blind in the light, but her vision was quite poor.

"You're the deer!" she gasped in amazement. "How did you break the spell? How do you talk at all?"

"Your spells cannot hold me for long," he told her. "That which inhabits this simple vessel is your superior. But it *does* bind my companions, and it is for their sake that I charge you."

"You have three charges only!" she spat, looking at the still smoking, blackened tree. "Consider them carefully, lest I kill you for what you have done to my home and my honor!"

"Honor be damned," Brazil replied disgustedly. "If you had any, there would have been no need to invoke a reversal. Remember *that* well. Should you default on the charges, it is I who will be Swarm Queen and you who will be a deer!"

"State the charges, alien," she responded in a bitter tone. "They will be honored."

Brazil thought carefully.

"One," he said. "My three companions and I shall cross the border into Ghlmon, traversing the distance from here to there without spell or any form of interference that would cause danger or delay."

The Swarm Queen's eyebrows rose, and she said, "Done."

"Two: the spells shall be removed from my three companions, and they shall regain all mental faculties, all memory, and shall be restored to their original forms."

"Done," the Swarm Queen agreed. "And the third?"

"You shall cast a spell to be effective when we cross the Ghlmon border that will erase all memories, effects, and signs of us four having been here, including those from your own mind."

"A pleasure," she said. "So shall it be when darkness falls."

"Until midnight at the Well of Souls," he responded.

And she was stuck. Should any of the conditions cease to function or be unfulfilled, the original spell would bounce back at her.

Nightfall came in about two hours. There were still

275

some wisps of smoke from the tree, but little else to show the struggle. When the swarm emerged from its thousands of holes in the surrounding trees, it found the queen disturbed, but they sensed that a battle had been fought and that she had lost. Since their power could only be focused through her, they had to go along.

The three does had scattered during the fire, but all had timidly returned by dusk and were herded into the toadstool circle without much difficulty.

The Swarm Queen's eyes burned with hatred, but she followed orders. As the swarm gathered in the circle and hummed its strange music, she pronounced the first charge, for their safe conduct, then turned to the second.

"The three within the circle shall be restored in mind and body to their original selves!" she pronounced, and as she said it, it was so.

Brazil gasped, cursing himself for a fool in remembering the literalness of charges.

In the circle stood Vardia, not as a Czillian, but as she had looked those first days on his ship—human, about twelve years old, thirty or so kilos, with shaven head.

Next to her, looking even more confused, was not the Dillian Wuju but Wu Julee, obviously a healthy and unaddicted one, but about forty-five kilos, long black hair, and decent-sized but saggy breasts.

And there was a stranger there. He was a boy, about Vardia's apparent physical age, with short hair and prepubescent genitals, about 150 centimeters tall, muscled, and fairly well proportioned.

"Well, Master Varnett," Brazil said, bemused. "Out of the woodwork early, I guess."

276

Ekh'l

THE DIVINER AND THE REL AND THE SLELCRONIAN in Vardia's body surveyed the towering, snow-capped mountains ahead of them.

The mountains, majestic and all-encompassing, ran right to the sea. A small beach was visible, composed of blackish sand. Out into the water they could see sea stacks, the remnants of long-extinct volcanic activity. The sky was a leaden gray, and the air was terribly cold off the ocean.

"Clouds will be moving in soon," Hain remarked behind them. "Rain or snow likely all along the beach. We'd better get started."

"Can we make it without going into the mountains?" the Slelcronian asked apprehensively. "What if we run out of beach?"

"Friend Hain, here, can cling to the sheer walls if necessary," The Rel replied confidently, "and she can ferry us around that way. No, this looks like rough, slow going but one of the easiest steps. The border with Yrankhs is just a few meters beyond the waterline, so we're not likely to meet the denizens of Ekh'l—a kind of flying ape, I believe. The Yrankhs are not ones we'd like to meet—flesh-eaters all—but they are water-breathers and not likely to bother us unless we decide to swim."

"The fog's coming in," Skander noted. "We'd better get going."

"Agreed," responded The Rel, and they started down to the beach.

It was easy going, relatively speaking. The beach did disappear for several miles at one point or another, but although it ate up a lot of time, there was no problem in Hain ferrying them across one by one.

277

After almost three days, including delays from both terrain and a cold, bitter rain that stopped them for several hours, they were about three-quarters of the way to the Ghlmon border. The only living things they had encountered were seabirds in the millions, crying out in rage at the intruders. Once or twice they thought they caught sight of something huge flying about the mountaintops on great white wings, but the creatures never came close and no one was sure.

At a particularly long break in the beach, which took Hain over an hour to negotiate each way, the only incident of the slow passage occurred.

Hain set off first with the Slelcronian and the supplies, leaving The Diviner and The Rel alone with Skander on the beach.

Skander sat munching some dried fish, apparently unconcerned about the pace or the rough portage ahead. Then, satisfied that Hain was out of sight and hearing along the rocky cliff, the Umiau looked up at The Rel. It was hard to tell the front from the back of the creature even if she knew the Northerner *had* a front or back.

Slowly, almost imperceptibly, she started edging down toward the nearby ocean breakers.

Less than five meters from the water, The Rel noticed, and started coming toward Skander at a surprisingly fast speed. "Stop!" the creature called. "Or we shall stop you!"

Skander hesitated a fateful moment, then made a break for the beckoning waves.

The Diviner's glowing, winking lights became extremely intense, and something shot out from the globe, striking with a loud crash just in front of the mermaid. Skander rolled but did not stop.

Another bolt shot out, striking Skander in the back, and she gave a cry then went limp, the water actually touching her outstretched arm. The body was motionless, eyes staring, but the sharp rise and fall of the chest showed that she lived.

The Rel glided up to the creature and halted next to the body.

"I wondered just how long that mind of yours would be controlled by that silly hypnotism," it said in its even, toneless voice. "But you forgot the Slelcronian lesson. Don't worry—you will be able to move soon. A fraction more voltage and your heart would have stopped, though. The only reason that you live is that we need you. The same for the others—Hain for transportation, the Slelcronian because its powers might be useful in a pinch. Now, you'll be coming around shortly. But remember this! If you escape you are of no use to me. If we must choose between losing you and killing you, you are most surely dead. Now, you may move—the *correct* way. And shall we say nothing of this to our companions, eh?"

Skander surrendered, as movement returned. She still felt numb, but not merely of body. The Rel continued in control, and she had no doubt that she was trapped.

Hain returned in a little over two hours, and, after a short rest, was able to handle the two of them.

"We're almost there," the great insect told them. "You can see the damned place from the last stretch of beach. It looks like a piece of hell itself."

Hain was right. Ghlmon looked like a place one would run *from*, not to. The shoreline curved off to the northwest, and the land of Ghlmon started abruptly, the last of the Ekh'l mountains just slightly inching into the new hex. It was a land of blowing sand, dunes ranging in all directions right down to the sea. Outside of the ocean, there was no sign of water, vegetation, or any break in the oranges and purples of the swirling sand.

"You really would have to be crazy to go there willingly, wouldn't you?" Hain said slowly, more to herself than to the others.

"No water at all," Skander sighed.

"No soil, nothing but sand," the Slelcronian added unhappily.

"The first truly pleasant place we've seen in the South," said The Rel.

Sander turned to The Rel. "Well, O leader, how do we proceed?" she asked sarcastically.

"We keep to the coast," the Northerner responded casually. "Hain can continue to catch fish. The Slelcronian will have to go without vitamins for a day or

279

two, but it will get plenty of sun. Better water in that stream back there," The Rel told the plant creature.

While the Slelcronian did so, Skander asked, "What about you, Rel? Or don't you eat?"

"Of course we eat," The Rel replied. "Silicon. What else?"

In a few minutes, they crossed the border.

The wind was close to forty kilometers per hour, the temperature around forty degrees Celsius. It was like going from midwinter into the worst day of summer, and the swirling sand bit deeply into all of them.

They were still within sight of the Ekh'l mountains when they had to stop for the day. Skander collapsed on the hot sand and shook her head exhaustedly. "What kind of creatures could possibly live in this hell?" she mused.

Almost as if to answer the question, a tiny head popped out of the sand near them. Suddenly, it leaped out of the sand, revealing a small, two-legged dinosaur, about a meter high, with short, stubby arms terminating in tiny but very human hands. It had a very long tail which seemed to balance it.

It was a darker green than the Czillian, but this was broken by what appeared to be a tiny, rust-colored vest and jacket. The creature came up to them and stopped. Its flat head and raised eyes set on each side of a spade-shaped mouth surveyed them with quick, darting motions. Suddenly it leaned back on its tail in a relaxed posture.

"I say, old fellows," it said suddenly in a casual tenor that seemed to come from deep inside its throat—suggesting a translator in use—"Are you the good guys or the bad guys?"

Ivrom

"THIS TURNING YOU ALL BACK INTO WHAT WE THINK of as human has some definite drawbacks," Nathan Brazil, still a giant stag, complained as they walked up the beach. The packs were on him, since none of the other three could now manage the heavy load.

"You think *you* have problems," Wu Julee responded. "We're all stark naked and none of the clothing in the packs fits anymore."

"Not to mention feeling hunger, and pain, and cold again," Vardia put in. "I had forgotten these sensations, and I don't like them. I was happier as a Czillian."

"But how is it possible?" Wuju asked. "I mean, how could things done by the Markovian brain be so undone?"

"Why not ask Varnett?" Brazil suggested. "He's the brain that got this mess started, anyway."

"You all are yelling about trivialities," Varnett sulked. "I could *fly*. And before I set out to catch you, Brazil, I experienced sex. For the first time, I experienced sex. Now I'm back in this retarded body again."

"Not that retarded," Brazil responded. "You were arrested chemically, but that's all out of your body now. Just as the sponge is out of Wuju. You should mature normally, in a couple of years, depending on your genes and your diet. Good looking, too, if I remember rightly, since you're based on Ian Varnett. I remember him as one hell of a womanizer—particularly for a mathematician."

"You *knew* Ian Varnett?" the boy gasped. "But—he's been dead some six hundred years!"

"I know," said Nathan Brazil wistfully. "He got

281

caught up in the great experiment on Mavrishnu. What a waste. *You* know it was a waste, Varnett—I saw your Zone interviews."

"There has always been trouble with Varnetts on Mavrishnu," the duplicate of the great mathematician, made from cells of the long-dead original's frozen body, said with a gleam in his eye. "They tried three or four early on, but I'm the first one in more than a century. They needed him again, at least, his potential. I wasn't the first to interrupt Skander at his real work and inquiries—a lot of skillful agents put everything together. They were raising me for a different, more local set of problems, but I was already proving to be, I think, too much of a problem. They set me up on Dalgonia to see if I could crack Skander's work, figuring that whether I did or didn't they could get me when I returned."

The group continued talking as they walked down the beach, unhampered—as the charge to the Faerie required—by any obstructions.

"How much *do* you know, Varnett? About all this, that is," Brazil asked.

"When I saw the cellular sample of the Dalgonian brain in the computer storage, I recognized the mathematical relationship of the sequence and order of the energy pulses," the boy remembered. "It took about three hours to get the sequence, and one or two more to nail it down with the camp's computers. I only had to look at the thing to see that the energy waveforms represented there bore no resemblance to anything we knew, and the matter-to-energy-to-matter process within the cells was easily observed. I combined what I saw with what we theorized *must* be the reason the Markovians had no artifacts. The planetary brain created anything you wanted, stored anything you wanted, on demand, perhaps even by thought. That gave me *what* was going on in that relationship, although I still haven't any idea *how* it's done."

Vardia was impressed. "You mean it was like the spells on us here—they just *wished* for something and it was there?"

"That's how the magic works here," Varnett affirmed. "The only way such a concept is possible is

282

if, in fact, *nothing* is real. All of us, these woods, the ocean, the planet—even that sun—are merely constructs. There is nothing in the universe but a single energy field; everything else is taking that energy, transmuting it into matter or different forms of energy, and holding it stable. That's reality—the stabilized, transmuted primal energy. But the mathematical constructs that are so stabilized are in constant tension, like a coiled spring. The energy would revert to its natural state if not kept in check. These creatures —the Faerie—have some control over that checking process. Not enough to make any huge changes, but enough to change the equation slightly, to vary reality. That's magic."

"I don't understand what you're saying too well," Wuju put in, "but I think I get the basic idea. You're saying that the Markovians were gods and could do or have anything they wished for, just like that."

"That's about it," Varnett admitted. "The gods were real, and they created all of us—or, at least, the conditions under which we could develop."

"But that would be the ultimate achievement of intelligence!" Vardia protested. "If that were true, why did they die out?"

Wuju smiled knowingly and looked to Nathan Brazil, once the only human, now the only nonhuman in the party, who was being uncharacteristically silent.

"I heard someone say why they died," Wuju replied. "That someone said that when they reached the ultimate, it became dull and boring. Then they created new worlds, new life forms here and there— and all went off as those new forms to start from the beginning again."

"What a horrible idea," Vardia said disgustedly. "If that were true, it means that even perfection is imperfect, and that when our own people finally reach this godhood, they'll find it wanting and die out by suicide, maybe leaving a new set of primitives to do the same thing all over again. It reduces all the revolutions, the struggles, the pain, the great dreams

—everything—to nonsense! It means that life is pointless!"

"Not pointless," Brazil put in suddenly. "It just means that grand schemes are pointless. It means that you don't make your own life pointless or useless—most people do, you know. It wouldn't make any difference if ninety-nine percent of the people of the human race—or any other—lived or not. Except in sheer numbers their lives are dull, vegetative, and nonproductive. They never dream, never read and share the thoughts of others, never truly experience the fulfilling equation of love—which is not merely to love others, but to be loved as well. That is the ultimate point of life, Vardia. The Markovians never found it. Look at this world, our own worlds—all reflecting the Markovian reality, which was based on the ultimate *materialist* Utopia. They were like the man with incredible riches, perhaps a planet of his own designed to his own tastes, and every material thing you can imagine producible at the snap of his fingers, who, nonetheless, is found dead one morning, having cut his own throat. All his dreams have been fulfilled, but now he is there, on top, alone. And to get where he was, he had to purge himself of what was truly of value. He killed his humanity, his spirituality. Oh, he could love—and buy what he loved. But he couldn't buy that love he craved, only service.

"Like the Markovians, when he got where he'd wanted to be all his life, he found he didn't really have anything at all."

"I reject that theory," Vardia said strongly. "The rich man would commit suicide because of the guilt that he had all that he had while others starved, not out of some craving for love. That word is meaningless."

"When love is meaningless, or abstract, or misunderstood, then is that person or race also meaningless," Brazil responded. "Back in the days of Old Earth one group had a saying, 'What shall it profit a man, if he shall gain the whole world, and lose his own soul?' Nobody listened then, either. Funny—haven't thought of that group in years. They said God was love, and postulated a heaven of communal

284

love, and a hell for those who could not love. Later on that got crudded up with other stuff until the ideas were gone and only the artifacts were left. Like the Markovians, they paid more attention to *things* than to *ideas*—and, like the Markovians, they died for it."

"But surely the Markovian civilization was heaven," Vardia said.

"It was hell," Brazil responded flatly. "You see, the Markovians got everything their ancestors had ever dreamed of, and they *knew* it wasn't enough. They *knew* that something attainable was missing. They searched, poked, queried, did everything to try and find why the people were miserable, but since everything they had or knew was a construct of themselves, they couldn't find it. They decided, finally, to go back and repeat the experiment, little realizing that it, too, was doomed to failure—for the experiment, our own universe, was made in a variety of shapes and forms, but it was still in their own image. They didn't even bother to make a clean start—they used themselves as the prototypes for all the races they'd create, and they used the same universe—the one they'd lived in, rose in, and failed in. That's why their artifacts are still around—the two artifacts they had—their cities and their control brains."

Varnett let out a gasp. "Suddenly I think I see what you mean. This Well World we're on, if you're right, not only provided the trial-lab runs for the new races and their environments, and the way of changing everything to match—it was also the control!"

"Right," Brazil affirmed grimly. "Here everything was laboratory-standard, lab-created, monitored, and maintained by automatic equipment to keep it that way. Not all of them—just a representative sample, the last races to be created, since they were the easiest to maintain."

"But our race here destroyed itself," Varnett protested. "I heard about it. Does that mean we're out of it? That the best we can do is destroy ourselves, destroy others, or, perhaps, reach the Markovian level and wind up committing suicide anyway? Is there no hope?"

"There's hope," Brazil replied evenly. "And despair, too. That religion of Old Earth I told you about? Well, those who believed in it had the idea that their God sent his son, a perfect human being filled with nothing but goodness and love, to us humans. Son-of-God question aside, there really *was* such a person born—I watched him try to teach a bunch of people to reject material things and concentrate on love."

"What happened to him?" Wuju asked, fascinated.

"His followers rejected him because he wouldn't rule the world, or lead a political revolution. Others capitalized on his rhetoric for political ends. Finally he upset the established political system too much, and they killed him. The religion, like those founded by other men of our race in other times, was politicized within fifty years. Oh, there were *some* devoted followers—and of others like this man, too. But they were never in *control* of their religion, and became lost or isolated in the increased institutionalizing of the faiths. Same thing happened to an older man, born centuries earlier and thousands of miles away. He didn't die violently, but his followers substituted *things* for *ideas* and used the quest for love and perfection as a social and political brake to justify the miseries of mankind. No, the religious prophets who made it were the ones who thought in Markovian terms, in political terms—the founder of the Com, for example, saw conditions of material deprivation that made him sick. He dreamed of a civilization like that of the Markovians, and set the Com on its way. He succeeded the best, because he appealed to that which everyone can understand—the quest for material Utopia. Well, he can have it."

"Now, hold on, Brazil!" Varnett protested. "You say you were there when all these people were around. That must have been thousands of years ago. Just how old are you, anyway?"

"I'll answer that when we get to the Well," Brazil responded. "I'll answer all questions then, not before. If we don't get to the Well before Skander and whoever's with him, it won't make any difference, anyway."

"Then they could supplant the Markovians, change the equations?" Varnett asked, aghast. "I at one time thought I could, too, but logic showed me how wrong I was. My people—my *former* people, those of the night—agreed with me. It was only when word came that Skander might make a run for it that they decided to send me to head him off. That's why I joined up with you, Brazil—you said you were going to do the same thing back in Zone. Our mysterious informant told us to link up with you if we could, and I did."

"Now how could—" Brazil started, then suddenly was silent for a moment, thinking. Suddenly the voice box between his antlers gave off a wry chuckle. "Of course! What an idiot I've been! I'll bet that son of a bitch has bugged every embassy in Zone! I'd forgotten just what kind of a devious mind he had!"

"What are you talking about?" Wuju asked, annoyed.

"The third player—and a formidable one. The one who warned Skander against kidnap, got Varnett to link up with me. He knew all along where Varnett, here, and Skander were. He just wanted to be there for the payoff, as usual. I was his insurance policy, in case anything went wrong—and it did. Skander was kidnapped, and out of control or immediate surveillance. At least he has managed to delay one or another party on the way to the Well so that we're supposed to get there at about the same time—where he'll have a reception party waiting for us. He warned Skander so I'd have time to get to Czill, about even with them on the other side of the ocean. When we were trapped with the Murnies, he pulled strings to get the Czillians to put pressure on The Nation to bottle them up until we were even again! I don't wonder that he might have some influence with the Faerie—maybe the Skander party somehow got bogged down, too!"

"Who the hell are you talking about, Nathan?" Wuju persisted.

"Look!" Brazil said. "There's Ghlmon, the last hex before the equator! See the burned-out reddish sand? It goes across two hexes in width, a half-hex tall."

"*Who?*" Wuju persisted.

"Well," Brazil replied hesitantly, "unless I am

wildly mistaken, somewhere out in that sunburned desert we'll meet up with him."

"Are we going to cross the border today?" Varnett asked, looking at the sun, barely above the horizon.

"Might as well," Brazil responded. "It's going to be pretty tough on all of us there, so we'd better get used to it. The heat's going to be terrible, I think, and my fur coat's going to be murder, while your naked skins will be roasted. So we'd better push on into the night as much as we can, following the shoreline as we have. Days may be unworkable there."

Wuju had an infuriated look on her face, but Brazil speeded up, forcing them into a jog to keep up, and within a few minutes they crossed the border.

The heat hit them like a giant blanket, and it was humid, too, this close to the ocean. Within minutes of crossing the border, they had slowed to almost a crawl, the three humans perspiring profusely, Brazil panting wildly, tongue hanging out of his mouth. Finally, they had to stop and rest. Dusk brought only slight relief.

Wuju looked again at Brazil with that I'd-like-to-kill-you expression. Hot, winded, the sand burning her feet and, when she sat down, her rear, she remained undeterred.

"Who, Nathan?" she persisted, gasping for breath.

Brazil's stag body looked as uncomfortable as anyone's, but that mechanical voice of his said evenly, "The one person who could know for certain that I would go after Skander, and that I would get to you in Dillia before going anywhere, was the only person who could tell Varnett where to find me and why. He was a pirate in the old days. You couldn't trust him with anything if he could make a shekel going against you, yet you could trust him with your life if there were no profit in it. That's what I forgot—the stakes are high here; there's a bigger profit potential than anyone could think of. He told me I could get help from everyone of all races, but trust none—including him, as it turned out. Although he figured I wouldn't think of him as an opponent since we'd been good friends and I owed him. He was almost right."

Understanding hit her at last, and she brightened. "*Ortega!*" she exclaimed. "Your friend we met when we first entered Zone!"

"The six-armed walrus-snake?" Vardia put in. "*He's* behind all this?"

"Not *all* this," came a voice behind them—a clipped, casual male voice that carried both dignity and authority. "But he still is happy everything has turned out right."

They all whirled. In the near-darkness, it was hard for any of them to see properly, but the creature looked for all the world like a meter-tall dinosaur, dark green skin and flat head, standing upright on large hind legs, while holding a curved pipe in a stubby hand. He also appeared to be wearing an old-fashioned formal jacket.

The creature puffed on the pipe, the coals glowing in the dark.

"I say," it said pleasantly, "do you mind if I finish my pipe before we travel? Terrible waste otherwise, y'know."

West Ghlmon

THE FOUR OF THEM LOOKED CURIOUSLY AT THE strange creature. Brazil could only think that he should have been in *Alice in Wonderland*. The others took the appearance of the new arrival more calmly, having grown used to strange creatures and strange ways by this time.

"You were sent by Serge Ortega?" Brazil asked evenly.

The creature took its pipe out of its mouth and assumed an insulted expression. "Sir, I am the Duke of Orgondo. This is Ghlmon. The Ulik have no authority here. They are merely our neighbors. We were approached only a few days ago by Mr. Ortega about this matter, and we are, of course, much concerned. The Ulik interest is—well, frankly, closer to ours. We know them and understand them. We've gotten along for thousands of years with them. With their help we managed to survive when the environment here changed and the soil turned to sand. But all of you—Mr. Ortega included—are here at our sufferance, and we will brook no intrusions into sovereignty."

"What's he saying?" Vardia asked, and the others added their confusion. For the first time, Brazil realized that now they could understand only people with translators and those speaking Confederacy. Their own translators had gone along with their former bodies.

"Pardon me, Your Grace," Brazil said politely. "I will have to translate, for, I fear, my companions have no translators."

The lizard looked at the three humans. "Hmmm.... Most curious. I had been told to expect a Dillian, Czillian, and a Creit. We heard that you would be an antelope, and that so far is the only correct information. You are Mr. Brazil, are you not?"

"I am," Brazil replied. "The male is Mr. Varnett, the female with breasts is Wuju, and the undeveloped female is Vardia. We did, after all, have to come through Ivrom. That, in itself, is an accomplishment, I should think—to have come through unaltered would have been a miracle."

"Quite," nodded the Ghlmonese. "But we had no doubt you would come through, although there's been hell to pay for the three days you disappeared. We figured you'd been bewitched, and started moving some diplomatic mountains to find who had you."

"Then that bewitching stuff wasn't part of Ortega's tricks?" Brazil responded. "He seemed awfully confident we'd get through."

"Oh, no, he figured that you would get stuck," the duke replied casually. "But we of Ghlmon are more adept at the arts than those filthy savages in Ivrom. It was only a matter of finding you. We already had the other party, so nothing was disturbed no matter how long it took."

"So what's the next move now?" Brazil asked calmly.

"Oh, you'll be my guests for the night, of course," the duke said warmly. "Tomorrow, we'll get you on a sandshark express and take you to the capital at Oodlikm, where you will link up with Ortega and the other party. From that point it will be Ortega's show, although we'll be watching."

Brazil nodded. "This game is getting so crowded you need a scorecard." He provided a running translation of the conversation so that the others could follow what was going on. Finally the creature's pipe went out, and it tapped the bowl and shook out the last remains of whatever it had been smoking. It smelled like gunpowder.

"Places have been prepared for you," the duke told them. "Ready to go? It's not far."

"Do we have a choice?" Brazil retorted.

The little dinosaur got that hurt look again. "Of course! You may go back across the border, or jump in the ocean. But, if you plan to stay in Ghlmon, you will do what *we* wish."

"Fair enough," the stag replied. "Lead on."

They followed the little dinosaur along the beach in silence for a little over a kilometer. There, by the side of the sea, a huge tent of canvas or something very similar had been erected. A flag was flying from the tent's center mast. Several Ghlmonese stood around nearby, and tried not to look bored to death.

Two by the tent flap snapped to attention as the duke approached, and he nodded approvingly. "Everything ready?" he asked.

"The table is set, Your Grace," one replied. "Everything should be suitable."

The duke nodded and the sentry held back the flap so he could enter and kept it open for the others to pass through.

Inside, the place looked like something out of a medieval textbook. The floor was covered with thick carpeting like a handwoven mosaic. Actually made up of hundreds of small rugs, it looked like a colorful series of lumps.

In the center was a long, low wooden table with strange-smelling dishes on it. There were no chairs, but the human members of the party were quickly provided with rolls of blankets or rugs that propped them up enough to make things comfortable.

"Simple, but it will have to do," the duke said, almost apologetically. "You will find the food compatible —Ambassador Ortega was most helpful here. We didn't expect you in these forms, of course, but there should be no problem. Pity you couldn't be entertained in the castle, but that is impossible, I fear."

"Where *is* your castle?" Brazil asked. "I haven't seen any structures but this one."

"Down below, of course," the duke replied. "Ghlmon wasn't always like this. It changed, very slowly, over thousands of years. As the climate became progressively drier, we realized that we couldn't fight the sand, so we learned to live beneath it. Air pumps, constantly manned by skilled workmen, keep the air coming in from vents to the surface—which crews keep clear. Sort of like living under the ocean in domes, as I have heard is done elsewhere. The desert's our ocean —more than you think. We can swim in it, albeit slowly, and follow guide wires from one spot to another, coming up here only to travel long distances."

Brazil translated, and Vardia asked, "But where does the food come from? Surely nothing grows here."

"We are basically carnivores," the duke explained after the translation of the question. "Lots of creatures exist in the sand, and many are domesticated. Water is easy—the original streams still exist, only they now run underground, along the bedrock. The vegetable dishes here are for your benefit. We always keep some growing in greenhouses down under for guests."

They ate, continuing the conversation. Brazil, not knowing how much the Ghlmonese were actually in on the expedition, carefully avoided any information in that direction, and it was neither asked for nor brought up by his host.

After eating, the duke bade them farewell. "There's a good deal of straw over there for padding if you can't sleep on the rug," he told them. "I know you're tired and won't disturb you. You have a long journey starting tomorrow."

Vardia and Varnett found soft places near the side

of the tent and were asleep in minutes. Wuju tried to join them, but lay there awake for what seemed like hours. Her insomnia upset her—she was tired, aching, and uncomfortable, yet she couldn't sleep.

The torches had been extinguished, but she could make out Brazil's large form in the gloom near the entrance. Painfully, she got up and walked over to him.

He wasn't asleep either, she saw. His head turned as she approached. "What's the matter?" he asked.

"I—I dunno," she replied hesitantly. "Can't sleep. You?"

"Just thinking," he said, an odd, almost sad tone in his electronic voice.

"About what?"

"This world. This expedition. Us—not just the two of us, all of us. It's ending, Wuju. No beginnings anymore, just endings."

She looked at him strangely in the darkness, not comprehending his meaning. Unable to pursue it, she changed the subject.

"What's going to happen to us, Nathan?" she asked.

"Nothing. Everything. Depends on who you are," he replied cryptically. "You'll see what I mean. You've had a particularly rough time, Wuju. But you're a survivor. Tough. You deserve to enjoy life a little." He shifted uncomfortably, then continued.

"Just out of curiosity, if you had a choice, if you could return to our sector of the universe as anything or anybody you wanted to be, what would you choose?"

She thought for a minute. "I've never considered going back," she replied in a soft, puzzled tone.

"But if you could, and you could be who and where you wanted—like the genie with the three wishes—what would you choose?"

She chuckled mirthlessly. "You know, when I was a farmer, I had no dreams. We were taught to be satisfied with everything. But when they made me a whore in the Party House, we'd sometimes sit and talk about that. They kept the males and females separate—we never saw any males except Party locals and favored workers. We were programmed to be supersexy and give them a hell of a time. I'm sure the male jocks were equally fantastic for the female bigwigs. They shot us full of hormones, thought we couldn't think of anything but sex—and, it's true, we craved it, constantly, so much so that during slack times we were in bed with each other.

"But the Party people," she continued, "they knew things, went places. Some of them liked to talk about it, and we got to know a lot about the outside world. We'd dream about getting out into it, out perhaps to other worlds, new experiences." She paused for a moment, then continued in that dreamy, yet thoughtful, somewhat wistful tone.

"Three wishes, you said. All right, if we're playing the game, I'd like to be rich, live as long as I wanted, and be young all that time, and fantastically good-looking, too. Not on a Comworld, of course—but that's four, isn't it?"

"Go on," he urged. "Never mind the three. Anything else?"

"I'd like to have you under those same conditions," she replied.

He laughed, genuinely pleased and flattered. "But," he said, serious again, "suppose I wasn't there? Suppose you were out on your own?"

"I don't even want to think about that."

"Come on," he prodded. "It's only a game."

Her head went up, and she thought some more. "If you weren't there, I think I'd like to be a man."

If Brazil had had a human face, it would have risen in surprise. "A man? Why?"

She shrugged, looking slightly embarrassed. "I don't know, really. Remember I said young and good-looking. Men are bigger, stronger, they don't get raped, don't get pregnant. I'd like to have children, maybe, but—well, I don't think any man could turn me on except you, Nathan. Back in the Party House—those men who came. I was like a machine to them, a sex machine. The other girls—they were real people, my family. They *cared*. That's why the Party gave me to Hain, Nathan—I'd gotten to the point where I couldn't turn on to men at all, only women. They felt, they cared, they weren't—well, weren't *threatening*. All of the men I met were—except you. Can you understand that?"

294

"I think I can," he responded slowly. "It's natural, considering your background. On the other hand, there are many worlds where homosexuality is accepted, and you can get children by anything from cloning to artificial insemination. And, of course, men have just as many problems and hang-ups as women. The grass isn't greener, just different."

"That might be the fun of it," she replied. "After all, it's something I've never been—like I'd never been a centaur before, and you'd never been a stag. I *know* what it's like to be a woman—and I don't particularly care for it. Besides, we're only playing."

"I guess we are," he responded. "Since we are, would you rather go back to being a Dillian than what you are now? You can, you know—just go back to Zone through the local Gate and back through again. You'll be readjusted to the original equation. That's the most common way of breaking spells around here, you know. That's the way I'd have handled things if I'd had the time back in Ivrom rather than risking that facedown with the Swarm Queen."

"I—I'm not sure I *could* go back to Dillia," she said softly. "Oh, I loved being that big and strong, loved the country and those wonderful people—but I didn't fit. That's what was driving me crazy in the end. Jol was a wonderful person, but it was *Dal* I was attracted to. And that doesn't go over in Dillia socially—and, if it did, it's impractical."

He nodded. "That's really what you meant when you told me long ago about how people should love people no matter what their form or looks. But what about me? Suppose I turned into something *really* monstrous, so alien that it bore almost no resemblance to what you knew?"

She laughed. "You mean like the bat or a Czillian or maybe a mermaid?"

"No, those are familiar. I mean a real monstrosity."

"As long as you were still you *inside,* I don't think anything would change," she replied seriously. "Why do you talk like that, anyway? Do you expect to turn into a monster?"

"Anything's possible on this world," he reminded her. "We've seen only a fraction of what can happen—

you've seen only six hexes, six out of *fifteen hundred and sixty*. You've met representatives of three or four more. There's a lot that is stranger." His voice turned grim. "We have to meet the new Datham Hain shortly, you know. He's a giant female bug—a monster if ever there was one."

"Now his outside matches his foul inside," she snapped bitterly. "Monsters aren't racial, they're in the mind. He's been a monster all his life."

He nodded. "Look, trust me on this. Hain will get what he deserves—so will everybody. Once inside the Well, we'll all be what we once were, and then will come the reckoning."

"Even you?" she asked. "Or will you stay a deer?"

"No, not a deer," he replied mysteriously, then changed the subject. "Well, maybe it's better over. Two more days and that'll be it."

She opened her mouth to prod, then closed it again. Finally, she asked, "Nathan, is that why you've lived so long? Are you a Markovian? Varnett thinks you are."

He sighed. "No, not a Markovian—exactly. But they might as well continue to think I am. I may have to use that belief to keep everything from blowing apart too soon."

She looked stunned. "You mean all this time you've been dropping hints that you were one of the original builders, and it was all a *bluff?*"

He shook his head slowly. "Not a bluff, no. But I'm very old, Wuju—older than anyone could imagine. So old that I couldn't live with my own memories. I blocked them out, and, until arriving here on the Well World, I was mercifully, blissfully ignorant. No mind in history can function long with this much storage input. The shock of the fight and transformation in Murithel brought the past back, but there's so *much!* It's next to impossible to sort it all out, get a handle on it all. But these memories still give me the edge— I know things the rest of you don't. I'm not necessarily smarter or wiser than you, but I do have all that experience, all that accumulated knowledge of thousands of lifetimes. That gives me the advantage."

"But they all think you're going to work the Well for them," she pointed out. "Everything you've said indicates that you know how."

"That's why Serge kept us alive," he explained. "That's why we've been coddled and prodded. I have no doubt that the little voice box on top my antlers has an extra circuit monitored by Serge. He's probably listening right now. I don't care anymore. That's why he could help us, know where we were and what happened to us. That's why we're going to meet him; that's how all this was prepared in advance. Just in case he can't use me, he'll use Skander, or Varnett— he thinks."

"I can see why he'd be concerned with you three," she replied, "but why the rest of us? Why me, for example?"

If Brazil could have smiled, he would have. "You don't know Serge—the old Serge. I'd been so lulled by that talk about a wife and kids I'd forgotten how little this world changes the real you, deep down. Hain —well, Hain is useful to keep Skander in check as well as for transportation. I don't know who else is along, but be sure they're there only because Serge has some use for them or he hasn't been able to figure out how to dispose of them properly."

"But why me?" she repeated.

"They must have some tame nasties on the Comworlds," he replied sardonically. "You're a hostage, Wuju. You're his handle on me."

She looked uncertain. "Nathan? What if it really came down to that? Would you do what he asked for me?"

"It won't come to that," he assured her. "Believe me, it won't. Varnett has already figured out why, although he's forgotten in his youthful excitement."

"Then what *will* you do?"

"I will lead them all to the Well—Skander can do that anyway, so could Varnett. I intend to show them everything they want. But they will learn that this treasure hunt is full of thorns when they discover what the price really is. I'll bet you that, once in the control room of their dreams, they will think the price is too high."

She shook her head in wonder. "I don't understand any of this."

"You will," he replied cryptically, "at midnight at the Well of Souls."

The trip was uncomfortable and bumpy. They traveled on a huge wooden sled with runners. Pulling them swiftly were eight huge beasts they could not fully see—sandsharks, the Ghlmonese called them. Only huge gray backs and huge, razor-sharp fins were visible as they pulled their heavy load and were kept in check by a Ghlmonese driver with reins for each of the huge creatures.

The sandsharks were giant mammals who lived in the sand as fish lived in water. They breathed air— a single huge nostril opened whenever their great backs broke the surface—and moved at eight to ten kilometers per hour.

By the end of the day the travelers were all sore and bruised, but more than halfway there. They spread rugs out on the sand, and ate food heated by the fiery breath of their driver. There was no problem sleeping that evening, despite the hot air, blowing wind, and strange surroundings.

The next day was a repeat of the first. They passed several other sleds carrying Ghlmonese, and occasionally saw individuals riding in huge saddles on the backs of sandsharks. Once in a while they would see a cluster of what appeared to be huge chimneys with crews keeping the openings from being blocked by sand. Far below, they knew, there were towns, perhaps large cities.

Finally, near dusk of the second day, structures appeared ahead of them, growing rapidly larger as they approached. These proved to be a network of towers and spires made of small rocks, reaching fifty or more meters in the air, like the tops of some medieval fortress.

They slowed, and came to a halt near two towers with a wide gate between. A number of Ghlmonese stood around; others were busy going to or from unknown places.

An officious-looking dinosaur, in ornate red livery,

came up to them. "You are the alien party from Orgondo?" he asked gruffly.

"They are," their driver replied. "All yours and welcome. I have to see to my sharks. They've had a tough journey."

"Which of you is Mr. Brazil?" the official inquired.

"I am," Brazil replied.

The official looked surprised, since Brazil was, after all, still a giant stag, but he recovered quickly. "Come with me, then. The rest of you will be taken to temporary quarters." He motioned to some other Ghlmonese, also in the red livery, and they came up to escort the party. Although the smallest of the humans was a head taller than any of the guards, no one felt like arguing.

"Go with them," Brazil instructed his group. "There'll be no problems. I'll join you as soon as I can."

They had no choice, and walked to the tower nearest them. Brazil turned to the official. "What now?" he asked.

"Ambassador Ortega and the other alien party are camped out near the base of The Avenue," the official replied. "I am to take you to them."

"Lead on," Brazil urged, unconcern in his voice.

The Avenue proved to be a broad trench, thirty or more meters across, that was just beyond the towers and spires. It was also more than fifteen meters below ground level, but, despite only the most rudimentary stone buffers, the sand didn't seem to blow into the obviously artificial culvert, but over and past it.

Broad stone stairs led down to the flat, almost shiny surface below. Brazil had some trouble negotiating the stairs, but finally made it. The buildings of Oodlikm seemed to line The Avenue on both sides, like medieval castles used to be built into the sides of steep river valleys back on Old Earth. There were many stairways and hundreds of doors, windows, and even ports for defense along both sides of The Avenue wall. As for the valley itself, its level, jewellike surface seemed to stretch to the ocean on Brazil's right, and off to the horizon on his left.

Brazil's hooves clacked on the shiny surface. He

towered over countless stalls selling all sorts of things and over the crowds which gaped at him and made way as he passed. He and his escort walked toward the ocean, past the last shops, and finally to what was obviously a more official, less commercial section, across which had been hastily erected a barricade with a heavy wooden gate and armed guards.

The official approached the gate, showed a pass he produced from his coat pocket. After the guards inspected his pass carefully, the gates opened and they passed through. Inside were more guards—huge numbers, in fact. In the center of The Avenue were an Akkafian, a Czillian, a Umiau in what looked like a square bathtub, and—something else.

Brazil studied The Diviner and The Rel, and the last pieces fit into place. The role of the Northerner had been unclear to him from the start, and he knew nothing of the creature's hex, physically or culturally. He was certain that the thing was at the heart of much of the mischief that had been worked, though.

Darkness had fallen, and the stars started showing through. Small gaslights had been lit, giving the entire scene an eerie glow.

"Remain with the others," the official instructed him. "I will get Ambassador Ortega."

Brazil went over to the alien creatures, ignoring all except the Umiau.

"So you're Elkinos Skander," he said flatly.

The mermaid gave a puzzled look. "So? And who or what are you?"

"Nathan Brazil," he replied crisply. "That name means little to you? Perhaps it will be better to say that I am here to avenge seven murders."

The Umiau opened her mouth in surprise. "Seven —what the hell do you mean?"

Brazil's independent eyes showed Skander on the right, and the interest of the other three on the left. The others were all watching the two tensely.

"I was the captain of the freighter who found the bodies on Dalgonia. Seven bodies, charred, left on a barren world. None of them ever did you harm, nor was there any reason for their deaths."

"I didn't kill them," Skander responded in a surly

tone. "Varnett killed them. But, what of it? Would you have preferred to open this world to the Coms?"

"So that was it," Brazil said sadly. "The seven died because you feared that their governments would get control. Skander, *you* know who killed them, and *I* know who killed them, but even beyond that is the fact that they needn't have died even for so dubious a reason. The Gate would not have opened for them."

"Of course it would!" Skander snapped. "It opened when Varnett and I found the mathematical key to the computer. And it was still open for you and your party to fall through!"

Brazil shook his head slowly. "No, Skander. It opened only because the two of you *wanted* it to open. That's the key, you know. Even though you didn't know that the Gate didn't lead to the Dalgonian brain, but to here, you knew that some sort of Gate must exist and you wanted desperately to find it. You had already decided to kill Varnett and the others before you found it. Varnett knew it. He had a desire to find the Gate, and the fear of death to fix it. That's what opened it up, not your mathematical discoveries. It hadn't opened since the Markovians, and it wouldn't have opened again unless the conditions were right."

"Then how did *you* fall through?" Skander retorted. "Why did it open for you?"

"It didn't," Brazil replied evenly. "Although I should have known it was there."

"But it *did* open for us, Brazil," Hain put in.

"Not for you, Hain, or for me, or for Vardia, either," Brazil told them. "But, within our party, there was one person who had lost all hope, who wanted to die, to escape fate's lot. The brain, sensitized to such things, picked this up and lured us to Dalgonia with the false emergency signal. We went up to where the shuttles left by Skander and Varnett were still parked, walked out onto the Gate floor, and, when Wu Julee was well within the field, the Gate triggered—sending all of us here."

"I remember you, now!" Skander exclaimed. "Vardia told me about you while we were imprisoned in The Nation! She told me how the ships seemed to vanish. When I heard all that, I assumed you had engineered the whole thing, that you were a Markovian. The evidence fitted. Besides, it stands to reason that you don't leave a control group like those on the Well World without someone to monitor the control."

"The fact that it was the girl and not Brazil who triggered the Gate doesn't necessarily invalidate your conclusions, Doctor," came a smooth, husky voice behind them. They turned to see the huge form of Serge Ortega, all five meters of snake and two meters of his thick, six-armed body.

"Serge, I should have known better," Brazil said good-humoredly.

All six arms of the Ulik shrugged. "I have a pretty good racket here, Nate. I told you I was happy, and I am. I have most of the embassies at both zones bugged, and the conversations recorded. I find out what's happening, who's doing what to whom, and if there's anything of interest to me and to my people I act on it."

Brazil nodded, and would have smiled if the stag body allowed it. "It was no accident that you were the one who met us, was it? You already knew I was there."

"Of course," Ortega replied. "Small cameras installed in two or three points around the Well go on whenever someone comes through. If they're old-human I get there first. Nobody cares much, since the Zone Gate randomly assigns them to other hexes."

"You didn't meet me when I came through," Skander pointed out.

Ortega shrugged again. "Can't *live* in the damned office. Bad luck, though, since I then lost sight of you for a long time. These others were already in and assigned before I managed to track Varnett down, although the Umiau are so lousy at secrecy your cover was blown about a month after you came."

"You've been following me since Czill, haven't you, Serge?" Brazil asked. "How did you manage it?"

"Child's play," the Ulik replied. "Czill has a high technological level but no natural resources, and some problems in handling hot metal anyway. We supply parts for their machines—we and many others— only ours have slight modifications. A resonator for the translator, for example, takes only one almost invisible extra circuit to broadcast—if you know the right frequency. The range isn't fantastic, but I knew where you were, and in most instances mutual back-scratching, past IOU's, and the like were all that was needed. I think I know what you are, Nate, and I think you know you should play the game my way."

"Or you'll kill the others?"

The snakeman looked hurt, but it was exaggerated. "Why, Nate! Did I say any such thing? But, regardless, I have Skander, here, and, if all else fails, Varnett. I'd prefer you, Nate. I don't think you're any different from the Nathan Brazil I've known all these decades. I'm willing to bet that that personality of yours isn't a phony front or a construct, but the real you, no matter what your parents were. You know me better than anybody, so you know my actions and what I'll do in any case. Will you lead the party in?"

Brazil looked at his old acquaintance for a moment. "Why everybody, Serge? Why not just you and me?" he asked.

"Ah, come on, Nate! What do you take me for? You know how to get in; I don't. You know what's in there—I don't. With the others I get an expert check on your actions and descriptions, and a little insurance from their own self-interest. The Northerner, here—it's working for a group so different from any of us I can't figure out anything about them. Nonetheless, like Hain, here, and the plant, they're all looking out for their own interests. So are your people, really. Nobody's going to let anybody else get the upper hand. You'll all even be armed—armed with pistols that can kill any of you, but can't kill me. I've taken immunity shots from Hain's stinger, so that's no threat, and I am so much physically stronger than any of you that I'll be happy to take you on. Nate knows how quick I can move."

Brazil sighed. "Always figuring the angles, aren't you, Serge? So tell me, if this was your game all along, why did we have to fight and walk so far? Why not just get us all together and bring us to this point?"

"I hadn't the slightest idea where you were going," replied Ortega honestly. "After all, Skander was still

303

looking, Varnett had given up, and nobody else knew. So I just let the expeditions lead me here. When it became clear where *both* expeditions were headed, I arranged to slow things down until I could get here ahead of you. Easier than you think—Zone Gate to Ulik, then over. Hell, man, I've been to that Equatorial Zone hundreds of times. There's no way in that anybody's ever found, and a lot have tried over the years."

"But we now know that the entrance is at the end of The Avenue," The Rel said suddenly. "And, from Skander, I perceive that the time of entry is midnight."

"Right on both counts," Brazil admitted. "However, that knowledge alone won't get you in. You need the desire to get to the Well center, specifically, and a basic equation to tell the Well you know what you're doing."

"The Varnett relationship," Skander said. "The open-ended equation of the Markovian brain slides. That's it, isn't it?"

"Sure," Brazil acknowledged. "After all, it wasn't supposed to keep any Markovians out. The conditions of this world are such that the relationship is simply indecipherable. It's only one in a million that the two of you discovered it, and almost one in infinity that you'd get to where you could use it. You could never have used it on Dalgonia since it requires an answer for completion, an addition. It's sort of 'What is your wish?' and you have to give that wish in mathematically correct form. In this case, though, the simple completion is done by the brain if you ask the question—the reverse."

"But if he is a Markovian, why could he not just contact the brain and save himself all the problems he's had here?" the Slelcronian asked.

Brazil turned to the plant person, a puzzled tone in his voice. "I thought you were Vardia—but that tone just doesn't sound like her."

"Vardia merged with a Slelcronian," The Rel explained, telling of the flower creatures and their strange ways. "It is possessed of a good deal of wisdom and some fairly efficient mental powers, but your friend is such a tiny part of the whole that the Czillian is essentially dead," The Rel concluded.

"I see," Brazil said slowly. "Well, there were too many Vardias here anyway. Ours is the original—back to human, again." He turned to Serge again. "So are Wuju and Varnett."

"Varnett?" Skander sat up suddenly, spilling water. "Varnett is with you?"

"Yes, and no tricks, Skander," Ortega warned. "If you try anything on Varnett I'll personally attend to you." He turned back to Brazil. "That goes for you, too, Nate."

"There will be no problems, Serge," Brazil assured him tiredly. "I'll take you all inside the Well, and I will show you what you want—what you all want. I'll even answer any questions you want, clear up any uncertainties."

"That suits us," Ortega responded, but there was a note of caution in his voice.

The Avenue—at the Equator

THE JOURNEY UP THE AVENUE HAD BEEN WITHOUT event, and none had tested Ortega's defenses. They were all going where they wanted to go, and, as the Ulik had said, each one had his own selfish interests at heart. All during the journey Brazil had been talkative and friendly, yet there was a sadness deep within him they could all feel, although he tried to laugh it off. The four members of Brazil's party kept to themselves. Hain kept looking at Wuju strangely, but bided her time, and Skander seemed resigned to Varnett's existence in the party.

And now, in the afternoon's waning sun, they stood at the Equatorial Barrier itself, imposing and seemingly impenetrable.

It was like a wall, partially translucent, that rose up until it merged with the deep blue, cloudless sky. The barrier itself didn't look thick, and felt smooth and

305

glassy to the touch, yet it had withstood attempts by many races on both sides to make as much as a mark on it. It went off to each side of them from horizon to horizon, like a giant, nonreflecting glass wall.

The Avenue seemed to merge into it, and there was no sign of any small crack, fissure, or even juncture of the odd paving of The Avenue with the surface of the barrier. They seemed to become one.

Brazil went up to the wall, then turned to face them. They waited expectantly.

"We can't enter until midnight, so we might as well be comfortable," he told them.

"Do you mean twenty-four hundred?" the real Vardia asked.

"No, of course not," Brazil replied. "For one thing, the Well World's days are about twenty-eight and a quarter standard hours, as you know, so the time twenty-four hundred has no meaning here. Midnight means exactly that—the middle of the night. Since a total day is exactly twenty-eight point three three four standard hours, and since the axis is exactly vertical, that means the light period is fourteen point one six seven hours, and so is the darkness. Midnight, then, comes seven point zero eight three five hours after sunset. The figures were determined by physical necessity when building the place. They just came out that way. Believe me, Markovian clocks were quite different from ours, and the time could be precisely determined."

"Yes, but how will *we* determine it?" The Rel asked. "There are a couple of timepieces here, but they are by no means that exact."

"No need," Brazil assured the Northerner. "Hain, fly up to the surface there and watch the sun. When it vanishes to the west, then tell us immediately. Be conservative—err on the side of sunlight. We'll check watches for seven hours from that point. After that, we can simply wait to open the wall. We'll have only about two minutes, so it's important that everyone goes as soon as the wall opens. The ones who don't will be left out here."

"What about the atmosphere inside?" Skander asked. "We have only a few pressure suits here."

"No problem there, either," Brazil responded. "All of us are compatible with the oxygen-nitrogen-carbon mix that's common, in one sense or another, with the sectors on both sides of The Avenue. There will be a compromise adjustment, but while the mixture might make a few of us temporarily light-headed, it shoudn't pose any problem. This system will automatically follow us, section by section, as we go down. The only problem we might have, and it's minor, is some strongly differing gravitational pulls due to the lines of force flowing from here. None will be a *real* problem, just uncomfortable occasionally."

His explanation seemed to satisfy them, and they sat down or otherwise relaxed, waiting for the proper time.

"Are you really—really me?" Vardia hesitantly asked the Slelcronian, who was awake only because of a small, lamplike gadget fastened over the headleaf.

The Slelcronian paused and thought carefully. "We are you, and we are more than you," it replied. "All your memories and experiences are here, along with the millions of the Slelcronians. You are a part of us, and we are a part of you. Through the Recorder, you are a part of the total synthesis, not just the isolated portion in this body."

"What's it like?" she asked.

"It is the ultimate stage to which any can aspire," the creature told her. "No individuality, no personality to corrupt. No jealousy, greed, anger, envy, or those other things that cause misery. All alike, all identical, all in communion. As plants we require nothing save water and sunlight, and carbon dioxide to breathe. When another is needed, we make a seed and mate it to the Recorders; it grows, and immediately after bloom becomes as we. The Recorders do not think, and get their food from our bodies."

"But—what do you *do?*" she asked curiously. "What is the purpose to your life?"

"Universal happiness in a stable order," the Slelcronian replied unhesitatingly. "Long have we yearned to spread the synthesis. Now, through this body and your experience, we can return to Czill and multiply.

307

We shall work with the devices of Czill to create a synthesis of animal with plant. We shall expand, eventually, to the Well World, and, with the aid of the Well, to the corners of the universe. All shall become one with the synthesis, all shall enjoy perfect equality and happiness."

She thought a minute. "And what if you can't do it with the animals?"

"We will," the Slelcronian replied confidently. "But, should it not be so, then the superior shall eliminate the inferior, as it is in the laws of nature since the beginning of time."

This isn't me, she thought. This can't be me. Or—or is it? Is this not what my society strives for? Is this not why we clone, why genetic engineering is eventually planned to make everyone identical, sexless, equally provided for in every way?

A sudden question struck her, and she asked, "And what will you do once you have accomplished this all-encompassing synthesis? What then?"

"Then there will be perfection and harmony and happiness," replied the Slelcronian as if reciting a litany. "Heaven will be ours and it will be forever. Why do you ask such a question? Are we not you? Did you not in fact accept the offered synthesis?"

The question disturbed her, for she had no answer. What had changed? How had the paths of Vardia I and II differed so radically in the last few weeks that such a question would even occur to her?

She turned away, and her eyes fell on Wu Julee and Nathan Brazil. They had some sort of symbiotic relationship, she thought. It was observable, no matter what form they had been in. When he could have clearly escaped the Ivrom spell, he had risked himself to free her.

She sat down, the chill of the night making the hardness of The Avenue feel like an ice cube on her bare behind.

What had she seen that her sister had not? Emotion? Love? Some different sort of relationship? Kindness? What?

What had her sister seen? A nation of great bugs all out to do each other in and lord it over the others.

Hain. Skander. That weird Northern creature. A world of machines. They represented something far different from Nathan Brazil, Wuju—and Varnett, with guilt over seven dead people he probably couldn't have saved anyway. Guilt over doing the right and proper thing? Impossible! Yet—she remembered him coming in in the early morning, carrying Brazil's battered and broken body. Exhausted, weak, half-crazed from the burden, yet unwilling to sleep or eat until Brazil had been tended to. Standing over that body, only technically alive, and weeping.

Why?

She thought again of the Slelcronian and its dreams. The perfect society. Heaven. Forever.

The Markovians had it, had the ultimate in material existence.

And they had deliberately wrecked it for death, misery, pain, and struggle on countless worlds in countless forms.

What *was* perfection, anyway? What did the Markovians lack that gave the lie to the grand dream?

They forgot how to love, Brazil had said. But what was love?

Have we already forgotten it?

The thought upset her, and she couldn't explain why. For the first time in her life, she felt alienated, alone, outside, left out.

Cheated.

And she had no idea what was missing.

For the first time, and perhaps the first of any being on the Well World, she knew what it must have been like to be a Markovian.

Was this, then, what Nathan Brazil felt? Was this why he felt he was cursed? Did he live all those millennia searching for the missing factor in the Markovian dream, hoping that someone would discover it?

But, no, she concluded. He knew what it was. He had tried to explain it.

Suddenly she shivered, but not from the chill. She had never thought, never brooded like this before, never faced the chill of reality before.

Oh, nonexistent, uncaring gods! she thought bitterly. What a curse more horrible than anything imaginable.

Suppose Nathan Brazil had what was missing, deep inside—and no one else did?

"Hello, Vardia," said a voice behind her. She turned with a start, and saw Wuju standing there. "You've been sitting there looking strange for the longest time."

She smiled weakly, but said nothing.

Wuju smiled and sat down beside her. "Yikes! This pavement's cold!"

"If you just sit you don't notice it," Vardia told her.

"Everyone's so somber and serious now," Wuju noted. "Even me."

Vardia looked at her strangely. "It's the mission—the end of the mission. In there is anything you want. Just wish for it. And all of us are going in. I don't know about anyone else, but I just discovered I don't know what to wish for."

"I wish we weren't going," Wuju said grimly. "If I had one wish, it'd be that this never had to end. Here —this journey, Nathan, all of you. It's been the happiest time of my life. I'm afraid that nothing will be the same after we're in there. Nothing."

Vardia took her hand and patted it. Now why did I do that? she wondered, but she continued doing it.

"I don't know what's going to happen," Vardia said calmly. "I only know that I must change. I *have* changed. Now I must understand how and why."

"I don't like this at all," Wuju responded in that same tone of foreboding. "I don't like the idea of things being changed by a whim. No one should have that kind of power—least of all these sorts. I don't like being a figment, an afterthought. I'm scared to death. I told Nathan, but he just shook his head and went away. I don't understand that, either. I can face death, now—and evil, too. But I can't face the fear of what's in there. Not alone."

"You're not alone," Vardia said with a gentleness that surprised her.

Wuju looked over at Brazil, standing facing the wall, unmoving, stoic, alone. She started to tremble.

"I can't face it alone!" she wailed weakly.

"You're not alone," Vardia repeated, squeezing her hand tighter.

Elkinos Skander watched the two women with interest. So the robots have retained a little humanity after all, he thought with satisfaction. But it's buried so deep within them that it took the Well World to bring any of it out.

And for what?

Things weren't working out quite the way he had planned at all, but except for the Slelcronian and, perhaps, that Northerner, it was all right, particularly if the robots like Vardia could feel.

Surely they wouldn't object to his requests of the Well.

He looked over at Hain, motionless in the darkness.

"Hain? You awake?" Skander asked softly.

"Yes. Who could sleep now?" came the bug's response.

"Hain, tell me. What do you expect to get in there? What do you want of the Well?"

Hain was silent for a moment. "Power," she replied at last. "I would make the Baron Azkfru emperor of the Well World, this galaxy, perhaps the universe. But, with this mob, I'll settle for his being emperor for the longest of time in Akkafan, with such other power left to future effort. My Lord, the baron, can do anything except fight this machine."

Skander raised his mermaid's eyebrows in surprise. "But what do *you* get out of it?"

"I shall be the baron's queen," Hain replied excitedly. "I shall be at his throne, second only to him in power. I shall bear the broods that will rule for eternity, the product of Azkfru and myself! The workers, even the nobles, shall defer to me and my wishes, and envy me, and my subjects will sing my praises!" Hain paused, carried away by her own vision.

"I was born in a run-down shack in a hole called Gorind on Aphrodite," she continued. "I was unwanted, sickly. My mother beat me, finally cast me out into the mud and dust when she saw I'd never be a miner. I was nine. I went into the city, living off the garbage, stealing to make do, sleeping in cold back doorways. I grew up grubbing, but in the shadow of the rich, the mineowners, the shippers from whom I stole. One day, when I was fifteen or so, I raped and killed a girl. She struggled, called me names—tried to scratch me, like my mother. They caught me, and I was about to be psyched into a good programmed worker when this man came to see me in my cell. He said he had need of people like me. If I agreed to serve him and his bosses, he would get me out."

"And you accepted, of course," Skander put in.

"Oh, yes. I went into a new world. I found that the rich whom I'd envied dreamed of greater riches, and that power came not from obeying the law but from not getting caught. I rose in the organization. I ate well, grew fat, ordered people around. I have—had —my own estate on a private world of the bosses. Staffed all by women, young women, held to me by sponge. Many were slaves; others I had reduced to animals. They roam naked in the forest on the estate, living in trees, eating the swill I put out for them like barnyard animals."

Skander had an eerie feeling in his stomach, yet he followed Hain's statements with morbid fascination. "But that's gone now," Skander said as calmly as he could manage.

"Not gone," Hain replied, agitated. "I will be mother now."

There was nothing Skander could say. Pity was for what Hain was or could have been, not what the creature was now.

"What do you want out of all this, Skander?" Hain asked suddenly. "Why all this trouble, all this effort? What do you want to do?"

"I want to restore humanity to itself," Skander replied fiercely. "I want to get rid of the genetic engineers, the philosophers of political sameness on the Comworlds. I want to turn us around, Hain! I want to make people human again, even if I have to destroy civilization to save mankind. We're becoming a race of robots, Hain. We wipe out the robots or we abdicate the universe to other races. The Markovians died of stagnation, Hain, and so will we unless it's stopped!"

Hain had never liked fanatics, saviors, and visionaries, but there was nothing else to do but talk. "Tell me, Skander. Would you go back? If you could, I mean. Suppose you get your wish. Would you go back or stay here?"

"I think I could end my days here if I got what I want," Skander replied honestly. "I like this place—the diversity, the challenges. I haven't had time to enjoy being Umiau. But, then, I'd like to see what our little race would be if my plan were fulfilled. I don't know, Hain. Would *you* go back?"

"Only as the Queen Mother of the Akkafians," Hain responded without hesitation. "At the side of my beloved Lord Azkfru. Only to rule would I return, Skander. For nothing less."

Ortega slithered over to them. He had small pistols in his hands, and he put one next to Skander and the other in front of Hain.

"Pistols for all," he said lightly. "Nice little energy jobs. They will work in there, like in any high-tech hex. They'll work on everybody except me. A dandy little circuit prevents that."

Skander reached over, picked up the pistol, felt it. Suddenly the Umiau scientist looked into Ortega's wide brown eyes.

"You expect us to kill each other, don't you?" he said softly. "You expect all hell to break out after we get to the Well and learn how it operates. And then you'll finish off the winner."

Ortega shrugged, and smiled. "Up to you," he replied calmly. "You can compromise with me, or with each other, or do as you say and shoot. But I will be in at the payoff no matter what." He slithered away to distribute guns to the others, chuckling softly.

"That bastard," Hain commented. "He hasn't seen what The Diviner and The Rel can do, has he? Wonder what sort of defense he has for that?"

"I think he knows," Skander responded. "That's one slick pirate there. He's counting on us to take care of the Northerner. And, damn his eyes, we have to! We have to, or that blinking little son of a bitch will zap all of us!"

"Just be thankful that snake *did* get transported to

the Well World," Hain said flatly. "Otherwise, he'd be running the whole damned galaxy by now."

Varnett came over to Brazil, who was still standing facing the Equatorial Barrier. "Brazil?" he said softly. "You awake?"

Nathan Brazil turned slowly, looking at Varnett.

"Oh, yes, I'm awake," Brazil told him. "I was just thinking. I've enjoyed this escapade, you know. Enjoyed it a great deal. Now it's over, ended. And it ends like all the other episodes in my life. So I have to pick up and keep on once again."

Varnett was puzzled. "I don't understand you at all, Brazil. You're in the pilot's seat. You alone know what's in there—you *do* know, don't you? You have a girl who loves you, and a future. What's eating you?"

Brazil shook his head slowly.

"I have no future, Varnett," he replied. "This part of the great play is over. I already know the ending, and I don't like it. I'm trapped, Varnett. Cursed. This diversion helped, but not much, because it brought back too much pain and longing as well. And as for Wuju —she doesn't love *me,* Varnett. She has a deep need to be loved. She loves a symbol, something that Nathan Brazil did to and for her, something in the way he reacted to her. But she wants of me what I can't give her. She wants her dream of normality." He shifted, stretching his legs out in front of him. He continued to face not the others, but the barrier.

"I'm not normal, Varnett," he said sadly. "I can give her what she wants, needs, deserves. I can do it for all of you. But I can't participate, you see. That's the curse."

"Sounds like grandiose self-pity to me," Varnett said derisively. "Why not take what you want if you can do all that?"

Brazil sighed. "You'll know soon enough. I want you just to remember this, Varnett. I want you to keep it in your head throughout all that happens. Inside, I'm no different from the rest of you."

"What would you want, if you could have anything at all?" Varnett asked him, still bewildered.

Brazil looked at the other seriously, sadly. There was agony and torment within him.

"I want to die, boy. I want to die—and I can't. Not ever. Not at all. And I want death so very much."

Varnett shook his head uncomprehendingly. "I can't figure you, Brazil. I just can't figure you."

"What do *you* want, Varnett?" Brazil asked sharply, changing tone. "What would you wish for yourself?"

"I've thought a lot about that," the other replied. "I'm only fifteen years old, Brazil. Just fifteen. My world has always been dehumanized people and cold mathematics. I'm the oldest fifteen of my race, now, though. I think, perhaps, I'd like to enjoy life, enjoy a *human* life—and somehow make my contribution to progress. To stop this headlong rush of the human race into a Markovian hell and try to build the society they hoped would evolve from their tens of thousands of cultures and races. There's a greatness here in the Markovian Well, a potential unrealized, perhaps, but great nonetheless. I'd like to see it reached, to complete the equation the Markovians couldn't."

"So would I, boy," Brazil replied earnestly. "For only then could I die."

"Seven hours!" Ortega's voice broke through the stillness. "It's almost time!" His voice cracked with excitement.

Brazil turned slowly to face them. They were all scrambling to be near the barrier.

"Don't worry," he assured them. "It'll open for me. A light will go on. When that light comes on, walk into the barrier. When you do, it'll be as nothing. Only *I* will change, but be ready for it. And understand something else—*I* will lead. I have no weapons, but the Well will give me a form unfamiliar to you. Don't be upset by it, and don't get trigger-happy with each other. Once we're all inside, I'll take you down to the Well of Souls, and I'll explain everything along the way. Don't do anything hasty, because I'm the only one who can get you down with certainty, and I'll not forgive any breaches. Clear?"

"Big talk, Nate," Ortega said confidently, but there was an unease in his manner. "But we'll go along if you do."

"I gave you my word, Serge," Brazil said. "I'll keep it."

"Look!" the Slelcronian cried. "The light's gone on!"

In back of Brazil a section of the floor corresponding to The Avenue was lit into the Equatorial Barrier.

"Let's go," Brazil said calmly, and turned and stepped into the barrier. The others, tension on their faces, followed him.

Suddenly Skander cried out, "I was right! I was right all along!" and pointed ahead. The others looked in the indicated direction.

There were several gasps.

Wuju stifled a small scream.

The Well had changed Nathan Brazil, just as he had warned.

Midnight at the Well of Souls

THE CREATURE STOOD AT THE END OF THE AVENUE, where it passed through a meter-high barrier and stopped.

It looked like a great human heart, two and a half meters tall, pink and purple, with countless blood vessels running through it, both reddish and bluish in color. At the irregular top was a ring of cilia, colored an off-white, waving about—thousands of them, like tiny snakes, each about fifty centimeters long. From the midsection of the pulpy, undulating mass came six evenly spaced tentacles, each broad and powerful-looking, covered with thousands of tiny suckers. The tentacles were a sickly blue, the suckers a grainy yellow. An ichor of some sort seemed to ooze from the central mass, although it was thick and seemed to be reabsorbed by the skin as fast as produced, creating an irregular, filmy coating.

And it stank—the odor of foul carrion after days in

the sun. It stung their nostrils, making them slightly sick.

Skander began babbling excitedly, then turned to them. "See, Varnett?" he said. "See what I told you? Six evenly spaced tentacles, about three meters tall! That's a Markovian!" All traces of animosity were gone; this was the professor lecturing his student, in pride at the vindication of his theories.

"So you really was a Markovian, Nate," Ortega said wonderingly. "Well, I'll be damned."

"Nathan!" Wuju called out. "Is that—that thing really you?"

"It is," Brazil's voice came, but not as speech. It formed in each of their brains, in their own languages. Even The Diviner received it directly, rather than through The Rel.

Skander was like a child with a new toy. "Of course! Of course!" he chortled. "Telepathy, naturally. Probably the rest, too."

"This is a Markovian body," Brazil's voice came to them, "but I am not a Markovian. The Well knows me, though, and, since all lived as new races outside, it was only natural that we be converted to the Markovian form when entering the Well. It saved design problems."

Wuju stepped out ahead of them, drawing close to the creature.

"Wu Julee!" Hain shouted insanely. "You are mine!" The long, sticky tongue darted out to her, wrapped itself around her. She screamed. Ortega spun quickly toward the bug, pistols in two hands.

"Now, now, none of that, Hain!" he cautioned carefully. "Let the girl go." He pointed the pistols at the Akkafian's eyes.

Hain hesitated a second, deciding what to do. Finally the tongue uncoiled from Wu Julee, and she dropped about thirty centimeters to the floor, landing hard. Raw, nasty-looking welts, like those made by rope burn, showed on her skin.

The creature that was Nathan Brazil walked over on its six tentacles, until it loomed over her. One tentacle reached out, gently touched her wound. The smell was overwhelming. She shrank from the probe, fear on her face.

The heartlike mass tilted a little on its axis.

"Form doesn't matter," it mocked her voice. "It's what's inside that counts." Then it said in Brazil's old voice: "What if I were a monster, Wuju? What then?"

Wuju broke into sobs. "Please, Nathan! Please don't hurt me!" she pleaded. "No more, please! I—I just can't!"

"Does it hurt?" he asked gently, and she managed to nod affirmatively, wiping the tears from her eyes.

"Then trust me some more, Wuju," Brazil's voice came again, still gentle. "No matter what. Shut your eyes. I'll make the hurt go away."

She buried her head in her hands, still crying.

The Markovian reached out with a tentacle, and rubbed lightly against the angry-looking welt on her back and sides. She cringed, but otherwise stayed still. The thing felt clammy and horrid, yet they all watched as the tentacle, lightly drawn across the wound, caused the wound to vanish.

As the pain vanished, she relaxed.

"Lie flat on your back, Wuju," Brazil instructed, and she did, eyes still shut. The same treatment was given to her chest and sides, and there was suddenly no sign of any welt or wound.

Brazil withdrew a couple of meters from her. There was no evident front or back to him, nor any apparent eyes, nose, or mouth. Although the pulpy mass in the center was pulsating and slightly irregular, it had no clear-cut directionality.

"Hey, that's fantastic, Nate!" Ortega exclaimed.

"Shall we go to the Well?" Brazil asked them. "It is time to finish this drama."

"I'm not sure I like this at all," Hain commented hesitantly.

"Too late to back out now, you asshole," Skander snapped. "You didn't get where you were without guts. Play it out."

"If you'll follow me," Brazil said, "and get on the walkway here; we can talk as we ride, and probably panic the border hexes at the same time."

They all stepped onto the walkway on the other side

318

of the meter-tall barrier. The Avenue's strange light went out, and another light went on on both sides of the walkway, illuminating about half a kilometer to their left.

"The lights will come on where we are, and go out where we aren't," Brazil explained. "It's automatic. Slelcronian, you'll find the light adequate for you despite its apparent lack of intensity. You can get rid of that heat lamp. Just throw it over the barrier there. It will be disposed of by the automatic machinery in about fourteen hours." The Markovian's tentacle near the forward part of the walkway struck the side sharply, and the walkway started to move.

"You are now on the walkway to the Well Access Gate," he explained. "When the Markovians built this world, it was necessary, of course, for the technicians to get in and out. They were full shifts—one full rotation on, one off. Every day from dozens to thousands of Markovian technicians would ride this walkway to the control center and to other critical areas inside the planet. In those days, of course, The Avenue would stay open as long as necessary. It was shortened to the small interval in the last days before the last Markovian went native for good, to allow the border hexes some development and to keep out those who had second thoughts. At the end, only the three dozen project coordinators came, and then irregularly, just to check on things. As any technician was finally cleared out of the Well, the key to The Avenue doors was removed from his mind, so he could not get back in if he wanted to."

They moved on in eerie silence, lighted sections suddenly popping on in front of them, out in back of them, as they traveled. The walkway itself seemed to glow radiantly; no light source was visible.

"Some of you know the story of this place already," Brazil continued. "The race you call the Markovians rose as did all other species, developed, and finally discovered the primal energy nature of the universe— that there was nothing but this primal energy, extending outward in all directions, and that all constructs within it, we included, are established by rules and laws of nature that are not fixed just because they are

319

there, but are instead *imposed*. Nothing equals anything, really; the equal sign is strictly for the imposed structure of the universe. Rather, everything is relative to everything else."

"But once the Markovians discovered the mathematical constructs governing stability, why didn't they change them?" Skander asked. "Why keep the rules?"

"They didn't dare try to tackle the master equations, those governing physical properties and natural laws," Brazil replied. "They could alter things a little, but common sense should tell you that in order to change the master equation you first have to eliminate the old one. If you do that, what happens to you and the rest of the universe? They didn't dare—so they imposed new, smaller equations on localized areas of the preexisting universe."

"Not gods, then," Vardia said quietly. "Demigods."

"People," Brazil responded. "Not gods at all. People. Oh, I know that this form I've got is quite different than you'd think, but it's no more monstrous or unusual than some of the creatures of this world, and less than some. The many billions of beings who wore bodies like this were a proud race of ordinary people with one finger on the controls. They argued, they debated, strove, built, discovered—just like all of us. Were their physical forms closer to the ones we're familiar with, you would possibly even like them. Remember, they achieved godhood not by natural processes, but by technological advancement. It was as if one of our races, in present form, suddenly discovered the key to wish fulfillment. Would we be ready for it? I wonder."

"Why did they die, Brazil?" Skander asked. "Why did they commit suicide?"

"Because they were not ready," Brazil replied sadly. "They had conquered all material want, all disease, even death itself. But they had not conquered their selves. They reveled in hedonism, each an island unto itself. Anything they wanted, they just had to wish for.

"And they found that wasn't enough. Something was missing. Utopia wasn't fulfillment, it was stagnation. And that was the curse—*knowing* that the ultimate was attainable, but not knowing what it was or how to attain it. They studied the problem and came up with no solutions. Finally, the best amplified Markovian minds concluded that, somewhere in their development, they'd lost something—the true fulfillment of the dream. The social equation did not balance, because it lacked some basic component. One plus two plus three equals six, but if you don't have the plus two in there, it can't possibly reach more than four.

"Finally, they came to the conclusion that they were at a dead end, and would stagnate in an eternal orgy of hedonism unless something was done. The solution seemed simple: start over, try to regain the missing factor, or rediscover it, by starting from the beginning again. They used a variety of races and conditions to restart, none Markovian, on the idea that any repetition of the Markovian cycle would only end up the same."

"And so they built this world," Varnett put in.

"Yes, they built this world. A giant Markovian brain, placed around a young but planetless sun. The brain *is* the planet, of course, everything but the crust. Gravity was no problem, nor was atmosphere. They created an outer shell, about a hundred kilometers above the surface. The hexagons are all compartments, their elements held in all directions by fields of force."

"So it was built to convert the Markovians to new forms?" Skander asked.

"Double duty, really," Brazil told them. "The finest artisans of the Markovian race were called in. They made proposals for biospheres, trying to outdo one another in creativity. The ones that looked workable were built, and volunteers went through the Zone Gate and became the newly designed creatures in the newly designed environments. Several generations were needed for even a moderate test—the Markovians didn't mind. A thousand years was nothing to them. You see, they could build, pioneer-style, but they were still Markovians. A lot of generations born in the biome and of the new race were needed to establish a culture and show how things would go. Their numbers were kept relatively stable, and the fields of force were much more rigid then than now. They had to live in their hex, without any real contact with other hexes. They had to build their own worlds."

They were riding *down* now, at a deceptively steep angle. Down into the bowels of the planet itself.

"But why didn't the first generation establish a high civilization?" Varnett asked. "After all, they were just like us, changed outside only."

"You overestimate people from a highly technological culture. We take things for granted. We know how to turn on a light, but not why the light comes on. None of us could *build* most of our artifacts, and most civilized races become dependent on them. Suddenly dumped in a virgin wilderness, as they all were, they had no stores, no factories, no access to anything they didn't make themselves out of what was available. A great many died from hardship alone. The tough ones, the survivors, they built their own societies, and their children's societies. They worked with purpose—if the test failed, then they died out. If they succeeded—well, there was the promise that the successful ones would someday go to the Well of Souls at midnight, and there be taken to a new world, to found a new civilization, to grow, develop, perhaps become the progenitors of a future race of gods who would be fulfilled. Each hoped to be the ones whose descendants would make it."

"And you were here when that happened," Wuju said nervously.

"I was," he acknowledged. "I assisted the creator of Hex Forty-one—One Eighty-seven, the hundred and eighty-seventh and last race developed in that hex. I didn't create it, simply monitored and helped out. We stole ideas from each other all the time, of course. Dominant species in one hex might be a modified pattern of animals in another. Our own race was a direct steal from some large apes in another hex. The designer liked them so much that not only did the dominant race turn out to be apes, but they were almost endlessly varied as animals."

"Hold on, Brazil," Skander said. "These others might not know much about things, but I'm an archaeologist. Old Earth developed over a few billion years, slowly evolving."

"Not exactly," Brazil replied. "First of all, time was altered in each case. The time frame for the develop-

322

ment of our sector was speeded up. The original design produced the life we expected, but it developed differently—as giant reptiles, eventually. When it was clear that it wouldn't do to have our people coexist with them, a slight change in the axial tilt caused the dinosaurs to die out, but it placed different stresses on other organisms. Minor mammals developed, and to these, over a period of time, we added ours to replace the ones logically developing in the evolutionary scale. When conditions seemed suitable for us, when apelike creatures survived, we began the exodus. Soon the temperate zones had their first intelligent life. Again, with all the resources but nothing else. They did well, astonishingly so, but the long-term effects of the axial tilt produced diastrophism and a great ice age within a few centuries. Our present, slow climb has been the product of the extremely primitive survivors of those disasters. So, in fact, has it been with all your home worlds."

"Is there a world, then, or a network of worlds of the Akkafians?" Hain asked.

"There was," Brazil replied. "Perhaps there is. Perhaps it's larger and greater and more advanced than ours. The same with the Umiau, the Czill, the Slelcronians, the Dillians, and others. When we get to the Well itself, I'll be able to tell you at least which ones are still functioning, although not how, or if they've changed, or what. I would think that some of the older ones would be well advanced by now. My memory says there were probably close to a million races created and scattered about; I'll be curious to see how many are still around."

They had been going down for some time. Now they were deep below the surface, how deep they couldn't say. Suddenly a great hexagon outlined in light appeared just under them.

"The Well Access Gate," Brazil told them. "One of six. It can take you to lots of places within the Well, but it'll take you to the central control area and monitoring stations if you have no other instructions. When we get to it, just step on it. I won't trigger it until everyone is aboard. In case somebody else does, by

323

accident, just wait for the light to come back on and step on again. It'll work."

They did as instructed, and when all were on the Gate, all light suddenly winked out. There followed a twisting, unsettling feeling like falling. Then, suddenly, there was light all over.

They stood in a huge chamber, perhaps a kilometer in diameter. It was semicircular, the ceiling curving up over them almost the same distance as it was across. Corridors, hundreds of them, led off in all directions. The Gate was in the center of the dome, and Brazil quickly stepped off, followed by the others, who looked around in awe and anticipation.

The texture of the place was strange. It seemed to be made up of tiny hexagonal shapes of polished white mica, reflecting the light and glittering like millions of jewels.

After they stepped off the Gate, Brazil stopped and pointed a tentacle back over it.

Suspended by force fields, about midway between the Gate and the apex of the dome, was a huge model of the Well World, turning slowly. It had a terminator, and darkness on half of its face, and seemed to be made of the same mica-like compound as the great hall. But the hexagons on the model were much larger, and there were solid areas at the poles, and a black band around its middle. The sphere seemed to be covered by a thin transparent shell composed of segments which exactly conformed to the hexagons below.

"That's what the Well World looks like from space," Brazil told them. "It's an exact model, fifteen hundred sixty hexagons, the Zones—everything. Note the slight differences in reflected light from each hex. That's Markovian writing—and they are numbers. This is more than a model, really. It's a separate Markovian brain, containing the master equation for stabilizing all of the new worlds. It energizes the Well, and permits the big brain around us to do its job."

"Where are the controls, Nate?" Ortega prodded.

"Each biome—that is, planetary biome—has its own set of controls," Brazil told him. "This place is honeycombed with them. Each hex on the Well World is controlled as a complement to the actual world. Most

324

controls, of course, do not have corresponding hexes. What we're left with today are the last few hexes created and some of the failures—not necessarily the ones that died out, but the ones that didn't work out. The Faerie, for example. Some of them snuck into the last batch of transits, and several of the others who were leftovers from closed and filled projects, some Dillians, some Umiau, and the like, who wanted to get out of the Well World and thought they could help, came, too. Not many, and they were disrupted by civilization's rises and falls, and became the objects of superstition, fear, hatred. None survived the distance on Old Earth, but we didn't get many to begin with, and reproduction was slow. But, come, let's go to a control center."

He walked toward one of the corridors on his six tentacles, and they followed hesitantly. All of them held their pistols tightly, at the ready.

They walked for what seemed an endless time down one of the corridors, passing closed hexagonal doors along the way. Finally Brazil stopped in front of one, and it opened, much as the lens of a camera opens. He walked in, and they followed quickly, anxious not to lose sight of him even for a moment.

The room lit up as they approached. It was made of the same stuff as the great hall and the corridors. There were, however, walls of obvious controls, switches, levers, buttons, and the like, and what looked like a large black screen directly ahead of them. None of the instruments held any sort of clue as to what they were, or had anything familiar about them.

"Well, here it is, and it's still active," Brazil announced. "Let me see," he murmured, and went over to a panel. Their faces showed sudden tension and fear, and all of the pistols were raised, trained on him. The Diviner's blinking lights started going very, very fast.

"Don't touch nothin', Nate!" Ortega warned.

"Just checking something here," Brazil responded, unconcerned. "Yes, I see. In this room is the preset for a civilization that has now expanded. It's interstellar, but not pangalactic. Population a little over one and a quarter trillion."

325

"If it's a high-tech civilization, then it is not ours," the Slelcronian said with some relief.

"Not necessarily," Brazil replied. "The tech levels here on the Well World were not imposed on the outside at all. They were dictated by the problems you might find in your own world. A high-tech world had abundant and easily accessible resources, a low-tech much less so. Since the home world had to develop logically and mathematically according to the master rules of nature, some worlds were better endowed than others. By making the trial hex here a low-tech, no-tech, or the like, we simply were compensating for the degree of difficulty in establishing technological civilization on the home world, not preventing it. We made them develop alternatives, to live without technology so they'd be better prepared on their home worlds. Some did extremely well. Most of the magic you find here is not Well magic, but actual mental powers developed by the hexes to compensate for low-tech status. What they could use here, they could use there."

"The Diviner says you are truthful," The Rel commented, one of the first things the Northerner had said since they set out. "The Diviner states that you were responsible for its prophecy that we would be here."

"In a way, yes," Brazil replied. "When I went through the Zone Gate, the Markovian brain recognized me as a native of Hex Forty-one and sent me there. However, in its analysis, it also found what I, myself, didn't know—that I had an original Markovian brain-wave pattern. It then assumed that I was here to give it further instructions or to do work. When it concluded this, The Diviner, extremely sensitive to such things, picked up the message, however garbled." He paused, and that central mass tilted toward them a little.

"And now," he said, sadness in his voice, "here we are, in the control center, and you've all got fear on your faces and your guns trained on me." *Even you, Wu Julee,* he thought, immeasurable sadness coarsing through him. *Even you.*

"I tried to give mankind rules for living which would avert a second disaster like the first, would keep it from

326

self-destruction. Nobody listened. Nobody changed. Type Forty-one was badly flawed—and it beat the odds anyway, this time. It made its way to the stars, and that was an outlet for its aggression, although, even there, even now, its component parts are looking at ways to dominate one another, kill one another, rule one another. And the drive for domination is there even in the nonhumans, you, Northerner, and you, Slelcronian. Look at you all now. Look at yourselves! Look at each other! Do you see it? Can you feel it? Fear, greed, horror, ambition burning within you, consuming you! The only reason you haven't killed one another by now is your common fear of me. How dare you condemn a Hain, a Skander—a society? How dare you?

"How many of you are thinking of the people these controls represent? Do you fear for them? Do you care about them? You don't want to save them, better their lives. That fear is inside you, fear for your own selves! The basic flaw in the set-up equation, that burning, basic selfishness. None of you cares for any but yourself! Look at you! Look at what monsters you've all become!"

Their hearts pounded, nerve ends frayed. The Diviner and The Rel were the first to respond.

"What about yourself, Nathan Brazil?" The Rel chimed. "Isn't the flaw in us simply a reflection of the flaws in yourself, in your own people, the Markovians, who could not give us what we lack because they did not themselves possess it?"

Brazil's reply was calm, in contrast to his previous outburst.

"The Markovians wanted to live in this universe, not run it. They had already done that. Destiny was a random factor they believed necessary to the survival of us all. That's why they closed down the Well. None of us would be here except for a freak set of circumstances."

"Where are the controls, Nate?" Ortega asked.

"We'll find them ourselves," Hain snapped. "Varnett cracked the big code, he should be able to crack this one, too."

Brazil's voice held deep sorrow. "Pride is a weak-

327

ness of all things Markovian, and you're a reflection of it. Now, if you'll ease up and allow me one touch on the panel in back, I'll show you the controls. I'll tell you how to operate them. Let's see what happens then."

Ortega nodded, pistols at the ready. Brazil reached out with a tentacle and touched a small panel behind him.

The large black screen went on—but it wasn't exactly a screen. It was a great tunnel, an oval stretching back as far as the eye could see. And it was covered with countless tiny black spots, trillions of them at the best guess. And between all the various black spots shot frantic electrical bolts in a frenzy of activity, trillions of blinking hairline arcs jumping from one little black area to another.

"There's your controls," Brazil said disgustedly. "To change the ratios, all you have to do is alter the current flow between any two or more control spots."

He looked at them, and there was the deepest fear and horror on their faces. They're afraid of me, he thought. All of them are in mortal fear of me! Oh, my God! Wuju who loved me, Varnett who risked his life for me, Vardia who trusted me—all afraid. I haven't harmed them. I haven't even threatened them. I couldn't if I wanted to. How can they ever understand our common source, our common bond? he thought in anguish. We love, we hate, we laugh, we cry, live— that I am no different from themselves, only older.

But they did not understand, he realized. I am God to the primitives, the civilized man of great power at a point where knowledge is power, surrounded by the savages.

That's why I'm alone, he understood. That's why I'm always alone. They fear what they can't understand or control.

"One control panel," he said softly. "One only. What are a few trillion lives? There is their past, their present, their potential future. All yours. Maybe their equation is the basis for one or more of you in this room. Maybe not. It's somebody's. Maybe it's yours. Okay, anybody, who wants to touch the first and second control spots, change the flow? Step right up! Now's your chance to play God!"

Varnett walked carefully over to the opening, breathing hard, sweat pouring from his body.

"Go on," Brazil urged. "Do your stuff! You might cancel out somebody, maybe a few trillion somebodies. You'll certainly alter someone's equation in some way, make two and two equal three in somebody's corner. Maybe none of us will be here. Maybe none of us will ever have been here. Go on! Who cares about all those people, anyway?"

Varnett stood there, mouth open, looking like a very frightened fifteen-year-old boy, nothing more. "I—I can't," he almost sobbed.

"How about you, Skander? This is where you wanted to be. And you, Hain?" His voice rose to a high, excited pitch. "Diviner? Can you divine this one? Vardia? Serge? Wuju? Slelcronian? *Any of you?*"

"In the name of God, Brazil!" Skander screamed. *"Stop it!* You know we don't dare do anything as long as we don't understand the panel's operation!"

"He's bluffing!" Hain snarled. "I'll take the chance."

"No!" Wuju screamed, and swung her gun around on the great bug. "You can't!"

"I'll even show you how," Brazil said calmly, and took a step.

"Nate! Stay away from there!" Ortega warned. "You can be killed, you know!"

Brazil stopped, and the pulsating mass bent toward Ortega slightly. "No, Serge, I can't. That's the problem, you see. I told you I wasn't a Markovian, but none of you listened. I came here because you might damage the panel, do harm to some race of people I might not even know. I knew you couldn't *use* this place, but all of you are quite mad now, and one or more of you might destroy, might take the chance, as Hain just showed. But none of you, in your madness, has thought to ask the real question, the one unanswered question in the puzzle. Who stabilized the Markovian equation, the basic one for the universe?"

There was a pumping sound, like that of a great heart, its *thump, thump, thump* permeating them. Their own hearts seemed to have stopped, all frozen in an eerie tableau. Only the thumping seemed real.

"I was formed out of the random primal energy of the cosmos," Brazil's voice came to them. "After countless billions of years I achieved self-awareness. I was the universe, and everything in it. In the aeons I started experimenting, playing with the random forces around me. I formed matter and other types of energy. I created time, and space. But soon I tired of even those toys. I formed the galaxies, the stars, and planets. An idea, and they were, as congealed primal energy exploded and flung transmuted material outward from its center.

"I watched things grow, and form, according to the rules I set up. And yet, I tired of these, also. So I created the Markovians and watched them develop according to my plan. Yet, even then, the solution was not satisfactory, for they knew and feared me, and their equation was too perfect. I knew their total developmental line. So I changed it. I placed a random factor in the Markovian equation and then withdrew from direct contact.

"They grew, they developed, they evolved, they changed. They forgot me and spread outward on their own. But since they were spiritually reflections of myself, they contained my loneliness. I couldn't join with them as I was, for they would hold me in awe and fear. They, on the other hand, had forgotten me, and as they rose materially they died spiritually. They failed to grow to my equal, to end my loneliness. Their pride would not admit such a being as myself to fellowship, nor could their own fear and selfishness allow fellowship even with each other.

"So I decided to become one of them. I fashioned a Markovian shell, and entered it. I knew the flesh, its joys and its pains. I tried to teach them what was wrong, to tell them to face their inner fears, to rid themselves of the disease, to look not to a material heaven but within themselves for the answers. They ignored me.

"And yet the potential was there. It is still there. Wuju's response to kindness and caring. Varnett's self-sacrifice. Vardia's need for others. Other examples abound, not just about us, but about all our people. The one who sacrifices his life to save others. The com-

330

passion there, sometimes almost buried by the overlying depravity. It peers through—isolated, perhaps, but it is there. And as long as it is there, I shall continue. I shall work and hope for the day when some race seizes that spark and builds on it, for only then will I no longer be alone."

They said nothing for several seconds. Then, quietly, Ortega responded, "I'm not sure I believe all this. I've been a Catholic all my life, but somehow God to me has never been a little spunky Jew named Nathan Brazil. But, assuming what you say is true—which I don't necessarily accept—why haven't you scrapped everything and started again? And why continue to live our grubby little lives?"

"As long as that spark is present, I'll let things run, Serge," Brazil replied. "That random factor I talked about. Only when it's gone will I go, give up, maybe try again—maybe, finally die. I'd like to die, Serge—but if I do I take everything with me. Not just you, everybody and everything, for I stabilize the universal equation. And you are all my children, and I *care*. I can't do it as long as that spark remains, for as long as it remains you are not only the worst, but the best of me."

The *thump, thump, thump* continued, the only sound in the room.

"I don't think you're God, Nate," Ortega replied evenly. "I think you're crazy. Anybody would be, living this long. I think you're a Markovian throwback, crazy after a billion years of being cut off from your own kind. If you was God, why don't you just wave your tentacles or something and get what you want? Why all this journey, and pain, and torment?"

"Varnett?" Brazil called. "You want to explain it mathematically?"

"I'm not sure I don't agree with Ortega," Varnett replied carefully. "Not that it makes much difference from a practical point of view. However, I see what you're driving at. It's the same dilemma we face at that control board, there.

"Let's say we let Skander do what he wants, abolish the Comworlds," the boy continued. "Let's say Brazil, here, shows him exactly how to do it, just what to press and in what sequence and in what order. But the Com concept and the Comworlds developed according to the normal human flow of social evolution, right or wrong. They are caused by countless past historical events, conditions, ideas. You can't just banish them; you've got to change the equation so that they never developed. You have to change the whole human equation, all the past events that led to their formation. The new line you created would be a completely different construct, things as they would be without any of the crucial points that created the Coms. Maybe it was an outlet. Maybe, bad as it was, it was the only outlet. Maybe man would have destroyed himself if just one of those factors wasn't there. Maybe what we'd have is something worse."

"Exactly," Brazil agreed. "For anything major you have to change the past, the whole structure. Nothing just vanishes. Nothing just appears. We are the sum of our past, good as well as bad."

"So what do we do?" wailed Skander. "What can we do?"

"A few things can be done," Brazil replied calmly. "You—most of you—sought power. Well, *this* is power!" With that the Markovian moved toward the control panel.

"My God! He's going in there!" Skander screamed. "Shoot, you fools!" The Umiau fired its pistol at the Markovian. In a second, the others followed, pouring a concentrated energy pulse into the mass sufficient to disintegrate a building.

The Markovian creature stopped, but seemed to absorb the energy. They poured it into him, all of them, even Wuju, with great accuracy.

He was still there.

The Diviner's lights blinked rapidly, and searing bolts shot out, striking the Markovian body. There was a glow, surrounding the creature in stark outline, and then it faded.

Brazil was still there.

They stopped firing.

"I told you you couldn't hurt me," Brazil said. "None of you can hurt me."

"Bullshit!" Ortega spat. "Your body was torn to ribbons in Murithel! Why wasn't this one?"

"Of course! Of course!" Skander exclaimed excitedly. "This body is a direct construct of the Markovian brain, you fools! The brain won't allow it to be harmed, since it's really part of the brain itself!"

"Quite so," Brazil responded. "Nor, in fact, do I have to go in there at all. I can instruct the brain from right here. I've been able to do that since we first entered the Well itself. I merely wanted to give you a demonstration."

"It would seem that we are at your mercy, Markovian," The Rel said. "What is your intention?"

"I can affect things for anyplace from here," Brazil told them. "I merely feed the data into the brain through this control room, and that's that. It's true there's a control room for each type, but they are all-purpose, in case of problems, overcrowding when we built the place, and so on. Any control room can be switched to any pattern."

"But you said——" Ortega started to protest.

"In the words of Serge Ortega," Brazil replied, a hint of amusement in his voice, "I lied."

Wuju broke from them and ran up to him, and prostrated herself in front of him, trembling. "Please! Please don't hurt us," she pleaded.

There was infinite compassion in his voice. "I'm not going to hurt you, Wuju. I'm the same Nathan Brazil you knew from the start of this mess. I haven't changed, except physically. I've done nothing to you, nothing to deserve this. You know I wouldn't hurt you. I couldn't." The tone changed to one not of bitterness, but of deep hurt and agony, mixed with the loneliness of unimaginable lifetimes. "*I* didn't shoot at *you,* Wuju," it said.

She started crying; deep, uncontrollable sobs wracked her. "Oh, my god, Nathan! I'm so sorry! I failed you! Instead of trust, I gave you fear! Oh, god! I'm so ashamed! I just want to die!" she wailed.

Vardia came over to her, tried to comfort her. She pushed the girl away.

"I hope you're satisfied!" Vardia spat at him. "I hope

you're pleased with yourself! Do anything you want to me for saying this, but don't torture her anymore!"

Brazil sighed. "No one can torture someone like that," he replied gently. "Like me, you can only torture yourself. Welcome to the broader human race, Vardia. You showed compassion, disregard for yourself, concern for another. That would have been unthinkable in the old Vardia. If none of you can still understand, I intend to do something *for* you, not *to* you. For the most part, anyway." He angled to address all of them.

"You're not perfect, none of you. Perfection is the *object* of the experiment, not the component. Don't torture yourself, run away from your fears. Face them! Stand up to them! Fight them with goodness, mercy, charity, compassion! Lick them!"

"We are the sum of our ancestral and actual past," The Rel reminded him. "What you ask may indeed be possible, but the well of fate has accented our flaws. Is it reasonable to expect us to live by such rules, when we find it difficult even to comprehend them?"

"You can only try," Brazil told it. "There is a greatness in that, too."

The *thump, thump, thump* continued.

"What is that noise?" Ortega asked, ever the practical man.

"The Well circuits are open to the brain," Brazil replied. "It's awaiting instructions."

"And what will those instructions be?" Varnett asked nervously.

"I must make some repairs and adjustments to the brain," Brazil explained. "A few slight things, so that no one can accidentally discover the keying equation again. I'm not sure I'd like to go through this exercise again—and, if I did, there's no guarantee that some new person might not take that chance, damage the structure, do irreparable harm to trillions who never had a chance. But, just in case, the Well Access Gate will be reset to respond only to me. Also more of an insurance factor has to be added, to summon me if things go wrong."

Skander gave an amazed chuckle. "That's *all?*" he said, relieved.

"It is most satisfactory to me," The Rel pronounced. "We were concerned only that nothing be disturbed. For a short while there, we lost sight of that—but we are back in control of ourselves again."

"Very minor adjustments are possible without disturbing anything," Brazil told them. "I can't do anything grandiose without upsetting a few things. I will, however, do some minor adjustments. For one thing, I am going to make sure that nothing like the Ambreza gas that reduced Type Forty-one humans on this world to apes will pass again, and I'm going to slap some local controls on technological growth and development, so that such an adjustment won't be necessary again, not here.

"And, because I can't bear to see them like that, I'm going to introduce a compound to the Type Forty-one atmosphere that will break the gas molecules down into harmless substances, while at the same time I'm going to make it a nontechnological hex absolutely. I don't know what they'll come up with, but I'll bet it's better than their current lot."

"What about us?" Hain asked.

"I will not change what you are inside," Brazil told them. "If I do that, you will not have lived at all. To do anything otherwise would be to invite paradox, and that might mess up everything. Thus, I have to deal with you as you are."

Brazil seemed to think for a moment, then said, in a voice that sounded as if it came from thunder, "Elkinos Skander! You wanted to save the human race, but, in the process, you became inhuman yourself. When the end justifies *any* means, you are no better, perhaps worse, than those you despise. There are seven bodies back on Dalgonia. Seven human beings who died trusting you, helping you, who were victims of your own lust for power. I can't forget them. And, if I alter the time line, bring them back, then all this didn't happen. I pity you, Skander, for what you are, for what you could have become. My instructions to the brain are justice as a product of the past."

Skander yelled, "It wasn't me! It was Varnett! I wanted to save the worlds! I wanted—"

And suddenly Skander wasn't there anymore.

"Where did it go?" The Rel asked.

"To a world suited for him as he is, in a form suited to justice," Brazil responded. "He *might* be happy there, he might find justice. Let him go to his fate."

Brazil paused a moment, then that huge voice came back. "Datham Hain!" it called. "You are the product of a horrible life. Born in contagion, you spread it."

"I never had a chance except the way I took!" Hain shouted defiantly. "You know that!"

"Most products of a bad environment turn out worse," Brazil admitted. "And yet, some of the greatest human beings came out of such miserable lots and conquered them. You didn't, yet you had the intelligence and potential to do so. Today, you stand as a contagion. I pity you, Hain, and because I pity you I will give you a localized wish."

Hain grew slightly larger, her black color turning to white. She saw it in the fur on her forelegs.

"You turned me noble!" she exclaimed, pleased and relieved.

"You're the most beautiful breeder in the kingdom of the Akkafians," Brazil said. "When I return you to the palace, you won't be recognized. You'll be at the start of a breeding cycle. The Baron Azkfru will see you and go mad with desire. You will be his brood queen, and bear his royal young. That is your new destiny, Hain. Satisfied?"

"It is all that I could hope for," Hain replied, and vanished.

Wuju looked at Brazil, a furious expression on her face. "You gave that son of a bitch *that?* How could you reward that—that monster?"

"Hain gets the wish, but it's not a reward, Wuju," Brazil replied. "You see, they withheld from their newcomer one fact of Akkafian life. Most Marklings are sterile, and they do the work. A few are raised as breeders. A breeder hatches a hundred or more young —but they hatch *inside* the mother's body and eat their way out, using the breeder's body for their food."

Wuju started to say something, then formed a simple, *"Ooooh,"* as the horror of Hain's destiny hit her.

"Slelcronian!" Brazil pronounced. "You present me with a problem. I don't like your little civilization personally, and I don't like you much, either. I've adjusted things slightly, so the Recorders now only work with Slelcronians, not with any sentient plant. But you, personally—you're a problem. You're too dangerous to be let loose in the technology of Czill; you know too much. At the same time, you know too much of what is here to go back to Slelcron. It occurs to me, however, that you've really not altered the expedition in any significant way. If you had *not* taken over Vardia, nothing would have changed. Therefore, you didn't—and, in fact, couldn't."

Nothing seemed to change, but there was a difference in the Czillian body.

"So what are you going to do with me and my sister?" Vardia the Czillian asked. As far as everyone in the room was concerned, except for Brazil, the Slelcronian takeover had never happened. Slelcron was merely the funny place of the flowers and the giant bees, and their passage had been uneventful. Even so, the human Vardia had found her sister the Czillian as cold as the Slelcronian had been. She had gone through the same mental anguish as she had before and felt alienated from her sister.

Everything was as it had been before.

"Vardia, you are your old self, and no longer your sister," Brazil pointed out. "I think you'd be happiest returning to Czill, to the Center. You've much to contribute, to tell this story the way it happened. They won't be able to make use of what you say to get in, but it may cause the thinkers there to consider what projects are really worthwhile. *Go!*"

She vanished.

Now only Brazil, The Diviner and The Rel, Varnett, Wu Julee, Ortega, and the original Vardia were left.

"Diviner and Rel," Brazil said, "your race intrigues me. Bisexual, two totally different forms which mate into one organism, one of which has the power and the other the sensory input and output. You're a good people, with a lot of potential. Perhaps you can carry the message and reach that plateau."

"You're sending us back, then?" The Rel asked.

"No," Brazil replied. "Not to the hex. Your race is on the verge of expanding outward in its sector. It is near the turning point where questions of goals are asked. I'm sending you to your own people on their world with the message I gave you here. The Diviner's gift will distinguish you. Perhaps you can turn your people, perhaps not. It's up to you. Go!"

The Diviner and The Rel vanished.

"Varnett," Brazil said, and the boy jerked as if he was shot.

"What's in that little bag of tricks for me, Brazil?" he asked with false bravado.

"There are degrees of Comworlds, some better than others," Brazil noted. "Yours isn't too far gone yet. Even Vardia's can change. The worst of the lot is Dedalus. It went the genetic engineering route, you know. Everyone looks alike, talks alike, thinks alike. They kept males and females, sort of, but the engineers thought of even that. The people are hermaphroditic —small male genitals atop a vagina below. They breed once, in an exchange, then lose all sexual desires and prowess. Each has one child, which is, of course, identical to the parents, turned over to and raised by the state. It's a grotesque anthill, but it may represent the future.

"They don't even have names there. Obedience and contentment are engineered into them. Yet, the Central Committee retains power. This small group retains its sexual abilities, and the members are slightly different. The population is programmed to obey any one of those leaders unquestionably. The Committee was a perfect target, and they're controlled by the sponge syndicate. That sort of genetic engineering is, I fear, what the spongers have in mind for everyone eventually—with themselves on top.

"I give you the chance to change things. As the Murnies did with me, I do to you. You will be the Chairman of the Central Committee of Paradise, formerly called Dedalus. You'll be the new Chairman. The old one just kicked the bucket, and you're now unfrozen to take command. If you meant what you told me, you can kick the spongers out of their most secure planethold and restore that planet to individual initia-

338

tive. The revolution will be easy—the people will obey unquestionably. Your example and efforts could dissuade others from taking the Dedalus course. It's up to you. You're in charge."

"What happens to the new Chairman's mind?" Varnett asked. "And my body?"

"Even swap," Brazil told him. "The new boy will wake up a bat over in your old hex. He'll make out. He's born to command."

"Not *that* madhouse," Varnett chuckled. "Okay, I accept."

"Very good," Brazil told him. "But, I leave you this out. Should you ever want, any Markovian Gate will open for you—to bring you back here, for good. You'll be in a new body, so nobody knows what you would wind up as. You'd be here until you died, but you have that option."

Varnett nodded soberly. "Okay. I think I understand," he said, and vanished.

"Serge Ortega," Brazil sighed. "What in hell am I going to do with an old rascal like you?"

"Oh, hell, Nate, what's the difference?" Ortega responded, and he meant it. "This time you won."

"Are you really happy here, Serge? Or was that just part of the act?"

"I'm happy," the snakeman replied. "Hell, Nate, I was so damned bored back in the old place I was ready to kill myself. It's gotten too damned civilized, and I was too old to go frontier. I got here, and I've had a ball for eighty years. Even though I lost this round, it's been great fun. I wouldn't have missed it for the world."

Brazil chuckled. "Okay, Serge."

Ortega vanished.

"Where did you send him?" Vardia asked hesitantly.

"Eighty's about the average life span for a Ulik," Brazil replied. "Serge didn't start as an egg, so he's a very old man. He has a year, five, maybe ten. I wouldn't put it past him to beat the system, but why the hell not? Let him go back to living and having fun."

"And so that leaves us," Wuju said quietly.

There was a sudden flicker in the image of the

Markovian, then a sparkling graininess. The shape twirled, changed, and suddenly standing there in front of them was the old, human Nathan Brazil, in the colorful clothes he had first worn on the ship a lifetime ago.

"Oh, my god!" Wuju breathed, looking as if she were seeing a ghost.

"The God act's over," he said, sounding relieved. "You should see who you're really dealing with."

"Nathan?" Wuju said hesitantly, starting forward. He put up his hand and stopped her, sighing.

"No, Wuju. It couldn't work. Not now. Not after all this. It wouldn't work anyway. Both of you deserve much better than life's given you. There are others like you, you know—people who never had the chance to grow, as you did. They can use a little kindness, and a lot of caring. You know the horrors of the sponge, Wuju, and the abuse to which some human beings subject others. And you, Vardia, know the lies that underlie the Com philosophy. I've talked to both of you, observed you both carefully. I've fed all this information plus as much data as could be obtained from a readout by the brain while you were in this room. The brain responded with recommendations on what would be best for you. If we're wrong—the brain and I—after a trial of what I'm going to do, then you both have the same option that is open to Varnett. Just get near a Markovian Gate—you don't have to jump into it. Just get passage on a ship going near a Markovian world. If you want, the Gate will pluck you out without disturbing the ship, passengers, or crew. You'll somehow mysteriously vanish. And you'll wind up in Zone again. Like Varnett, you will have to take potluck with the Zone Gate again. Once here, again, there will be no returning.

"But try it my way for a while. And remember what I said about your own contributions. Two people *can* change a world, if they wish."

"But what—" Wuju started to ask, but was cut off in midsentence.

The two bodies didn't vanish, they just collapsed, like a suit of clothes with the owner gone. They lay there in a heap on the floor.

Brazil went over and carefully rearranged them so they looked as if they were sleeping.

"Well, now what, Brazil?" he asked himself, his voice echoing in the empty hall.

You go back, and you wait, his mind told him.

What about the bodies? he wondered. Somehow he couldn't just vaporize them. Though their owners were gone, they lived on as empty vegetables.

But there was nothing else to do, of course. They were just memories for him now, one a strange mixture of love and anguish. He was prolonging the inevitable.

There was a crackle, and the bodies were gone, back to primal energy.

"Oh, the hell with it," said Nathan Brazil, and he, too, vanished.

The control room was empty. The Markovian brain noted the fact and then dutifully turned off the lights.

On "Earth," a Planet Circling a Star Near the Outermost Edge of the Galaxy Andromeda

ONE MOMENT ELKINOS SKANDER HAD BEEN PERCHED atop Hain's back, looking at the control room and those in it. Then, suddenly, he wasn't.

He looked around. Things looked funny and distorted. He was color-blind except for a sepia tone that lent itself to everything.

He looked around, confused. I've gone through another change, he realized. My last one.

A rather pleasant-looking place, he thought, once he got used to the distorted vision. Forests over there, some high mountains, odd-looking grass, and strange sort of trees, but that was to be expected.

There were a lot of animals around, mostly grazing. They look a lot like deer, he noted, surprised. A few differences, but they would not look out of place on a pastoral human world.

He looked down at himself, and saw the shadow of his head on the grass.

I'm one of them, he suddenly realized with a shock. *I'm a deer. No antlers like those big males over there, so I must be a doe.*

A deer? he thought quizzically.

Why a deer?

He was still meditating on this, when suddenly the grass seemed to explode with yells and strange shapes; great, rectangular bodies with their facial features in their chest, and big, big teeth.

He watched as the Murnies singled out a large doe not far from him and surrounded it. Suddenly they speared it several times, and it went down in wordless agony and lay twitching on the ground, blood running, but still alive.

The Murnies pounced on it, tearing at it, eating it alive.

To be eaten alive! he thought, stunned, and suddenly blind panic overtook him. He started running, running away from the scene.

Up ahead another band of Murnies leaped out of nowhere and cornered another deer, started to devour it.

They're all over! he realized. *This is their world! I'm just food to them!*

He ran narrowly avoiding entrapment several times. There were thousands of them here, and they all were hungry.

And even as he ran in exhausted, dizzy circles, he knew that even if he avoided them today he would have to avoid them tomorrow, and the day after, and the day after, and wherever he ran on this planet there would be more of them.

Sooner or later they'll get me! he thought in panic. *By god! I'll not be eaten alive! I'll cheat Brazil of his revenge!*

He reached the highlands by carefully pulling himself together.

Now that he had decided on a course of action, he felt calm.

There! Up ahead! his mind said joyfully. He stopped and looked over the edge of the cliff.

Over a kilometer straight down to the rocks, he saw with satisfaction. He ran back a long ways, then turned toward the cliff. With strong resolve, he ran with all his might toward the cliff and hurled himself over it.

He saw the rocks coming up to meet him, but felt only the slight shock of pain.

Skander awoke. The very fact that he awoke was a shock, and he looked around.

He was back on that plain at the edge of the forest. His shadow told him.

He was a deer again.

No! his mind screamed in horror. *I'll cheat the bastard yet! Somehow I'll cheat him!*

But there were a lot of deer and a lot of Murnies on that world, and Skander still had six more times to die.

Paradise, Once Called Dedalus, a Planet Near Sirius

VARNETT GROANED, THEN OPENED HIS EYES. HE FELT cold. He looked around him and saw a number of people peering at him anxiously.

They all looked exactly alike. They didn't even look particularly male or female. Slight breasts and nipples, but nothing really female. Their bodies were lithe and muscular, sort of a blend of masculine and feminine.

All of them had small male genitals where they should be, but, from his vantage point, he could see a small cavity beneath them.

None of them had any body hair.

If you did it upside down and the other was right side up, he thought, you could give and receive at the same time.

"Are you all right?" one asked in a voice that sounded like a man's voice but with a feminine lilt.

"Do you feel all right?" another asked in the identical voice.

"I—I think so," he replied hesitantly, and sat up. "A little dizzy, that's all."

"That will pass," the other said. "How's your memory?"

"Shaky," he replied carefully. "I'm going to need a refresher."

"Easily done," the other replied.

He started to ask them their names, then suddenly remembered. They didn't use names on *his* planet.

His planet! *His!*

"I'd like to get right to work," he told them.

"Of course," another replied, and they led him from the sterile-looking infirmary down an equally sterile corridor. He followed them, got into an elevator, and they rode up to the top floor.

The top floor, it seemed, was an office complex. Workers were everywhere, filing things, typing things, using computer terminals.

Everybody else was slightly smaller than he was, he realized. Not much, but in a world where everyone was absolutely identical such a slight difference was as noticeable as if Cousin Bat had entered the room.

His office was huge and well-appointed. White wall-to-wall carpeting, so thick and soft his bare feet practically bounced off it. There was a huge desk, and great high-backed chair. No other furnishings, he noted, although their lack made the place look barren.

"Bring me a summary of the status of the major areas of the planet," he ordered. "And then leave me for a while to study them."

They bowed slightly, and left. He looked out the glass window that was the wall in back of his desk.

A complex of identical buildings stretched out before him. Broad, tree-lined streets, some small parkland, and lots of identical-looking shapes walking about on various business.

The sky was an off-blue, not the deepness of his native world, but it was attractive. There were some fleecy clouds in the sky, and, off in the distance, he saw signs of cultivated land. It looked like a rich, peaceful, and productive place, he thought. Of course, weather and topography would cause changes in the life-styles planet-wide, but he wagered those differences were minimal.

The aides returned with sheaves of folders bulging with papers. He acknowledged them curtly, and ordered them out.

There were no mirrors, but the lighting reflected him in the glass windows.

He looked just like them, only about fifty millimeters taller and proportionately slightly larger.

He felt his male genitals. They had the same feel as the ones he had had as Cousin Bat, he thought.

He reached a little lower, and found the small vaginal cavity.

He spread some papers around to make it look as if he had been studying them. He would, in time, of course, but not now.

He saw a small intercom on the desk and buzzed it, taking a seat in the big chair. At the far end of the room a clerk almost beat the track records entering, coming up to the desk and standing at full attention.

"I have found indications," he told the clerk seriously, "that several members of the Presidium may be ill. I want a team of rural doctors—based, as far as possible, away from here—to be brought to my office as soon as possible. I want that done *exactly* and at once. How long before they can get here?"

"If you want them from as far away from government centers as possible, ten hours," the clerk replied crisply.

"All right, then," he nodded. "As soon as they arrive they are to see me—and no one else. *No one* is even to know that they have been sent for. I mean absolutely no one, not even the rest of the office."

"I shall attend to it personally, Chairman," responded the clerk, and turned to leave. So much for the spongies, he thought.

"Clerk!" he called suddenly, and the other halted and turned.

"Chairman?"

"How do I arrange to have sex?"

The clerk looked surprised and bemused. "Whenever

345

the Chairman wishes, of course. It is a great honor for any citizen."

"I want the best specimen here in five minutes!" he ordered.

"Yes, Chairman," responded the clerk knowingly, and left.

His eyes sparkled, and he rubbed his hands together gleefully, thinking about what was to come.

Suddenly Nathan Brazil's visage arose from the corners of his mind.

He said he'd give me my chance, he thought seriously. And I'll make good on it. This world will be changed!

The door opened, and another inhabitant of Paradise entered.

"Yes?" he snapped.

"I was told to report to you by the clerk," the newcomer said.

He smiled. The world would be changed, yes—but not right away, he thought. Not until I've had much more fun.

"Come on over here," he said lightly. "You're about to be honored."

On the Frontier— Harvich's World

HE GROANED, AND OPENED HIS EYES. AN OLDER MAN in overalls and checkered shirt, smelly and with a three-days' growth of beard, was bending over him, looking anxious.

"Kally? You hear me, boy? Say somethin'!" the old man urged, shouting at him.

He groaned. "God! I feel lousy!" he managed.

The old man smiled. "Good! Good!" he enthused. "I was afeared we'd lost you, there. That was quite a crack on the nog you took!"

346

Kally felt the left side of his head. There was a knot under the hair, and some dried blood. It hurt—throbbed, really.

"Try to stand up," the old man urged, and gave him a hand. He took it, and managed to stand shakily.

"How do ya feel, boy?" the old man asked.

"My head hurts," he complained. "Otherwise—well, weak but okay."

"Told ya ya shoulda got a good gal ta help with the farm," the old man scolded. "If'n I hadn'ta happened along you'd be dead now."

The man looked around, puzzled. It *was* a farm, he saw. Some chickens about, a ramshackle barn with a couple of cows, and an old log shack. It looked like corn growing in the fields.

"Somethin' wrong, Kally?" the old man asked.

"I—uh, who are you?" he asked hesitantly. "And where am I?"

The old man looked concerned. "That bump on the noggin's scrambled your brains, boy. Better get into town and see a doctor on it."

"Maybe you're right," the other agreed. "But I still don't know who you are, where I am—or who I am."

"Must be magnesia or somethin'," the old man said, concerned. "I'll be damned. Heard about it, but never seed it afore. Hell, boy, you're Kally Tonge, and since your pa died last winter you've run this farm here alone. You was borned here on Harvich," he explained, pronouncing it *Harrige,* "and you damned near died here." He pointed to the ground.

He looked and saw an irrigation pump with compressor. Obviously he had been tightening the top holding nut with the big wrench and had kicked the thing into start. The wrench had whirled around and caught him on the head.

He looked at it strangely, knowing what it must mean.

"Will you be all right?" the old man asked concernedly. "I got to run down the road or the old lady'll throw a fit, but if ya want I can send somebody back to take ya inta the doc's."

347

"I'll see him," Kally replied. "But let me get cleaned up first. How—how far is it into town?"

"Christ, Kally! Ya even talk a little funny!" the old man exclaimed. "But Depot's a kilometer and a half down the road there." He pointed in the right direction.

Kally Tonge nodded. "I'll go in. If you get a head injury, it's best to walk. Just check back in a little while, just in case. I'll be all right."

"Well, okay," the old man responded dubiously. "But if I don't hear ya got in town, I'm comin' lookin'," he warned, then walked back to the road.

He's riding a horse! Kally thought wonderingly. And the road's dirt!

He turned and went into the shack.

It was more modern than he would have guessed, although small. A big bed with natural fur blankets in one corner, a sink, a gas stove—bottled gas underneath, he noted—and the water was probably from a water tank near the barn. A big fireplace, and a crude indoor shower.

There was a small refrigerator, too, running off what would have been a tractor battery if he had had a tractor.

He noted the toilet in one corner, and went over to it. Above it hung a cracked mirror, some scissors, and toiletries.

He looked at himself in the mirror.

His was a strong, muscular, handsome face in a rugged sort of way. The hair was long and tied off in a ponytail almost a meter long, and he had a full but neatly trimmed beard and mustache. The hair was brown, but the beard was reddish.

He turned his head, saw that the knot was almost invisible in the hair. Brushing it back revealed an ugly wound.

He died in that accident, he thought. Kally Tonge died of that wound. And I filled the empty vessel.

He stripped and took the mirror off its nail hanger, looking at himself. He saw a rugged, muscular body, well toned and used to work. There were calluses on the hands, worn in from hard farm labor.

The wound *did* hurt, and while he was certain it wouldn't be serious now, it would be better to go into

348

town. It would also help to explain his mental lapses.

He put on a thick wool shirt and work pants, and some well-worn leather boots, and went back outside.

The place was interesting, really. It looked like something out of ancient history, yet had indoor plumbing, electricity, albeit crude, and several other signs of civilization. In the midst of this primitiveness, he noticed with amusement that he wore a fancy wristwatch.

It was not cold, but there was a chill in the wind that made him glad he had picked the thicker shirt. They were short on rain here, he noted; the dirt road was rutted and dug up, yet dry and caked.

He walked briskly down the road toward the town, looking at the scenery. Small farms were the rule, and many looked far more modern than his. There wasn't much traffic, but occasional people passed on horseback or in buckboards, giving him the impression that modern vehicles were either in short supply or banned.

And yet, despite the lack of recent rain, the land was good. The tilled soil was black and mineral-rich, and where small compressors pumped water from wells or nearby creeks into irrigation ditches, the land bloomed.

He came upon the town much faster than he had anticipated. He didn't feel the least bit tired or uncomfortable, and he had walked with a speed that astonished him. The town itself was a study in contrasts. Log buildings, some as tall as five stories, mixed with modern, prefabricated structures. The street wasn't paved, but it went for several blocks, with a block or two on either side of the business district composed of houses, mostly large and comfortable. There was street lighting, and some of the businesses had electric signs, so there was a power plant somewhere, and, from the look of things, running water and indoor plumbing.

He studied some of the women, most of whom were dressed in garb much like his own, sometimes with small cowboy hats or straw broad-brimmed hats on their heads. There weren't nearly as many women as men, he noted, and those that were here looked tough, muscular, and mannish.

The town was small enough so that he spotted the doctor's office with no difficulty and headed for it.

The doctor was concerned. He had quite a modern facility, with a minor surgery and some of the latest machines and probes. Clearly medical care was well into the modern era here. The X-rays showed a severe concussion and fracture. The doctor marveled that he was alive at all, as he placed medication and a small bandage on the wound after sewing seven stitches.

"Get somebody to stay with you the next few days, or look in on you regularly," the doctor advised. "Your loss of memory's probably only temporary, and not that uncommon in these cases. But a lot of damage was done. The brain was bruised, and I want someone to see that you don't have a clot in there."

He thanked the doctor, assuring him that he would take care of himself and be watched and checked.

"Settle the bill at the end of the month," the doctor told him.

This puzzled him for a minute. The bill? Money? He had never used it himself, and, back on the street, he pulled out a thin leather wallet, which looked like the survivor of a war, and opened it.

Funny-looking pieces of paper, about a dozen of them. They had very realistic pictures, almost three-dimensional, on them, the fronts showing the same man three times, the others two other men and a woman. The backs showed a remarkably realistic set of farm scenes. He wished he could read the bills. He would have to find out what each one was and remember the pictures.

A three-story log building's lights went on in the coming twilight, and he saw from the symbol on the sign that it was a bar and something else. He didn't recognize the other symbol, and couldn't read the words. Curious, he walked over to it.

There was a rumbling of thunder in the distance.

She awoke, feeling nauseated, and threw up.

The bile spilled on the cheap rug, and in it, as she gagged uncontrollably, she could see bits and pieces and even whole pills of some kind.

The spasms lasted several minutes, until it seemed there was nothing else to give. Feeling weak and exhausted, she lay back on the bed until the room steadied. The stench of the bile permeated her.

Slowly, she looked around. A tiny room, with nothing but a bed much too large for it and a wicker chair. There was barely fifty centimeters' clearance on either side of it.

The walls and ceiling seemed to be made of logs, but the construction was so solid it might as well have been rock. It was dark in the room, and she looked for a light. Spying a string hanging above her, she pulled it, and a weak, naked light bulb suspended from the ceiling flicked on. The glare hurt her eyes.

She raised her head slightly and looked down at her body. Something was definitely different.

Two extremely large but perfectly formed breasts met her eye, and her skin seemed creamy smooth, dark-complexioned but unpigmented.

Her gaze slid down a little more, and she saw that the rest of her body matched the breasts—curving in all the right places, definitely.

She felt—strange. Tingly all over, but particularly in the areas of her breasts and crotch.

She was nude from the waist up, but hanging on sultry hips was a pantslike garment of fine-woven black lace, to which hundreds of tiny sequins of various colors were attached.

She felt her face, and found that she had some sort of hairdo. There were also long, plastic earrings hanging from pierced ears.

She looked around in the gloom, found a small cosmetics case with a mirror in it, and looked at her face.

It is a beautiful face, she thought, and she was not being vain. Maybe the most beautiful face I've ever seen. Cosmetics had been carefully applied to bring out just the right highlights, but the face was so perfect that they seemed almost intrusive on its beauty.

But whose face was it? she wondered.

She noticed a box next to the cosmetics case on the floor, and picked it up idly. It was a pillbox—open, and empty. There was a universal caution symbol on it, but she couldn't read the writing. She didn't need to.

This girl, whoever and whatever she was, had killed herself. She had taken all those pills and overdosed. She had died here, in this room, moments before—

alone. And the moment that girl had died, she had been somehow inserted into the body, and the physical processes righted.

She stared again at that beautiful face in the mirror.

What would make someone who looked like this and experienced such feelings as she now did commit suicide? So very young, she thought—perhaps no more than sixteen or seventeen. And so very beautiful.

She tried to get up, but felt suddenly light-headed and strange. She flopped back down on the bed and stared up at the light bulb, which, for some reason, had become fascinating.

She found herself gently caressing her own body, and it felt fantastic, like tingling jolts of pleasure at each nerve juncture.

It's the pills, a corner of her mind told her. You didn't get all of them out of your system.

The door opened suddenly, and a man looked in. He was dressed in white work clothes, like kitchen help. He was balding and fiftyish, but he had a tough, hard look to him. "Okay, Nova, time to—" he began, then stopped and looked at her, the empty box, and the bile and vomited-up pills on the floor and the side of her bed.

"Oh, shit!" he snarled angrily, and exploded. "You went for the happy pills again, didn't you? I warned you, dammit! I wondered why a sexy high-top like you would work this jerkwater! They tossed you out of the others!" He stopped, his tone going from fury to disgust.

"You're no good to anybody, not even yourself," he snapped. "I told you if you did this again, I'd toss you in the street. Come on! You hear me?" he started yelling. "You're going out and now! Come on, get up!"

She heard him, but the words didn't register. He looked and sounded somehow funny, and she laughed and pointed to him, giggling stupidly.

He grabbed her by the arm and pulled her up. "Jesus!" he exclaimed. "You're a hell of a piece. Too bad your insides don't match your outsides. Come on!"

He pulled her out into the hall and dragged her down a flight of wooden stairs. She felt as if she were floating, and made flying motions with her free arm and motor sounds with her voice.

A few other young women peered out from second-floor rooms. None of 'em pretty as me, she thought smugly.

"Stop that giggling!" the man commanded, but it sounded so funny she giggled more.

The downstairs was a bar, some sawdust on the floor, a few round tables, and a small service bar to one side. It was dimly lit, and empty.

"Oh, hell," he said, almost sadly, reaching into a cash drawer behind the bar. "You ain't even earned your keep here, and you burned your clothes on the last flyer. Here—fifty *reals*," he continued, stuffing a few bills in the lace panty. "When you come to out in the street or the woods or the sheriff's office, buy some clothes and a ticket out. I've had it!"

He picked her up as if she weighed nothing, and, opening the door with one hand, tossed her rudely into the darkening street. The chilly air and the hard landing brought her down a bit, and she looked around, feeling lost and alone.

She suddenly didn't want to be seen. Although there were few people about, there were some nearby who would see her in a few moments. She saw a dark alley-way between the bar and a store and crawled into it. It was very dark and cold, and smelled a little of old garbage. But at least she was concealed.

Suddenly the streetlights popped on, and deepened the shadows in which she sat confused. The shock of where she was and her situation broke through into her conscious mind. She was still high, and her body still tingled, particularly when rubbed. She still wanted to rub it, but she was aware of her circumstances.

I'm alone in a crazy place I don't know, practically nude and with the temperature dropping fast, she thought miserably. How much worse can things get?

As if in answer, there was a rumbling and a series of static discharges, and the temperature dropped even more.

Tears welled up in her eyes, and she started crying at the helplessness of her position. She had never been more miserable in her life.

A man was crossing the street, walking toward the bar. He stopped suddenly. Lightning flashed, illuminating her for a brief moment. He looked puzzled, and came toward the alley. She was folded up, arms around her knees, head down against them. She rocked as she cried.

He saw her and stared in disbelief. Now what the hell? he thought.

He reached out and touched her bare shoulder, and she started, looked up at him, saw the concern on his face.

"What's the matter, little lady?" he asked gently.

She looked up with anguished face and started to speak, but couldn't.

She was, even in this state, the most beautiful thing he had ever seen.

"Nothing's that bad," he tried to soothe her. "Where do you live? I'll take you home. You're not hurt, are you?"

She shook her head negatively, and coughed a little. "No, no," she managed. "Don't have a home. Thrown out."

He squatted next to her. The lightning and thunder continued, but the rain held off still.

"Come on with me, then," he said in that same soft tone. "I've got a place just down the road. Nobody there but me. You can stay until you decide what to do."

Her head shook in confusion. She didn't know what to do. Could she trust him? Dare she take this opportunity?

A strange, distant voice whispered in her brain. It said, *"Can you feel it? Fear, greed, horror, ambition, burning within you, consuming you! . . . Perfection is the object of the experiment, not the component. . . . Don't torture yourself, run away from your fears. Face them! Stand up to them! Fight them with goodness, mercy, charity, compassion. . . ."*

And trust? she wondered suddenly. Oh, hell! What have I got to lose if I go? What do I have if I don't?

"I'll go," she said softly. He helped her up, gently, carefully, and brushed the dirt off her. He's very big, she realized. I only come up to his neck.

"Come on," he urged, and took her hand.

She hesitated. "I don't want—want to go out there looking like this," she said nervously.

"There's nothing wrong with the way you look," he replied in a tone that had nothing if not sincerity. "Nothing at all. Besides, the storm's about to break, I think. Most folks will stay inside."

Again she looked uncertain. "What about us?" she asked. "Won't we get wet?"

"There's shelter along the way," he said casually. "Besides, a little water won't hurt."

She let him lead her down the deserted street of the town and out into the countryside. The storm continued to be visual and audible, but not as yet wet. The landscape seemed eerie, illuminated in the flashes.

The temperature had dropped from about fifteen degrees Celsius to around eight degrees due to the storm. She shivered.

He looked at her, concerned, feeling the tremors in her hand.

"Want my shirt?" he asked.

"But then you'll be cold," she protested.

"I like cold weather," he responded, taking off his shirt. His broad, muscled, hairy chest reactivated those funny feelings in her again. Carefully he draped the shirt around her. It fit her like a circus tent, but it felt warm and good.

She didn't know what to say, and something, some impulse, caused her to lean into him and put her arm around his bare chest. He responded by putting his arm around her, and they resumed walking.

Somehow it felt good, calming, and her anxieties seemed to flee. She looked up at him. "What's your name?" she asked in a tone of voice she didn't quite comprehend, but was connected, somehow, in its throaty softness to those strange feelings.

"W——" he started to say, then said, instead, "Kally Tonge. I have a farm not much farther down the road."

She noticed the bandage on the side of his head. "You're injured."

"It's nothing—now," he replied, and chuckled. "As a matter of fact, you're just what the doctor ordered

355

—literally. He said somebody should be with me through the night."

"Does it hurt much?" she asked.

"Not now," he replied. "Medicine's pretty advanced here, although as you know the place is rather primitive overall."

"I really don't know much about this world," she replied truthfully. "I'm not from here."

"I could have guessed that," he said lightly. "Where *do* you come from?"

"I don't think you've ever heard of it," she replied. "From nowhere now, really."

"What's *your* name?" he asked.

She started to say "Nova," the name the man had called her, but instead she said, "Vardia."

He stopped and looked at her strangely. "That's a Com name, isn't it?" he asked. "You're not from any Comworld!"

"Sort of," she replied enigmatically, "but I've changed a lot."

"On the Well World?" he asked sharply.

She gasped, a small sound of surprise escaping her lips. "You—you're one of the people from the Well!" she exclaimed. "You woke up in that body, as I did! That head wound killed Kally Tonge and you took over, as I did!"

"Twice when I needed someone you comforted me, even defended me," he said.

"Wuju!" she exclaimed, and an amazed smile spread over her face. She looked him over critically. "My, how you've changed!"

"No more than you," he replied, shaking his head wonderingly. *"Wow!"*

"But—but, why a man?" she asked.

His face grew serious. "I'll tell you sometime. But, good old Nathan! He sure came through!"

The storm broke, then, and the rain started coming down heavily.

They were both soaked through in seconds, and her fancy hairdo collapsed. He laughed, and she laughed, and he picked her up and started running in the mud. Just ahead he saw his shack, outlined in the lightning flashes, but he misjudged the turn to his walk with his burden. They both tumbled into the road, splashing around and covered with thick black mud.

"You all right?" he shouted over the torrent.

"I'm drowning in mud!" she called back, and they both got up, laughing at each other.

"The barn's closer!" he shouted. "See it over there? Run for it!"

He started off, and she followed, the rain getting heavier and heavier. He reached the door way ahead of her, and slid it aside on its rollers. She reached it, and they both fell in. The place had an eerie, hollow sound, the rain beating on the sheet-metal roof and wood sides of the barn. It was dark, and smelled like the barn it was. A few cows mooed nervously in their stalls.

"Wooj?" she called.

"Here," he said, near her, and she turned.

"Might as well sit it out here," he told her. "There's a pile of hay over there, and it's a thousand meters to the shack. Might as well not go through the deluge twice."

"Okay," she replied, exhausted, and plopped into the hay. The rain continued to beat a percussion symphony on the barn.

He plopped beside her. She was fussing with her lace pants.

"The mud's all caked in them, and the sequins are scratching me," she said. "Might as well get them off, for all the good they'll do as clothing anyway, even if they are all I've got in the world."

She did, and they lay for a while side by side. He put his arm around her and fondled her breast.

"That feels good," she whispered. "Is—is that what I've been feeling? I thought it was still the pills. Is this what you felt with Brazil?"

"I'll be damned!" he said to himself. "I always wondered what an erection felt like to a man!" He turned and looked at her. "I'll show you what it's really like, if you want," he said softly.

"I—I think that's what he wanted," she replied.

"Is it what *you* want?" he asked seriously.

"I think I do," she whispered, and realized that it *was* what she wanted. "But I don't even know how."

"Leave that to an expert," he replied. "Although

I'm not used to this end of things." He put both arms around her, kissed her and fondled her.

And he kicked off his pants, and showed her the other side of being a woman, while discovering himself what it was to be a man.

The rain was over. It had been over for a couple of hours, but they just lay there, content in the nearness of each other.

The door was still half-open, and Vardia, still dazed and dreamy from her first sexual experience, saw the clouds roll back and the stars appear. "We'll get you some clothes in the morning," he said at last. "Then we'll tour the farm. This rain should do everything good. I was born on a farm, you know, but not my own farm."

"People—non-Com people—they do that *every* day?" she asked.

He chuckled. "Twice if they're horny enough. Except for a couple of days each month."

"You—you've done it both ways," she said. "Is it different?"

"The feeling's definitely different, but it's the same charge," he replied. "An important part, male or female, is that you do it when you want with someone you want."

"Is that love?" she asked. "Is that what Brazil was talking about?"

"Not the sex," he replied. "That's just a—a component, as he would say. Without the object—without love, without feeling for the other person, without *caring,* it's not pleasant at all."

"That's why you're a man now," she said. "All the other times—they were the wrong kind, weren't they?"

"Yes," he replied distantly, and looked out at the stars. She clenched his hand tightly in hers.

"Do you think he was really God?" Vardia asked quietly.

"I don't know," he replied with a sigh. "What if he wasn't? When he was in the Well he had the power. He gave me my farm, a good, healthy young body, a new chance. And," he added softly, "he sent you."

She nodded. "I've never lived like this," she said. "Is it all as wonderful as tonight?"

"No," he replied seriously. "There's a lot of hard work, and pain, and heartache—but, if it all comes together, it *can* be beautiful."

"We'll try it here," she said resolutely. "And when the fun is gone, if ever, or when we're old and gray, we'll take off for a Markovian world, and go back and do it again. That's a good future."

"I think it is," he responded. "It's more than most people ever get."

"This world," she said. "It must never become like the others, like the Com. We must make sure of that."

At that moment there was a glow far beyond the horizon, and suddenly a bright arrow streaked upward in the dark sky and vanished. A few seconds later, a distant, roaring sound came to them.

"Poor Nathan," he said sadly. "He can do it for everyone but himself."

"I wonder where he is now?" she mused.

"I don't know what form he's in," he replied, "but I think I know where he is and what he's doing, and thinking, and feeling."

They continued to gaze at the stars.

Aboard the Freighter <u>Stehekin</u>

NATHAN BRAZIL LAY IN THE COMMAND CHAIR ON THE bridge and gazed distantly at the fake starfield projected in the two window screens. He glanced over to the table atop the ancient computer.

That same pornographic novel was there, spread open to where he had last been reading it. He couldn't remember it at all, but, he reflected, it didn't matter. They were all alike anyway, and there was plenty of time to read it again.

He sighed and picked up the cargo manifest, idly flipping it open.

Cargo of grain, bound for Coriolanus, it read. *No passengers.*

No passengers.

They were elsewhere now—the rotten ones in their own private hells, the good ones—and the potentially good—with their chances. He wondered whether their dreams were as sweet as they had imagined. Would they forget the lessons of the Well, or try for change?

In the end, of course, it didn't really matter.

Except to them.

He closed the manifest and threw it across the control room. It banged against the wall and landed askew on the floor. He sighed a long, sad sigh, a sigh for ages past and the ages yet to be.

The memories would fade, but the ache would remain.

For, whatever becomes of the others or of this little corner of the universe, he thought. I'm still Nathan Brazil, fifteen days out, bound for Coriolanus with a load of grain.

Still waiting.

Still caring.

Still alone.